ELEUTHERIA

THE RUNIC HISTORIES OF EFELLDOR

BOOK 1

RUTH CANTU

Hardcover ISBN: 979-8-9988855-2-5

Paperback ISBN: 979-8-9988855-1-8

Book cover by Selkkie Designs – www.selkkiedesigns.com

Line and copy editing by Simply Spellbound Edits, LLC

Map and illustrations by FantasySpriteStudio

First edition 2025

ELEUTHERIA

THE RUNIC HISTORIES OF EFELLDOR
BOOK 1

RUTH CANTU

The Island Of

Temple Ruins

Amethyst Hall

the Blackwood

Vinnith Mountains

Lyris's Cottage

Sorrelikah Jungle

AUTHOR'S NOTE

If we're related—please, put this book down and walk away.

Eleutheria comes from the Greek word for freedom. Like the title, much of the story was loosely inspired by my childhood fascination with western mythology (such as Roman, Greek, Norse and Welsh) and combined with my Mexican heritage. Neither the western mythology nor the references to Mexican/Latine culture are intended to be an accurate portrayal but, rather, a foundation for the world of *Eleutheria*.

None of *Eleutheria's* content was created with AI. Each part of the story, from the characters to the prose to the em-dashes is a product of by my brain. I do not support nor condone generative AI in the arts.

Because I value your mental state, I've included a list of content warnings below. Please, look through them before deciding if Eleutheria is for you.

Eleutheria includes graphic language, graphic violence, battle warfare, magical torture, death of a teenager, female oppression, trafficking attempts, reference to off page sexual assault, violent confrontation of a sexual abuser, heavy grief of on page deaths, discussion of parental death, discussion of children's murders, alcohol/drug use and abuse, fantasy world prejudice, reference to off page suicide, discussion of self-harm, and open-door sex.

PRONUNCIATION GUIDE

ELEUTHERIA (ελευθερία) in Ancient Greek is correctly pronounced eh-*lef*-theh-ree-ah but for the sake of this fantasy novel, the pronunciation is eh-*loo*-theh-ree-ah.

in order of appearance...

Alys Sathos: Al-is Sath-ohs

Lilain: Lih-layn

Elenna Makim: Eh-len-nah Mah-keem

Ansil Makim: An-sell Mah-keem

Corryn Stellanati: Ker-rihn Stella-nah-tee

Rilessa: Ree-less-ah

Melisandre: Mel-is-ahn-drah

Maddox Lexsidus: Mad-dex Lecks-sigh-dus

Yori Denox: Yor-ee Deh-nocks

Morithia: Mor-ith-ee-ah

Morgenna: Morg-en-nah

Sylinia: Sil-in-ee-ah

Rugard: Roo-gard

Nyxinthi: Nix-in-thee

Zelah Zarrata: Zay-lah Zah-rah-ta

Olyvr Felumbra: Ah-leh-ver Fel-um-brah

Agria Grafeas: Ah-gree-ah Grah-fey-ahs

Sorrelikah: Sor-rel-eh-kah

For the ones who found their voice and used it to break free.

And for Andy—
Thanks for daring to believe we were more than our circumstances.

Part One

The Mother of All Creation began life with a seed of hope...
-from 'Duality of Witches'

1

DEATH IS EASY

Alys

Death was too simple. A final gasp before oblivion. What Queen Lilain deserved was terror—the kind of mind-numbing terror she adored inflicting. Either that or falling into a vat of flesh-eating insects.

That would work too.

The Day Realm witch queen gestured me forward with a single finger. Her crimson-varnished fingernail could have passed for a nymph claw. I took a deep breath of stale cavern air and stepped toward her throne hewn into stone. I might as well have stepped off a cliff. At least then, I knew what waited below.

"I won't allow goblins across my borders, Captain Sathos," Queen Lilain began. Her throaty, low voice evoked satin sheets and moans in the dark, but I was no longer fooled. "They toe the borderline one day, and the next they're pillaging Day Realm villages. I cannot allow that. You and your squad shall

1

eliminate the encroaching goblin camp. Without their clan leader they're blind. Kill him."

I bowed low and said, "It is done. The 22nd Airwitch Squad of the Day Realm's Aerial Squadrons is honored to serve our queen."

Honored. A bitter taste remained in my mouth, coppery and foul. Uneasy squeaks of shifting leather armor creaked from behind. Someone else in my squad agreed. Serving the Day Queen held no honor—certainly, not slaughtering goblins seeking refuge—but I hadn't clawed my way up the DRAS ranks by spewing every traitorous thought that popped into my head.

I waited for Lilain to dismiss us. Instead, she tapped a pale finger to her lips. Malice slithered behind the beautiful façade like an asp wondering where to strike. Gritting my teeth until my jaw ached, I held her stare—a pathetic bit of defiance against power I couldn't match.

She rose and loomed over me on the dais, never blinking. The hairs on the back of my neck prickled one by one. I knew what came next. A silver glow bloomed over her blue irises.

Shit.

Smiling like a hungry nymph who'd discovered a deer with a broken leg, she said, "*You will take your squad and hunt down Ko, leader of the Bonebreaker Clan. You won't rest nor retreat until he is killed.*"

Compulsion.

Icy fingers sank into my mind, ripping through my will. The perverse magic stung as if I'd dunked my head in a barrel of frigid mountain water. Ko's pale green face replaced any other thought. I needed to run a sword through him. He had to die. The need overtook everything: my hopes, my dreams, my will that had formed an airwitch captain from an orphaned street rat.

Find Ko, the icy magic hissed in my head. *You want to please your queen.*

I shuddered, grunting against the urge to flee the underground palace and skewer the goblin. No—Lilain hadn't said immediately. The frigid compulsion relaxed in agreement, but it wouldn't uncoil from my mind. Not until I found the goblin clan leader and ended him.

There was nothing natural in Lilain's power to manipulate our desires. Witch magic revolved around the natural world and its dual balance. Day versus night. Shadow versus light. Compulsion, and its mind thievery, was anything but balanced. No other witch could do it—which explained why no one had overthrown the queen who never aged, yet another perversion.

I, on the other hand, would probably die before I reached thirty—barely more than two years away.

One by one, my squad of airwitches stood before Lilain. Some took her compulsion resolutely, stone-faced with short bows. Not the Makim twins. They steeled their jaws, lips curling into sneers. Elenna and Ansil Makim were idiots, *my* idiots, who'd been through every Lilain-induced horror alongside me since we were adolescent pages, but still idiots who couldn't veil their disgust.

Elenna bowed too low. Her nose nearly scraped her knees.

A hip-length, golden braid slid over her shoulder to curl on the stone floor. She extended an arm in a dramatic flair, the other tucked to her stomach in a mockery she didn't bother concealing. Gasps rippled from the back of the cavern where the Day Realm's courtiers hugged the wall, standing as far from Lilain's range as they dared.

I suppressed a groan. Of all the days to flout her disrespect, why pick the one when Lilain was fingering our brains?

The queen tilted her head and sharpened an unblinking gaze on Elenna. Smoke trickled from her clenched palms. At least she was using ordinary Day Witch magic now. If one could call her freakish command of it *ordinary*.

Jasmine-scented magic, sticky and pervasive, lined my nostrils. I stopped breathing, heart leaping with the rising smoke.

Elenna straightened and clicked her heels in salute. She eyed Lilain's smoking fingers with a rare whiff of contrition, but didn't back down, returning to the lined 22nd with squared shoulders and a characteristic impudent grin.

Lilain's pride wouldn't suffer another proud witch. "Lieutenant Makim." Despite the new wobble in her grin, Elenna inched back to the throne.

Enormous tallow candles on the walls flared to life with a flick of Lilain's wrist. Their flames scraped the hanging stalactites like blazing fangs. The courtiers pressed further into the wall in a chorus of whispering silks. Squinting against the sudden light, I prayed to any listening god to spare my stupid friend—but then when had the gods bothered with a witch's prayers?

"Your bravery is said to be unmatched in battle, Lieutenant"—Lilain smiled down at the snake of smoke curling around her fist—"but humility would better serve you in this court, don't you think?"

Elenna shifted from one foot to another, vigorously working her jaw. *Deep breaths,* I wanted to encourage. *Let her mock, but for gods' sake, you big-mouthed fool, don't take the bait.* Elenna jerked her head once as if flicking off an irksome fly.

"Perhaps," Lilain said in a dry drawl. "Your courage isn't what it used to be. I hope it won't fail against Ko. Rumor claims he's a fearsome Creature, capable of great violence. What a shame it would be if you didn't return."

My nails bit halfmoons into my palms.

Lilain's unblinking sweep halted on me. The tilt of her head begged me to intervene. What could be more entertaining than punishing witches in front of an audience? I kept my face blank, refusing to betray the thunder in my chest.

Finally, she laughed low and dropped her stare. The candles dimmed and plunged us back into shadow. She waved Elenna away with another deep chuckle to herself. No one was fooled. Someone would eventually pay for Elenna's disrespect.

I sank into the dark recess and slowly breathed out. One of these times Elenna would go too far and never leave this gods-forsaken throne room again. Grinning sheepishly, the insolent idiot hurried to my side. I scowled but didn't dare reprimand her this close to Lilain. Ansil had the same idea. An inverted mirror of Elenna, his tawny skin glowed in the dim candlelight like an onyx-haired masculine reflection of his sister. I could practically see him admonishing her through their mental twin bond.

What I wouldn't give to hear the tongue lashing between their joined minds.

Finished with Elenna, Ansil sidled up to me and muttered, "We need to talk."

I shot him a burning glare before fixing my attention on the Day Queen compelling the remaining airwitches. The last thing I needed were his ridiculous—and traitorous—notions. Mindful of each word Lilain used to compel the 22nd, I searched for a loophole from her control. She was careful. She wouldn't dare leave a hole for the 22nd to slither through.

With the last airwitch compelled, Lilain dismissed us. Relief trickled like a leaky spigot. The sooner I rid myself of Ko and Lilain's compulsion, the better. As if sensing my unease, the icy spiderweb tightened around my will. If I had to rip Ko's head off with my bare hands to get rid of it, then so be it.

"Captain Sathos?" a throaty voice called from behind. "A final word."

My leaky spigot of relief abruptly shut off.

I gestured the others down the maze of halls to the cavern's exit. Elenna wanted to argue, but Ansil wrenched her away. He sent me a pained glance of commissary over his shoulder before vanishing around a bend.

Smoothing the pinched lines in my expression, I spun toward Lilain.

She was running her fingers through knee-length, gilded hair, inspecting the ends. "You are a good soldier, Alys Sathos. Loyal to the innocents of your realm. Fierce and brave. Your reputation as the best swordswitch in the Day Realm Aerial Squadron is well-earned. Especially for a nearly magicless witch. You are a remarkable testament to your mother's memory."

A too-familiar pit of guilt opened in my chest at the mention of my mother. Physical pain wasn't the only knife in Lilain's arsenal of cruelty.

She looked up from her hair, smiling without warmth. "However, I do not believe Captain Federikka Sathos would allow insubordination."

Foolish me thinking I'd walk away. A clever fish might avoid the dangling bait but what hope did it have if a net waited?

"I am deeply sorry for Lieutenant Makim," I began, holding up two hands, but their trembling revealed too much. Clutching them behind my back, I said, "Rest assured, Your Majesty, it won't happen again."

Lilain chuckled. She rose and stepped from the dais with slow precision. Knee-length white robes of fine silk whose price could've fed a village for a year swished in a whisper. From a sheath at her side, she drew a knife. This time I couldn't hold my flinch.

"Shall we call Elenna back into the throne room?" she asked, never blinking.

"Please, Your Majesty. She reacts without thinking—"

"Who is to blame for her arrogance? Who failed to stamp out her defiance?"

"Me." I stuck out my hand as an offering. "As Elenna's captain, I'll take responsibility for her defiance."

I would take a thousand hours of Lilain's malice over a minute of Elenna's screams. As I did everything else in my miserable life, I'd take this punishment alone. At her core, the Day Queen didn't care who she punished. Screams and tears held a power more precious than magic—control.

She pricked my longest finger, studying the blood bead against my tawny-olive skin with a curious frown. Lifting my hand to her mouth, she whispered a spellcast. I didn't speak the dead Mother tongue, but I was overly familiar with these particular words. Worse than her natural Day magic of fire and air, her manipulation of magic through this spoken spellcast brought unspeakable pain.

The moment she released me, I cradled my hand to my chest and bit my cheek until I tasted blood. The cavern grew hot. The dim candles too bright. I couldn't catch my breath in the stuffy air. Sweat dotted my forehead, and my eyes burned.

Lilain swept back to her throne, calling for a glass of wine.

The burn began at my feet, like I'd propped them too close before a fire. It climbed up my legs, stretching tight across my skin. A slow gurgle pumped fire through my limbs. My swollen heart slowed, pressing against my lungs. And then an inferno exploded from every pore. Everything centered on the fire forcing its way through my veins, shredding reality until only agony remained.

Someone screamed. Maybe me.

Then it stopped. The burning vanished in an instant. Lilain's punishment finished, her pride smoothed over.

"Get her out," someone commanded.

I lay on my back, unable to recall falling. Wilted across the roughhewn cavern floor, I blinked up at the glowing stalactites. Someone slid an arm beneath me and pulled me up. A gruff voice muttered a healing spellcast somewhere above me. Familiar magic forced the poison from my system. I knew this magic. How many times had it floated through me when I cut myself on a sword as a page?

"Up you get, girl," Thysia rasped in my ear. My old mentor helped me to my feet, swinging a scarred arm around my shoulders when I swayed for the floor. He must have been summoned from his post as Lilain's DRAS adviser. "Not a word. We go out the doors, one step at a time. There we go. Good."

We shuffled through the stone doors and exited the cavern. With each exhale, Lilain's poison faded. By the time we reached the desert sunlight streaming into the underground palace, I limped unaided. Patting Thysia's arm, I thanked him even as shame crested my cheeks. A captain of the Day Realm's Aerial Squadron shouldn't need help. It made me look weak, and weakness was another poison.

Not that Thysia would ever see past the skeletal page, fresh off the streets, struggling to hold a sword aloft.

He shook his head. "Be careful, girl. You run a tight squad, but those Makims will bring nothing but trouble." He glared toward the entrance to the cavern where the twins waited, already floating on their brooms, arms crossed, brows drawn.

I grinned, my cheeks stretched too tight as I took my broom from a waiting page. "With all respect, sir, we're already neck deep in trouble."

Swinging a leg over the crooked notch in the broom handle, I summoned a meager gust of air magic and shot from the cavern on the pulsing air. I hadn't been born with much magic. I didn't have fire or light like most Day Witches, but at least I had enough air magic to get my broom up.

A thin cotton scarf protected my lower face from the biting sands as I raced the wind above the sandy streets of Kazadorah. Air forced itself down my nose and throat. The blistering wind roared its indignation, but I wouldn't bow to gravity. I climbed higher, ignoring the sting pricking any exposed skin. Exhilaration coursed through my veins and devoured any residual fear.

I needed more.

Anything to block the ice lingering in the back of my mind, reminding me my will wasn't mine.

I shut my eyes and leaned sideways. With a tight grip on the broomstick, I released the magic keeping the broom aloft—and plummeted toward the desert.

Wind gulped my laughter. I plunged back into the wet clouds, clutching the broom to my chest. My insides screamed in protest, tumbling and revolting against the unnatural feeling of falling too long. The untethered sensation snapped at something inside, straining to be freed.

Here in the sky, I was almost free. Nothing but gravity touched me. I was well and truly alone.

I opened watery eyes to the muddled brown mass below. Cacti and mangy shrubs dotted the desert's never-ending beige. When the city's streets became visible lines, I shoved the broom beneath me and slowed.

Ansil and Elenna waited in air above the city. The rest of the squad was a blur flying toward the DRAS tower.

"So, the 22nd heads back to the Borderlands, eh?" Elenna called when I neared. Tight lines around her mouth belied her irreverent tone. Thank the gods she didn't bring up Lilain's punishment. "Worse, we're headed for the Blackwood. A graveyard of DRAS airwitches. Home of goblins, witch-eating nymphs, and the Mother knows what else."

The Mother Goddess of life Created six Creatures of this world, each less powerful than the ones Created first. Witches came second in Creational Order, goblins fourth. The nymphs—along with banshees and the primal beasts and animals—were sixth.

"Better a goblin than a Night Witch," Ansil said with a dry laugh. We spread into a line and flew for the tower. "At least a goblin won't rip you apart with magicked shadow for the sake of it."

I rolled my eyes, but the pull to the Borderland's eerie forest tugged my gaze north. Unlike the rest of the Creatures, witches had been split into two:

those whose magic belonged to the day and those whose belonged to night. We were the Mother's second attempt at naturally balanced Creatures, and her biggest failure.

"It's one small camp. We fly in, we eliminate Ko, and we fly out. We'll be fine."

We landed on the DRAS tower top and hurried to the dining hall. Long past dinner, most airwitches were tucked into their bunks. A few remained in the hall, lounging at tables holding the remnants of dinner. They scowled when we appeared, weighing full bellies against a fight with the 22nd.

They could have Lilain's favor.

Along with her greed, her lust, and her compulsion.

"I hope one of those shits picks a fight tonight," Elenna began in an exaggerated drawl. "A good brawl before a long flight is just what I need."

I snorted and heaped fragrant rice onto my plate. Ridiculous as it was, her fiery spirit warmed me. I'd suffer Lilain's poisonous spellcasts to keep it lit. From fourteen-year-old pages to DRAS airwitches, the twins and I had seen it all together through the next fourteen years—goblins, near marriage bonds, drunken fights.

Ansil eyed the nearest witch over his loaded plate. His rain-and-soil scented magic tickled my nose, and a moment later flames blossomed from his fingertips.

"Don't," I warned. "Save your magic and strength for the coming flight. Can't have you falling asleep on your broom because you've emptied your magic for a pointless brawl."

"I'll save the reckless flying for you, Captain." But his flames vanished.

Around a mouthful of beans and flatbread, Elenna said to her brother, "They're not *that* stupid. *If* they managed past you and me, Alys would kick their asses. Or gut them." She nodded to the double dimachairi hilts rising above my shoulders. Golden hilts framed my ebony braid. The long thin swords waited snug in their sheaths, ready to be drawn. I didn't possess much magic, but my dimachairi blades had crowned me DRAS combat champion more than once. They'd also rewarded me with a captaincy: a feat Elenna proudly shoved into the jealous sneers of other squads.

I flicked a black bean at her. "Shut your mouth when you chew, pig."

She opened her mouth wider, snickering when I mimed gagging. The warmth fell from her expression as she ducked her head and swallowed. "What happened with Lilain?" I shook my head. She shoved her plate back. Worry creased the skin between her brows. "Alys—we need to talk."

"We really don't. Now, go pack."

In my rooms, I crammed everything I needed in my canvas bag and made it to the corridor before pausing. I groaned and retraced my steps, quietly shutting the door. At the window, I knelt and listened. Rhythmic thumps came from several rooms down. No doubt a pair engaging in airwitches' favorite pastime, but nothing that warned someone came my way.

I pried open the hollow windowsill and pulled out a book. A beautiful woman adorned the linen cover behind a hundred smudged fingerprints. She peered through long lashes at the man holding her, content in a world where falling in love wasn't liable to get you killed.

Lucky her.

Alone was better.

Cat-like footsteps padded down the corridor, only heard because I'd been listening for them. I slammed the windowsill shut, wincing at the sound. The doorknob twisted, and I dove, shoving the book into the stuffed bag.

Ansil stood at the door and let out a pained whine. "Please, tell me that wasn't what I think it was."

"All right. It wasn't what you think it was."

"Again, Alys?" he hissed, checking the empty corridor behind him. He eased the door shut and leaned against it, wide lips angling down. "First Elenna, now you with your damned book. Are you two desperate to die today?"

"Don't be ridiculous. Unless you rat me out, no one will know."

"There are dozens of airwitches on the other side of this door who wouldn't think twice about turning you in for contraband. Would you actually read during a goblin raid? If you're caught—"

"I can't leave it behind for someone else to find. Besides, I'll be damned if Lilain controls one more facet of my life."

Two years ago, Lilain had abruptly ordered a total book ban after something dodgy erupted in the Sorrelikah Jungle between the Mother's priestesses and Lilain. Something that sent the Day Queen on a murderous spree and slaughtered the priestesses and anyone associated with them.

Then she'd promptly banned all books.

Even the smutty ones.

Ansil dragged a hand down his pinched face, attempting a semblance of patience. He held out a hand to help me up but didn't release me. His warm, black eyes swallowed me in concern.

"You won't be damned, Alys. You'll be dead. There are better ways to fight Lilain than hiding contraband in a tower full of witches who will do anything to snatch your captaincy."

I shoved him away and shouldered the bag. He could try to talk me out of them, but in books I found the safe space I craved. In their stories, I found a happiness that didn't exist in reality. Brushing past him, I headed for the tower top's open sky.

Muttering about reckless fools, Ansil stomped behind me. A whole head taller, his shoulders dwarfed my frame. He dropped his voice, grave and sharply edged. "Things need to change, Alys. I shouldn't have to worry about my closest friend being beheaded over her obsession with romance books."

"Careful, Makim. Those are dangerous words." I paused and grinned over my shoulder. "And I'm not obsessed."

Any urgency in his voice vanished with his laugh. The velvety sound usually turned rational witches into fools for the handsome idiot. I'd seen Ansil through his gangly limb period, his lousy mustache period, even his brief period when he'd convinced himself we should become marriage bonded.

I'd quickly squashed that idea.

If anyone was immune, it was me.

Elenna and the 22nd waited at the tower top. I took my broom from a page and ran my fingers over the worn runes over the crooked handle. Three slanted lines, each with a forked tip. Standard issue, the carved runes enhanced air magic coursing through a Day Witch, even my weak magic.

Elenna, more powerful than most witches, sometimes flew brief distances without a broom if her magic reserves were full.

Oh, to be powerful.

Shooting into the stars, I glanced behind me. Tension filtered out my muscles. Twelve airwitches flew out of formation, teasing and recounting their day. Hooting loudly, the squad's young scouts—Oris and Hecuba—recalled a drunken night when Oris had fallen face first into his own vomit. Laughter filled the warm night. As close as any family, we trailed the stars, dodging moonlit clouds.

Relaxed around one another, our shoulders dropped. Laughter became more frequent. The further we flew from Kazadorah—from Lilain's unblinking gaze—the more we came alive.

But like a frigid reminder, Ko's image shoved aside any warmth.

"You will take your squad and hunt down Ko, leader of the Bonebreaker Clan. You won't rest nor retreat until he is killed."

Another whisper reminded me there would *never* be rest or retreat. Not with Lilain breathing down our necks.

2

COMPULSION IS EASIER

Alys

"All right, Ansil. Let it out."

As much as I dreaded this conversation, I couldn't bear their exchanged loaded glances behind my back any longer. Might as well get it done and over with.

Flanking me, Elenna signaled the rest of the 22nd back into the desert night sky.

"Right," Ansil began, twisting midair to make sure we were out of earshot, "our *hobby* hit a snag."

The Makims jokingly called treason their *hobby*, but firebombing Lilain's summer homes in the grassland peninsula wasn't leisurely. Nor was riling Kazadorah's market crowds into violence. Our compelled vows to protect Lilain and her court meant little to Elenna's talent for finding loopholes. She twisted every letter of Lilain's word until she created a hole to wriggle through. And it was godsdamned dangerous.

"The less I know the better," I reminded with a pained sigh.

Again, they eyed one another. A nasty little beast of jealousy reared, sniffing their bond. I squashed it, remembering moving through this dangerous world was easier alone.

Elenna shook her head. Wisps of sandy hair slipped from her scarf as she drifted closer. "Alys, I love you dearly, and I say this as a sister and not your lieutenant. You need to pull your head from your ass. The realm is dying under Lilain, and we have to do *something*."

I cast a wary gaze behind my broom toward the rest of the squad far behind. Trust only went so far when compulsion was possible.

Elenna lowered her voice. "How much more can the Day Realm endure? We don't have enough food or water. We're at war with the more powerful Night Realm over something no one even remembers. Centuries fought with blind prejudice because we wield different magic, but if they don't wipe us out, starvation will. Beyond that—think of the evil Lilain allows in the city's alleys. What kind of ruler sits back and accepts *children* suffering? You, of all people, should think about those children—"

"Don't tell me who I should think about," I snarled, slowing my flight to float beyond their reach. Guilt dissolved into shame and memory. Federikka Sathos had plucked me from those alleys. She'd saved me from the fate most orphaned Kazadoran street rats couldn't avoid. "I never forget them. When I sit down to eat, when I get into bed. I'm *well aware* of what they suffer."

The twins couldn't meet my eyes.

Bitter rage bubbled inside me, spewing out as cruelty. "You think blowing up empty buildings will change *anything*? That Lilain will suddenly grow compassion? Who'd go against the undying Day Queen and her compulsion? You, Elenna? Did you succeed today when she compelled you?"

Elenna puffed out her chest and a sneer formed, but Ansil shot her a warning glare.

Turning to me, he tried a different angle. "Sooner or later, someone will rise against her. Why not now? We need someone who can lead, who's clever. A figurehead for the realm. That's not me."

Realization sank like lead in my belly. He was pleading with me to volunteer to a cause that was little more than suicide.

"You're clever and passionate, Alys. Loyal to a people who'd look down on you because of your magic, but those of us who know better would follow you to the death. Not because of your power or origins, but because of your indelible ability to overcome everything thrown at you. We could spread much needed hope if more followed your lead—mind over sheer power."

My scoff was deafening in their hopeful silence.

"I'm a powerless witch who gained the captaincy by the skin of my teeth. I'll forever ride Federikka Sathos's coattails. Lilain would laugh before burning me to cinders and scattering what remained over the desert. I am nothing—*nothing*—against her."

"You are much more than you realize," Elenna blurted. "Gods, Alys. You're fucking brilliant. No one finds compulsion loopholes or navigates the courtiers' schemes like you. You don't need magic. We just need someone who *thinks* like you."

"*No.* When Lilain finds out—because she always does—you will sentence everyone you know, guilty or not, to painful death."

Snarling, Ansil spun my shoulder, nearly yanking me from my broom. "The Day Realm is full of hungry people craving more than food. They're tired of barely surviving. They want to *thrive*. And if I die striving for freedom from a tyrant, then I go to the Soul Lands fighting for something worthwhile."

Elenna took a ragged breath, tears brimming in her dark eyes. "I know we're asking too much, and failure is nearly certain. But think of the hope we could bring if we *succeeded*. Think of how different the realm could be if a few had courage."

The shifting clouds revealed glimpses of the moon-brightened sand below, but I shut out the desolate beauty. Instead, I imagined the squalor of the streets; the children with smudged cheeks; knives waiting in dark alleys. I thought of the underground palace with its pompous courtiers like engorged ticks living off the back of the Day Realm, of the queen and her unblinking eyes.

"You two are more than this realm deserves, but courage isn't enough to break Lilain's hold, and I won't be a part of something that eventually kills you."

Their silence followed me into morning, full of a thousand unsaid words. Disappointing them smarted, but I wouldn't risk our lives for something fruitless. Lilain held a sword over our heads, and she'd wield it with the slightest provocation.

Night dissolved into day. Sand became sparse grasslands before the Blackwood Forest rose on the horizon. Mangled trees spanned the Borderlands, halving the island between the two witch realms. Here, the dark shadows hid secrets only the Mother knew. I'd take the beasts of the Sorrelikah Jungle over the Blackwood where beasts weren't the only predators. Goblins, elves, Night Witches—all keen to bleed a DRAS airwitch.

With a readying inhale, the 22nd fanned out on my signal and ducked into the trees. The scouts, Oris and Hecuba, had already darted ahead to search what awaited. Earthy decay greeted my nose on a breeze. The chittering of squirrels and birds was conspicuously absent, as if they didn't dare wake the forest.

A high-pitched whistle broke the eerie silence and Oris exploded from the trees. He signaled us to halt and ripped the scarf from his neck, releasing a waterfall of inky hair down his back. "The goblins are gone. The whole Mother bleeding camp is empty."

Growls burst behind me. The bond-married pair, Uzza and Rami, cursed louder than the rest.

I held up a hand and the squad fell silent.

"Where's Hecuba?"

Oris jerked a thumb over his shoulder. "Sweeping the camp's perimeter."

Another series of shrill whistles pierced the forest in the direction of the Bonebreaker's camp. The 22nd shot forward in attack formation, winding around snagging branches. Breaking the tree line, we entered a meadow of tents. Burnt oil and chicken lingered fresh on the air. Scraggly tents circled a campfire, each held up by tight lines of damp clothing. Something prodded my memory, but the pull of compulsion reminded me I was after Ko's head.

Hecuba floated on her broom at the edge of the camp. She'd summoned a fiery ring in the tall grass where a single goblin sat at its center. As one, the 22nd surrounded me in a tight formation. Uzza and Rami claimed the front, fire leaping from their palms.

I signaled the wary airwitches, and a path formed toward the goblin.

"Please," he whispered. Meadow-green hands wavered above his balding head. "I mean no harm."

My feet skimmed the grass as I descended onto the meadow's plush bed. I raised two fingers in signal and dismounted my broom. Immediately, Ansil and Uzza were on the ground beside me. Another signal and Elenna whizzed away to loop the perimeter.

Even for the short, stocky goblins, the Creature shivering in the grass was small. The top of his head barely reached my shoulders. Liver spots pocked his green skin. His slicked jet-black hair couldn't hide the missing chunks.

Sickness ran rampant in the unforgiving goblin camps. Even the most loyal of clans would've left behind one of their own if it meant survival.

I crouched outside the fiery ring and pulled down my scarf.

Uzza rumbled a warning. Her smoky-scented magic swarmed, ready to attack, but I nodded at Hecuba who lowered the ring.

The goblin remained on his knees, swaying back and forth, wheezing an incoherent prayer. My heart softened, wondering what sort of life he'd led to end up alone and forgotten. It wasn't unlikely I was already on the same path. I reached out and steadied him. Reading something in my gesture, he sagged against my hand. We both knew how this ended, but I wouldn't be cruel.

Motioning to the empty camp, I asked, "How did your clan know we were coming?"

The goblin laughed, a sound like swords scraping across stone. "Your Day Court has more leaks than a broken pot."

I frowned, but compulsion prodded an icy finger. "Where is your clan leader?"

"Please . . ."

"The clan leader, goblin."

"Kazen." He burst into a wet cough before wiping purple blood from his mouth. "I am Kazen of the Bonebreakers, and I'm all that remains of our clan's camp."

Ansil crouched beside me. With my nod, he said, "You've been abandoned, Kazen. Would you protect those who'd sacrifice you to run? Help us find Ko. He's all we want."

"What do witches know of sacrifice?" the goblin wheezed. He sniffed the smoky air and grimaced. "Ko would sacrifice himself for his people in glorious death. Can you say the same of your queen?"

Ansil dove for the shrinking goblin, flames licking his fingers.

"No," I snapped, wrenching Ansil back by the back of his collar. "We need him."

To Kazen, I said, "I can give you what goblins want most. A glorious death. Not one brought by sickness, but one with a sword in your hand, your enemy stealing your last breath. Just give me Ko."

He narrowed tar-black eyes devoid of any white, but a tinny quality entered his breathing. "Northwest of here there is a valley at the base of the Vinnith Mountains, near the Miner's Pass. You'll find Ko and my clan gathered there." Purple-stained teeth widened in a grin. "But you won't bring him down."

"Give Kazen a sword."

With a sharp steel ring, Ansil extended his dimachairi. Kazen snatched the long, thin blade, but the sudden movement brought on another cough that rocked his frail frame.

I waited for it to subside before drawing my sword.

Glancing skyward, he muttered something in the Mother tongue, a final prayer. With a deep breath, he launched forward. His strikes were shallow, his blade slipping against mine. I let him take the offensive for a few moments, but his withered body couldn't handle it long.

He dropped to his knees in the grass and moaned. I mentally offered remorse to the Mother and ran the blade through his heart. Purple blood stained the crisp white linen shirt. Again, something tugged at my memory.

Find Ko. Kill Ko.

"Th-thank you, witch. May y-you also find glory . . . in . . . in death."

His hand dropped to the ground, the sword tumbling from his grip.

Hecuba burned the body, allowing the goblin one final honor before his soul traveled to the Soul Lands. The breeze around us swelled and gathered his ashes, returning them to the circle of our world.

We found Elenna and flew for the Vinnith Mountains and Ko. The land beneath tumbled in a mass of trees and hills. Oaks became evergreen giants, towering over soil no longer golden with sand. Gone was the warm, arid air, replaced by a chill penetrating our scarves. Even the birds became less familiar. The red desert hawks had long vanished. Above us, golden eagles shrieked and dove as if recognizing Day Witches didn't belong this far north.

Out here shadows hid Night Witches and their strange magic. Wholly different from Day Witches, yet eerily alike. Two balancing ends of the Mother's nature. Light and flame versus shadow and water. A Day Witch's ability to fly matched by a Night Witch's unholy way of moving through shadow and appearing out of thin air.

The thought did not sit well.

Goblins were one thing. A trained Night Witch army led by the Night Princess General another. Princess Melisandre and I had crossed swords more times than I cared to recall, and each time I'd barely survived. If I didn't see the calculating Night Princess on this trip, I'd count it a success.

The mountains came into view, but a brewing thunder cloud did too. I signaled for a stop and the 22nd halted above a stony ridge. The Miner's Pass waited beyond the ridge, the goblin's valley surely on the other side.

"Perfect," Elenna yelled into the mounting wind. She nodded to the incoming dark sky. "A bit of cloud cover and rain will hide us."

Gathering the squad, I warned, "Don't try anything stupid. We find Ko, we end him and compulsion. We get out."

"But there's more than a camp now. Can we take on a whole clan?" someone asked.

"They don't know we're coming," I answered. "They think they've escaped. Remember, goblins don't have much magic on their own. On the other hand, one clan's combined magic is powerful, but goblins have to gather it together. If we sneak up on them, they won't have time to bind their magic into one source."

I was reminding myself as much as them. "We fly in and out. No unnecessary lollygagging."

Elenna laughed; all earlier consternation gone. She swung her arm around my shoulder, waggling her brows. "Give me the right kind of lolly, and I'll happily gag."

I bit my tongue on a snicker and shoved her away. Amidst Elenna and Oris's gleeful hoots and innuendos, I signaled the squad back into formation. We split into two lines: Ansil leading one, I the other. I took the eastern end of the valley and lead Elenna, Oris, and the others into the storm. Ansil and his line took the western end.

Over the ridge, the hills flattened, giving way to the valley. I squinted through the incoming rain, but the storm had darkened the valley below. Lightning crackled inside the clouds as the thunder's booms shattered the wind.

To the west, Ansil and the others flashed in the lightning before a shrouding rain curtain descended.

Elenna fought the gale with impatient hands. She attempted to carve an easy path with air magic, but the storm wouldn't budge. Screaming winds pushed us west, to the center of the valley. To my left, Oris and Uzza lifted arms, each battling the gales. If Elenna's powerful magic couldn't fight it, neither could they. I signaled them to stop and conserve their magic.

A dancing light below caught my eye—our target—but I couldn't see much more through driving rain.

I signaled for descent, and we lowered, struggling through the winds forcing us westward. I searched for Ansil and the others but found only impenetrable sheets of rain. My scarf was soaked, my face numb beneath it. Frigid fingers slipped on my broom as I struggled to keep it level.

To the west, lightning lit the clouds from within, briefly displaying the silhouettes of Ansil's line against the foreboding sky. The shrieking winds pushed them eastward as they fought to slow down.

No, that wasn't right.

The winds blew westward, not east.

I glanced at Ansil's line, but they'd disappeared. The winds blew me west and yet—Ansil blew eastward . . . pushing us both toward the goblin camp.

Oh, gods.

We'd flown into a fucking ambush.

3

AS FAR AS THE ARROW FLIES

Alys

The goblin arrows flew before I whistled a warning. Streaks of wood and feather fletching burst from the darkness below. Cursing, I jerked my broom higher. Frigid rain stung my eyes. An arrow brushed over my foot, and a scream exploded somewhere to my right.

Retreat.

Icy compulsion clenched around my desire to save us. *Retreat.* Trapped by compulsion, the word couldn't escape. Whatever waited for us, we couldn't turn back. Only killing Ko would get us out.

On my signaling whistle, we dove for the valley, weaving through a torrent of arrows and rain. Fire bloomed across my line of airwitches in an answering volley.

In reply, the sky boomed.

Goblin magic and their ability to control the skies and ground wasn't supposed to be a threat. A single clan pooled their magic into one source, a clan leader or priest. Surely one clan didn't hold enough power for a deadly thunderstorm. I squinted down at the ring of lights, trying to see beyond the cloaking darkness. This attack had been coordinated, ready and waiting.

Godsdamn Kazen.

I signaled the line into a defensive formation in a series of whistles. We should've been keeping high from reach. Instead, compulsion forced us further below.

Another volley of arrows whizzed past.

I dropped in the air, flattening against the broom handle. Without magic, I was useless against air attacks. I needed to get to the ground.

"Conniving bastards," Elenna howled. She flung out both hands, and a dragon of silver and blue flames formed midair. Snapping jaws blasted fire into the darkness below. Blue tinged light lit up rows of tents before rain smothered the fire. Gods, how many goblins were there besides Ko's clan?

I whistled again, warning the line to prepare for the worst. Not that it made a difference.

No retreat.

Across the valley, Ansil's line burned arrows out of the sky in flashes of red and gold. Faint whoops of triumph bounced off the nearby mountains. Ansil's golden dragon joined Elenna's, and the two magicked beasts stormed for the ring of lights.

The arrows began again.

Heavier than before, they swarmed the sky in wall of fletching and wood. Oris sent a wall of flame, but he wasn't fast enough. A hiss nicked my neck, slicing through my scarf.

Uzza's scream split the air, and a gurgling cry answered her before fading into the valley.

"Rami!" she called in a broken wail.

"*Hold*," I roared over my shoulder. She fixed a stare on the ground, shoulders heaving. Rami was gone. Uzza's magic-imbued bond to another for life, shattered. Smoke and steam poured off her, but she remained with the line—caged by compulsion.

Lightning forked across the sky in an explosion of revealing light. Rows of goblins waited below. Hundreds of tents lined the valley with unlit campfires. Thousand more bows aimed high. The ring of light had been a false beacon, leading the 22nd into a thousand-strong ambush.

Gods help us.

One airwitch squad against thousands of goblins. All pooling magic into a powerful force. With this many together, I didn't know what they were capable of. I couldn't risk more of my squad's lives. We'd already lost too much.

A cold grip tightened around my will.

No, it hissed. *Kill Ko. Nothing else matters.*

Against all reason, the 22nd dove into the waiting carnage. I gave into Lilain's compulsion, letting it shove aside the bubbling horror.

Elenna and Uzza whizzed across the valley on trails of magic. A dragon of fire sprang to life, a sparking tornado following. The powerful display inhaled tents and goblins in a fountain of fire and air, leaving behind scorched earth.

I dove lower and scanned the tents. As clan leader, Ko would be at the center of the Bonebreaker camp. Not among the archers. But the clever goblins had wrapped the valley in a thick sheet of rain, making visibility impossible.

Across the valley, two airwitches plummeted to the earth. I searched the sky, loosing a breath when a golden dragon burst through a tent and roared.

The air hummed, and I had a moment's warning before lightning struck.

Fingers of electricity forked, striking the air inches from my face. I hurtled sideways, blinking furiously against white spots.

Ahead, Hecuba froze. Lightning outlined her before the boom came.

Blood splattered across my face. A coppery, burnt scent masked everything else.

Shit. Shit. Shit.

Something sticky slipped down one cheek and off my chin. Heart galloping, I searched the air for the girl. She'd been just ahead of me . . .

Another soft hum broke my horror. Lightning sliced the air ahead.

Everything went white.

I hauled my broom blindly to the side, breathing through my mouth against the stench of charred flesh.

The hiss of arrows joined the chaos. Uzza's final roar faded to the ground. Something sliced my shoulder. I jerked further left, praying to any listening god I wasn't flying into another volley.

Under the goblins' rain cover, I dove for the ground. The blurry tent tops were an empty maze of sodden canvas. The goblins had amassed around the archers leaving most of the tents empty.

I rubbed my eyes and hissed through the sting, willing my vision back. The last thing I needed was to walk into another ambush.

A familiar clash of steel dimly rang to south—with it a rush of relief. Following the sound, I wound on my broom through tents, narrowly dodging flapping banners.

There.

Elenna and Oris were back-to-back in the mud. Each shot magic from one hand, the other swinging dimachairi. Dozens of goblins surrounded them, howling and brandishing axes and pikes.

Silently, I drew my own dimachairi and landed behind a tent. I tipped my broom and sent it into the sky, waiting to be summoned. Nearby archers aimed for Ansil's line. Shouts of glee erupted when an airwitch plunged to the ground. Hands shaking, I breathed deep and steadied my rage. Elenna and Oris first.

No, Ko first, Lilain's compulsion reminded, a frigid parasite feeding on my adrenaline.

I shook my head, trying to clear its hold. I needed Elenna and Oris to get Ko. I couldn't do this alone. Hoping that was enough of a loophole, I took a testing step in their direction.

Nothing.

I edged around the tents.

The sigil of Ko's fiercest rival clan hung limp off a nearby tent post. I squinted at the next banner and rubbed my eyes again before inspecting the rest of the sigils. The banners of every other rival clan who'd ordinarily attack Ko on sight dotted the valley. Every goblin clan was here. What the bleeding Mother had we flown into?

Ko's Bonebreaker banners became more prevalent. The skull and crossbones of their sigil flags hung motionless, saturated in the pouring rain.

I heard Elenna before I saw her.

"You bastards think you have me?" she shrieked. A teeth-rattling boom followed. "I'll ram your axe so far up your ass you'll choke on your own shit!"

I'd known Elenna for thirteen years. There was no mistaking the tremor in her voice.

I leapt from the shadows and ran. Ducking beneath a surprised goblin's outstretched arm, I darted for Elenna. Two more goblins lunged, swinging battered swords. I spun and dodged low, sinking sword into belly.

More goblin howls followed, but I ran, fighting not to slip in the mud. Heart pounding, breath gasping, I hacked through goblins. I had to reach Elenna.

Parry, thrust, slash. Another goblin fell. Then another.

A jagged iron blade veered for my throat. I threw my weight back and arced my dimachairi.

Through the smoke and rain, I spotted Elenna's golden head drenched in rain and purple blood. Nearby, Oris hurled waves of fire, erecting a thin wall from the incoming horde, but his flames had begun to falter.

They'd nearly depleted their magic.

We needed Ko.

I sprinted the final distance, swerving around a crumpled goblin on fire.

"Mother curse you, Alys," Elenna snarled before throwing me a bloody, toothy grin. She launched another ball of flame before closing the gap between us. Her arms swung around my neck, smearing blood across my cheek. "After that lightning storm I thought you were dead."

I winced and thumped her back. "Give me an hour."

Thrusting my dimachairi at an incoming blade, I scanned the brightly lit clearing.

"Ko?"

"He ran through like I'd lit his ass on fire. Missed him by a hair's breadth. Then the bastard vanished. Couldn't follow. Too many goblins."

We spun, backs together, trying to trace a path toward Oris who held back a dozen goblins. Countless crude blades smashed against our swords. Blood splattered purple and red in the black mud. Goblin claws found exposed skin until my face stung with mud, blood, and sweat.

Oris reached us first, panting and clutching his thigh. Another wicked gash oozed blood across his hairline. But he was grinning.

"I found Ko."

He jerked his head to a clump of tents before dashing through a mass of howling goblins. Together, we flung magic and swords to form a path. Dozens more goblins poured from tents.

After a few dizzying minutes of winding around tents, we vanished into their own wind-wrapped rain.

Oris ducked behind a crate smelling of oranges, stopping to point at a tent a few paces ahead. "Ko's up ahead. See that banner? It's his personal Bonebreaker sigil."

Larger than the others, the tent's walls bulged with activity. A thunderous voice rivaling the storm bellowed out orders from within.

I tugged Elenna back when she started to rise.

"Wait. Where's Ansil and his line?"

She tilted her head, then winced. "Still in the air. West of our position. His line's gone."

Only four remained of the once powerful 22nd Squad. Pushing aside the rising panic, I ordered, "Tell him to create a distraction and cover us from the air. Let's pull Ko from the tent."

Elenna nodded and a moment later a boom rattled the valley. Ansil's golden dragon roared, followed by the clan leader's booming curse. Goblins streamed from the tent, each nocking arrows they pointed into the sky.

Ko finally appeared, ripping past the tent flap and bellowing orders. Taller than the nearest goblin, he carried himself with the pride of a leader and the swagger of a battle-worn warrior. An ancient crossbow sat cradled like in infant in his muscled arms.

"Get that witch down, or I'll serve your livers for breakfast," he roared.

A female goblin dressed in knee-length robes of shocking violet dogged Ko's steps. She raised a staff adorned with a glowing blue orb toward the sky. Merciless black eyes fixed onto Ansil, and she began chanting in the Mother tongue.

"Watch for the priestess," I whispered. "That orb contains their combined magic. Break it if you get the chance. Otherwise, avoid her."

Elenna whistled low through her teeth. "Got it. Kill Ko. Purple-robed bitch is extra." With a flick of her fingers, a blue flamed dragon roared past, riding on a wave of spring-scented magic—a vibrant contrast to Elenna's destruction.

We rose from our hiding place and barreled for Ko's back.

A young goblin met my eyes.

He let out a warning shriek, and every goblin in the clearing spun.

The priestess spotted us first. She thrust the staff high, and the storm surged for Elenna's dragon. Steam exploded into the clearing as rain swallowed fire. It drenched us in stifling, sticky air. Grunting, Elenna fell to her knees, trying in vain to keep the dragon alive. But not even a powerful Day Witch could hold back the magic of every goblin on the island of Efelldor.

The dragon hissed into vapor, and everything vanished in a blanketed haze.

I could hardly make out Oris an arm's length from me. Breath held, we slowly spun, searching the steam for Ko or Elenna. The priestess too had vanished.

A frantic whisper muttered a spellcast in the Mother tongue somewhere to the left.

I swung my dimachairi and found flesh and robes.

Purple blood splashed my chest. The priestess released a gurgled cry, but it was too late. The pulsing orb toppled into the mud, threatening to roll beyond reach. Diving, I slammed the sword hilt onto the glass. Blue light exploded from the shattered orb.

Take that, you murderous bitch.

The pouring rain halted. A thousand goblins burst into howls as their magic streamed back. We'd halfway done it. If we could take out Ko, we were headed home.

Oris let out a wild whoop, then clamped a hand over his mouth, eyes wide.

Shit.

Somewhere in the steam, a squelching boot lifted out of the mud. Then the telltale *click* of a loaded crossbow.

I lunged for the young scout. An iron bolt slammed through my shoulder, ripping leather and bone. Pain exploded, and I couldn't think past the burning in my arm. My collar bone snapped on impact, but the bolt had gone clean through.

Sprawled across Oris, I inhaled a scream with a whimper. Every bone in my arm threatened to give way in protest of my collar. I rolled off Oris who scrambled up and hauled me to my feet. Sheathing one useless sword, I clutched the other in my good hand.

Kill Ko and get out. We were *close*.

Nodding once, Oris and I sprinted toward the bolt's origin. Now or never. I signaled Oris, and he adjusted his grip on his dimachairi. I'd go low for the goblin leader. He'd go high. We'd rip Ko in half and end this Mother cursed nightmare.

But we were not fast enough.

A wind swept the fog aside. We jerked up in horror and found Elenna clearing the steam. Ko, too, materialized across the clearing.

He roared and slammed his hand across the reloaded crossbow trigger.

Time slowed to a crawl.

On and on, the bolt barreled.

Oris's young features twisted into shock. He lurched one hand up as if to block the bolt. It ripped through his sternum with a snap. The heavy momentum threw him into the mud. Frowning at the iron protruding from his chest, he opened his mouth as if to argue. He swayed, once, twice. Surprise etched his carefree face before he slumped into the mud.

And then he was still.

No, no, no. He was too young. Barely old enough to be a scout.

I lurched for him, but a shadow fell over me.

An axe slammed into my wounded shoulder. My scream spurred time back into place and I careened face first into the mud. Scrabbling in the mud through the fire in my shoulder, I heaved my head free. Blazing agony dotted the edges of my conscious. My arm throbbed uselessly—but it was still there.

Gasping, I rolled over, ready to leap. Another shadow crossed me.

This was it. The moment I died—alone in the filth.

Golden flames lit up the sky. The axe-wielding goblin shrieked, trying to rip off his flaming furs. Another goblin crashed into him. This one's green skin melted to reveal bone.

The soothing scent of soil after a rainstorm washed away the horrors of the slaughter. Above, Ansil wove in and out of tent poles like a heroic god of fire.

A sob heaved out. Relief overtook pain. I scrambled up with a single dimachairi, slashing through goblins with new vigor.

"One last chance," I snarled to Elenna, smashing a sword hilt into a howling goblin's nose. "We run for Ko, and we escape this shithole."

"I'm down to the dregs of my magic. Basically—one good shot."

Throwing one another rueful grins in silent goodbyes, we dove into the fray of goblins. We knew this day would come from the moment of enlistment. Airwitches rarely lived long lives.

Icy fingers around my mind urged me onto the huge goblin reloading the godsdamned crossbow. Only a bit further. If I reached Ko before he finished reloading . . . Baring his teeth, he lifted the weapon onto his shoulder and aimed the crossbow into the sky.

Ansil wasn't watching Ko. Intent on clearing our path to the goblin leader, he hurled balls of flickering fire into the goblin masses.

The bolt slid into place. The anchoring string snapped.

Ko wrapped his hand around the trigger and squeezed.

"No!"

Elenna's scream pierced the shrieks.

Fire evaporated from Ansil's hands. He looked down and found me, but I was transfixed on the bolt sticking out from his chest. I was imagining it. Surely. Not Ansil. He was too quick, too clever for an iron bolt to end his vivid life.

Blinking too slowly, he slipped from his broom and plummeted to the ground. Graceful long limbs pointed toward the sky as his braid fluttered like black rope around his neck. He hit the ground with silent force. Unmoving.

I staggered toward the body, but my feet whipped toward another path. Toward Ko.

Everything went numb. As if ice replaced my blood. *Kill Ko.*

No. I needed to get to Ansil. He might still be alive. He might—

Elenna's screams rang in my ears, but the ice shut her out.

Kill Ko.

One step and then another. Away from Ansil's body.

Elenna flailed her arms toward her brother, even as her feet sent her to Ko. Throwing her head back, she screamed. The heart-wrenching wail forced even the goblins to pause.

She reached Ko first. Both her dimachairi sailed for the goblin leader fumbling with his crossbow. One sword missed, disappearing into the maze of tents. The other sank into Ko's throat.

I didn't bother to watch him die. Compulsion retreated and I knew Ko was dead.

With Elenna's daggers and my swords, we carved a path through goblins to Ansil's body.

But he didn't move. His chest didn't rise and fall.

"Answer me, you stupid prick," Elenna begged, but their mental link had died with him.

"The compulsion's gone—"

"I'm not leaving him."

"Elenna, we need to go while we can."

I summoned my broom with a whistle, kicking a goblin from inching closer before mounting with one arm. A horde of goblins raced for Elenna's unguarded back.

"Summon your broom, Lieutenant. That's an order."

"I'm not *leaving* him." She looked up, and my heart crashed into the mud. Her smile was final. "You were meant for something special, Captain. Even Lilain can see it. Go take that bitch off the throne."

"Elenna, no. *No!*"

Head thrown back between a sob and a laugh, Elenna gathered her final dregs of magic and flung me into the sky.

My mind spun like the broom. Too much had happened too quickly.

I focused on keeping my seat on the wayward broom. Flattened against the handle, I refused to give the winds purchase, but Elenna's wind had no aim. My arm on fire, I screamed into the gale. One hand wasn't enough to control the bucking broom. Rolling midair, I lurched from the valley. Elenna's magic was too much. It overpowered my meager attempts to gain control.

A towering pine loomed dead ahead.

The broom abruptly sank.

No. If Ansil was too clever to die, then Elena was too bright. She was supposed to be the ray of light, the one who could pull me from my dark thoughts. But the vanished magic said there was no one pulling me out of anything.

Heart in my throat, I tried to guide the falling broom's descent. I couldn't keep hold of the slick handle. My good arm was going numb. With an abrupt dip, the broom slipped out from under me, and I plunged for the Blackwood below.

4

MORE THAN FIRE BURNS

Corryn

As an instructor of the Night Realm's Amethyst Hall, the daunting smell of adolescence was altogether familiar. The smell of a burning tapestry—on the other hand—was not.

"Fire!"

Chairs squealed across the dining hall's stone floors immediately following the student's shriek. Flames engulfed an ancient tapestry as the threadwork of an ancient elven queen crumbled into ash.

Scurrying around fleeing students, I conjured a wave of water from the air's moisture. Calls from fellow instructors rang through the hall, directing too-helpful students from the fire. A year-one girl began a chorus of wails. Others followed.

I smothered a sigh and flung water at the blaze, mentally apologizing to the elven queen. Behind me, an instructor calmed the wailing. Weeks-long punishment awaited whoever had left a candle unattended. Why was a candle necessary at breakfast? The dining hall's soaring windows with views of the Vinnith Mountains provided enough light.

Unless—Gods, I hoped not.

Leaning forward as if to inspect the damage, I sniffed the tapestry. Smoke and musty fabric met my nose. Nothing untoward. But as I turned, the slight scent of summoned magic wafted past. Soft and sweet, like lilacs in a field.

And terribly bad news.

I sent another wave onto the tapestry; this one wobbly. A whoosh of mountain breeze scented magic obliterated any sign the lilacs had been there. Unfortunately, it wouldn't stop the rumors of a mysterious fire from spreading straight to the Night Realm capital and its queen.

Spinning, I faced the dining hall and examined the young Night Witches.

Pillars of lavender-veined white marble stood sentinel over instructors shepherding students back to breakfast. At the head table, the headwitch frowned. Her sharp gaze swiveled between me and the extinguished tapestry. I didn't dare confirm her worse fears this publicly, but my flat expression said enough. Blood vanished from her high cheeks through a tight smile.

I couldn't blame her. A Dual Realm Witch had summoned fire in the middle of breakfast before any and all eyes. Few knew Dual Witches even existed. If they did, they'd be horrified by the unnatural magic they wielded—magic from *both* kinds of witches. Worse, they wrought an imbalance capable of tipping the delicate scales of power between the two realms.

As if the abnormal conception between enemy realms wasn't worry enough, the poor Dual Witches had to contend with the Night Queen's beast. Whatever it was, the thing caught and slaughtered the innocent witches.

Pulling my pearl bracelet loose from my blouse's cuff, I scanned not quite corporeal shadows flitting over the students—young *Night* magic. Amongst those eager faces, a Dual Witch hid; more than likely one of the newly arrived year ones. I knew the older students well, but the new ones held dangerous secrets.

The children of well-to-do merchants or courtiers of the Night Queen's court didn't spare me a glance as I passed, but they were not who I was after. I focused on the few staring at their loaded breakfasts with distrust or fidgeting with their brand-new uniforms. Those whose magic, not family or coin, had earned them a place at Amethyst Hall. A magic powerful enough to gain the school's attention, but not enough to garner the friendship of their wealthy peers—something I recalled all too well.

Centuries ago, the most powerful Night Witches gathered to form the royal Night court, bloodlines which thrummed with magic into modern day. Power begat power after all. Although, sometimes, the Mother did not abide by bloodlines. Sometimes, a mere nobody manifested more power than even the Night Queen's royal bloodline. Amongst these distrustful students—poor and too world wise—I would find the Dual Witch.

Before Queen Morgenna found them first.

Head lost in a cloud of memory, I stepped into the school's courtyard, hurrying through the heavily scented flowers to my runes class.

"Corryn," an elegant voice called. "A moment, please."

Rilessa Stellanati, the current headwitch of Amethyst Hall—and my mother—squeezed between two trellises of climbing roses to cut across the courtyard's garden. She flicked her wrist, muttering, *"Sonus abiit."*

The air shifted iridescent in a sparkle of pink and gold. Spellcasted magic encased us in a thin bubble, blocking our voices from listening ears. Rilessa's ink-smeared hands quaked as they reached for me.

"The tapestry, Corryn. Are you certain it was summoned fire magic?"

"I'm certain. There's another Dual Witch."

Rilessa sank against the trellis. Thorns snagged at her woolen skirts, no doubt pricking the skin beneath, but she paid them no mind. Silver threaded her jet-black hair, reflecting decades of her mission to save as many Dual Witch children as she discovered. Time and headwitch responsibilities weighed on the once unobtrusive instructor who'd raised a lonely, odd child on her own at Amethyst Hall.

I squeezed her shoulder, wishing strength into her. "We'll find the child before Morgenna and hide them. We'll do it again."

"But her beast—"

"Can't find the student if Morgenna doesn't."

"If you were suspicious of the fire, someone else could be too. Spies are everywhere—amongst the instructors, the students. How long until Morgenna discovers a child summoned fire in a crowd of Night Witches and sends her beast to kill the child? What excuse will she make for *this* death?"

"In our years of protecting the students, we've never lost one."

We'd heard stories of others less fortunate. Whispers of families hidden in the Blackwood found inexplicably murdered, one parent a mystery to anyone who knew the family—a secreted Day Witch, Rilessa and I would furtively realize. No Dual Witch hid from Morgenna's beast for long—whatever it was. She found them and her beast slaughtered them. Only children who made their way to Amethyst Hall found safety. Rilessa and I bound their magic inside them, and we released them to live a magicless life.

If Morgenna uncovered what we'd been doing—I seized my pearl bracelet, counting each pearl to soothe the rising anxiety.

Twenty pearls. Always twenty.

"We won't fail," I said, lifting my chin. "We'll outmaneuver her again. We're two unassuming instructors, content to play the part of bookish witches with our heads in the clouds."

"She'll know about the tapestry within the week. If the child publicly displays Day magic again, she'll know within a day." She clasped my hand, gripping my knuckles until they went white. "We are not invincible. The chance of Morgenna or her beast catching us grows with each child we hide."

A spark of unfamiliar defiance tingled through my fingertips. In the middle of the morning, the courtyard darkened. Shadows from the nearby columns slithered through the garden at my unintended call, reaching like serpents for my skirt's hem.

"I will not roll over in cowardice because of her power-hungry vendetta. Dual Witches don't ask to be born. If Morgenna seeks to destroy them out of fear of their power, then I'll stand between her and the child. Dual Witches are Creatures of the Mother with lives worth saving too."

Rilessa loosened her grip on my hand, sighing softly. She straightened and plucked a rose from the trellis. "You are everything good in this world, even when the world offers you little in return, but Morgenna will never rest. If both realms knew they could create a new power together, they'd never stand for separation. Morgenna will always hunt Dual Witches. She *will* protect this threat to her power at all costs."

She crushed the rose and let it fall to the gravel.

I shook my head, almond-colored curls flying in every direction. "I don't care about politics or power. I *will* find this student, and I *will* save them from Morgenna."

Rilessa smiled. A lingering sadness softened the lines of her cheeks. She wove her arm through mine and pulled me close. "May that purity keep you safe from those who would seek to destroy it, my darling."

5

THE CAGED SNAKE

Alys

E verything hurt.

Every bone ached from the fall. My shattered collarbone bordered on agony Lilain would've been proud of. Cushioned amongst pine needles and springy moss, I gulped in air, glaring up at an enormous pine. Pale bark flaked off where I'd grappled for a hold as I fell.

I rolled onto my belly, but a fresh wave of nauseating pain forced me to halt. Breathing deep through my nose, I listened for goblin shrieks. Nothing. Scattered rays of dying sunlight barely lit the Blackwood. I had no idea how far Elenna had flung me. For all I knew, I was deep in the Vinnith Mountains.

Gods, Elenna.

Elenna, Ansil, Oris. My airwitches now waited at the Crone's mercy—all except me—the one who should've saved them.

Throat tightening, I tried starving the rising emotion, but it swept over me in a red wave. I slammed my fists into the ground and let loose a scream. Burning hot pain shot up my injured arm with the fire of a thousand suns. Embracing the throbbing, I pounded the mossy earth, accepting it as proof I lived when others didn't.

The northern Blackwood's unfamiliar groans crested with my screams. Peculiar creaking from somewhere behind me rose the hairs on my neck. Tales of succubi and witch-eating wood nymphs colored the stories of airwitches who ventured too close to the Night Realm border. I had to get out of the forest. If I could fly from the Blackwood with one arm, the rest of the journey home was simple.

I scanned the nearby brush for a broomstick handle. Then the fallen leaves. The moss. Even crawled to search a rotting log.

Nothing.

Snarling, I drew a sword, ready to obliterate a nearby bush, but something had beaten me to it. The top center of the bush had collapsed on itself. Ripped leaves and broken twigs circled the hole. I plunged into the bush, wading deep into green thorns until my palm met something smooth. Triumphant, I closed my hands around the polished handle and pulled.

A single shard of the carved handle sat in my palm.

Worthless. Shattered in the fall.

"No." I wouldn't let this end me so easily. There had to be a way out. Maybe only one piece had snapped off.

I dove back into the bush. Thorns tore my cheeks, snagging my hair. I only found more wooden shards. Sinking to my heels, I cradled the remains of my way out of this nightmare. Which god had I pissed off so thoroughly to earn such a day? I was as good as dead out here.

Think, I reminded myself. I was alone, yes, but wasn't that when I excelled?

Images of falling witches pricked sharper than the thorns. I was alone because they were *dead*.

Flinging the useless broom, I surrendered it to the darkness. Who was I to live when greater, more powerful witches died for me? Who was I but an orphaned nobody saved by luck and a kind heart? I slammed my fist to the earth again and welcomed the pain. Compared to guilt, pain felt tangible, like it had an end.

I lifted my fist again, but a voice snapped the air, sounding as if a dozen women spoke together.

You will cease at once.

The voice didn't belong to this world. Ethereal, ageless, powerful—undoubtedly a god. A bright light exploded beyond the nearby tree line.

Yelping, I scrambled backward, raising my good arm to shield my eyes.

From the light, a figure formed. Shadows drifted in unnatural movements from her naked figure. Rays of light beamed out like arms. Where a face should've been, a smooth shadow writhed beneath hair of every color and texture. Witchkind rarely saw the gods on the island of Efelldor. The few instances a god graced our island didn't end well. Too many centuries had passed since witchkind earned their favor.

The goddess floated closer on unmoving feet. Beneath her, the grass grew. Stretching emerald blades reached for her bare legs. Pine giants above creaked and bent in half with low bows. Even the starlit sky glowed brighter.

Mouth gaping like a dying fish, I stared. What had I done to deserve *this*? The Mother of all Creation stood before me. The Creator of life—elves, witches, vampyres, goblins, humans, beasts; we all bowed to this Mother of life.

Do not falter, child. The road is long, and you have barely begun.

Her multifaceted voice echoed inside my head, meant only for me.

The Mother studied me, hands gracefully folded over a soft belly. I didn't know where to set my gaze. On the swirling light? The faceless head? She beckoned me closer.

Rising, I inched for her side. A warmth unlike any fire emanated from her, heating more than my skin. Her glow seeped into my soul, warming me from the inside out.

"Have I done something to displease you?" I asked in a smoky rasp.

I sensed a smile growing beneath the shadows, but it didn't soothe the sinking feeling in my gut.

The end of an era is nigh, the realms shall fall. You, my child, are an instrument divine, one sword upon which Efelldor shall fall.

"Oh—no. I think you—you have the wrong witch."

Shadows exploded and darkness engulfed the wood.

I threw an arm over my head and fell to my knees, waiting for the blow.

She sighed and then the dark retreated. Lowering my arm, I found her crouched inches from me. Shadows slid from her faceless head, revealing mismatched eyes. One was fiery, orange and gold. The other black as the deepest shadow, reminding me of Kazen's dead black eyes.

I obeyed her gesture for me to rise.

Do you believe the Mother of all Creation would mistake one of her Creatures for another?

"No, Mother," I whispered. Wiping clammy hands on my pants, I swallowed hard. "I'm not a powerful witch. I can barely fly—"

I know what you are, Alys Sathos.

"But—"

If you lock a snake in a cage, how long before the snake realizes it can slither through the bars?

I shook my head, eyeing the unnatural moving shadows. Why couldn't the gods speak plainly? The shadows swirled impatiently, diving for the forest floor before shooting back into the sky.

Do not equate might with power. How quickly witchkind neglects their history. Did you not experience exile for your underestimation of humankind?

How could any witch forget? The firstborn witches of Gilgador the continent had once enslaved humanity before humans rose against their oppressors. In retaliation, witchkind nearly extinguished them. Only an act of the gods and the Mother herself stopped them. Punished, the witches were cast from the Mother's homeland of Gilgador to the island of Efelldor where—two millennia later—we remained.

"What would you have me do?"

Both eyes fogged over in colorless white. *The Night Realm must fall. The Night Queen shall no longer be allowed to suffer the throne. Her people deserve more, and I hear their pleas. You will be the swinging blade of execution, my child. Fate wills it.*

A strangled laugh tumbled out. For two thousand years the gods wouldn't hear a witch's plea. Why now? Why the *Night Realm*? "Do Day Witches not deserve freedom from their queen? With all respect, Mother, I am a Day Witch. Why should I care about the Night Queen or her people?"

Worry not for the witches of the south. I do not ask dismissal of their suffering. Only patience. Lilain's time will come. Witchkind has suffered poison too long. You shall provide a bitter antidote.

"And if I don't?"

The Mother stood motionless. Too still for a Creature of this world. The light beams dropped, collapsing to shine on pine needles. Even the trees, bent in solemn bows, groaned as if wondering what idiot would question the Mother. She gripped my uninjured shoulder and Federikka's booming laughter rose in a torrent of memory. Her scolding. Her sighs. Her never-ending counsel for my wild behavior egged on by Elenna—a mother's love.

Fate is a path we choose, the Mother said in a weary voice. *Choose the wrong path and witchkind will fall and this time there will be no salvation. You are the final hope. Should you fail, you doom witchkind to permanent slumber.*

No pressure, then. Just a magicless witch sneaking off into an enemy realm to destroy their all-powerful queen or risk dooming the entirety of my kind.

The Mother loosened her grip. *You are not alone. Five others join you, but you must hold firm to your part. You are more than you believe. Power you have not yet found, but will need in the coming seasons, awaits you. Find your power and you will find your strength.*

I didn't want power. I wanted to survive long enough to find an inkling of happiness. But Elenna and Ansil's pleading voices surfaced. This was what they wanted, maybe not for the Night Realm, but they would never have stood for the oppression of *any* people. And yet . . . I wasn't half the witch they thought I was.

If there were five others who could tell the Night Queen to go rot in a hole, why did they need me?

Imitating Elena's most innocent smile, I lied and said, "All right. I'll accept my fate and do my best to bring down the Night Queen."

How I could ever dream of doing it remained to be seen. Escape the Blackwood and run seemed like a better idea than sacrifice my life for *any* Night Witch.

Hopefully, the Mother couldn't read minds.

Hold onto faith and triumph shall be your prize. Above all else, do not deviate from fate's path.

The Mother ignored my bewildered frown and cradled my chin. *The way forth is heavy with sorrow, but you are not alone. When you find the others trust shall become your most powerful weapon. Find the trust in your heart where your mind finds fault.*

Mist bloomed from the ground, absorbing the Mother's lower half. *Believe you are more than you allow yourself to be. You are one of destiny.*

The mist swelled and her figure vanished as the Blackwood's shadows rushed back.

I spun, searching for a sign I hadn't imagined the whole thing. Instrument divine. Fall of the realms. *Me* somehow inciting a coup to dethrone the Night Queen *and* somehow staying away from her equally terrifying heirs—the princess general and her brother, the crown prince. If Princess Melisandre sparked rage in the DRAS, her brother spun nightmares.

No, thank you. Running it was then. Fuck the Night Realm.

Feeling feverish, I eased off my filthy leather armor and let it fall to the ground. The tunic beneath was little better, but the hem was clean enough to wipe blood and mud from my face. I scowled at the filthy remains and examined my options.

The twinkling sky offered its own idea. Silvery moonlight bathed the northern end of the clearing toward the Night Realm . . . *If* I wanted to go there, how would I infiltrate the northern witches? At the very least, I'd have to cut my hair and take out the gold lining my ears just to blend in. Then what? My accent would give me away. Not to mention I needed someone to heal my shoulder before it became infected.

And Lilain? She'd compelled many horrors from me, but nothing compelled me to return. Desertion was punishable by death and the only reason Lilain didn't compel our loyalty was because she enjoyed hunting deserters. Few succeeded. Besides, what was there to return to? I'd rather become a deserter then return to another blood boil spellcast—alone.

Mouth dry, I made the first step in my new plan—a drink and a quick rinse.

A dribbling brook cut through one end of the clearing, perfect for what I needed. I could've crossed the small stream in one long bound, but it flowed quick and clear. Icy water numbed my hands as I gulped down clean mountain water.

The muddied gash on my shoulder still bled and the break would require a healing spellcast. Wincing, I set to work cleaning the wound.

Ansil was the 22nd's healer. His affinity for spellcasts, including healing, was legendary among the DRAS. He was the reason I wasn't a mangled mess. Few witches could spellcast, fewer still could do it without using all their magic in one go.

But Ansil wasn't here.

Yanking my tunic back up, I hung my head, taking deep breaths to halt the squeezing in my throat. There would be time to grieve. Not now.

Something twitched in the shadows beyond the stream. I went motionless and watched. The darkness watched back, as unmoving as I was. Nothing crept out. Somewhere an owl hooted. After a few moments, I turned back to the creek, contemplating scrubbing my hair. As icy as the water was—

A prickling sensation skittered across the back of my neck, and I straightened.

Something was watching me.

Pearly fingers of fog crept from the trees, moving too rapidly to be natural. Parting, they swept in a circle, cutting off my view of the forest.

I rose to a crouch, raising my good hand to a dimachairi hilt. The unmistakable smell of witch magic hit my nose—cedar and something sharp. The spicy scent plunged into my lungs, filling me until I smelled nothing else.

Heart ratcheting, I searched for movement in the dense fog. Across the stream, the fog grew impossibly thick, lowering to the ground before it parted to reveal deep shadows.

Two hooded figures stepped from the peculiar dark. Black leather and wool encased the lithe figures striding for me. All-too familiar black cloaks embroidered in gold rippled in the soft breeze. It might've been an impressive entrance if I didn't realize what the black and gold signified.

Mostly that I was dead.

The DRAS often took on the Night Army without much loss. But the black-and-gold clad Night Guard was another matter. They were the villains of the chilling stories told to DRAS pages to make them obedient. *Watch how you speak or Lilain will serve you as fodder for the Night Guard.* In fourteen years of service to the DRAS, I'd never come across the elusive Night Guard. Figures tonight would be the first.

The two Night Witches halted across the stream. One was a woman. Beneath her hood, pinched lips twisted into a mocking smile. The other—this one male—remained partially behind her, hooded and motionless but for the slight drumming of long pale fingers against his leg.

Breathing through a spasm of pain, I unsheathed my dimachairi.

The Mother had said my fated path was amongst the Night Witches. Surely, *this* wasn't what she meant? Then again, I was on track for the worst day ever, so it was probably *exactly* what she meant.

6

RUN LITTLE WITCH

Alys

"Covered in blood, mud, and looking like shit. You're a walking DRAS advertisement, Sathos."

Princess Melisandre, General of the Night Realm Army, flipped back her hood and cocked her straw-blonde head. My heart slowed to a dull thud.

"All alone without your faithful twin shadows?" The princess scanned the woods. "Elenna Makim never could keep her mouth shut. Did something finally silence the noisy bitch?"

A thousand of Lilain's baiting words had hardened my temper, but hearing Elenna's sacrifice mocked nearly broke me. No—I'd break for Lilain before I broke for Melisandre. I focused on the sounds of shuffling feet in the magicked fog.

Three more Night Witches waited behind me. The hooded Night guard behind the princess remained motionless, but if he and his long fingers controlled the strange fog, I wouldn't dare give him my back.

The princess tried a different tactic. "I can't decide if you're incredibly brave or ridiculously stupid." She cocked her head again. Blunt cut hair knocked against her chin. "I'm leaning toward stupid. Why else would you trespass in the Night Realm?"

Shit.

No airwitch returned from the Night Realm.

Soft shuffles continued in the fog. Shadow coiled around the princess's arm, a reminder of her unmatched magic I had never managed to overthrow. If any other Night Witch had caught me, I might've out maneuvered them. *If* I hadn't been one arm down and more than twenty-four hours without sleep.

Fuck it.

I spun and leapt into the fog.

White instantly swallowed me. My own feet vanished from view. Beyond the haze, the Night Guard exploded with orders as they dove into the fog after me. Someone cursed not even an arm's length to my right. Stumbling through, I shot a prayer to the goddess of luck I'd find the other side of the fog before I found a witch.

Magicked shadows lunged, splitting the fog. A Night Witch twice my size materialized at my side. Massive arms swung for my chest. Twisting, I spun from the giant, gasping through the knife-like pain down my arm. The fog swirled, no doubt called back to its master. I was seconds from discovery.

Taking a chance, I barreled forward.

A stroke of luck later, I burst from the milky fog and into the Blackwood.

Hurtling through the trees, I sheathed my dimachairi and veered north through brambles. My would-be captors followed. A Night guard hurtled through a brush behind me, faster than the others. Every twist, he followed; through every stream and thorny bush, he remained a few paces behind. Just when I'd begun to lose him, he'd materialize closer, leaping out of a shadow.

I threw myself down a ravine, smacking my broken shoulder against the sides of packed earth. I swallowed back nausea and blinked away bright spots. Creeping through the pitch-black empty gorge, I clapped a hand over my mouth, forcing myself to breathe through my nose.

Think. How to lose the guard?

Feeling my way through the brush, I listened. The muffled yells of the princess and the others drew closer. They were still too far to be a threat. The Night Witch behind me though—where had he gone? I bit the inside of my cheek and tried to quiet my breathing. I couldn't keep this chase up. I would pass out from pain or sheer exhaustion. Straining to listen, I clapped a hand over my mouth and nose. The heavy silence bore down, thick and viscous.

Then a thud of someone landing in the ravine.

Quiet footsteps drew near.

Easing into a bush, I shrank among the twigs, praying they wouldn't break. I groped the base of the shrub, searching for a stone. Or a root ball. Anything I could use. Decaying leaves shriveled under my touch. A feather. Handfuls of dirt. Nothing useful.

The soft steps neared.

"I know you're there." The Night Witch's short, clipped accent couldn't hide the dangerous calm in his voice. Low and smooth like a blade slicing through water, it sent chills peppering across my skin. "You're injured. We both know you won't last much longer."

I clawed the ground, searching. Another feather. A rodent's tiny jawbone. Gritting my teeth, I palmed a fistful of dirt and exhaled.

There.

The slimy skin of a large mushroom appeared under my fingers. Perfect.

Popping off the mushroom cap, I eased it from the bush. The Night Witch hadn't made it this far down the ravine, but it was a matter of seconds before he stepped on me. Begging the goddess of luck for one more blessing, I hurled the mushroom. A splash came from down the ravine, sounding exactly like a slipped foot.

Brilliant.

The Night Witch only laughed. The low, silky sound was like a fingertip sliding down my spine. "Did you really think that would work?"

Terror strangled the glee right out of me.

I hadn't survived a goblin ambush, lost my closest friends, been blind-sided by a goddess, only to be murdered in some muddy ravine.

Fuck that—I was going to live.

I shot from the bush, and the witch lunged. A blind hand snagged my sleeve slick with blood. With a twist and a scream, I hurtled free, stumbling through brush, muck, and gods knew what else.

My fumbling fingers skimmed the packed earthen sides of the ravine, searching for a way out. A protruding tree root pricked my thumb. I hissed a triumphant curse and latched on. Fire shot down my shoulder, but I wasn't about to let it stop me. Climbing the root, I rolled over the ravine's lip and took off into the Blackwood.

Because I had no luck left, the Night Witch followed.

Don't stop, I pleaded with my burning legs. Refusing to become an easy target for the Night Witch's swarming shadows, I weaved through the forest's dense brush, swerving around fallen logs. A heavy burn settled in my ribs, inching into my lungs. Tight spasms shot down my calves.

A little longer.

I scrabbled over a partially petrified log when a boom of thunder reverberated from the ground. Sparing a glance behind me, I found the witch skidding to a halt. The forest floor gave another growl, and he took a step backward.

Let him pause, because I sure wouldn't.

Ducking under a willow, I made it halfway through a clearing before a loud creak split the Blackwood. A sprig of green whipped toward me. I stumbled out of its way, nearly face planting into a tree trunk. Was that—*oh shit.* The willow snapped its limb again, this time connecting with my stomach. The impact seized my lungs *and* my scream as I soared backward. A waiting pine wrapped a limb around my waist, flinging me into the air. Another pine bound my legs and flung me toward the stars.

I clawed for something, *anything* to hang onto.

The trees stilled as quickly as they'd come alive.

The mossy ground didn't bother to cushion my landing. Muffled sobs forced air into my grateful lungs. Rolling onto my back for breath, I blinked dirt from my lashes.

Something flashed in the corner of my periphery, and then the Night Witch was on me. His knees slammed my legs shut, rough hands pinning my wrists to the dirt.

"Get off me," I snarled. I thrashed against him, but the Night Witch shifted his weight and trapped me to the forest floor. Frantic, I slammed my head toward his nose and missed. He reared his head and his hood fell back, revealing the brightest eyes I'd seen on any witch. Forest green and flecked generously in gold, they narrowed into predatory slits. Wavy strands of hair, darker than even mine, tumbled down onto a pale forehead.

"Just surrender," he snapped. The smooth mocking voice from earlier had dissolved into breathless frustration.

"So you can slit my throat? Go fuck a shadow, Night Witch."

I tried headbutting him again but barely skimmed a razor-sharp jaw. Caged against the ground, I searched for a way out. He had every advantage over me. Weight, strength, magic. *Power.*

Panic-fueled rage bubbled like an insidious spring. Every muscle and bone wilted under the day's repeated failures.

Shuddering, I took a deep breath and screamed.

The Night guard's too-bright eyes widened. His horror snaked a sick thrill through me, but it vanished when he dropped his weight. He slapped a hand over my mouth. The other clamped my wrists in one hand, thrusting them above my head.

Fire bloomed in a wave up my arm.

"What is wrong with you?" he hissed, scanning the trees. "Do you have any idea what roams the Blackwood at night?"

I did, but I couldn't think past the fire in my arm wrenched above my head. Blistering white fogged everything, and I swore the grass screamed with me.

"I'm pulling your arms down." The guard's grip eased, and he released my mouth. "If you scream or try to run, I'll break your other shoulder. Do you understand?"

Two of him now floated above me. I nodded once and he lowered my arms. Blood and relief whooshed back into my burning arm. Gods, it stung like a thousand hornets. Shadows darted from somewhere behind him and splayed out my arms—nowhere near my knives. Not that I could've drawn one if I tried.

Even in the dark, the bright pinpricks in his pine-green eyes skewered me in place like golden daggers. Never taking them off me, he unsheathed my dimachairi at my back and the stilettos at my ribs. I should've slammed my head into that long, straight nose, but I couldn't decipher which of the two floating above me was real.

"Godsdamn." A man's heavy breathing broke from the nearby brush, "Was that a banshee? I thought we were too far south for those."

The enormous Night Witch from the stream hurried forward. He helped my captor yank me to my knees. Another wave of nausea. Gods, I couldn't feel my shoulder. Granted, I couldn't feel my entire arm and half of my side, but—small miracles—at least I was alive.

"Your Highness," a new voice called to the bright-eyed witch. A young, shrewd-looking Night guard darted forward, wiping sweat off his mahogany forehead. *Your Highness*? My heart plummeted, but the young guard's next words sent it leaping back into my throat. "Princess Melisandre insists we kill the Day Witch and move on."

Before I could so much as protest, the princess emerged from the trees. Her short hair was pasted to ruddy cheeks, eyes glassy but triumphant.

"Why is she sitting unbound?" She flicked her wrist, and the shadows darted forward, rising to weave a cage around me. "I said she was magicless, not defenseless."

I leapt up, but I didn't make it two steps. The shadows lengthened into black lines, crisscrossing to reach a point above me. Tentatively, I reached to touch the shadows and met solid black bars. Freakish Night magic. Shadows shouldn't be solid, but there would be no passing through these.

Satisfied, the princess peered down with familiar dark green eyes rimmed in gold.

Right. The other *highness*.

I swiveled to glare at my captor. Eyes almost identical to Melisandre's were already on me. They narrowed back before turning to his sister.

Fortuna, goddess of luck, must've truly hated me.

I'd not only stumbled upon the princess general, but her twin brother, Crown Prince Maddox of the Night Realm, Heir to the Night Queen. I'd fabricated countless tales of him to frighten pages. Eyeing his empty, cold expression, I wondered if I'd unwittingly told the pages a few truths.

Still . . . I didn't mind a discreet perusal.

The Night Prince had ripped off his cloak, revealing a long, lean body I didn't doubt was honed to destroy as much as his magic. He exuded an elegance that screamed entitled power, glaring everyone down his nose.

And yet . . . I couldn't deny every feature was carved by a master of stonework. Soft waves of midnight hair contrasted the sharp lines of his jaw and nose. His skin reminded me of the desert's ivory sands, unblemished and perfect. But he could've been the ugliest witch on Efelldor, and I still would've been drawn to his eyes. Uneasy intensity sparkled golden even in the silvery moonlight, measuring me against an impossible standard.

One I failed every time.

"We slit her throat," Melisandre said. "Leave her for the wood nymphs and pretend it never happened—"

"*You* might easily break the Night Queen's law," her brother interrupted, lifting a single brow, "but the law demands any trespassing Day Witch must appear before the queen and the Night Guard *will* uphold it."

Melisandre threw her hands in the air. "Then we umbranate her to the capital."

Umbranate? Was that what they called their travel through shadows?

"Fine." The prince gave her an unaffected shrug. "*You* take her. *You* risk losing her to the shadows and landing gods know where. Or better yet—*you* risk her killing you both mid-umbranation. If she's as dangerous as you say"—the prince shot me an unimpressed look—"then you should recognize what an awful idea that is. I will escort her, and we will *walk* to Morithia. It's only a few days. She can face judgment then."

Morithia—the Night Realm capital and seat of the Night Queen.

I steeled my spine against a shiver of relief. I wasn't dying. At least not yet. If this was fate's attempt to prod me onto my path . . . I had no intention of going to their capital.

Melisandre scowled. A low growl conceded her brother's point. "Then I'm going too. You clearly haven't seen the little bitch rip out a spine with nothing but a dagger." She stepped closer to her brother, clenching a fist as she hissed. "*I* won't let her escape because *your* pride won't see what she's capable of."

"Right," the prince said, lips twisting into a sneer. "If only we could reach your undefiled ivory tower standard. Never wrong. Always right no matter how drunk or high you are."

Melisandre's fist soared, but the prince's shadows snatched it midair. He spun her and shoved her toward the younger guard who righted her. For a brief moment, the haughty prince mask slipped, revealing someone who looked as worn as I felt.

"Go sleep off whatever you're on, Melis."

She pushed the guard's offered arm away, throwing her brother a look that could've flayed stone. "You're a miserable prick, Maddox. And one day it'll catch up with you."

I blinked and his icy disdain returned.

Elenna and Ansil argued often, but their bond went above everything else. Even me. Whatever lay between these Night twins had destroyed their bond and any respect for one another.

Ignoring Melisandre's curses, the prince's gaze flicked to me. As he stood motionless, shadows from beneath nearby trees slunk forward and began undoing my cage. One formed into a black rope and wound around my arms and legs. Another tightened around my shoulders.

I swallowed a muffled groan.

The prince instructed the giant, "Take her to camp and see Melis heals her."

Shoving his hands into his pockets, he strode off. He moved with an unnerving cold calm. As if he hadn't kidnapped another witch. As if I was nothing but a drag on his evening. A powerless, *nameless* little annoyance.

I vowed then never to utter his own name.

Not even to myself.

The giant approached with a wary grin. He hesitated a pace away and bit his lip. "No trouble, right?"

I rolled my eyes. "I can barely move, Night Witch. Broken shoulder, remember?"

Mind made up, he nodded and hefted me onto his shoulder, muttering, "Sorry," and adjusted me until I could breathe through the pain. "I'll go as slow as I can."

I raised my head, holding onto one last dignity. Sweeping over the forest, I met the prince's narrowed stare over his shoulder and froze. Something in his stare was too probing. Like he'd plunged into my soul's depths and found nothing of value. A vicious urge to claw his eyes out rose. To wipe that haughty mask off and show him he held no power over me.

But my shoulder screamed for me to lower my neck, and I broke first, slumping face first into the giant's back. Ansil and Elenna's deaths hadn't been enough to keep the god of misery sated. Now, I was fated to an impossible task I had no intention of fulfilling and captured by a Night Witch who knew exactly what I was—powerless and pathetic. What could possibly make this day worse?

7

SPEAK INTO THE DARK

Alys

Waxed canvas tents spotted the Blackwood meadow. Pages and Night guards alike prepared for the evening watch. I certainly wasn't going anywhere that night. After they'd clamped pointless manacles preventing me from wielding magic onto my wrists, two guards armed to the teeth took positions standing sentry over me. Meanwhile, I could barely keep my eyes open. Even the pain in my shoulder wasn't enough to keep me awake.

Beneath an immense oak, the giant prepared a spot for the night. While he hadn't offered a tent or cot, he spread a frayed bedroll that looked as if it predated the realms. He tapped his chin, then dug through a lumpy bag before tossing a moth-eaten blanket over the bedroll.

"Right," he said, testing the new ropes binding me. "If you promise not to do anything you shouldn't, I'll tuck you in like the good little witch you are."

Letting loose a startled laugh, I wiggled into a sitting position. I hadn't expected a bedroll. More like a dropkick into the dirt.

The giant threw the blanket over my legs and eyed me. He must've approved whatever he saw because he nodded and fished out a pillow rivaling the bedroll in age. Tucking it behind me, he tossed me a wink and patted the pillow.

Floppy blue-black spiral curls on top skimmed the giant's ears. The back and sides of his head had been shaved smooth. A thick beard framed a russet face leading to round, warm amber eyes. He carefully undid his own bedroll with enormous hands capable of snapping me like a twig. Small scars crisscrossed his fingers in a timeline showcasing a soldier's life.

Feeling my stare, he smiled up at me. There was no mockery in it. He genuinely looked pleased to be there—with me.

"What's your name?" I asked.

Caution warred with curiosity, but the latter won. "Yori Denox, First Lieutenant to the Commander of the Night Guard."

Of course. The prince's right-hand witch.

"I already know who *you* are," he added with a cheeky grin. "I've heard Melis's battle tales a thousand times. Never thought I'd meet the wicked Alys Sathos, the bloodthirsty demon Melis never pinned down. Until now."

I snorted. The bitch hadn't done shit. It had all been her brother's doing.

"Do you often escort Day Witches to Morithia?"

The giant spread out his bedroll with meticulous care, careful not to come within arm's reach of me. "No, you're the first. The Night Guard serve from Morithia and go wherever we're needed throughout the realm. We don't typically go beyond our borders. We serve at the queen's judgment."

"And what exactly should *I* expect from her judgment?"

Yori bit his lip, watching the nearby guards sharpen their swords with too much concentration. "Probably the work camps."

Certain death, then. Camps no witch was meant to survive, a capital punishment. I flexed my hands but couldn't budge their restraints. The gentle giant's willingness to answer my questions came from his faith in his impenetrable knots. Like his prince, he had full confidence I wasn't going anywhere.

"Tell me, Captain Sathos," he began, "how have you crossed swords with Melis as often as you have and *lived*? Magicless no less."

"Because I'm better than her." Ignoring his scoff, I pasted on an ease I didn't feel. "Magic makes you valiant until you've spent it all and have to rely on your sword. I've *only* ever relied on my sword. That sort of reliance tends to sharpen a skill even your princess can't match."

Seeing my chance, I leaned back against the tree and grinned. "Why is she with the Night Guard? Did your queen finally take the generalship from her?"

Yori frowned as Melisandre yelled at a page struggling to pick up an overturned soup tureen. Clearly, even her own people were not spared her ire. He turned owlish eyes onto me and grinned back, no doubt seeing right through my information fishing. His unshakable confidence didn't waver.

"Occasionally our queen requires the royal heirs to work together. Twin magic is too rare to set aside even for their personal squabbles. From their ability to share magic to their mental link, it's a gift the queen won't waste. She sent them here to soothe the nearby villages. A united front against the wild rumors claiming we've left the border villages to the vampyres."

I sat up and gaped. "Vampyres? This far north?"

Unlike the witches and participating goblins and elves cast out of the Mother's continent for their part in the human genocide, vampyres were allowed to remain on Gilgador. But as punishment for their part, they'd been cursed to burn in the daylight. Still, stragglers found their way to Efelldor, hunting the few human refugees who lived beneath the canopies of the Day Realm's jungle or the wilds of the west coast.

He shrugged massive shoulders, but a line remained between his brows. "Merely villager gossip. It's why Melis and Maddox were sent by our queen. To bring supplies to the nearby villages in hopes of quelling rumors." Gossip indeed. If true, it explained why the goblin clans had massed together. If vampyres were as far north as the Blackwood, goblins would become the natural prey.

"You sound as if you know your royals well."

Yori's booming laughter turned several heads. "I like you. You're caught in the worst circumstance, and yet you scheme like you're sure you've got the upper hand."

He sank against braced hands and beamed wider at the single finger I offered him. "I knew Maddox and Melis—or Melisandre—long before they became commander of the Night Guard and general. We attended the same school of magic, Amethyst Hall. Maddox befriended a village oaf trapped in a debacle of aristocratic children and we've been stuck together ever since."

Before I could press him for more, gleeful howls exploded from the nearby guards. With Melisandre at their center, they hooted over her shoulder as she flicked through a book. The young guard from earlier stood beside her, digging through a canvas bag—

I sat up straight.

My canvas bag. It must've come loose and fallen into the Blackwood when my broom shattered.

Melisandre held the romance book I'd packed, *Hot Blooded Love*, and was reading aloud. Well, at least books weren't banned in the Night Realm. Here my biggest crime was an expansive taste in reading.

The princess strode for us, and read aloud, " *'His fangs gently pierced her neck, and she moaned in pleasure.'* Gods, is this awful drivel what gets Day Witches off?"

"I'd say you could borrow it and learn something, Princess," I said, pleased with my even voice, "but even I wouldn't wish a liquor-soaked witch like you pawing at some poor soul's pants."

Melisandre snapped the book shut and stalked closer. Her dark eyes were clearer now, brimming with a years-long rage that had nearly run me through once or twice. Whatever she'd imbibed, had left her system. Unfortunately, a sober witch who very much wanted me and my big mouth dead remained.

A shadow fell across my bedroll. Black strands like curious snakes slithered for my bound hands before something yanked them back. I didn't need the cedar and clove scent of the prince's magic to know who stood there.

"Ward the camp," he commanded in a low voice, brokering no argument. "Set a perimeter guard. When you return, two of you remain with the Day Witch through the night. No mistakes." He never raised his voice. I'd heard him swear, heard his commands, but when he spoke everyone else fell silent. It was a testament to the control he held over the Night Guard as their commander.

Scoffing, Melisandre tossed the book to Yori and disappeared amongst the tents. The giant rose then saluted, fist over heart with one more grin I couldn't help but return. A feeling of familiarity like Elenna's raucous laughter or Ansil's smirk gripped me. Breathing through a sudden tightness in my throat, I slumped against a tree, hissing when my shoulder collided with the bark.

"Are you still injured?"

The prince remained behind me, scowling with his hands shoved into his pockets. His bright eyes glowed more gold than green in the firelight but held none of its warmth. He'd caught me, bound me, and he wanted to know if I was *all right*?

I gave him my back and glared into the fire Yori had lit for me.

He crouched and blocked my view, meeting me at eye-level. "If you're hurt, you'll only slow us down. Did Melis heal you or not?"

I straightened as best I could and spat, "I'm fine."

"Then this won't hurt." He swooped forward and shoved me, shoulder first, into the tree.

I cried out, ricocheting off the rigid bark. Lightning pain struck my shattered bones. White stars flecked everything, and my lungs sucked in glass.

The prince stared down his nose at me with an imperiousness only a royal ass could sustain. An unfamiliar, hungry urge to prove I was better than him erupted; I needed to prove I could shatter that cold, emotionless mask.

Biting my lip until I tasted iron, I eased onto my knees. "That was well deserved, wasn't it? Let's punish the nasty Day Witch for ruining your evening. She's not worth anything anyway. If only I could be like *you*. Tell me, Prince. What's it like to be a queen's lapdog?"

He was on me before I blinked, my cheeks tightly gripped between long, pale fingers. Icy contempt never faltering, his eerie eyes burned inches from mine. His breath warm against my cheek, he murmured, "The only reason you're alive is because *I* allow it. Keep that in mind and keep your mouth shut." His grip dug deeper into my cheeks, and his bright gaze fastened to the blood pooling at the corner of my lips.

"We could have more fun if my mouth was open."

He made a noise of disgust and released me before striding away.

Snickering, I scrubbed my cheek on my uninjured shoulder. "That's twice now," I called to his back, hoping for one more dig at that unflappable demeanor. "Twice you've put your hands on me."

"And twice you've done nothing about it."

I spluttered a string of incoherent curses, but he strode off with the last word, hands in pockets, pausing to snipe something at Melisandre. He stepped into a shadow and vanished, swallowed whole by a pine's shadow.

Umbranation—while admittedly interesting—couldn't beat flying in the air.

The prick hadn't bothered to remain behind. He'd caught me and left the unimpressive Day Witch for the comfort of his royal bed.

Rumors among Lilain's courtiers insisted the Night Prince had infiltrated their ranks with his infamous network of spies. Other rumors claimed he was among them, playing assassin. I'd always chalked those rumors up to courtier dramatics but seeing him vanish into nothingness had sown a seed of doubt. Perhaps he was right, and I shouldn't mouth off to one of Efelldor's most powerful witches.

Or perhaps I'd found a sickening way to burrow under his skin.

The princess sauntered over. She grinned down and reared her boot back.

I sprang into a ball, but I wasn't fast enough. The gleaming boot slammed into my stomach. I doubled over in silence, refusing to give her any satisfaction even as my shoulder pleaded with me to be still.

Melisandre clicked her tongue.

"I'm to heal you, Sathos." Another kick. "But I don't think I shall." A kick to my bent knees. "It'll be our secret. I suspect you'd rather chew your arm off than tell Maddox you're hurting."

A whimper popped out, betrayed by lungs desperate for air. I couldn't move, curved into a ball to prevent the worst of her blows from landing on my shoulder.

"So"—she crouched, whispering into my ear—"this is us pretending." Then she rose and rammed her foot into my ribs before sauntering away without a backward glance.

Wheezing, I coughed around newly broken ribs. The fire there reared up to join the flames in my shoulder. A pathetic mewl followed. I wouldn't cry. Not for a Night Witch. I spat out a mouthful of blood from my ruined cheek. The Night Princess was nothing to me but the unpleasant taste of bitterness.

I rolled over and through blurry eyes, found my assigned guards drawing closer. One leaned over to inspect me. He spat at my feet and crowed with laughter at my flinch. They were all the same. Each a pointless waste of Creation. This was whom the gods wanted saved? I'd sooner gut myself and wear my entrails as a necklace.

8

AN ORDINANCE OF FATE

Corryn

F ortuna's luck had finally turned against me, and time was ticking. I'd
found nothing in my search to locate the Dual Witch student. A handful of the year-one students came from village orphanages—the ones most
likely to come from Dual backgrounds—but when pressed for examples of
their magic, they'd gone terribly shy and awkward, unable to summon even
a wisp of shadow.

I couldn't very well force their magic from them.

Dinner finished and the students were off to bed. Joining their throng, I
ran an absent thumb over the glossy texture of my pearls, scratching an itch
in my mind with their comforting shape.

A shriek burst from the courtyard followed by a dozen more.

For a split second, I caught Rilessa's eye before dashing for the commotion—and the smell of smoke.

The Dual student had accidentally lit another fire.

I rushed around the columns, swimming through students streaming
from the courtyard. Flames devoured the garden as smoke billowed into a
pink sky. Instructors rushed past me to the garden, throwing water onto
a carnage of lilies and roses. A trellis crashed to the ground and launched
embers into the fleeing students.

Leaving the fire to water-wielding instructors, I searched the students
for the scent of sweet lilacs. Smoke hung thick, covering the scent of any

summoned magic making it impossible to pinpoint one scent. That wasn't my only dilemma. The courtyard crawled with students and instructors. News of a second fire this close after the tapestry would travel quickly.

Morgenna would know by morning.

I needed to find the Dual student *now*.

A lone girl stood pressed into a column, mouth agape watching the flaming garden in terror. Alone, terrified, and looking as if she'd made the worst mistake of her life—I'd found the Dual Witch.

Surging forward, I nearly walked into a gaggle of breathless girls. All year ones, they clung to one another, taking turns peeking behind a column. When several male, year six students passed, I realized they weren't watching the fire at all. Of all the times . . .

Huffing, I hurried past the boys, calling over my shoulder for them to usher the gigglers to their dormitories.

By the time they corralled the girls, the lone girl against the column was gone.

I spun, desperate to locate the poor girl. Nothing. I couldn't lose her. Without me, she was dead before dawn. Diving back into the fray of students, I winced as another surge of wind threw sparks over us.

On the blasted wind came a blessedly familiar scent—lilacs.

But the wind didn't blow from the columns. It drifted from the gaggle of girls I'd sent away. The eldest of them, a gangly redhead, threw a wide-eyed glance over her shoulder. A single, despondent tear slid down her cheek before she swiped it away. Curls flying like a blazing tree in the wind, she took off and disappeared into the crowd.

A solid body careened into me, sending us both to the ground.

Untangling myself from the fallen instructor, I lurched for the girl before jerking to a halt. If I gave chase, I'd draw attention. Something neither of us could afford.

"Mother damn you, Stellanati."

The instructor got to his feet, his bushy white brows slanting. "First the damn fire pranks. Now, you nearly breaking my hip. We don't all bounce back." An herbologist, one who taught General Law of Potions to year ones and was more at ease with medicines than witches.

"Forgive me," I said, helping him upright. "I was getting onto a group of girls, and one dashed off. A year-one girl, older than most, curly red hair, plenty of freckles."

The white bushes on his forehead straightened. "That'll be Seren Mercatura. Fifteen is too old for a year-one. I'm surprised the school admitted her. Must have some damn magic."

I offered vague agreement, but every blood drop had gone cold.

Powerful magic indeed.

Seren was the Dual Witch.

Hunting the girl now would be catastrophic. No, Rilessa and I would wait until Seren was alone. The sooner we bound her magic and ferried her out of the school, the better our chance of saving her.

Before Morgenna's beast came sniffing.

The ticking clock boomed; each strike louder than the one before.

Rilessa and I waited in her office, watching the clock inch past curfew. The skin on my wrist had been rubbed raw from spinning my pearls. I fidgeted with each smooth, white bead, counting them as if I didn't know there were twenty. Always twenty.

When the clock chimed midnight, we rose, reaching for the cloaking shadows. With a spellcast muffling our steps, we reached the student dormitories unseen. A dozen lights lingered in the windows, students hopefully studying.

The servant stairwell door creaked open, and we were in.

On the first landing, we stepped onto the dormitory floor. Memories tightened around my chest in a vise-like grip of regret. Nearly a decade should've been enough time to forget.

Counting the doors, we reached Seren's room, and my heart plummeted. Her door was partially opened.

"Not a sound," Rilessa warned, lips barely moving. She pushed open the cracked door and stepped inside. Sucking in a breath, I followed.

Seren's room was neat, everything in its place. The only disturbance came from the sheets sliding off the four-poster to pool onto the floor. Seren lay on the bed, her tumble of red curls visible from her position facing the wall. She wasn't moving.

Ignoring Rilessa's hissed warning, I scrambled for the girl. The bed creaked beneath my weight, but Seren didn't move. With a shaking hand on her thin shoulder, I rolled her over.

"No."

Her lovely brown eyes were wide, glassy and unseeing. A puddle of red gathered beneath her, seeping into the sheets in a wet crimson blot against white. Tiny flecks of blood sprayed across her freckles. More blood stained the front of her nightshirt, leaking from the thin line at her throat.

We'd been mere *minutes* too late.

Morgenna's beast had reached Seren first.

An innocent life had been murdered for the sake of holding power. My tears smeared the flecks on her freckled face as I gathered her. An entire life wasted. A chance to discover who she was, who she was meant to be—gone because I'd failed.

A murmured spellcast came from behind, then the iridescent shimmer of a sound-blocking bubble swallowed me. The door snicked shut, and Rilessa was there, prying the girl from my arms.

"We'll make it appear a suicide." Rilessa didn't meet my startled stare, running a hand over the girl's blood-dampened curls. "By all accounts she was lonely. It'll be convincing. Only an aunt who gained custody of her a few months ago will grieve."

I shot from the bed, wiping my sleeve across my cheeks. "How can you be so callous? She's freshly dead in your arms, Mother. Barely an adult—no—still a child."

"Because," Rilessa snapped, mouth twisting into an unrecognizable snarl. She shut her eyes, face softening. In a quieter voice, she said, "Because there will be more, my darling. More Dual children will enter Amethyst Hall. We must remain anonymous to save them. We failed Seren, yes, but we must not let emotion fail the others."

I shook my head, trying not to compare my own wild curls to Seren's wet with blood. "But to lie, to hide the injustice—"

"Is to save the others. If parents discover a student was murdered, it will open a flood of questions Morgenna will not want answered. Further digging will lead to us and what we've done all these years to save others. If you and I are dead, who will save them from her and her beast?"

"It's wrong," I choked out.

Rilessa's shadow rose from the bed and floated to Seren's desk before selecting a knife used to sharpen pencils and dropping it into her palm. She dipped the knife in Seren's blood before placing it into the girl's limp hand. The thin blade matched the line across her throat.

She was right. No questions would be asked about a quiet nobody. Perhaps a buzz would go through the school, but only until the next scandal. And then Seren would be forgotten.

"We've saved many, Corryn. Count the wins. Not the losses."

I laughed, a stark sound in the small room stinking of blood.

"*Are* we winning? Is that what we're doing when we bind young witches and send them into a world where they'll never belong, forever caged by their own magic?"

"We are all caged, my darling. It is the tithe we pay to our queen for life. But, remember, a caged bird lives in hope of freedom. Focus on those you've saved and pray to the gods they've been kept for a better future."

I didn't pray that night, but perhaps I should've. After scrubbing Seren's blood off me, I brewed a cup of lavender tea with hands rubbed raw. The calming herb wasn't enough. The powerful spellcast I cast over the tea to transform it into a sleeping potion wasn't exactly recommended by healers, but I'd earned it.

My head had barely hit the pillow when the dream began.

The bottle-green meadow didn't resemble anything in Efelldor. Silver specked the meadow from the pale moon dangling in the inky sky. I spun in a circle, wondering if I'd fallen through the pillow and awoken in a new world. Strange flowers with a spicy perfume speckled one side of the field with their thorny, yellow blooms. On the other side, deep wine-colored flowers waved on long stalks. Shimmering prongs jutted from their centers, puffs of pink occasionally spewing out.

I bent over the bloom to sniff.

"I wouldn't touch a hydalimus if I were you. Much less smell it."

A woman watched me from beyond the flowers. Moonlight highlighted her raven hair, floating as if it were caught underwater. She smiled and revealed a row of pointed teeth, somehow whiter than her skin.

I blinked twice, wondering if my sleep potion had gone rancid.

"You're questioning if this is real." The woman gestured to the meadow. "It is and it isn't. But that's not the point. You're here, and I have a message from the Mother, Corryn Stellanati."

"*We* have a message." A golden-haired man shimmered into view behind the woman. Barefoot in the emerald grass, his naked upper half revealed an impossibly defined chest dusted with hair. His blue eyes would have put the brightest skies to shame. "I am Baldyr, god of the day and light and all that resides in its splendor."

Mother bless me.

This would teach me to meddle in potion magic.

The woman snickered, a soft sound like a cat toying with a bird. "You never were one for subtlety, Bal." She maneuvered through the flowers, avoiding the wine blooms swaying for the hem of her midnight robe. The closer she drew, the stronger the air smelled of lavender and smoke. When she was within reach, she held out a hand. In it, a swirling mass of shadow flickered with silver pinpricks.

"I would tell you this proves who I am, Nyx, the goddess of night and darkness"—she clenched her fist, and the stars vanished—"but in this place titles become meaningless, and you wouldn't believe me."

"This is a dream," I whispered, feeling for my pearl bracelet. It wasn't there.

The Creature that called himself Baldyr held out my pearls. "Consider this proof we are more than a dream."

"A dream god might say that."

Nyx grinned with teeth like a wolf. "But would a dream god tell you how to bring down Morgenna and end your silent battle?"

I took a step back.

If there was a chance this was real, that the gods had appeared in a dream ready to answer a prayer I'd never bothered praying . . .

"If such a god existed, why wait until now?" I asked. Burgeoning fury dogged each word. "Why not come when the battle began, before a child was *murdered*? Why let us suffer?"

Her grin fell. "We are bound to the wheel of fate, Corryn Stellanati. Until this moment, we couldn't interfere—"

Baldyr placed a massive hand on Nyx's shoulder. "There are many things we should not yet speak of, sister." To me he said, "You are not lost to the Mother. You are ordained by fate to change this world. It begins with the Night Queen."

I shook my head, trying to clear the buzz. I had no place outside Amethyst Hall. My task lay in passing knowledge to younger generations. I certainly had no business changing the world. That was for princes and princesses, magistrates, and courtiers.

Nyx shrugged off her brother's hand and stepped closer. A cloud of lavender and smoke washed over me like a calm night. "If you desire to save innocents like Seren Mercatura, look past your selfish misgivings. This is your chance to do more than stanch the bleeding of Morgenna's attacks on Dual Witches. If you choose this fated path toward freedom, you must listen carefully. Find and unite the five destined alongside you. Find the other witches destined by portents of fate. Find and unite the Mother's fated six."

Portents—powerful prophecies of great, untold future feats.

I, a mere instructor, was a portent of change.

Laughing in her face was, perhaps, not a wise idea.

Nyx began chanting in a guttural growl that prickled the hair on my arms. "Two are swallowed by the river's claim and all it supposes. One hides behind a veil of self-hatred that must be burned by forgiveness's harsh light. One is caged, the bars sealed by malice and woe, waiting for the key that was torn asunder. And the last is your hope of refuge. Find your hope, and you shall find the rest."

As if expelled from the dream, I sat up in bed, choking on an inhale and dripping in sweat. The meadow was gone, the gods vanished.

The evening came rushing back. Seren, her death, the beast. How I'd failed. How I might continue failing no matter what I did. I rubbed my palm, remembering the fading warmth of Seren's limp hand. I could do *more* than stanch the bleeding if I followed the gods' plans, if I found the other five witches bound in fate alongside me. I could not only save, but *free* the Dual Witches.

But what if it'd been a dream?

I lay back onto my pillow, jolting at the smell of lavender and smoke permeating the pillowcase. It smelled like a calm night—no, like hope.

9

THE MANIPULATION OF WORD

Alys

C haos is particularly beautiful when it's not my problem.

The morning after my capture, Yori escorted me to a mess tent where I sat rope-bound at a table with bread for my breakfast. He offered bitter swill and called it tea. I nearly refused, but the ceramic cup held certain promise.

When pink-faced pages burst into the tent begging for help umbranating pack mules into a nearby village, Yori had left me behind with two young guards before exasperatedly trailing the pages. Perhaps the goddess of luck was switching sides? I hadn't seen Melisandre since the night before, but I caught her occasional shouts. Thank the Mother the prince hadn't reappeared since umbranating the night before.

Good riddance.

The young guards Yori left behind were idiots. One looked like a slicked rat, with hair doused in over-perfumed oil. The other—like an overgrown infant who couldn't grow a beard. From the magic they wielded, they were *powerful* idiots. Then again soldiers weren't chosen for their brains. These two had spent the last half hour arguing over a bet and its outcome.

"You said ten coin. Fess up," Rat Hair demanded.

"No, *you* said if Prince Maddox caught the Day Witch. He didn't. The trees did."

With bound feet, I nudged a nearby stone under the table, angling it beneath the table's edge. Coins jingled as Rat Boy waved a coin purse.

"The trees didn't do a bleeding thing. It must have been his magic, you dolt. Therefore, *he* caught her, and I get ten coin."

Smooth Cheeks dug in, oblivious to my bound wrists dragging my teacup across the table. "He doesn't have power over trees, *you dolt.* That's elven magic. You trying to pass the prince off as elven now?"

"Could be god magic too, you know. Maybe the gods wanted her ass caught. Filthy Day Witches, spreading like vermin."

"For the love—you hear yourself? If it was the gods, it wasn't Prince Maddox which means I owe you shit."

The teacup shattered over the rock. Both guards whipped toward me, shadows rearing from the tent's corners. Rat Boy rushed forward only to slow when he spotted the broken teacup in the grass.

I raised my bound hands and grinned weakly.

"Sorry. Hard to drink like this."

They scowled, closely watching me pick up the broken teacup. "You know," I said, tossing the shards onto the table. "Technically, your prince *did* catch me. The trees grabbed me, but they didn't throw me at him. He took advantage when they dropped me."

Rat Boy whirled onto Smooth Cheeks, finger in his face. "I told you. He caught her, fair and square. Even the Day Witch agrees."

Unseen, I slipped the sharpest shard between my palms, concealing a grimace when an edge nicked my palm. Good. This would be sharp enough to cut through rope. Hands tucked beneath the table, I sawed through the fibers. The guards continued arguing, sparing me occasional glances. This wasn't good enough. I needed them completely diverted for a good half minute.

When the rope fell, I pulled my legs up beneath the table, sitting oddly cross-legged with my ankles bound. This angle cut off my feet's circulation, and if I didn't cut the rope quickly, I'd be stumbling out of here. And probably be caught. With my broken shoulder—and newly broken ribs thanks to a self-righteous princess—I'd have a difficult time fleeing at a wounded pace anyway.

The second set of ropes dropped soundlessly to the grass. I eased my legs back down, trying to slow the blood rushing into them.

"In the Day Realm," I interjected over Smooth Cheek's whines, "honor is quite serious. Day Witches have died over insinuations of dishonor. You'd never hear of a Day Witch refusing to pay a bet. It would be an automatic duel to the death."

Well, not really, but they wouldn't know that.

Smooth Cheeks swelled up to his full height. His broad chest puffed out. "How dare you, you filthy—"

"She's right again, isn't she," Rat Boy interrupted, looking as if his birthday had come early. "You have no honor. You'd sell your mother for a cup of tea."

Smooth Cheeks howled and dove for Rat Boy. His meaty fist smashed into Rat Boy's nose with a sharp crack. Screaming obscenities, they rolled across the grass, paying no heed to the chairs they knocked over. Or their momentarily forgotten charge.

Grinning, I bee-lined for the tent flap and ducked into the morning air. The sudden bright light nearly blinded me, but I aimed for the closest trees and their cover. North would be better. Away from the—

Shit.

Melisandre strode in my direction, leading a page by the ear. If she looked up, she'd see me. But my only open path led straight to her. More tents lined my way, waiting to be torn down.

Squashing my rising panic, I dipped into the nearest tent, praying to the Mother no one occupied it. Again, my prayers went unanswered.

A single young page—the first Night woman I'd seen since Melisandre—sat in a chair rolling maps into leather canisters. She blinked hooded blue eyes at me, hands hovering over worn cartography.

I rushed the girl and threw an arm around her neck. She stumbled up, pulling tight against my good shoulder until she was gasping. She didn't have time to reach her dagger before I'd ripped it from her side. Angling the sharp edge against her throat, I hissed through erupting fire in my arm.

"Don't scream. I don't want to kill you, but I won't be caught by your princess." I grinned down at the girl. "On the other hand, I would definitely kill *her* if given the chance. Just not today."

To my surprise, the page lifted an auburn brow before saying, "Too bad. I might've held her down for you."

The dagger dropped a hair. "Another time. I have to survive the day first. Keep quiet until I leave the tent. After that, do what you want." I figured I had half a minute before she sounded the alarm. Half a minute to spin their conceptions on their heads and go north.

"Until next time then, Day Witch."

I winked and slid her dagger into the back of my waistband. Without waiting for the page's reaction, I ducked into the humid air.

Melisandre was gone. The path to the north woods lay empty.

Wild joy spread warm across my chest the moment the forest's shadows engulfed me. My cheeks split wide with the first smile in days. The elation of escape nearly surpassed the throbbing pain in my arm, but I barged ahead, plowing through ferns and over logs.

Minutes later, distant whistles and shouts began—all fading south. I wondered if the page ever gave me up or if the two idiots finally noticed I'd escaped.

Well, it was about time Fortuna smiled on me.

10

POSIONED HONEY

Maddox

"We have a problem. It has big doe eyes and a sharp mouth."

Yori and a pounding headache greeted me when I stepped from the Blackwood's shadows. Godsdamn it. How hard was it to keep a tiny witch tied up and guarded? I'd expected the tents dismantled, the guard umbranating back to Morithia after our utter failure to pacify the villages.

Nose to the ground, Melis and I had searched the realm's border all night and found no evidence of truth to the vampyr rumors. To add insult to injury, I'd wasted the past few days trying to convince village leaders everything was fine with supplies and coin. Why the magistrate council thought that would work was beyond me. The villagers were poor, not stupid. Throwing coin at a problem didn't solve anything if the problem was trust.

Now this.

I took a deep, slow breath through the drums in my head. "Tell me that little demon's restrained and sitting quietly in a tent."

"Well, I could but you'd probably prefer the truth." Yori shuffled from one foot to the other and sighed. "Melis is gathering a unit. They're heading south to cut Sathos off."

Cursing, I sprinted for the south end of camp.

To return home, the Day Witch would cross the Blackwood, a danger to any witch. Traversing the Blackwood alone was certain death, but airwitches were resourceful. DRAS pageships ensured only the most savage became airwitch soldiers. The higher up the DRAS ladder, the more conniving the airwitch, and, as Lilain's favorite captain, Alys Sathos had clearly scaled all the rungs.

A nagging thought slowed my steps.

Sathos hadn't secured a captaincy by doing what everyone expected. She knew our first instinct would chase her south. To the west lay the mountains—more impassable than the Blackwood. And east? Too far east and Sathos would run into elven scouts. She was reckless, but she wasn't stupid enough to tangle with the airwitch-hating elves.

That left one direction.

I whirled for the northern Blackwood, throwing over my shoulder, "Tell Melis to pack up camp and be ready to move out when I return."

"Where are you going?"

"To make this pointless trip worth something."

The Blackwood instantly swallowed me. An unnatural chill replaced the clearing's sunlit warmth. Gods, I hated this place. Following the tree line's edge, I crept north, hoping I wasn't wrong. I needed *something* to go right—*anything* after the night before. A northern breeze skittered through the forest—thick with decay. But another scent drifted on it, soft and faint.

Barely a note in the Blackwood's rot, the unmistakable scent of Sathos's magic floated past. Triumphant, I tore after the delicately sweet scent coated in a sharp edge—like honey laced with poison. No matter what the rumors claimed, she was clearly *not* magicless. Ready to claim at least one victory, I chased the scented breeze through the Blackwood, slowing when it grew intense.

A deer stepped across my path, forcing me to halt.

Unafraid, the doe kept one eye on me as it nibbled on an evergreen. Remembering the animated trees, I eased around the deer. Too many things in the Blackwood were inexplicable. I didn't fancy being mauled by a cursed deer.

It twitched its head, as if gesturing behind it. When I didn't move, the doe gestured again, more violently. I glanced beyond the deer, past a thicket of pines with a brook running through them. Something small knelt beside the water.

I nodded once and circled around the deer, refusing to look away. I'd seen all manner of strange shit in the Blackwood, but a deer helping me hunt was new. The doe nodded her head and with one last pointed look at the pines, sauntered deeper into the forest.

The Day Witch knelt beside the shallow brook, feverishly drinking from cupped palms. Her skin had taken a greenish hue and sweat beaded her forehead. She rose awkwardly, one hand clamped to her side, the other swinging uselessly.

Melis hadn't healed her.

An annoying twinge burrowed deep. Sathos took a tottering step and winced. Rubbing her ribs, she grew greener and clapped a hand over her mouth.

The twinge deepened.

Melis's vindictiveness was legendary, but I should've known better than to leave the Day Witch at Melis's mercy. There was justice. Then there was cruelty.

I weighed my options. Sathos was injured, but she'd already tossed the magic-warding manacles, and I couldn't trust her not to wield magic. No matter Melis's insistence of her magicless nature, I smelled it. Even if I seemed to be the only one. I'd have to surprise her.

Tugging at the pinprick within my soul, I veiled from view. With my body vanished from sight, I inched into the clearing.

The Day Witch abruptly straightened, sniffing the air. Eyes widening, she took off into the trees, searching the forest over her shoulder. Holding in a curse, I followed. She sped up with a sharp cry of pain, weaving through the pines, and lurching from my shadows.

I dropped the magic hiding me and plunged after her.

So much for the element of surprise.

She stumbled more than once, muffling her cries. I had to admit grudging respect. Bigger witches would've given in before now.

A ravine with rushing white waters came into view, and she veered for it. She must have been desperate if she was attempting the same tricks from the night before. I summoned the ravine's water and forced her back—slamming her into me.

She gasped, struggling to use her momentum to propel herself out of reach, but her narrow frame bounced off my chest, nearly sending us both into the water.

Diving for the Blackwood's shadows, I encased us in a sphere of darkness. Sweet, spiced honey forced me to blink and clear my head long enough to wrench her arms behind her. She gasped and went limp, but I didn't let go, pulling tighter instead. A choked whimper broke through our struggle and we both froze.

"If you stop fighting me," I hissed through clenched teeth. "I'll relax my hold."

"I'd rather run my eyeball through with a rusty knife than stop fighting. You might as well—" She broke off with a breathy gasp that didn't match the razor edge in her tone.

Against my better sense, the shadows eased back, and I loosened my grip. She dropped to her knees, cradling her arm.

The stupid twinge returned.

The Day Witch squinted up at me through shallow panting. I could almost see cogs spinning in her mind, calculating her chances of running. The witch before me was physically unimpressive, and I wasn't convinced this small, mouthy witch led the Day Queen's most brutal squad, magicless or not.

She sat on her heels, a bead of sweat sliding down her pointed face. Everything about her was sharp—her nose, her chin, even the angle of her black brows. In a peculiar way, she was pretty. As if the Mother had taken a black fox and turned it into a witch. Then as an afterthought added enormous doe eyes that missed nothing.

The effect was disconcerting.

Breathing deeply through her nose, Sathos gritted her teeth and said in that odd, lyrical accent, "I'll try escaping again."

"I'm aware."

She narrowed her eyes, looking more foxlike than ever. "Then you should kill me. No one would know. Unless you don't think you can. Do princes get squeamish over blood?"

I clamped my jaw shut to keep a retort from popping out. It had been a long time since someone had crawled under my skin this effectively.

Shadows flared from the trees and wound like ropes over her wrists, cinching them together. The manacles followed. I wasn't taking any chances. She winced, but her skin remained the same pallid shade. A small snarl escaped as I yanked her to her feet, but she didn't fight me. From the green tinge to her skin, I suspected she was focused on not vomiting.

"Melis didn't heal you?" I already knew the answer, but my sick sense of pride wanted to see Sathos swallow hers. A punishment for leading us on this wild chase.

She pursed pouty lips, and I focused on examining the shadows at her wrists. Hissing between her teeth at the tightening shadows, she experimentally flexed her hands, but the shadows wouldn't give. "No, she didn't heal me," she finally snapped. "Truth be told, I'm surprised she didn't just finish me off last night. Maybe she's going soft. Like you."

"Are you always this provocative?"

I shoved her backward, forcing her to sit on a nearby boulder.

Sathos remained silent, studying me. She had an unnerving way of assuming control of every situation. Like she was confident of her every move. Either she had the frightening ability to bluff her way through anything or she had an enormous ego. Probably a bit of both.

"Take off your tunic."

Her eyes somehow became larger, and she jerked an uninjured arm to cover herself. "You sick, twisted—"

"I need to *heal* you," I snapped. What kind of monster did she think I was? "As much as you deserve to be dragged injured to Morithia, we need to move quickly. Now, take off your tunic so I can *heal your shoulder*."

I slid the bonds from her wrists to her ankles and knelt, impatiently gesturing her to move.

Sathos remained motionless, arm tight over her chest. "Maybe *I'll* be the one to kill *you*."

"And then what?" I lifted an unimpressed brow. "Limp off until Melis catches you?"

"Maybe that's what I want. Rid myself of both of you."

Forget egotistical. She was flat out insane. I leaned in, breathing poisonous sweet magic and holding it inside. "Then do it."

Her dark eyes flashed, clearly unused to challenge. She dropped her arm with a leery squint and began unbuttoning her tunic's top button. Then the next. All the while watching me watch her in the world's oddest cat-mouse game.

"I would think a prince as pretty as you," Sathos began in a slow drawl, "wouldn't resort to drastic measures to see a witch naked." She paused on the fourth button and shot me a wicked grin. This was going to become a game of how far she could go. "You should work on your seduction technique. Maybe less brooding and more—"

"Finish that thought and I'll drag your unhealed sack of bones back to camp."

I was aware of how proportionately set my features were. I'd rather not be reminded by someone who wielded them like a weapon.

She snickered softly, undoing the final button. Another shirt lay beneath the tunic, sleeveless and coated in blood. Gritting her teeth, she maneuvered her arm from her sleeve, turning a sickly pale green again. A gruesome cut bisected her shoulder, back to front. Blue and purple mottling spiderwebbed from the wound.

She caught my stare and rolled her eyes.

"Hurry up. I'm cold."

Her braid hung between us, a long black rope that signified how different she was. Gingerly, I pinched it between two fingers and tossed it back over her uninjured shoulder. Day witches held onto many ancient customs, but long hair was the strangest. I eyed her ears where small gold hoops snaked the skin. I took it back. Purposefully poking holes repeatedly into their skin until their ears glinted gold was the strangest.

"Why are you taking so long? Do you even know the healing spellcast?"

I slid my hand beneath the fraying strap of her top, squeezing harder than necessary. She yelped a creative curse but didn't back from my other hand sliding beneath the bloody fabric to her broken ribs. I'd expected a maze of scars from the captain of the 22nd, not smooth skin, warm and soft beneath a narrow frame—completely at odds with the venomous glare she pointed at me. Gooseflesh pricked down her bare arm.

"Your hands are freezing."

"You'll live. *Sana corpus.*" The spellcast wound through me, latching onto my magic, and flowing out my fingers. This spellcast was the easiest. Not because I excelled at it. I'd never been able to heal anything greater than broken bones—at least not without Melis. But passing off a bit of my magic to another witch felt . . . natural. Even a Day Witch. It wasn't as if she could heal herself. No witch could break a natural law of magic. To heal, a witch passed on a thread of their magic onto another. Healing oneself was cyclical and therefore impossible.

Sathos tucked her head to the side, breathing shallowly and squeezing her eyes shut. Mending bones creaked and straightened beneath my hands.

I snuck another glance at her face and my stomach gave another uncomfortable lurch. Her complexion evened, greenish pallor fading into smooth tawny. The sharp angles of her face blurred with relief, softening into an almost dainty elegance. Eyelids fluttering open, she let out a soft sigh.

This time, *everything* inside me lurched. I froze, transfixed beneath a pair of velvety brown irises—who belonged to an enemy witch doing gods only knew what in my realm.

I snatched my hands back, the spellcast complete.

She cleared her throat and stood, swaying on bound feet. Stretching arms above her head, she tested her mended collarbone.

Rising slowly, I avoided the thin line of golden skin below her rising tunic. She was an odd puzzle of sharp words and confidence; one I itched to solve.

Pointing at the tunic she'd begun rebuttoning, I asked, "How many goblins does it take to soak a DRAS captain in blood? A hundred? Two hundred?"

That sort of bloodshed spoke of an unheard-of battle between the DRAS and goblins. Usually, it was a display of airwitch dominance.

She raised a brow, concentrating on the final button. "What a strange compliment. Your seduction attempts truly need more work."

A neat sidestep.

Scowling, I yanked the shadows from her ankles, ready to wind them around her wrists when she darted a hand behind her back.

I caught her wrist a second before the blade ripped through me. Angling my body to the side, I slammed her wrist down, sending the knife clattering to the ground. The unbalanced movement was all she needed to rip out of reach and take off.

Healed, she was godsdamned *fast*.

Weaving through the trees, I sprinted after her, cursing myself for letting my guard down when she hadn't. That would be the last time I'd let those doe eyes outmaneuver me.

Spotting the shadows of a pine, I sprinted into their darkness, allowing them to swallow me. A second later I reappeared in front of her. She shrieked, failing to stop and rammed into me with the force of a man, sending us barreling to the ground.

I should've caught her this way the night before. If it hadn't been for the treachery of the Blackwood in the dark, I might have saved us a pointless chase.

"You cheating prick," she howled, shoved into the dirt by waiting shadows.

"*Cheating*? You tried to *stab* me."

Breathless, I pushed the little demon deeper into the ground. She clawed at the dirt, screeching and sending pine needles flying. Her caterwauling would attract something neither of us wanted.

"Shut up," I hissed, ringing shadows around her wrists. "Get up and walk before something finds and eats us."

She went rigid, making it damned near impossible to heft her up. Fine. I'd *drag* her back. Shadows swarmed, lifting and slamming her against a pine. I patted down her body and searched for anything sharp. She stiffened almost imperceptibly but mercifully kept any more suggestive quips to herself.

Finding nothing, I slid the dagger she'd nearly stabbed me with beneath her chin and leaned toward her. To her credit she didn't flinch.

"Save both of us the effort and give in, Sathos."

"Give in?" she repeated, a hitch catching in her throat. Ignoring the knife, she leaned forward. "To what? Marching to my death at your queen's hands? What do you think I am? A lamb cheerfully trotting off to the slaughter-house?"

We were nose to nose. Too close. I could make out each black lash framing almond-shaped eyes. Dozens of swirling shades of brown opened wide with a white ring. Looking into them gave me the unsettling sensation of leaning over a cliff.

"Perhaps you shouldn't have trespassed then." I angled the knife higher. "Tell me what you're doing here. Why is a DRAS captain—the 22nd's no less—in the Night Realm?"

Full lips twisted into a wry smile. "There are many terrifying Creatures in these woods, Prince. You aren't one of them."

"Fine." I pulled back, nearly missing her tiny shiver of relief. Not bothering to hide a smirk, I summoned a shadowy tether between her bound wrists and my hand. Without glancing back, I yanked hard. A delightful yelp was followed by the thud of her ass hitting the ground. Ignoring her inventive curses, I dragged her behind me and started for the camp.

Served her right.

"If I don't get the truth from you, Sathos, someone else will."

"Is that a threat?"

"No." An icy reminder crept through me. "A threat implies a *chance* of harm. If you make it to the Night Queen, there isn't a chance."

"Why not?"

"Because it's a *certainty*."

A certainty Morgenna would obliterate this defiant Day Witch.

11

GILDED WATERS

Alys

The Mother clearly played favorites with the realms because the Night Realm had been given all the beauty. The village of Grelgesco sat like a perfect miniature model between the Blackwood and the Vinnith Mountains. Neatly thatched roofs above whitewashed cottages rested in the cove of a lake shimmering gold in the setting sun. Behind the lake, jagged mountain peaks stood guard over the picturesque landscape.

That morning the prince had returned me to an empty camp clapped back in worthless magic-warded manacles. Only a handful of guards, including Melisandre and Yori, waited.

Bound and dragged by the prince's shadows, the journey to the Night Realm capital began in silence. In my frustrated stewing, I shut down each of Yori's attempts at conversation. My irritation only grew when the prince's flat mask occasionally slipped when he caught one of my glares. Each instance brought on a smirk, one I spent hours imagining smearing into the dirt.

Evening washed us in pink rays, and Melisandre insisted we stop for the night in a nearby village instead of camping. The prince gave his twin a grimace when she named Grelgesco but agreed. By that point, I was practically salivating at the thought of a bed and bath, praying to the Mother I'd be allowed both.

Shadows at my wrists snapped, and I stumbled forward, barely catching myself.

"Keep up, Sathos. The village of Grelgesco does not tolerate Day Witches. Their sons proudly serve the Night Army."

Ah, the Night Army the DRAS tore apart. The sons the 22nd sent running back for their borders. Right.

I let out a snort the prince ignored.

A tower of white marble veined in violet stood sentinel outside the village, stark against the quaint cottages. I nudged Yori, nodding my chin to the tower. "What's that?"

"An outpost library." He pointed across the lake to the mountaintops. "Scholars and instructors up there at Amethyst Hall use the outposts for research. They contain the isle's most heavily warded books. You'll find tower libraries scattered across the realm. Of course, the best library is Albulus Tower in Morithia."

Melisandre grunted. "Don't let the instructors at Amethyst Hall hear you. They're rather partial to their library rotunda."

The tower's shadow fell over us as we neared the village outskirts. All those books inside. All that information. The lack of a book ban *almost* made the Night Realm palatable.

Yori 's head swiveled between Melisandre and her brother like a pendulum with tight ringlets. "Perhaps coming this close to Amethyst Hall was a bad idea."

Neither twin responded.

Melisandre fixed hungrily on the mountains while the prince muttered something vulgar under his breath and tugged me closer. Only the crunch of pebbles beneath our feet broke the weighted silence. The young guard from my capture, barely twenty, stared openly between the fractured twins, as intrigued as I was by their history.

The wilting creak of an opening door snapped the silence. As one, we spun toward the tower. A woman not much older than me stepped out, squinting at the setting sun. Masses of fawn-colored loose curls fell around her shoulders, contradicting her neat, starched blouse gathered into a wool skirt. Her stack of precariously tucked books threatened to slip from her hold.

"Need a hand, Corryn?" Melisandre called. Her clenched hands betrayed any indifference in her voice.

The woman yelped and reared back. Her elbow slammed into the door behind her and the books slipped from her grasp, bouncing across the stone walkway. Cheeks going a muted pink, she bent to retrieve them. Yori hurried to help her. He spoke softly as if trying not to spook a horse, chatting about nonsense as he helped gather her books.

She was tiny, slightly frail-looking, with dusky olive skin that desperately needed more sun. Nothing about her screamed threat, and yet I sensed both twins' hackles rise. Shadows inched toward the bookish witch, detecting a greater threat.

With an irritated sigh, the prince blocked my nosey observations and motioned me to hurry along.

As we passed, the timid woman glanced at my bound hands, tracing the shadow tether to the prince. She winced—an almost apologetic expression—before sprinting into a deep shadow and vanishing. No—umbranating.

"We'll pass through Grelgesco quickly," the prince instructed when the woman had gone, "avoid attention and head for the inn. The last thing we need is the village's notice of *her*."

I shrugged, tossing my braid over my shoulder.

Not my problem.

The tether between the prince and I shrank, forcing me to walk directly in front of him through the dirt packed street. A few children playing a game of marbles stopped to watch us pass. They took in the black-and-gold cloaks of the Guard with large eyes, whispering to one another. Eager gazes fell on me and transformed into wicked delight. A prisoner—an airwitch no less—caught like a rat.

What a bloody treat.

When they scrambled for the whitewashed houses, Yori moaned. "They'll drag the whole village out to see her."

Not a minute passed before villagers began emerging from the cottages. Haggard faces roved over us. They took in the cloaks with surprised curiosity, lingering on the Night Prince and Princess. Sweeping gazes took in my braid and something dark bloomed. I couldn't mistake the undisguised grief and rage.

Something stiff like guilt prodded my gut.

A stone flew past my head, cleaving the air between the prince and me. That didn't bode well. I peeked over my shoulder at him and tried to ascertain if he'd go ahead and let the village stone me.

He didn't look any more irritated than usual. Muscles twitched in his jaw and the shadowy leash dissipated into my natural shadow. Snaking an arm around my middle, he yanked me to his side.

"Stay close."

Well, it wasn't as if he'd given me a choice. Besides, my hands were still bound. I was well and trapped against his side. He lowered his arm to my hips, crouching slightly.

"Don't you dare toss me over your shoulder," I hissed.

He glared down, pointing to the crowd inching forward as their murmuring became obscene shouts for my head. "Forgive me for trying to save your miserable life."

"Or," Melisandre drawled behind us, eyeing the prince's arm, "you could give her a shove. The villagers would do the rest."

Now came the stoning.

A statuesque woman lunged toward me, knocking villagers out of her way.

Yori was instantly there, blocking her with his girth. He gently pushed her back into the crowd, but she spat at him in defiance. Shadows rushed at his call, rising to block her when she reached for me again. She clawed at his shield with a wail that reminded me of Uzza's final cries.

The prince shook his head at his sister. His long fingers burrowed into my hip as he jerked me from a stone flung on a shadow wave. "The law is clear. She goes before the queen."

Massive shadows glided from the base of each cottage in a looming black cloud over the village. Another witch surged forward before faltering at the black cloud hovering over the youngest Night guard. I understood, then, why the young guard accompanied us. The Night Guard was made of power. And he rippled with it.

Another stone ripped through Yori's shield, bouncing off my knee. Sharp spasms shot down my leg. I stumbled back against the prince and hissed. A trickle of blood oozed down the inside of my pants. Unless the Night Guard calmed the villagers, we were minutes from a mob.

"Unbind me."

The prince shot me an incredulous glower before turning his attention back to an elderly man waving a bucket of dead rats, screaming about diseases Day Witches carried.

Lovely.

I pulled against the prince's grip. "I'm not dying bound and helpless while some village idiot beats me to death with a bucket of rats."

The old man went flying over the crowd on the prince's shadows, smashing into a group of caterwauling women. The villagers inhaled, quieting as the women disentangled themselves. Then the yells exploded into a new wave of flying spittle and shadow. Stones flew with abandon, no longer aimed only at me. Red-faced witches readied to rip us to pieces and avenge their grief. The mob shredded through the guards' shields; their shadows prying apart all that stood between us and the mob.

"Enough," the prince snarled. He shoved me into Yori's arms. The giant didn't hesitate, hefting me into his arms like an over-sized infant. The prince turned to the Blackwood and lifted his hands. Black clouds rose from the trees, merging to form a shapeless mass. He motioned to Melisandre who clenched her jaw but gave him a curt nod. To Yori, the prince ordered, "Don't let the Day Witch go, and for fuck's sake, *do not unbind her.*"

Where exactly did he think I would run off to? The mob's loving embrace?

With flicking hands, Melisandre and the prince coaxed an enormous spider of shadows from the forest, climbing over the trees on spindly legs. Mouth dropping open, I realized they were summoning the heart of the

Blackwood; the deepest depravity of the forest. Half the size of the village, the beast thrashed and growled. A yawning pit opened in its center—eager to swallow all light.

"I hate it when they do that," Yori muttered, upper lip curling as the shadow scurried for the retreating villagers. "That thing scares the shit out of me."

It scared the shit out of the villagers too. The mob stumbled back, throwing up their own shadows against the monster. Angry chants became prayers for the Mother's salvation, for the Crone's mercy.

Melisandre's cheeks flushed pink, eyes sharp, taking in the monster she'd created with unmatched joined magic. But the prince remained expressionless, focused on the villagers, scanning those closest to me. Long pale fingers tapped an erratic beat against his leg.

"Do you not trust your queen to uphold our laws?" His low voice cut through the muffled prayers. The villagers descended into silence, and horror began to dawn at what they'd done—*who* they'd nearly mobbed. Many fell to their knees, their pleas exploding once again. The snarling shadow beast drifted lower.

"The Day Witch will go before Queen Morgenna and find justice. Will you stand in the Night Queen's way?"

Desolate stares snuck past the prince and found me. The gut twinge returned, and I found I couldn't fault their blind rage. Not when I knew how stained my hands were.

Slowly, the villagers backed away, clearing the street.

The beast gave a ghastly moan and sank back into the Blackwood, waiting for the day it would be called again—a reminder of the power the Night Queen had at her heirs' fingertips.

Over Yori's shoulder, I caught the prince's eye and frowned. It was one thing knowing he had enormous power. It was another witnessing it. What had the gods been thinking when they fated me to dethrone the Night Queen? He was merely the queen's heir, and he had more magic in his pinky than I had in my entire body.

The modest inn wasn't anything special. Musty rooms. Beds of limp straw. Rusted copper baths. But each was a glorious sight for an exhausted witch who itched with crusted blood and sweat.

Allowed a quick bath, I washed off the grime and emerged a new witch. A pair of pants and a tunic set of brown wool waited for me. The pants fit with some rope as a belt, but the tunic hung off my frame and itched worse than crusted blood. Still, the innkeeper's token apologies for the village's antics were clean and that was enough.

Hair dripping, I padded barefoot and shadow-bound to my bed. Sharing a room with the prince and Yori meant I would have two guard dogs yet again. No chance of escape.

Melisandre hadn't been allowed near me. The prince had the decency to look annoyed by her casual suggestion to bunk with me. "You'll slit her throat, and then *I'll* have to deal with the consequences."

Lips twisting, he eyed my hair. He traced its length to my hips before throwing me a linen towel. "You're getting the floor wet."

"It's a part of my plan," I retorted. I squeezed excess water from my hair, struggling to maneuver around bound hands. "When you slip, I'll dash off to your murderous little village."

"Do it. Then I'll finally be rid of your mouth."

"Odd considering you can't seem to stop staring at it."

His head snapped up from his meticulously packed canvas bag. "Do you ever quit?" Tossing the bag to the bed, he crossed his arms, fingers drumming on his bicep. "You're a captive. On her way to certain punishment. At least one thought in that thick head should wonder if you should stay silent."

Worming under his skin was too easy.

Throwing the damp linen back at him, I flipped my hair over my shoulder and said, "My head's not thick. It's all this hair."

Yori watched our volleying from his bed with a wide grin and plenty of chuckles. His enormous frame pushed the limits of the bed's supports. Each booming laugh shook the termite-ravaged wood.

"I distinctly remember your mother telling you," he drawled to the prince, "one day you'd meet a witch who ran circles around you, and you wouldn't have a clue what to do with them."

"Don't give Sathos too much credit. You'll inflate that enormous head, and it might burst," the prince replied without missing a beat. He tossed a blanket onto my makeshift cot in the corner—opposite of the door.

I snorted and braided my tangled hair. At least it was clean. Mulling over Yori's words, I said, "That sounds rather maternal for the great and terrifying Queen Morgenna. I wouldn't peg her for motherly."

The room's mirth evaporated.

Yori sat up slowly, pity stamped across his rugged features like a shield.

A wall of flat ice slid over the prince. He took a step toward me, his spine impossibly straight. "Captain Sathos—once again you prove the ignorance of the Day Realm. Morgenna is not my mother."

I glanced at Yori for clarification, but the giant searched his blanket as if the pilled wool held the answer to life's mysteries.

Shadows slunk from the room's corners, slithering for their prince like black adders.

"Magicless. Squadless. Captured. Utterly ignorant. A pathetic excuse for a witch." His soft mockery aimed to hurt, retaliation for whatever my careless words unleashed. "Perhaps Melis was wrong. Perhaps you're not the threat she believes."

He wasn't dangerous because of his title or power. No, I'd dealt with my fair share of powerful pricks. But his unfathomable ability to see through me and skewer everything within? That had the potential to unravel everything I'd tied into a neat knot. He saw the nobody from the filth of Kazadorah who'd manipulated her way up the DRAS ranks. He saw the worthless rat.

I was *nothing* to the powerful like him.

More than that, I was alone, running from an impossible fate and caught in his grasp.

A spark of something unbridled reignited inside me, and I crept closer until we were toe-to-toe.

Heart hammering, I whispered, "Your sister is right about one thing, isn't she? You're a miserable prick and it's not hard to see why no one wants to be around you, why even your twin sister despises you."

He clenched his jaw, and the scent of spiced cedar rose on shadows, held back only by his thin restraint. But I wanted to fan the flaming anger creeping over him and melt that emotionless facade. "The question is—are you a miserable prick because no one likes you? Or does no one like you because you're a miserable prick? Chicken or the egg."

Shadows flung me onto the cot.

The impact left me gasping for air, and I scrambled up, ready for his blows.

But the prince stalked past me, soundless as he moved. At the door, he snapped to Yori, "Tie her to the cot and watch her. She won't think twice about stabbing you, so if she tries to escape"—his bright stare could've flayed me—"kill her."

12

CHICKEN OR THE EGG

Alys

I awoke to moldy straw poking through the thin mattress and promptly let loose the filthiest curse I knew. Elenna would've applauded my creativity. But instead of Elenna, a giant Night Witch peered blearily down at me.

Right.

I'd been captured, and Elenna was dead.

Yori took my storm cloud of a mood in stride and hauled me down the inn's stairs. Breakfast consisted of familiar oat porridge and nearly burnt pork. A bite later, I was convinced crispy pork made an excellent addition to breakfast. Perhaps the Night Realm did a few things right. Books and pork. Not enough to risk my life for them, though.

The Night Guard filed in, heaping plates with eggs, peculiar smelly fish, and pork. When the prince strode in, he sat as far from me as possible, refusing to meet my gaze.

Petulant baby.

At Melisandre's staggering entrance, the inn quieted. She wore the same clothes from the day before, rumpled and stained. Calling for tea, the Night Princess slumped into her seat. Even several chairs down, I could smell the village tavern.

Munching on pork—bacon, they called it—I studied the twins, wondering what their parents must've done to gain the Mother's favor and bear twins. Twins amongst witches were rare. Their duality was a symbol of the Mother's double nature. Able to share magic and pull from the other in a nearly bottomless river of power, twins bore extraordinary magic. Stumbling across two pairs of twins in a lifetime was unheard of.

An image of Ansil's falling body stormed my memories. My stomach churned and I flung the bacon back onto my plate.

"I can't decide if being a twin is a gift or a curse," I began to no one in particular. Latching onto the tension in the room, I fed it my souring mood. "Imagine being in one another's heads all day. Or worse. At . . . intimate moments."

Yori snorted beside me. "It doesn't work that way. They have to allow the other in."

I knew that, but I continued prodding, itching for a fight. Anything to block the awful image of Ansil's limbs bent skyward.

"Imagine fancying one witch and bursting into your twin's head to discover an eyeful of that witch on the other side. How awkward."

Yori groaned, shushing me.

Beside him, Melisandre dropped a partially started slice of toast and swerved her head to me. The cloudy haze of alcohol lifted, and she half-rose, clenched fists resting on top of the table.

Recalling the thick tension at the outpost library tower, I flicked my gaze to the prince who was watching me with a guarded frown. "I'm curious. That witch back at the library tower? Who had her first?"

Yori dove, barely blocking Melisandre's fist from crashing into my nose. "Bleeding Mother, Alys. Of all the things you could've said . . ."

Too bad the giant moved quickly. I wouldn't have minded one more chance to plant a fist in Melisandre's face. The younger guard—Nik—pulled her off Yori, throwing me a glare when she nearly bucked him.

"To be fair," I said, wiping bacon grease from my hands, "if I was in that woman's position, I probably would've picked the prince too. Why would anyone pick *you* when they could pick a more put together version who doesn't saunter into a battle drunk as shit?"

Melisandre's face crumpled, unnaturally delicate without its sharp-edged cruelty. Wrenching from Nik, she streaked for the door, slamming her hip into a chair and knocking it to the floor.

A heavy silence thicker than the forgotten porridge smothered the room.

"Cruelty won't free you," Yori murmured, bending to return the chair upright.

"Maybe not. But you forget she's tried to kill me for years. Nearly succeeded too. I'm not inclined to become her dearest friend when she's tried to see what my insides look like. Besides, I merely said what everyone else is thinking."

Yori's gaze was heavy. I tamped down the urge to squirm beneath his disappointed stare. What did I care if I didn't meet a Night Witch's standards? But he shook his head, and a stone settled into my belly, further churning my already rebelling innards.

The prince had remained silent, studying the entire exchange on a chair tipped back on two legs. Unlike his sister, he appeared unperturbed. Icy as ever, he finally asked, "The chicken or the egg, Sathos?"

E scape was never far from my thoughts. Every bend around a brook or dark shadow, I calculated my chances of escape. And the bleeding Night Prince was there each time an idea formed. Bound to him on a shadow leash, he saw each opportunity before I did, thwarting each attempt before I'd finished formulating a plan. Each time he blocked my way, a flash of a smirk shattered his princely contempt. He'd turned it into a sick game, and I couldn't decide if I wanted to escape or just fuck it all and try to strangle him before the others killed me.

"Just think," he drawled while our group rested beneath the shade of an enormous oak. We'd finally cleared the Blackwood and emerged onto rolling emerald fields strewn with lone trees. "If your broom hadn't shattered, you'd have reached Kazadorah by now."

And most likely be writhing under a blood boil spellcast.

No thanks.

"And you, Prince, would be cozied up with your queen, eager to—"

Yori shoved a waterskin into my hands, cutting me off. "Can all Day Witches fly? Most Night Witches can't umbranate."

"Now who's fishing?" Gulping down the offered water, I wondered if I could trade information for information. Anything to increase my odds of escape. "I suppose they can. It's the broom's amplifying air runes that let us fly. But rune-warded brooms are hard to come by, so DRAS airwitches make up the majority of fliers."

"Still doesn't explain how you ended up broomless in the Night Realm."

I smiled through an urge to wrap bound hands around the prince's neck and squeeze. Aiming for an unaffected shrug, I took a long sip from the waterskin. A single drop of water beaded on my lower lip. I wiped it away with my thumb, acutely aware he followed the movement. A tumultuous image of him licking it off plagued my poisoned brain.

Absolutely not.

Tossing the waterskin back to Yori, I took a gamble.

"How is water a natural magic of Night Witches? Shadows obviously belong to the night, but water?"

Yori snuck a glance at the prince who shook his head, but the giant rose and extended his hand to me. "It's the tidal power of the moon. The celestial power controls tides in the night and gifts us water summoning."

"Enough."

Before I could take Yori's hand, the prince hurled me onto my feet on a wave of shadow. He set us off at a brisk pace, and I wasn't about to let him drag me on my ass again. Hurrying to match his long-legged pace across the fields, I reached his side and said, "You might as well let me fish. Who will

I tell? If you're so convinced I can't escape, then what harm will come from answering my questions? Now, tell me about your shadows."

"You talk too much. Maybe I'll gag you."

"Depending on what you gag me with, I may not mind."

The prince's back went ramrod straight.

Behind us, Yori and Nik gasped then burst out in raucous laughter. The prince sent them a look that could've frozen the entire Eastern Sea. They cut off mid-howl, doing their best to look contrite.

To my surprise it was Melisandre who explained. "Our natural magic is similar to a Day Witch's. We connect the magic in our souls to the magic in nature. You lot draw from fire and air in the atmosphere. We draw from shadow and water. As for shadows, they're like water. Water has multiple forms—gas, liquid, ice. We manipulate those forms in shadows too."

I scrunched my nose.

"But how does shadow have more than one form?"

Sighing irritably, the prince answered, "Because unlike your magic, ours is sentient."

My brows flew into my hairline.

He summoned his shadow from the grass. It brushed against my bound wrists, but I felt nothing. "In its simplest form, shadow is merely the absence of light. But controlled by the right witch . . ."

The shadow shoved, and I went sprawling onto my ass.

He shot me a nasty grin that somehow enhanced his already perfect features. "It's drawn to powerful witches, wanting to be used. It remains shadow but with our soul's will attached. Most Night Witches only summon pure insentient darkness. It's uncommon to manipulate it as you've seen. But then again, the Night Guard is made up of uncommonly powerful witches."

I poured every drop of loathing into my glare.

It wasn't enough he'd been Mother blessed in every other aspect of his life. A dominating warrior, rich beyond measure, with a face that could've made a Second Order priestess beg for the unholy. That face remained impassive, but his strange eyes sparked with something nastier than his grin—power.

The living embodiment of everything I was not, the Night Prince crouched beside me, close enough he blocked the sweet scent of the field's milkweed with his overpowering cedar.

"Lest you think that's too much power, there's even more to our magic. The rarest Night Witch holds the power to balance a Day Witch's magic to create light from nothing—like this." He vanished. One moment he was taunting me, and the next he was gone. I knew he hadn't umbranated. Beneath a full sun, only my shadow darkened the grass, and he hadn't touched it.

Unseen hands snatched my bound wrists and hauled me to my feet. I yelped and tried to jerk from the phantom sensation. I could feel the force of his grip, his calloused fingers tight around my wrists, but I was looking right through him to the open fields.

Godsdamn it, this was weird.

"But it's not balanced at all, is it?" he hissed into my ear. The stubble of his jaw brushed against my cheek, rough and jarring, completely unseen. "What's the point of your light when it can't reveal what's veiled?"

He reappeared without warning and set off.

"I can't summon light. No magic, remember?" I called, somewhat breathless as I blinked away the fog feathering over me. He raised a dubious brow over his shoulder. Undeterred, I jogged to catch up. "What about the trees? Did you do something to them to catch me?"

"You ask a lot of questions for someone supposedly meek and magicless."

"I never said I was meek. The trees, Prince. Was that you?"

"No. You must have pissed off a number of gods to command such attention."

Well, shit.

I shot a nervous glance at a lone tree and its thick limbs. *Above all else, do not deviate from your path.* First thing I'd done after the Mother's warning? I lied to her face and ran from my path. In return, the Mother had *painfully* pushed me to the Night Realm, assuring I'd be caught by the Night Prince headed for the Night Queen and certain death.

The lone tree waved a single branch in mocking assurance

I nearly threw a middle finger up at the taunting tree before thinking better of it. If the Mother wanted to play this game, she could herd me all she wanted. I'd seen enough of the Night Witches to know they weren't worthy of my suicidal fate.

Yori nudged me with his elbow and pointed to a faraway herd of deer with a radiant smile, looking for all the world like we were lifelong friends off on an epic adventure.

Damn him.

"**W**hy do Day witches keep long hair?" the youngest guard asked, peering at my braid I was fiddling with between bound hands.

After the prince's eerie veiling display and the realization I might not be able to run from my fated path, I'd sulked across the fields. The land became flatter the further east we ventured, but the easier hike did little to help my mood. Yori refused to let me stew, bombarding me with questions about the Day Realm, with Nik occasionally butting in.

"It's an ancient witch custom you Night Witches seem to have forgotten," I finally answered.

The others all turned to me curiously.

"In the ancient days before the exile, when witches were the Mother's favorite, the other Creatures' jealousy often manifested in cursed energy—the casting eye it was called. I don't know if there was any actual magic to it or if the witches played victim, but the favoritism became a sore point between witches and the rest of the world. Even the gods. There was some ancient witch queen whose beauty was renowned. Her incredibly long, beautiful hair made her a target of the casting eye. When she died of an illness no one could heal, the casting eye was naturally blamed. Long hair became a symbol of defiance—a sort of 'fuck you and your casting eye' to the rest of the world. Unlike, the Night Realm, the Day Realm never forgot our continent roots."

I ran a finger across tiny gold hoops and studs hugging the curve of my ear. "Like these." My voice came out soft, nearly stolen by the winds whipping through the tall grasses. "The ancients also believed grief and physical pain wound the same. Both serve as reminders of what we've lost. Even when the pain fades, grief doesn't. The gold remains as a token of what we lost."

Each of them eyed the dozen rings and studs lining my ears with new appreciation. I had more than most. Most airwitches did. But one always stood out to me. The gold stud through the whirl of my ear had hurt the worst. I'd made sure of it when I picked the spot. Three years later, losing Federikka ached as if it had happened yesterday.

Pushing aside guilt, I turned my questions onto Yori and learned he'd been orphaned at an early age. He'd been raised by an elderly aunt until his extraordinary magic manifested and he accidentally flooded his village.

"Amethyst Hall scooped me up after that spectacle," he said, laughing. "From there a straight shot to the Night Guard—the only place for a powerful nobody."

The emerald fields eventually became golden with grain. Fields of waiting food. All for Night Witches who weren't starving to death in a back alley, alone and forgotten. In this realm, no one was dying of negligence or cruelty. So, why had the Mother insisted I free the Night Realm first?

Cued by the setting sun, we stopped in a field of trees lined as far as I could see. Shiny red fruit hung from each laden limb. Picking up a fallen fruit, I sniffed it. This one was half-rotted, its flesh smelling sickly sweet. I let it tumble to the ground with a splat.

Yori crept up behind me and gently said, "There are rumors much of the Day Realm lives in starvation. Is it true?"

"Most of the Day Realm is desert. Water is scarce, so very little grows." The group went silent, and heat crawled up my neck. I tried a nonchalant shrug, but I couldn't look up from the rotted fruit littering the ground.

Squinting at a lump of writhing maggots, I said, "DRAS pageships are highly competitive, not from loyalty to the realm or Lilain but because airwitches are guaranteed three meals and a bed. The Day Realm Aerial Squadrons are made of children who defied poverty—who stole, cheated, *killed* our way out. Too many didn't. Yet, a few days north, all *this* goes to waste."

Uncomfortable silence hovered like an eager vulture as we formed a camp. Nik found a ladder, and with Melisandre, picked fruit, promising to leave coin. I watched them work together with an itchy lump in my throat, remembering only a few days ago, I too belonged to a group.

"Come eat."

The shadowy leash jerked, as commanding as the prince's words. Behind him, the others pulled out squashed loaves of bread and cheese from the inn. Slicing into the red fruit, they ate with groans, juice dripping through their fingers. I eyed the fruit in a nearby basket, wondering how to eat the bleeding thing.

"You've never had an apple?" The prince watched me with a faint sneer, an uneaten apple in one hand, a knife in the other. He cut a slice and held it out.

"I can't decide if you're being kind or patronizing."

"What a terrible place you must come from if you misconstrue a basic right to food as kindness."

I scowled and snatched the slice before shoving it into my mouth. Nothing could have stopped my eyes fluttering shut nor the moan that escaped me. The things a Kazadoran child would do for one of these . . .

I opened my eyes to find the prince's eerie intensity had gone dark on my mouth.

An unsettling swoop in my belly like I'd nosedived off a broom forced me to reach for the basket and my own apple. I took a tentative bite through thin skin and let out a much more silent sigh.

Settling beneath the limbs of a laden tree, I soaked in the fading sunlight. The shadow tether relaxed. Not quite releasing me but giving me ample room to maneuver around its bonds.

The prince plopped down too close and tossed me a hunk of bread and cheese. I gave the shortened space between us a pointed look, but he ignored it and asked, "Why does Lilain not have an heir?"

"Lilain is . . . ageless," I answered around a mouthful of cheese. "She's lived for centuries, and she'll live for centuries more. Don't ask me how. No one knows. An undying witch doesn't need an heir."

The prince tossed his apple core and stretched his long legs before him. He leaned back on his elbows, the wool of his tunic pulling across his arms. Wool was supposed to be plain. Simple and obscure. With the muscles rippling underneath, *his* black wool was anything but.

I refocused on my apple and took a large, unnecessary bite.

"But both?" he muttered. Leaning further back, he studied the hanging apples. Our shadows twined into one mass and snaked the trunk to pluck two apples from a low hanging branch. One dropped into my lap.

"Both what?"

"More fishing?"

I took a bite from my new apple. "You're terribly insecure, Prince. Worried I might escape you and tell Lilain your secrets?" Apple juice ran down my wrist in a thin stream. I mumbled a curse and swiped my tongue to catch it.

He abruptly sat up, glaring at the shrinking sun.

"Morgenna isn't my mother. Like Lilain, she's somehow tapped into unnatural magic. She's lived for gods know how long. I'm her heir because I'm her nearest descendant."

Well, that was unexpected.

"What's the point of heirs if she outlives them?"

His disdain returned in force. "Unlike the Day Realm, the Night Realm is a complex, political machine. It requires multiple cogs of policy. Although she rarely leaves the Onyx Palace in Morithia, Morgenna is the head of that machine. You could say I'm the arm. She rules, and I implement her policy while providing an ear to the realm. For example, I'll report the growing frustration of the border villages. Rumors of vampyres are growing, causing unnecessary panic. It's my responsibility as heir to protect and serve not only the queen but the people of the realm, even if I never see the crown on my head, as my father never did, nor his mother."

Noble. Even for a prick.

"All right. I'll concede you lot are a *bit* more organized." I inspected an apple seed, marveling at how something insignificant could become a giant tree. "Do you know what first started the conflict between the realms?"

"No. It happened during the Lost Five Hundred Years."

"What Lost Years?"

"It's said the books containing Efelldor's history from the turn of the millennia to 500AE burned during a Day Witch raid two hundred years ago."

"*All* the books? They were *all* lost at once?"

"Yes." He dragged the word out, once again weighing how much to tell me. "Our records, spotty as they are, go back to the witches landing on Efelldor after our exile—two thousand years ago—up to the modern AE era when we ousted the elves from power a thousand years ago. Then our records pause for five hundred years. Somewhere in those missing centuries Morgenna—and possibly Lilain—came into power."

Lilain's penchant for control fit the prince's narrative. Compelling a DRAS squad to storm the Night capital library was within her scope of scheming for power. Especially if the books contained something she'd rather hide. Like a way to live forever. Or a way to undo it. Afterall, this was the same queen who'd banned books based on one incident in the jungle.

Flicking the apple seed at the prince, I asked, "You find nothing odd in erasing history so neatly?"

He plucked the seed from his tunic and flicked it back, hitting my nose. "I find many things odd. Like how a DRAS captain as *legendary* as you ended up in the Night Realm." A rather graceful dodge of my question. More telling than his answer could've been.

"An oddity you shall never unravel."

"I doubt that."

Twisting his lips into a grimace, he rose, an elegant unfolding of long limbs that came from a life of privilege and elite training. He held out his hand, eyes narrowed like he half-expected I'd bite him.

Equally wary, I studied his long fingers for a second too long. Nicked in a lattice of thin pale scars, they mirrored mine. Years of practice with a sword displayed beside earned callouses. There was no reason to take his hand. I could stand on my own.

He began lowering his hand, but I leapt forward and snatched it. Warm fingers clenched around mine, like a reflex he couldn't control. His eyes met mine, and I swore I saw something dark and hungry before ice frosted over. He yanked his hand back as soon as I was on my feet, flexing his fingers once before shoving them into his pocket.

Well, at least I wasn't the only one unable to keep the *really* bad ideas from creeping into my head. And other places.

13

THE JEWEL OF MORITHIA

Alys

"N o wonder Night Witches think we're boorish heathens," I muttered to the landscape below the hilltop.

Whatever I'd expected from the capital, it wasn't the sprawling city snaking down the seacoast. The Eastern Sea glinted silver, lapping against the massive gray smear of Morithia. I drank in the mess of stone and smoke, tracing miles of soot-stained roofs. Thick black stone encircled the city, daring anyone to plunder the Night Realm's jewel.

On a seaside cliff above the city, the Onyx Palace glittered like a dangerous black blade poised over its people. Towers topped with onyx spires jutted into the clouds. Golden ivy adorned much of the palace in a visage of black and gold. But what caught my eye was the iridescent dome capping the center wing. Its glass caught the midday sun, sparkling like a diamond encased in black.

In comparison, Lilain's citadel hewn into a canyon wall seemed pitiful.

"Move," the prince snarled from behind, shoving me down the hill toward the city gates.

The ancient, black gate mocked my failure to escape in a deep low groan as it opened. I stepped through the gateway and into my fate.

I blamed the Mother for this.

If I died within these walls, it was on her. Fate be damned.

Everything inside the gates was odd. Instead of Kazadorah's grid of sandstone streets, neat cobblestones wound around Morithia. Clipped accents sliced the air like knives. Street vendors called out unfamiliar foods from markets. Occasional drunken laughter escaped from taverns already overflowing in the late afternoon.

At least that remained the same between realms.

Nik and Yori took turns calling out different districts and their claim to fame as we passed through them. Pride coated Nik's voice when he spoke of the city where he'd grown up here as a courtier's son. When we crossed into the Water Wheel District, his pride vanished, replaced by something that sounded strangely like guilt. Yori didn't look any better.

A filthy river meandered through filthier streets of the Water Wheel. The familiar reek brought on a pang of memories, when finding food and shelter in Kazadorah's forgotten alleys mattered more than anything else. Thin faces peeked from windows and half-shut doors. Hard eyes skimmed over me to skewer the Night Guard instead.

How odd.

By the time we reached the path leading up the palace's cliffside my heart was ready to leap from my mouth. I was going to die a Night Realm captive and deserter. Shuddering breaths sawed in and out of me. Each step felt like an iron weight wrapped around my ankles.

Maybe I deserved this for running from my fate.

Even the Night Realm had innocents—children. Children like those in the Water Wheel.

I'd abandoned them, and now I was going to seal their fate with my death.

I jerked to a stop and all blood drained from my head.

Nik and Yori exchanged a sympathetic grimace above my head. Yori tugged me from the prince, ignoring his muttered warning. He drew his arm through my bound one and bent his head to whisper, "Whatever happens inside, Alys, I'm here. I can't stop whatever comes, but I'll find a way to soften it."

Startled, I jerked from my morose thoughts. "Why? What have I done to gain your loyalty?"

"I don't believe in black and white. It's the shades of gray that paint a more dimensional outlook. You remind me of someone I once knew. A kindhearted witch who was twisted into something else."

When I pulled my lips back into a sneer, he said, "You and I are more than the situation of our births or magical abilities. I have a gut instinct about intentions, and you, Alys Sathos, strive to be good. Whatever awaits in the palace won't change that. Bad circumstances either enhance or break you. You decide."

He didn't know me nor the list of atrocities I'd committed in Lilain's name. The countless goblins I'd slaughtered. The Night Witches I'd killed to bolster her power. Maybe I wasn't evil like Lilain, but I'd never done anything to hold the title of *good*. But one glance at the gentle, yet *powerful*, giant said he understood that never-ending search to belong in a world that breezed over nobodies like us until we forced it to pay attention.

I blinked back sudden warmth in my eyes and managed to croak, "Let's hope I prove you right."

He shook his head, and his affability returned with a soft smile. "You don't have to prove anything. You don't owe the world for being born."

More guards waited inside the palace gates. A familiar red-haired, young woman hurried to Melisandre carrying an armful of velvet fabric. The page from the tent who hadn't ratted me out took the princess's cloak, replacing it with one embroidered with golden dragon motifs. Another page helped the prince into a similar cloak.

Melisandre snatched a hairbrush from the page's hand, ripping the boar bristles through her blunt hair. "Next time bring oil, you stupid girl. My hair tears without it. I'd be bald if you were my personal page. You're utterly useless."

Nik snapped his head toward Melisandre with a frown. The prince did too, but whatever he mentally said to her, she replied with a single raised finger.

Barely twenty, the young woman bowed deeply, attempting to conceal the scarlet flushing her creamy skin. "Of course, General. My apologies." She straightened and caught my eye.

I grinned back and drew a line across my neck. The girl covered a snort with a cough before hurrying onto the palace grounds behind Melisandre.

Yori escorted me through the gate, pretending not to notice my shivers. A bead of sweat rolled down my nose, dripping onto bound hands. The prickling on my neck warned the prince was watching, expecting one final escape attempt.

For once, I surprised him.

We stopped before the center wing and its ornate door of hammered gold with handles of onyx. It would've been beautiful if it wasn't for whatever waited inside.

A sharp pull on the shadow tether sent me staggering backward and into the prince who spun me to face him.

Not a ray of emotion bled through his icy mask. A prince back in his domain.

"Two things, Sathos. One, you will obey Her Majesty in every command. Keep your snide mouth shut. You will speak with the utmost respect and only when asked." He leaned in, eerie irises gleaming too bright in the sunlight. "Two, whatever informalities you've come to expect from the Night Guard, wipe them from your mind. Behind that door you become nothing, an enemy of the realm and treated accordingly. Don't expect preferential treatment from anyone."

He aimed the last words at Yori who crossed his arms and scowled.

The prince swiveled back to me and leaned in further, ice-carved face a breath from mine. "Do you understand?"

I didn't yield an inch, only nodding once. Shadows leapt from the walls and swung the hammered-gold doors open. Yori clapped my shoulder with a wobbly grin—one I couldn't mirror—and ushered me through.

The Night Queen's throne room was centered beneath the massive glass dome I'd seen on the hill. Curved windows covered all but the wall behind us. The court of witches beneath the open sky were bathed in iridescent sunlight. Onyx floors sparkled in an illusion of infinite abyss. More onyx with golden runes adorned pillars soaring high to cradle the dome and clouds beyond. It was magnificent.

I most certainly didn't belong.

Courtiers in traditional knee-length robes lined each side of a golden carpet. At its end, a dais of black onyx held an intricately sculpted throne. Dragons carved into burnished gold clawed the armrests, bowing to the seat where the loveliest woman sat.

For a queen centuries old, the Night Queen Morgenna appeared younger than me. Raven black hair curled away from an unlined ivory face. Centuries of cunning pooled like murky water in her eyes. Something in the way she hungrily leaned forward as I approached reminded me of witch-eating nymphs. Dressed in knee-length black robes over a blacker dress with diamonds and pearls sewn along the hem, she looked every inch the dreaded Night Queen. As I drew nearer, I realized the golden crown atop her head was made of two warring dragons raising a chicken egg-sized ruby between them.

The courtiers whispered and pointed when we passed. Their sneers took in my baggy tunic and disheveled braid with silent judgment. I met each stare, refusing to be cowed. They may've stood in the Night Realm throne room, but they bore the same contempt and lust for power of their Day equivalents.

The prince took the lead and bowed before Morgenna. Yori placed a hand on my neck and shoved me into a deep bow with a muttered apology.

"What's this?" Morgenna asked. Her soft voice was an elegant clip to Lilain's throaty rasp, but they shared the same dangerous edge cloaked beneath a pleasing tone—a voice used to obedience.

"A DRAS airwitch, Your Majesty," the prince answered. "She was trespassing south of the village of Grelgesco."

The queen smiled, an easy gesture meant to disarm.

Then her eyes lit with a familiar glow.

"Tell me why she was trespassing."

Compulsion.

Lilain wasn't alone in her unnatural magic. The prince's warnings, the Mother's command this realm fall first—everything fell into place. Lilain's power was an unfettered display of cruelty, but here in Morithia, the city's economic progress shrouded her hold. If she—or rather her heir—took care of her people, most wouldn't peek behind the curtain.

But a caged animal remains captive no matter how well it's fed.

"I don't know." The words twisted from the prince's mouth. He clenched and unclenched his hands before stuffing them into his pockets.

"Then shall we hear it from her?" Morgenna waved me forward with a delicate hand. *"What is your name and rank?"*

Her compulsion burned like frost, ripping apart any inclination to run and hide. Unbidden words formed and leapt out. "Alys Sathos, Captain of the 22nd Squad of the Day Realm's Aerial Squadrons."

Satisfaction slid over glossy black eyes. "Queen Lilain's favorite captain. The stories I've heard of you, Captain Sathos . . . You've forced our general's hand many times." Animosity colder than compulsion impaled the Night Princess. "Too many times."

Melisandre's focus remained on the golden rug.

The queen faced me again with another simpering smile. *"Why are you in the Night Realm, Captain Sathos?"*

"An ambush. We—I—" I clamped my lips shut, fighting against the talons slicing into my will.

Morgenna's laugh skittered out of her like her creeping shadow. The unnaturally dense darkness leapt from the floor, shoving me to my knees.

Beside me, the prince's hands twitched in his pockets.

I tried to exhale, but words tumbled out instead. "We were compelled to destroy a goblin camp, but we—we failed. There was a storm—We didn't see the ambush. We were outnumbered and"—I choked on ice coating my tongue—"the goblins killed the 22nd. Only I and another remained. My—" Elenna's tear-stained face burst through the ice of compulsion. I didn't want to share this. This was mine. *My* grief.

But the words clawed free.

"My remaining lieutenant used the last of her magic to blow me out of harm's way. When her magic died with her, I fell from my broom into the Night Realm."

The burn of compulsion was nothing to the fire roaring in my soul. The memory of the 22nd dying one by one looped in my head. I'd led them into the ambush I should have foreseen.

I killed my squad.

Yori groaned a small noise of sympathy. The sound was a gentle hand on my shoulder, reminding me I wasn't alone. At least one Night Witch understood beyond the boundaries of our realms.

Morgenna sighed. She tapped a milky finger against her chin. "Your trespassing predecessors went straight to the work camps, but you, *the* Captain Sathos . . . Such a waste. Spin."

I blinked. She wanted me to . . . spin?

The prince nudged me with the toe of his boot, muttering, "Get up and spin so she can ascertain you."

I rose on rickety knees, fighting to keep from swaying at the sudden blood rush to my legs. He let out an impatient hiss and snatched at my arm, forcing me into a spin. Little did he know, he was the only thing keeping me from faceplanting.

"You appear healthy enough," Morgenna murmured thoughtfully. "Although, rumors of your magicless nature suggest otherwise."

She tapped her bow-shaped lips with a soft smile, and her eyes began to glow silver. "*Tell me, Alys. Do you have magic?*"

"I'm worthless." The answer burst out unguarded, and the courtiers tittered. My teeth sank into my lip, but the words broke free. "I only have enough air magic to fly a heavily runed broom."

Morgenna cocked her head and frowned. "Such a pathetic life for Lilain's most infamous airwitch. I expected more usage out of you."

I froze, barely breathing.

More usage.

The mockery of the more powerful had always been an axe over my head. I'd dealt with it, sat with it, learned to be content with who I was. That I would always be a tool to wield. I wasn't even that to Morgenna.

Just like the Night Witches in the Water Wheel below the palace.

More usage.

Origin of realm didn't mean anything to her. We were *nothing* but wasted time. No one would fight for us.

The Mother had promised *me* power, and even if it was metaphorical, I would wrench the throne from the thin, small hands of this woman who couldn't see beyond my lack of magic. *This* was my fated path, and I would no longer run from it.

"No," I snapped, all terror gone, replaced by a manic need to reveal the monster beneath the pretty veneer. "My life is *fulfilling*. I serve my realm, my people. I sacrifice to protect those who cannot protect themselves. I don't sit on a golden throne and let my heirs do the work while I reap the benefits of their power."

"*Shut up,*" the prince hissed. His grip on my arm tightened enough to leave a mark.

I tore from his hold and lifted my chin, pressing my shoulders back. My words echoed all the way to the Mother's own ears and, gods, I hope she heard them.

"If you can't see my value, then perhaps you should reevaluate what power means because unlike you, I have a purpose."

Morgenna's dainty expression cracked, and a snarl ripped from her lips.

She shot from her throne, javelin shadows exploding toward me.

But something shoved me sideways onto the golden carpet.

The javelins scattered before reforming and circling the prince who stood where I'd been. A dark warning overtook his brief horror. *Don't move.* Shadows oozed up his back, curling over his shoulders to slide like black silk down his jaw.

What game was he playing?

Face delicate again, Morgenna hummed and strolled toward me. Inky lace trailed her in a long veil attached to her crown. She tilted her head and frowned prettily. "Dear me. Is Amira and Mendrick's tragedy repeating?"

"Not at all, Your Majesty." The prince spun toward the queen, and his inscrutable mask slammed back down.

"What a relief." Morgenna's brows angled upward with a heavy sigh. "We both know how that ended . . . Still—"

She flicked her fingers, and the fawning shadows reared over him.

I shot upright, heart in my throat, but again he shook his head, darkening eyes pinning me in place. *Don't interfere.* The black specters tasted the air but never touched him.

This isn't Lilain's court, I reminded myself. Morgenna didn't brutally punish for sport.

"And they say the Mother doesn't have a sense of humor . . ." Morgenna chuckled, eyes flicking between us. "Shall we play a game, Captain Sathos?"

My heart threatened to catapult from my chest. I'd rather not, actually. I'd only begun believing my life had purpose after all. Couldn't we explore that a tad longer?

"We shall have a trial," she cooed, "a challenge for Queen Lilain's favorite."

An excited buzz descended on the throne room as I rose to my feet.

"Captain Sathos"—Morgenna began, and the buzz fell silent—"is reputed to be the most fearsome of Queen Lilain's airwitches. But how can that be? She said herself she's magicless. Worthless." The courtiers laughed in a tinkling of elegant snickers bouncing off glass. "Shall we see how she fares in combat against Prince Maddox's Night Guard? Perhaps, then, we shall see her true value to our realm."

She smiled, a vicious thing revealing a notion of the Creature beneath silk and lace. "Or perhaps we shall see the best the Day Realm offers is little more than a pest. If Captain Sathos defeats any guard who challenges her and survives, then she will earn a permanent place amongst the Night Guard. After swearing compelled fealty to me, of course. Do you accept, Alys Sathos?"

Whispers circled, poking holes in my physique, in my ability with a sword, with my fists.

An airwitch amongst the Guard? Surely, she wouldn't survive.

The Mother had never claimed my fate was easy. She certainly never said I'd waltz down my fated path without danger. Here lay the first dangerous step. And if I won? I'd be at the heart of Morgenna's court. A hairbreadth from a knife in her back.

Beside me, the prince raised a single dark brow, a challenge of its own. If I accepted Morgenna's offer, I might go through him too as the commander of the Night Guard, and I'd yet to best him. That alone was tempting enough.

"I accept."

The throne room erupted in a glass-rattling roar.

Morgenna's shadows lazily snaked around me, eels ready to strike. A soft smile lingered on her lips, as lethal as the swirling darkness. I thought Lilain was conniving, but I had a nasty feeling Morgenna was worse.

14

EVIL DOESN'T LINGER IN THE DARK

Maddox

T he door across from my rooms in the royal apartments remained firmly shut and a twisted part of me wanted the little demon to step out
and squabble with me.

Mercifully, only Yori came out.

"I couldn't tell if Alys was impressed or horrified by the royal grandeur of
her new rooms. For the record, no one needs a gilded bathtub. A porcelain
one will wash an ass the same."

He grinned wide at my pinched expression then glanced back at the shut
door. "Pretty sure she'll sleep on the floor out of spite, and something tells
me you'll never get a '*thank you*,' but better here than the barracks. I don't
know how you managed to sway the queen to give her Melis's old rooms."

I pushed off the wall and dragged my gaze from the Mother-bleeding
door. "A lot of underhanded coaxing and flattery. If the Day Witch is nearby,
the queen can keep an eye on her."

"*You* can keep an eye on her," Yori corrected, but his grin vanished.

A female airwitch with a long list of casualties wouldn't survive a night
in the guard's male-dominated dormitories. No woman deserved that.

I could still picture Morgenna's glee, the blinking bug-eyed excitement
between Sathos on the rug and me standing over her. I'd reacted thought-

lessly. Morgenna wouldn't have harmed her in front of the court. Instinct had shoved Sathos onto the floor the moment the shadows reared. If the mouthy little terror had kept quiet . . .

Wordlessly, I handed Yori Morgenna's summons. He didn't have to read it. He'd read a hundred of them before.

We set off for the end of the long corridor, to the ostentatious, gilded doors. Nodding once, he leaned against the wall, ready to wait—as he always did whenever Morgenna summoned me. Someone needed to heal whatever remained when she'd finished.

No matter how many times I faced these doors, my heart twisted in on itself, and I had to remember to breathe. Pain was nothing if it meant I was alive for her next summons. It was a pathetic piece of hope to cling onto, but it was better than nothing.

Inside, Morgenna beamed from her pink sofa and patted the spot beside her. "What a fascinating journey you must've had. Lugging the infamous Captain Sathos from the border. Quite a coup." A recognizable note of high-pitched glee set my teeth on edge. "Tell me more about your journey."

"Princess Melisandre and I redoubled our efforts along the border villages." This wasn't what she wanted to hear. Few realized she rarely dabbled in the realm's affairs, leaving them to me and the magistrates. Mother curse me if I knew what she actually did with her time. "But vampyr rumors persist. I think it's time to start taking them seriously. There are too many sightings to chalk up as mere rumor. The fear is real and spreading. If we set up a permanent presence in each border village, perhaps—"

"Dear boy, vampyres do not wander this far north. They certainly don't move in large groups as rumors insist. What hogwash. No, this is Lilain's problem. She and her precious DRAS can see to them. Well, those who remain. Now that I have the 22nd's captain, she'll have to make do."

She chuckled, pouring tea into a dainty teacup. "Now, let us talk of something more exciting. Do you think Captain Sathos will triumph in tomorrow's challenge? Will I add her to my Night Guard?"

I hadn't let myself think about the challenge, or how I'd undoubtedly end up testing what made Alys Sathos so legendary. The gleam in Morgenna's eye told me she'd orchestrated the entire challenge to see what would happen between us after my little stunt.

"She is not . . . inconsequential."

"Oh, pooh. No witch on Efelldor believes her inconsequential. *Tell me what you think will happen tomorrow.*"

The compulsion left little wiggle room. "She's capable of besting most of the Night Guard. Except—"

She leaned forward, her simpering smile going feral. "Yes?"

"Except perhaps . . . me."

"Would you kill the Day Witch to protect your realm? *Answer honestly.*"

The answer was yes, but what came out was, "I don't know."

I flinched, waiting for her strike. I might as well have declared I'd defected to the Day Realm.

Morgenna laughed, a perverse tinkling bell. She was in a good mood. That never bode well.

"Your mother would've been thrilled."

I shot forward, hovering over her.

But the shadows remained dormant in the room's corners, refusing my summons. No matter what she did, I couldn't harm the Night Queen, couldn't say a disparaging word or urge anyone else to do it. I was trapped within my own head, suffocating under her compulsion.

She sipped her tea, comfortably cloaked in power. "Do sit down."

I sank into a chair and forced my breathing to remain even. Images and sounds from the night my mother died dredged up a river of unwelcome memory. I latched onto the nearest thought and blurted, "Is it wise to keep Captain Sathos when she's Lilain's prized captain?"

"Finders keepers as children say."

The Night Realm was undoubtedly larger and more populous, but the DRAS outnumbered the guard and Melis's legions. It wouldn't be wrong to claim one airwitch was worth three Night soldiers. The Night Guard, on the other hand, might match the DRAS's brutal skill, but we were less than half the DRAS's numbers.

If Lilain wanted war, it would be long and bloody—without a clear victor.

"Is she worth whatever game you're playing?" The bite in my voice forced Morgenna to look up. A shadow skirted from beneath the sofa. It slithered up my body and cinched around my throat. Grappling with its wispy hand, I tried to pry it open, but the tendril tightened until spots dotted the pink room.

"I've known Lilain for centuries, boy. Do not pretend to understand the Day Queen or her games. Lilain adores schemes and challenges. Let us see what she makes of this one and have a bit of fun with Captain Sathos."

To my surprise, the shadows dropped, and she waved me away, ringing a bell for one of her many lovers to attend her. Daring to believe I'd leave unharmed, I hurried out.

I'd nearly made it to the door when she called, "Oh, Maddox? *Should Alys Sathos skirt our laws outside of what you know is in accordance with my word, you will report it to me.*"

She'd left no leeway, no room for the compulsion's interpretation. If Sathos won, if she became a Night Guard and skirted the line of loyalty, she was dead.

I nodded, grasping the door handle, ready to escape.

Morgenna wasn't finished. Any artificial simper died from her voice. "While I could inflict great pain upon Alys, I imagine you could do worse."

There it was. The threat hanging over me. Be a good boy or Morgenna would compel the unforgivable. No one deserved Morgenna's wrath. Not even the defiant and unpredictable Alys Sathos. Where everyone else saw power or a threat in me, Sathos found a target to hurl her contempt. Most of me still had no idea what to make of her and that made her infinitely dangerous. But a sliver I'd tried to bury wondered if those acrid words tasted as sweet as her magic smelled.

The Night Queen laughed. "Don't look so glum. There's an easy way out. Perhaps she'll die tomorrow, and all will return as it was."

If Sathos survived the next day. She hadn't seen what the Night Guard was capable of. What the second sons of the most powerful Night Witches in Morgenna's court could do. An unbidden image formed. Clever, sharp eyes glazed over; their fawn color dulled. Her blood smeared on my hands.

My throat went unbearably dry.

"But if she lives . . ." Morgenna trailed off with an exaggerated wince. "Are you noble enough to stay away from a pretty little Day Witch? To fight her draw for her sake? I won't compel you. No . . . I'm rather keen to see this play out. A melodrama performed just for me."

I bowed before retreating to the golden double doors and hastened out of her lair before she compelled something else out of me.

Yori pushed off the wall when I stepped into the corridor, scanning me for injuries. For once, there was none.

"We can't let Alys die." His expression was resolute. This was happening. "*We?*"

"Don't be dense. I've seen the way you look at her. You don't want her dead any more than I do. All sentimentality aside, she's an asset to the guard. Think of the help she'd be—"

"She's an enemy witch and a mouthy pain in the ass. What reason would I have to save her from Morgenna's challenge?"

Yori leveled a long look at me. "She's an invaluable ally. One we'd be foolish to let die. Stop fighting her and maybe fight *for* her?"

"She doesn't need me to fight her battles. She's Alys Mother bleeding Sathos."

"Who just lost her entire squad, unwittingly landed in an enemy realm, and is being forced to fight for her life just to be captive to an enemy queen. She's not invincible, much as she might think she is. She needs help but she will *never* ask *you* for it."

Fight for her.

I rubbed at my temples, trying in vain to stave off a headache. "Or we do nothing and let her fight her own way out of this. If she dies, then at least everything returns to normal."

15

WHAT HIDES IN DAYLIGHT

Alys

F uck the Night Realm. And the Mother. And fate and every godsdamned moment in time that led to this moment.

Anxiety clenched my stomach, and I leapt for the pot, retching. Any confidence I had the day before in the throne room vanished in the night's unknown. I was going to die by the hand of a Night Guard. Probably the prince.

No amount of begging the Mother for a sign I was on the right path had worked. I'd prayed to silence. Perhaps I could force a few guards to surrender their pride with my skill. But one long day of fighting powerful witches who wanted me dead? Then to end with a prince who'd *already* proven he could best me? He'd saved me once—an odd fluke, to be sure—but I doubted he'd show mercy again, our short history being what it was.

I was going to die on the first step of my path.

Pathetic.

Sprawled on the cold floor of my new bathing room, I groaned. Here was my chance to infiltrate the heart of the Night Realm. The first step to dethroning the Night Queen and fulfilling my fate, and I couldn't even keep my guts down.

The pink dawn had crested in the window when a knock interrupted my pacing. A guard had stood outside my door all night—I'd checked. What did he want now? I cracked the door open to find the red-haired page girl instead. She held a stack of clothing and a determined grin.

"Hello, Captain Sathos. I'm here to explain the trial and help you prepare." She grinned wider, finding confidence in my silence.

Yori had mentioned with a few exceptions like himself, most of the guard was made of lesser sons of courtiers. Daughters were saved for marriage alliances across the court and realm. Warfare was a man's duty. And these barbarians called the Day Realm savage . . . So, what was *her* story?

Opening the door, I allowed the girl in. She held herself with the elegant grace of a courtier, but sharp movements spoke of hardened years. She couldn't have been any older than Nik who was already deep in a guard career. Setting down a stack of clothing, she revealed a black woolen tunic and leather pants. Empty sheaths decorated their outer thighs—the uniform of a Night Guard. The black-and-gold cloak was noticeably missing.

"I'm Sylinia Creluna, a page to His Highness, Prince Maddox. For the time being he's redirected my service to you."

Probably one of his infamous spies.

"Why send you?"

"Because I volunteered."

I frowned, studying the tall, willowy girl. Built like most female soldiers, she was lithe with toned arms and calves, fostering speed over brute force. Thirst shone behind lively blue eyes, a craving to spin the world on its head and demonstrate what the world failed to acknowledge.

"Why would you volunteer to service a Day Witch?"

"Oh, I don't care about that. You're a woman. A bleeding effective one with a long list of successful campaigns. Every guard would beg on their knees for the chance to fight you today. I don't know how it is in your realm, but here my gender is an uphill battle I face each day. You're a legend, Captain Sathos. I want—"

Sylinia paused, picking at her unadorned page uniform. "I want to be seen for my efforts. Not because I succeeded in spite of my gender, but because I succeeded on my own merits. Perhaps we can come to an agreement? When you become a Night Guard, you'll need someone to guide you through our customs. In exchange for my help, would you train me the way women are trained in your realm? The guard has no idea what to do with me."

Opportunity stood before me—perhaps sad and desperate, pulling at my heart—but useful, nonetheless. "Deal. *If* by some miracle I become one of the Night Guard."

Beaming as if I'd granted her dearest wish, Sylinia shooed me behind a silk partition and handed me the Night Guard uniform. As I slipped the luxurious lamb's wool over my bare arms, I'd never felt more traitorous.

She strode for the door and, likely spurred on by my ashen complexion, said before leaving, "I've been informed magic will not be allowed by challengers on the queen's command. The point of the challenge is physical combat. You must force your opponent's concession to move onto the next round. Should you fight up the ranks to Prince Maddox, you'll be allowed a healing spellcast before facing him."

How generous—and probably pointless against the Night Realm's most lethal warrior.

Another retching session later, I inched open the front door. My heart leapt into my throat. The prince waited across the hall, leaning with one boot propped up on the door behind him. Dressed in head to toe black like me, he looked far too delectable for someone who would probably snap my neck before long. There was bad taste in men, and then there was a pathetic need to find comfort in all the wrong places. I erred on the latter.

He gave me a once over and sighed in that maddening way only he could do with such a tiny exhalation. He gestured for me to follow. It took every scrap of dignity not to slam the door shut on the day's unknowns and dive back into the overstuffed bed. I followed him through the twisting corridors of midnight stone and portraits of long dead royals. Sneaking a glance at the prince, I found his infamous frigid mask securely in place.

"Eager to finally kill me?"

"What makes you think you'll last that long? You might die in the first round."

"But then you'd never know if you could best me in combat."

He flicked his gaze in my direction, lingering a heartbeat too long on my new tight pants. "I doubt I'd miss anything."

Heat flushed my cheeks. Terrible taste, indeed. Elenna once told me I should find someone sweet instead of the menacing men who should be shoved off a cliff. Then again, the prince was more likely to shove *me* off a cliff.

We'd nearly reached the exterior doors when a portrait caught my eye. The painting had been shoved into a darkened corner—as if forgotten with time. Dressed in courtier finery, a golden-haired woman rested her hands on the narrow shoulders of two children. The round-cheeked girl was a replica of her mother, smiling shyly up at her. The other child—a boy no older than six—had his hands shoved into his pockets. He mirrored his mother's smile, a secret only they shared.

A shadow rose from the floor, pushing me from the portrait and toward the stairs where the prince waited—hands deep in his pockets. "Don't start with your fishing."

"Not even as my final request?"

He opened an exterior door and motioned me through with a nasty grin I'd begun to realize he saved specifically for me. "Ask whatever you want when you're bleeding out at my feet."

The barracks was a long building of gray stone up against the palace wall. Its neat, rigid atmosphere reminded me of the DRAS towers and the severity of soldier life. It would've been comforting if it wasn't where I'd probably die.

Yori and Nik waited at the entrance. Worry lined their foreheads. The prince passed me off to Yori and disappeared into the barracks to do princely things like perfecting his wavy locks that I certainly never entertained running my fingers through. Yori kept up a steady stream of conversation as we stepped inside, pointing to doors leading from the main corridor—armory, meeting rooms, dormitories. I didn't have the heart to tell him it didn't matter. Nik's occasional wince agreed.

We ventured deeper until we came to an open courtyard where Sylinia paced beneath the sunlight. Behind her, an enormous sparring ring beckoned. Allowing for several sets of sparring at once, the wooden platform sat high above the ground, encircled by ropes. A circular walkway hung above the ring. Already, several young witches dressed in courtier finery and page uniforms crowded the walkway. Sunlight glinted off the coins passing between hands.

Beyond the ring, a platform of rugs and velvet sofas waited for the courtiers streaming into the open air. They took their places, pouring tea from gilded teapots while openly pointing. I would be the day's entertainment—like a performing dog.

Charming.

The Night Queen entered, and the ring fell silent. Her towering heirs marched behind her, the prince on her right, the general on her left. Each should've been more menacing than the petite woman lowering onto a velvet sofa, but they never pulled their gaze from her or the shadows swirling over her hands. At her dismissal, they took chairs on either side as a nearby courtier rushed to serve them tea.

The display left my heart a ratcheting mess. *This* was power at Efelldor's highest level. *This* was whom I was supposed to somehow topple from power.

No . . . I'd done my fair share of the impossible and come away the victor—the street rat who'd proven a magicless page could obliterate the DRAS ranks with sheer determination. Who the Mother of all Creation chose to tear apart this realm and bring it to its knees.

It began in this sparring ring.

Head high, I marched up the stairs. A low buzz swept the crowd, growing louder the closer I drew. When I stepped onto the ring's wooden planks, the buzz became a rumble. Nik muttered something about hoping I'd made my peace. Throwing me one last pitying glance, he disappeared into the throng of guards assembling in the ring's corners.

A string of men lined the nearby ropes, stripped down to leather pants in the warming sun. Each of them leered, eager to smash me into oblivion and prove why a Day Witch—a woman no less—didn't belong amongst them.

While Yori droned on about the challenge's rules—mainly that *I* couldn't kill anyone—I studied the leering men, finding their weaknesses, tearing *them* apart before the fight started. I'd have to be faster than two of them. Their long limbs moved with a quick grace that reminded me of Ansil. But Ansil got lost in his limbs if I swerved enough. Two others had swollen legs—perpetual drunks—a good liver punch would do them in. A blond giant crisscrossed his legs as he paced—displaying an unbalance I could manipulate.

Yori finished and gestured me to my first opponent.

The blond giant began circling me.

"How many Night soldiers have you killed, Sathos?"

"I stopped counting when the evil pricks started slaughtering DRAS pages."

Snarling, the blond lunged. A massive fist flew for my exposed ribs. Leaping to the side, I barely rolled out of his way. Mid-lunge, he whirled, leg swiping for mine, again, barely missing. I saw an opening in his temporary unbalanced form as he prepared to lunge again.

I charged, swung around his neck, and forced him down onto his outstretched leg with a loud pop.

The blond giant rolled, and I managed to dive before he crushed me. He sprung up with a minor limp, newly wary. Circling, he studied me, looking for an opening in my relaxed stance. But I'd found his weakness long before he faced me. He crossed his feet too widely, typical for a bulky man with thick thighs.

When he charged, I pounced for the gap in his stance and feigned right. He lurched sideways and I went the opposite direction. Diving low, I hooked my foot around his ankle and twisted my body. My momentum brought him down with a booming thud. Fire shot through my ankle, but I sprung forward and dug my knees into his chest, effectively smothering him. He bucked, but I'd already gripped his head between my palms. Holding tight for dear life, I slammed it onto the wooden floor. Once. Twice. On the third hit he was out.

I rose to stunned silence and glanced at the courtier's platform. Open mouths of horror stared back. The whispers began in a rush and more than one bet moved hands.

Their prince lifted an unimpressed brow.

Morgenna clasped delicate hands to her breast in mock horror. "Next."

A long-limbed guard swaggered forward, spewing obscenities in a poor attempt to distract me. I'd heard first-year pages curse more creatively. Big Mouth swung with too much force, briefly unbalancing his form. I didn't have his strength, but I had a brain.

Ducking under a punch for my jaw, I aimed for his unguarded side. But he lurched and grabbed a handful of hair at my crown. Pain splintered through my scalp and a cry burst free.

Seizing his wrist in both hands, I dropped to the floor. He fell with me, his arm wrenched in an unnatural angle. Hand limp, he released my hair, but with my elbow tucked over his, I yanked it closer. His curse reverberated through the ring followed by the satisfying crack of bones snapping.

He lunged from me, but I was already scurrying back. Attempting to catch me off guard, he inadvertently swung into my waiting leap kick. My boot collided with his snapped shoulder with another crunch. The cheering hollers for Big Mouth went silent at his scream. If he was smart, he'd find a healer soon. His arm's angle looked as if I'd ripped an important nerve that might leave his arm paralyzed.

Falling onto his knees, he clutched his shoulder and growled, "I submit." Two down.

I nodded, turned onto the next guard. I could do this.

"If I get a hold of you in the dark, Day bitch," Big Mouth hissed from behind me. "I'll make you scream until blood runs down your legs."

I whirled and sent my boot careening into his teeth. Then his nose, his ribs, his skull. Anywhere I could reach. Anywhere I could make him hurt. He couldn't touch me if he was dead. I leapt onto his back, twisting his screaming head, ready to rip it off his godsdamned neck.

Two sets of arms tore me from the bloodied guard.

Yori's gruff voice was in my ear. "Let it go, Alys. He's scum. Not worth it.

125

"You can't kill your opponents," Nik snapped in my other ear. "Don't fuck up. You're Mother bleeding brilliant. You can win this, but not if he's dead."

His warning cleared the seething haze, reminding me what stood at stake—fate, Morgenna, the survival of witchkind. I shrugged them off. I didn't need coddling. Pink stained my cheeks, my chest heaving. I hadn't lost control in years, but the pressure of the day, everything on the line . . .

On the platform, Morgenna's hungry, wide eyes roved my body. Beside her, the prince watched Big Mouth limp off the ring with an utterly blank expression.

Shaking off the vestiges of rage, I faced my next opponent. And then the next. The memories spurred by Big Mouth fed into a storm I'd let stew for years. What I'd faced on the streets of Kazadorah, what any woman anywhere faced—it all spilled into a punch, a kick, a rip of tendons until each guard slammed a palm on to the ring's floor, submitting.

I dropped to the floor alongside the last guard, my entire right side screaming. One of them had thrown me to the floor—no doubt breaking something. My lip was swollen, and from the amount of blood dripping off my chin, I was fairly certain my nose was broken.

But I'd finished them.

Sylinia crouched beside me, sliding her hands over various cuts, whispering, "*Sana corpus.*" Warm, honeysuckle-scented magic flowed beneath my skin, undoing wounds, but while my body mended, my energy remained sapped. Sitting up was a hardship, let alone facing the prince. Cold dread slithered down my spine as I remembered the lethal grace with which he moved. He'd snap my neck in seconds.

I shoved at Sylinia's hands as she tried to heal my split lip. If I died, then I'd go out bloody and defiant.

Beneath a towel used to wipe blood, Sylinia pushed a vial into my hand. "Take this. It's an energy tea, magicked to work strong and quick."

"A potion?" I hissed, covering the vial from any wandering eyes. "These aren't allowed. Only healing spellcasts."

"Tell that to Prince Maddox. He's the one *technically* giving it to you."

On the platform, the prince reclined in a chair, one long leg crossed over knee, while chatting with a courtier. The picture of someone who didn't have a care. Only a single finger tapping against the armrest spoke differently. Was he so proud he wouldn't stand anything but an even match? Or was this another odd fluke of a save?

Sylinia threw a linen towel over me on the pretense of wiping my neck. Concealed, I swallowed the potion, putting far too much trust in the prince and his flukes. I slipped the empty vial back to Sylinia and shuddered. Adrenaline burned through my veins on a river of fire. Or maybe that was poison burning.

Shaking out my tingling limbs, I shut off my senses and focused on the prince, on the way he moved. He was faster than the others. He moved with graceful unpredictability, calculating and emotionless. I tried to recall his gait, wondering if I could twist him up in his long legs.

"You should know," Sylinia whispered, "Prince Maddox has freakish recollection. Whatever you've already tried on the others, he'll remember. Try something new."

Shit.

I was out of *new*. All I had was my brain and that was a slimy mass of fog. What if he wasn't trying to save me?

I couldn't depend on his flukes. I frowned at the courtiers, mind racing. Sunlight glimmered off their jewel-encrusted daggers made more for show than lethal ability.

The prince followed my gaze to the daggers with a barely veiled frown. Something ticked in his jaw. Brief exasperation slashed his face before he smoothed it back into disdain. Whatever he was up to, I had forced him to adjust.

Good.

Pressing a handkerchief to my bleeding lip, I stepped before the queen's platform and bowed. "I hope this has been enlightening, Your Majesty."

"Oh, it truly has, but the best is yet to come, wouldn't you agree?"

"Certainly." I shot a grin at the prince who remained unmoved. "In fact, I suggest we take the next round a step further. A true warrior demonstrates skill with a blade, not fists."

Morgenna smiled, slow and languid over the rim of her teacup. "Retrieve two swords, Lieutenant Denox."

"Might I suggest he retrieve my dimachairi?" I pointed to the prince and lowered my voice. "I know they're here."

The queen's smile stretched wider.

At her nod, Yori vanished into the barracks.

The prince rose from his chair and began toward the ring. He unbuttoned one tunic button. Then two. The courtiers straightened and whispers rippled through the greedy smirks. Annoyance crept over his usual mask. Men and women craned their necks as he shrugged his tunic off broad shoulders.

Mother damn me.

It wasn't enough his face looked as if it'd been carved by the Mother herself. No, she'd clearly spent a ridiculous amount of time making sure the rest of him was equally mesmerizing. Sunlight caught a thin sheen of sweat starting at the divot of his throat. A bead slid down to meet thin lines of runic prayer tattoos at his ribs, and I followed it down, down, down until it slid into the waistband of his pants.

Somewhere to my right, Nik snickered.

I jerked my gaze back up and found a slight smirk threatening one corner of the prince's mouth. I curled my toes inside my boots and spun away. I was not about to admit I was ogling someone who was about to run me through. If I lived, I would have to reexamine my priorities.

Yori dashed back into the courtyard with our swords. Before he could climb onto the ring, the prince quickly ate the space between us.

"Swords? What are you doing?" he hissed under his breath.

"Giving myself a chance, genius. You said you were going to kill me, remember?"

"Please tell me you drank the potion."

"The *poison*, you mean?" His teeth ground loud enough Morgenna probably heard them on her platform. I clicked my tongue. "Yes, yes. I drank it."

He squeezed his eyes shut, soft snarling under his breath, "You might as well shove a sword through me now, Sathos."

Scrunching my nose, I peered up at him, but he gave no indication of what that meant.

I still wasn't sure if he was trying to save or murder me.

Yori appeared with three swords, a long broadsword and a set of familiar sheaths. The prince swept past me and grabbed all three. Yori muttered something low. The prince nodded with a disgusted grimace that didn't offer me hope before returning to the center of the ring. He held out the dimachairi, but when I closed my hands around the hilts, he yanked them backward.

Startled, I reeled into his chest and into an intoxicating cloud of spiced cedar.

He lowered his head and hissed, "If you want to live, stop sticking your fingers in my plans and follow my lead."

His warm breath skittered over the shell of my ear and traitorous goose-flesh exploded down my neck.

Trust *him*? The one who'd landed me in this mess? Morgenna's right-hand witch?

Behind him, Yori stood with Nik and Sylinia, each wearing identical expressions of concern.

Not for the first time in days, I tossed caution over my shoulder and stepped into the first blade position. If this was a trick and he killed me, I swore on the Mother I'd find a way out of the Soul Lands and come for him.

Legs apart, I centered my gravity, waiting for an entrance.

"Stop dissecting me and move, Sathos," he drawled for all to hear, twirling the sword with practiced ease. His words were enough invitation.

Our swords clashed once, twice—six times—on my offensive. Sparks exploded from steel on steel, scattering across the ring. I sank back into first position as he circled me. He crossed his legs too narrowly for an opening, sword loosely held at an angle to his chest.

A tiny glimmer of fire cracked through his mask.

He spun his sword again, a flick of the wrist—slower this time. I frowned, studying his wrist, but he came at me, his hands shifting on the hilt. He slid his right hand up the hilt, taking the brunt of the sword's weight.

He *was* right-handed, wasn't he?

I leapt into fourth blade position, skimming over fifth and sinking into sixth to aim for a low blow across his legs. But he read my intentions and lunged backward. Again, I saw it, the subtle shift of his hands. He *was* right-handed. Swinging high, he arced the sword through the air. My answering dimachairi formed a low X, blocking the blow with a screech.

"Don't hesitate," he muttered before ripping away.

Don't hesitate for *what*? Not murdering him for being so godsdamned mysterious?

I saw the opening a moment later. His left hand gripped the upper hilt, holding the brunt of the sword. He'd also shifted into fourth position, skipping third and the balance it would've brought. If he lunged from fourth position this way, he'd leave his center of gravity too high.

He lunged.

Grunting, I blocked the too low sweep of his sword and angled down. The blade flew from his left hand's unstable grip and clattered to the floor. I snatched advantage of his lowered, unbalanced stance and leapt onto him. His back hit the wooden floor with a painful smack. In an instant, my dimachairi was at his throat.

The tattooed lines of his runic prayers glistened with sweat, and I was all too aware of his bare chest touching the insides of my thighs. Not staring became harder than the challenge itself. Heaving up and down with his labored breaths, I tried in vain to reel in my wandering thoughts.

His strange eyes brightened, flaring my soul open.

I'd won but I felt bare, vulnerable against the way he looked at me—like *he* was the one who'd won. For a moment, he wore the briefest grin, unfamiliar and real, before it slipped beneath the mask. He slapped his palm once on the platform. The echo of the wood silenced the crowd.

"Why?" I whispered.

In hindsight, his plan was obvious. With me in the dark, he wouldn't rouse suspicion. As long as I had energy to keep up with his pretense, he betted on me being clever enough to see through the ruse, giving me one small window to win—and live.

He'd saved me. *Again.*

"You won, Sathos. Don't be a sore winner."

Gold glittered like flaming sparks in forest-green irises, mocking and sharper than the blade at his neck. He tapped my leg, and I slid off.

My head spun trying to make sense of his motives and failing.

"And so, my melodrama begins," the queen called, clapping.

The crowd joined her, shock rippling through the courtiers.

Morgenna cocked her head and studied me, a spider watching a moth drift onto her web, wondering if she should strike immediately or watch and wait to see what I'd do.

"Welcome to the Night Realm, Alys Sathos."

16

DEATH RUNES

Corryn

R umor soured quicker than milk.

What began as romantic whispers of vampyres whisking young women into the night for scandalous trysts became a thread of doubt through the realm. Seren's death, while accepted as done by her hand, caused a stirring Rilessa hadn't anticipated. Between the compelled Day Witch in the capital, the vampyr rumors, and Seren's death, the courtier parents were on edge. They wanted reassurance of their children's safety.

A few weeks after Rilessa and I found Seren, we sat in the headwitch's office with a handful of instructors, waiting on a court representative—which meant Maddox.

I scrunched into my chair, trying to banish old memories. Counting my pearls didn't ease the pit in my stomach. Equal parts guilt, shame, and indignation were attached to the bracelet. Huffing softly, I pushed it deep into my skirt pocket. The world had thrown plenty at my feet in the last weeks. I chose not to add tragic history to my load.

The Night Prince entered the office to instructors bending in half to bow. A towering Yori followed. Petulantly, I refused to join the chorus of greetings, even when Yori offered me a tentative smile across the room.

Rilessa assumed the gracious headwitch persona and welcomed them in, offering tea and refreshments with a practiced smile. Ever fastidious of royal protocol, she addressed the normal formalities: small chitchat, the adoration of Morgenna, and tea.

The Mother forbid a Night Witch forget to offer tea.

I'd never trusted Maddox, but when he became the Crown Heir dangling off Morgenna's hand, I couldn't help but wonder how much he knew of Dual Witches, if he bothered to feel remorse for the horrors his queen and her beast inflicted. Or if he himself sicced the beast onto innocents.

I glared at the back of his head, wishing he'd leave. But Maddox seemed unusually unsettled, fidgeting in the high-backed, leather chair instead of his usual unnatural stillness. When Rilessa offered tea once more, he cut her off with a sharp, "Enough chitchat. Let's discuss the measures you'll take to protect the school."

Rilessa's smooth smile wavered. "Surely you don't think there's merit in the vampyr rumors, Your Highness?"

"Every rumor has a basis. I'd be remiss to ignore one spreading this wildly."

Oh, yes. Prince Maddox knew well the power of rumor.

Nodding, Rilessa handed him a list of the school's wards and new suggestions. We were warded against outsiders, save for the few of us whose blood was keyed to the wards, but with the possibility of vampyres in the realm, the courtier parents demanded more.

Maddox scanned the list, poking holes through several of the wards' magic capabilities before telling Rilessa most of them wouldn't work. I sighed wearily through my nose. It had taken several visits to academic outposts to find the necessary books on wards. A trip I'd rather have avoided if it meant not spotting Maddox and Melis in Grelgesco.

Mother curse my petty soul. I hoped the Day Witch wrecked his life.

When Maddox stood to leave, the thundercloud over me lifted with him. Rising with the rest of the instructors, I slipped out the door before anyone noticed, intent on my room and the stack of divination books awaiting me—not that they were of any use on portents.

I hadn't found much information on where the written portents were kept. I'd searched countless library towers and found little. Most books recounted the fraud science of reading tea leaves or animal bones. A rare few explained how to translate portents using numerology and astrology—those I'd studied feverishly. *None* explained where I might *find and study* specific portents.

How was I supposed to find the other fated five witches if I couldn't find the portents heralding them?

Crossing the ruined courtyard, I kicked a chunk of charred gravel back into the garden. Divinationists were a tight bunch, refusing to share research with outsiders. I'd like to think I was intelligent enough to figure out their translation on my own, but *finding* the bloody portents?

Mother curse me.

"Instructor Stellanati."

I froze, my hand on the door handle to the instructors apartments. Briefly, I considered making a run for it, but I'd never make it. I plastered on a smile and turned to face Maddox.

Stony as ever, he didn't bother with niceties. "Are you the runes instructor?"

"And if I am?"

"Then I require your knowledge on Death Runes."

My false smile slipped into a frown. Sharp dread nailed iron into my belly. "You should know what they are."

"Humor me and tell me what you know."

This was dangerous knowledge even the most curious researchers didn't seek out. But I wanted him gone and I had no desire to stand there arguing where anyone could discover us.

Slipping a hand into my pocket, I rubbed the slick pearls and launched into my lecture tone. "A typical rune is carved into a derivative of nature—mineral, earth, wood. With a correctly spoken spellcast at their inception, they harness the natural magic of nature to give a witch a small, temporary boost of magic or to guide the magic within the derivative—like the school's stone wall protection wards."

"But Death Runes are different," Maddox prodded, raising a brow.

I eyed the shadows, hoping no one hid within them as I counted the pearls in my pocket. He was asking after dark, illegal magic, the sort that summoned the Night Guard.

"Death Runes are cut into flesh and performed by two Creatures. A spell-cast incantation isn't necessary because instead of absorbing nature's magic, Death Runes draw magic from a Creature's soul. That magic can be used on the inscriber or the inscribed but... the problem lies in discipline. It takes great amounts of self-control not to bleed someone dry of magic and kill them. Hence its name."

The few depictions of the ritual I'd come across in my runic research came with numerous warnings. "It's unnatural magic, Prince Maddox. Most likely created by ancient witches greedy for more power. Most academics won't study them. It's too much of a temptation, and the risk of doing harm is too high."

Maddox shrugged. "As a runic instructor you have access to books on them, don't you?"

I laughed, high-pitched and warbled. "Are you asking *me* to risk my career and pull some of the darkest runic books for *you*? You don't even like me. Why would you ask this of me? I could report you."

"You won't. And I don't need to like you to trust you."

My mouth fell open in an unseemly gape.

Trust me? After the awful way we treated one another in school?

Pulling a hand from his pocket, he raked it through his hair. When I took a subsequent step back, he frowned. "Regardless of what happened between us, I know who you are—someone with a strong sense of morality."

Had he not heard a word I'd said? There was nothing moral about Death Runes. I ratcheted my spine to its tallest height and tried to glare down my nose at him. "Then you should know I won't break the law code. As commander of the guard, as the *crown prince,* neither should you."

"Morgenna's compulsion permanently ties me to the law. I *can't* break it. But you can. *You* can bend a rule or two, and I need your help with something you have no idea how important."

135

Perhaps I should've let bygones be bygones, but memory hung thick between us. I wouldn't risk my career for a patronizing prince with dubious intentions, no matter what his sister once was to me.

"Absolutely not."

17

THE DEPTHS OF THE QUIES RIVER

Alys

I n hindsight, I should've seen Morgenna's compulsion coming. Or predicted how thoroughly she'd wind icy ropes around my mind. Even merely thinking about her head on a—

I gagged on my mead as icy claws raked down the insides of my head, effectively stopping any thought of harming the queen. How the bleeding Mother was I supposed to dethrone a queen when I could only think boot-licking thoughts about her? What a pile of fated horseshit.

"I've been captured by an enemy realm, compelled to serve a queen possibly worse than my own, and *this* is how I'm compensated?" I gulped more mead and forced it down. The sickly-sweet alcohol wasn't better on the second swallow. If anything, it was worse.

"No Day Witch could enjoy this without half a tavern in their belly." I slid the tankard across the bar to a waiting Yori who threw back the rest with a cheerful grin bordering on maniacal.

One week after winning Morgenna's challenge, I'd limped into a sticky tavern deep in the Black Wall District. Every muscle screamed from countless rounds of sparring with eager pages and vengeful guards. Not to mention Nik and Sylinia. True to my promise, I'd begun training Sylinia. She proved no less violent than Nik—who was brilliant in the ring—leaving me violet and blue. In return, she brought me dozens of books on law code, which to my horror, my compelled mind latched onto and wove new compulsions with every law I learned.

Loopholes held the key to freeing myself *and* the lesser people of the Night Realm. I'd already decided the people of the Water Wheel took precedence over anyone else. Forget the Night Realm. Only the Water Wheel was worth saving. Elenna and I had unearthed plenty of loopholes with Lilain. Why not Morgenna?

Turning to Sylinia, I poked her arm and demanded, "Let's go over the Water Wheel District codes again."

She groaned before turning a vicious glare onto a chortling Nik who swung back a tankard of mead bigger than his head. "It's been *a week*, and you've managed to memorize nearly every law the Guard's compelled to obey. I'm reciting law code in my *sleep*, Alys. Give us a reprieve, I beg you. Go get drunk or—Mother forbid—have fun."

Snorting on my other side at the greasy bar, Yori said, "You memorized the entire law codex in a week? Did you eat or sleep?"

"No, but I pulverize Nik once or twice between learning who's who in the courtier hierarchy."

On Yori's other side, Nik gestured with a single finger before returning to his swill.

"Don't tell Maddox I said this," Yori began, throwing me a wink above his curly beard. "You might be the only witch who could outdo him in brainy endeavors. A thought that no doubt keeps him up at night. He could never stand having a rival."

Scrunching my nose, I ordered a new drink—not mead—and said, "I'd rather swallow every drop of mead in this city than compare myself to that self-righteous idiot."

Thankfully, I rarely saw the prince. Yori had mentioned he went in and out of the city, umbranating through the realm on political business. When the prince said he was the arm of the realm, I hadn't realized for all appearances, *he* ruled the realm while Morgenna sat her ass on a golden throne.

Not that I pitied him.

The one time I'd run into him in the corridor outside our rooms, he'd refused to acknowledge me. But late each night, I'd hear him pause before entering his rooms and it only irked me, knowing in some distorted way he'd won the push and pull between us by saving me in Morgenna's challenge.

Yori wiped the back of his hand across his mouth and frowned. He set the empty tankard down and motioned for another. "I know he comes across cold and unfeeling, but it's what he chooses to portray. Easier for him, I think, as the face of the realm."

He pointed to Sylinia who'd joined a robust game of cards. "Take Sylinia, for example. She's the daughter of Lord Creluna, a notable courtier and magistrate. When she was fifteen, she ran from her father's estate in the Vinnith Mountains to join the Night Army and escape a betrothal. She spent a few years hiding amongst the army, even serving in several goblin battles. When she was caught, the scandal was awful. Imagine a gently bred daughter of a magistrate, meant for tea parties and embroidery, and discovering she'd become a bloody soldier. Surrounded by the coarsest of men—and *disguised* as one."

Yori shook his head with an indulgent smile. "She was a sight to behold when a lieutenant dragged her before the throne. Sylinia's father, Lord Creluna, wanted her punished. Executed, actually. She'd made a fool of him, and the proud prick wanted her dead. If it hadn't been for Maddox, the queen would've agreed and executed her then. Maddox argued the same powerful blood running through the courtiers' Night Guard sons, also ran through their daughters. Why couldn't their daughters serve the Night Guard if they wished? The queen loves her entertainment and agreed, leaving the decision to Lord Creluna. It took Maddox days to convince the courtier to let his daughter live. Days more to let her find a purpose in the Guard, but eventually he did. Lord Creluna disowned Sylinia, and she was free to begin a pageship in the Night Guard."

"Free in more ways than one," Nik spat, never looking away from Sylinia. "Creluna doesn't deserve a daughter like her."

I studied the young woman across the tavern, her booming laughter easy—free. Under the glare of court, she would've withered. As much as I considered the prince an arrogant git, I couldn't deny he'd given the young woman her freedom. However, one good deed didn't wipe away his cold superiority.

"Your prince has decent moments," I admitted, sipping my spiced wine. "Doesn't mean I have to like him."

Nik snickered into his tankard. "He's your prince, too, now, *Captain*. Problem is, once you stop and think about it, you might find liking him isn't really necessary for what you want to *do* with him. I think—"

"Don't finish that thought," I interrupted. Horror inched a hot wave into my cheeks. "You're already too drunk for its repercussions."

"I can't be the only one who's seen it." He glanced at Yori for confirmation, but the giant held up massive hands with a snort. "Come on. Prince Maddox and Sathos eye each other as if they can't decide if they want to fuck or knife the other. It's creepy and weirdly erotic—"

"No, Alys, wait—"

I ignored Yori's plea and dove for the blathering young guard.

Nik beamed and we tumbled to the floor in a heap of fists and boots. Drunken laughter cheered Nik on, encouraging him to beat the Day Witch into oblivion. But Nik was four tankards in and couldn't land a solid hit.

Were these kicks supposed to be aimed at me or someone in the next room? The unruly attack was too tempting to pass up. With a grab and twist of his ankle, I sent him spiraling to the floor. His creative use of pig shit curses were terribly impressive. Laughing, I flounced beside him in a cloud of dust. He groaned and bobbed from my noisy kiss on his cheek, but his laughter echoed mine.

Like a wave, the buzzing tavern washed into memories. They hit me like a volley of arrows, one after the other. A similar tavern of airwitches. Fistfights that ended in song and cheers. Drunken laughter and brutal teasing after a hard-won battle.

I sat up and inhaled sharply, biting back tears, only to burst into a dust-induced coughing fit.

"Mother curse you, Sathos. You hit like a man," Nik said. He sat up with a low groan and whacked at my back. "But I'm glad you're here and not in some mine. A bleeding airwitch in the Guard . . ."

The rest of the evening flew by in a blur of laughter and fists from too-curious witches. News had spread across the city and every Night Witch angled to get a glimpse of me. Sneering and snide remarks had become commonplace, and I'd taken to wearing a cloak with a hood to hide my hair and ears on the streets. Morithia teemed with fresh experiences, and I wouldn't sit back and let this new world bow my shoulders.

When the tavern owner finally kicked Nik and Sylinia out for egging on a fight between a bear of a man and the one who'd cuckolded him, Yori and I slunk out with them. The young guards slurred their indignation, but Yori's enormous arms pried them from the tavern door.

"I think I'll wander a bit more," I called out to Yori when he promised to haul the others to their beds. "I haven't seen much of Morithia at night."

He frowned and glanced down the street leading to the Water Wheel District. "Be careful. Not just because you're a Day Witch. The city's monsters come out at night."

"I grew up on the streets of Kazadorah. I'll be fine."

He gave me one more searching look before nodding and prodding the two singing drunks back up the road to the palace. Slurring, Nik began a rousing song on the merits of tits, with Sylinia joining him. Their off-key jeering bounced off the wooden frames of nearby houses and soon several heads poked out from the windows, yelling for them to shut up.

Smiling, I tugged my hood over my head and wandered in the opposite direction. I'd spent most of my time in the palace, studying or sparring, or in the Black Wall District's taverns and markets. Occasionally, I'd pop into a book shop and buy books by my favorite novelist, Agria Grafeas, with Nik's infinite pocket money from his courtier father. *Hot Blooded Love* proudly sat on a bookcase in my rooms, displayed for all to see instead of hidden beneath a windowsill. It was almost worth the shit I'd endured to get it there.

Almost.

Unlike the cavorting laughter spilling out of the Black Wall, the taverns of the Water Wheel were ghostly quiet. Here, the shadows seemed darker, the motionless streets stiller. The churning Quies River meandered through the district, stinking of piss and rot. Odd shapes I didn't stop to think about bobbed in and out of the murky water. At the district's center, a square littered with empty bottles and bits of discarded refuse sat abandoned in favor of prettier, shiner things in the Black Wall.

I started to meander out of the district, when the faint sound of running caught my attention.

A figure barreled down the empty street at breakneck speed. Another in a cloak followed. The glitter of a blade shone in the moonlight. The first figure—a girl—ducked into an alley and the second followed.

Without thinking twice, I sprinted for the alley.

Many things occurred in a dark alley. Few of them holy.

"Don't touch me!" a feminine voice pleaded. "I swear, my grandmother will pay again."

"Too late, pet."

The dark alley was a dead end. A sliver of candlelight shone through a window high above, throwing light on a young girl no older than seventeen. She stood pressed against crates blocking the alleyway, leaving only one way in or out. His back to me, a thin man in a tattered cloak stood in her way, brandishing a rusted knife. Unlike the prince's summoned shadows, this man's drifted every which way, as though he didn't hold enough power to control them.

"You know Osrin's rules. Bleeding age means it's time to pay your family's tithe." The man inched closer to the trembling girl. "Your grandmother knows better, Simone. She shouldn't have let you out knowing its straight to the whorehouse for you."

Osrin Atercruor.

The crime lord of the Water Wheel—a foul witch Morgenna had compelled the Night Guard not to touch.

Simone pressed herself further into the crates, eyeing the thin space between the wall and Rusted Knife. Her desperate search found me, pleading wordlessly for intervention. I took a step, but an icy hand curled around my will. Gods, if this was one of Osrin's brutes, I couldn't harm a hair on his head. Morgenna had decreed the Guard leave the Water Wheel alone. It's crimes and victims left on their own. The Water Wheel was rotting from the inside out, and she'd compelled us to do nothing but watch.

But could I help the girl help herself?

I tapped Rusted Knife's shoulder.

He whirled, knife extended. In my best clipped Night accent, I asked, "Would you mind giving directions to the nearest tavern? Preferably one that doesn't serve mead?"

Bit shallow and my accent needed work, but it grabbed his attention.

"Get lost." Rusted Knife tried to spin back, but I lunged for the edge of his cloak.

The icy hand squeezed my will a little tighter. Instantly, my disobedient hand dropped the cloak. I shoved my hood off and let my Day drawl drip off my tongue, rolling my consonants in exaggeration. "I only want a good glass of wine. Know a place?"

Rusted Knife squinted at my ears, flipping his knife from one hand to the other. Greed clouded his beady eyes. A young girl was a nice prize for Osrin, but a Day Witch? I could practically hear the jingling coins in his head. *That's it, shit-for-brains.* I grinned wide. *Forget the girl. You want a go at me, instead.*

"Wine, eh? Yeah, I know a place. Take you there myself."

Oh, I bet he would. All the way to one of Osrin's whorehouses. He stepped closer, knife spinning between fingers. I eyed it, waiting for him to force me to defend myself, compulsion's only leeway. Then I'd beat the living shit out of him and throw him into the river.

The ice hissed, shooting frost down my spine.

All right. Not the river.

A shadow reared from the alley's far wall, thick and corporeal. It formed a razor thin blade of shadow inching for us.

I tensed, ready to run. What else waited in the alley with us?

The new shadows hissed like a blade through air and a wet slap spewed blood onto my face.

The headless remains of Rusted Knife swayed before slumping to the ground.

Well, that was unexpected.

Simone began to wail. Streams of tears flooded her amber cheeks as she stared at the body with heavy gasps.

"What are you waiting for?" I cried out, stepping over the remains and searching for the violent newcomer. "Go!"

She dashed through a puddle of blood and ran out into the street.

Wiping my face with the edge of my cloak, I peered into the shadows, heart high in my throat. Technically, I hadn't seen who'd thrown the shadow. Was I compelled to bring in the new witch for impeding Osrin in the Water Wheel?

The icy hand slithered away, any trace of compulsion no longer viable.

I grinned down at the bloody remains. As long as my own eyes didn't witness Morgenna's law broken, I could slither through her compulsion—a loophole.

A figure stepped from the alley's swirling shadows.

Stumbling back, I nearly tripped over Rusted Knife's head.

Slim and impossibly tall, the newcomer reminded me of folklore I'd once read about fae, fabled Creatures from the continent who lured young witches and elves to feast on their flesh. The witch cocked his white-blond head and smiled with teeth too small for his long face.

"What's this?" His spider-like legs ate the space between us. Shadows lifted my braid, examining the gold in my ears.

I couldn't move, my lungs paralyzed as the witch peered through the darkness. Something set off alarm bells in my head at his empty smile. Something was morally broken or missing in him. He stopped a breath from me, washing me in his magic's scent of crushed leaves and wildflowers—wolfsbane. He blinked two differently colored eyes and murmured, "A Day Witch saving a Night Witch brat? What is this world coming to?"

"She was defenseless." I steeled my spine. The witch's smile deepened and somehow grew more blank. I held in a shiver and spat, "She could've been a goblin, and I would've still saved her from that lecher."

"Day Witch you might be, but you can't save her, *Night Guard.*" The blue eye darkened. A razor-sharp shadow rose and veered dangerously close to my neck. "You'll only watch as they all do. Content to let the Night Queen bitch poison the Water Wheel."

He lifted my chin with one frigid, pale finger. "But then . . . Maybe a Day Witch is more useful than a Night Guard." He shoved past me and strode into the street. "Come. You should meet the girl's grandmother. Matilda will want to thank the witch who saved her wayward imp."

Throwing myself at the mercy of a strange Night Witch had the makings of a terrible idea. But Morgenna's compulsion remained unprovoked, and my curiosity of the Water Wheel and its people proved potent.

My hand strayed to the rows of stilettos at my thigh.

"If you try anything, I'll toss you into the Quies with the dead."

"An ironic twist considering how many I put there." He grinned at my sky-high brows. "I'm the only one in the Water Wheel with the balls to *take care* of the district's filth. Or mad enough. You pick."

He strode across a bridge, whistling a tune as eerie as he. If I'd survived Morgenna and Lilain *and* accepted my shitty destiny only to be knifed by this creepy bastard, I'd have a bone to pick with fate.

Curiosity trumped self-preservation, and I hurried after him.

We stopped outside a tavern leaning too far to one side. A sign swung on a rusted bent nail, depicting two dragons battling with flame. The Dueling Dragons tavern was no better on the inside. The musk of rotted wood swept over me, thick and ancient as the city. Not one chair wasn't in need of repair. A crooked bar shielded grime-covered bottles and tankards. Haggard witches stooped over roughhewn tables. Some were deep in their mead with unfocused stares. Others lingered in small groups, heads ducked together in whispers.

They straightened when we stepped inside.

Behind the bar, a massive witch slammed a glass onto the bar, fixing a glower onto my companion. Larger than Yori with tight curls darker than night and a matching complexion, he shoved through the swinging door separating the bar from the tavern.

"Fuck's sake, Ervik. You brought the Day Witch to Matilda's tavern?"

The crowd erupted in jeers. Someone wondered aloud if I'd start shooting sunlight from my ass. Others insisted the barkeeper—Rugard—throw me from the tavern. I kept my shoulders square, meeting each venomous glare with my own even as I noted each exit.

Ervik slung an arm around my shoulders and lazily grinned. "I found the answer to the Water Wheel's Osrin-sized problem."

The shoddy timbers supporting the ancient building groaned under the crowd's new howls. Dust and gods knew what else rained from termite-ravaged rafters.

A stout woman rose from a corner table. Her angular eyes missed nothing, exuding the kind of cunning I'd once seen in an osprey studying rabbits before diving. Perhaps her skin had once been smooth ivory, but the sun hadn't been kind. Heavily lined skin illustrated a long and weary life. She limped through the quieting crowd as they stepped back, ducking their heads in respect.

Behind her, the young girl from the alley inched forward, wide eyes on me. Rugard followed, an older replica of Simone—no doubt her father.

"How is a Day Witch our answer?" the woman asked Ervik. She ran a sharp gaze over me, lingering on the daggers at my sides.

"Some bastard trapped Simone in an alley. The Day Witch couldn't stop him, of course. Thank the bitch on the throne. But she distracted the creep long enough for me to get there." Ervik's shadow lifted my braid, forming a loop around my neck. "This isn't any Day Witch, Matilda. This is the legendary Captain Alys Sathos. Imagine what a *legend* could do with Osrin."

"I can't," I blurted, yanking my hair from around my neck. "I can't touch him or his ... work in the district."

"We are well aware," Matilda muttered. She sank into a chair and waved her arm toward the eagle-eyed crowd. Grumbling, the tavern returned to its conversations, obeying her need for privacy.

"Do you know who Osrin preys on with the queen's blessing?" she asked, motioning for me to sit across from her.

I nodded and eased into the chair. Osrin Atercruor was Morgenna's leash on the district who had rebelled against her decades ago. His established flesh trade used the district's young girls as product for the city's monstrous witches and it kept their families well in line. Morgenna had compelled the prince and the Guard to refrain from interfering. As long as the city's once rebellious district remained under a pressing heel, they'd never rise against Morgenna. Above anyone else, the Water Wheel saw through the queen, straight to the evil-crusted soul.

"Walking the streets tonight," Matilda began with a low gravel, "you wouldn't guess it, but the Water Wheel was once what the Black Wall is now. A prosperous market district. A safe place to walk at night. At least, before Osrin. The bastard may've been born one of us, but he had a heart made of coin. Started with illegal herb. The mind rotting kind that turns you against your kin. Then he moved onto young women. Anything to profit from Morithia's underbelly."

"Why don't you get out?"

"Who would have us and with what money? That monster on the throne made sure no one would employ us. Made it to where we became pariahs in our own city. No, we fix our own problems in the Water Wheel."

"So, why does *he* think you need me?" I pointed at the impossibly long-legged witch hovering over our table.

Matilda blew a sigh, tossing back a wisp of coarse silver hair. She crossed her arms and leveled a hard gaze at me over the table. "He believes if someone taught us how to fight back, it wouldn't matter if the Guard helped. We're not looking to make the same rebellious mistakes from before. But if we had a sharp mind leading us and a few tricks with a dagger, then maybe we stood a chance at taking down Osrin ourselves."

That still didn't explain why they wanted me.

"Sounds like you want a scapegoat to take the fall. If I could, why should I help you? Or *trust* you, for that matter?"

"If anyone hates Morgenna, it's her captive Day Witch. I'd wager you want her head too. But that's not what we're after. We only need a way from

Osrin's grip, and if we piss off Morgenna while we're at it—well, no one here gives a rat's ass. What more can she do to us?"

Sitting back, I crossed my arms and squinted around the noisy tavern. I shouldn't get caught in the Water Wheel's plight. I was supposed to free them from Morgenna, not Osrin.

An uncanny parallel rose. I'd spent fourteen years of my life on streets as perilous and filthy as these—only to end up in an alley and saved by a Captain Sathos. Too much of a coincidence to ignore. Maybe this was the next step of my fated path. Begin freeing the Night Realm—not by moving directly against Morgenna, but by loosening her hold.

But to jump in without certainty . . .

"Give me proof," I finally snapped.

Matilda sat up straight. Beside her, Ervik and Rugard leaned closer. I could almost smell their hope. Matilda leaned her elbows onto the table, hawkish eyes narrowing.

"What proof?"

"Something that proves you won't toss me over when everything goes to shit. Give me proof of your commitment to bring down Osrin, and I'll help you deal with him the best I can. You let me handle Morgenna's compulsion."

Rugard placed a hand on Matilda's shoulder. "Ma, you sure?"

"I've always been sure." Shrugging his hand off, she said to me, "Give me time to think, and I'll get you proof. I aim to finish this one way or another."

Elenna and Ansil's pleading faces flashed from a moonlit night high above the clouds. The last conversation we'd had together rang hollow. For them, I would do in Morithia what I'd refused to do in Kazadorah. Ansil's voice rang through a fog of guilt and memory.

They're tired of surviving. They want to thrive.

Holding out my hand to Matilda, I took another wobbly step down my path.

18

ONLY THE WIND KNOWS

Alys

A boot slammed into my jaw, launching me to the sparring ring floor.

"Fifth hit I've landed, Sathos," Nik whined and extended a hand. "You're getting sloppy."

He may have been my favorite sparring partner, but only because he'd picked up my airwitch maneuvers and turned them around on me. It was almost like sparring with Ansil again. He helped me up with a boyish smirk, giving me a light shove, trying to rouse me into another round.

"I'll give you a free shot. No defense."

"Tempting, but I'm done. I need tea and a bed."

I hated myself for picking up Night Realm customs, but here I was—craving their shit tea. What I wouldn't give for a carafe of steaming *kafeh* from a stall in Kazadorah's market. Sylinia and Yori did their best to guide me, one of them nearly always at my side as I navigated my new life. If I reached a hand in return, I might've called them friends. But losing Elenna and Ansil had gouged my soul. I couldn't replace them. Not with Night Witches.

For weeks, I'd floated in a new routine of sparring and training with the Guard, unsuccessfully reminding myself alone was better. But the bubbling grief I'd set aside waited beneath the surface, threatening to rip open and dump onto the onyx floors.

"Shit. What did you do now, Sathos?"

I followed Nik's gaze to find the prince watching us. Hands in his pockets, he leaned against a wooden post by the doors. Why was he always leaning on something? It only made him look more . . . climbable.

Icy as ever, he motioned me down.

Yori stood at his side, wildly gesturing ham-like hands as they argued. Marvelous. Had the prince discovered Matilda's offer? Technically neither of us broke Morgenna's law. Not yet anyways.

Nik clapped my shoulder and muttered, "Good luck" before heading to the barracks dormitories. For all his swagger, Nik hated confrontation.

Whatever shouting match this probably entailed, I wasn't in the mood. Everything ached: my bones, my skin, my soul. I wanted to drown my aches in a tub of perfumed water, drink my tea like a pretend Night Witch, and go to bed.

I climbed down and silently presented myself without a single quip.

The prince frowned, studying me from head to toe. "You look like shit."

"Unwell," Yori moaned. He muttered something indiscernible. "He means you look unwell."

I shrugged, unable to disagree. Dark stains under my eyes exposed how little sleep I found in my cold and mocking rooms—a constant reminder I didn't belong. My bronze skin had taken on a dull pallor without my daily desert flights. The stress of constantly watching my back didn't help either.

Shit was probably the only way to describe how I looked.

Yori bit his lip and gestured a hand over me. "This isn't the right time. Look at her!"

"She deserves to know," the prince snarled, straightening from the post. "Sathos is the last person you should coddle."

All thoughts of tea evaporated.

A sharp ping of exhilaration raced through my joints, ready to catapult me into whatever new catastrophe waited.

Yori's lips thinned into a line before pleading, "Don't do this. You'll crush her."

"Give her more credit or go find someone else to coddle." To me the prince snapped, "Come," and spun toward the doors.

I'd never heard him speak sharply to Yori and from the disbelief on Yori's features, it didn't happen often.

Shrugging apologetically at the giant, I jogged to catch the prince. We weaved through the barracks until we reached a set of stairs leading up a tower to the prince's office. I hadn't been allowed up there. Only officers were allowed in. My Night Guard captaincy was in name only. I wasn't a part of a guard unit, merely a nuisance forced upon the prince by the queen's questionable intentions. He may have saved me twice, but he'd made it clear I wasn't welcomed in the barracks.

I'd shown up anyway.

Rich mahogany paneling lined the walls of his office. A long table occupied most of the space. Dozens of chairs framed it—reserved for *officers only*. Tapestries of embroidered star charts hung across one wall facing a desk of mahogany. Neat stacks of paper made up one side of his desk. The other held several leather-bound books. More books lined the many shelves behind the desk, hundreds of them, varying in subject and age.

Oh, to be a rich prince with unlimited access to books.

Well, not entirely unlimited.

Sylinia had warned me not to delve too deep into bookshops. Most books were open to the Night Realm's public, but Morgenna's censorship had come down hard in the last thirty years. Fiction was allowed. Books on economics or farming encouraged. But history and magic were precious. Library towers like the one in Grelgesco were off limits to all except a registered few. Permission was granted by the queen or the literary magistrate in Albulus Library Tower.

A tower I desperately wanted into for all the supposedly infamous knowledge.

"Don't touch the books." The prince's voice sliced my thoughts like a blade through a page. He leaned one hip against the desk, arms crossed as he watched me study the bookcase. "You wouldn't understand half of them, anyway."

Without breaking from his stare, I ran a finger down each spine on a shelf. "You have no idea what I'm capable of understanding, and you better hope it doesn't bite you in the ass. Although maybe I *will* hope for it. Then you can come crawling back to me."

"As if I would get on my knees for you."

Raising both brows, I offered a slow grin. "You already did. Remember? In the Blackwood? When you had your hands up my tunic?"

I swear I heard his jaw pop. I could almost see him bite back a dozen nasty retorts, but he settled on a rather passive, "Next time, I'll let you bleed out."

Faint anticipation warmed my blood, a byproduct of our back-and-forth bickering. Grinning up at him, I sank into a worn leather armchair and said, "Why am I here?"

He narrowed his eyes, tapping his fingers on his thigh before reaching for a paper on his desk. "I received a missive from a spy in Lilain's court. It's about the 22nd Squad."

Any lingering mirth crackled and died.

I lunged for the paper, but he yanked it from my reach. Heart pounding in my ears, I eased back into my chair, breathing slowly, trying not to give into the urge to tear his eyes out.

"Give me the missive, Maddox." His name slipped out, decimating my weeks-long ban of stubborn will. It meant nothing to me now. Everything centered on the paper and whatever it held. Images of lightning and splattered blood flashed. Bodies falling through the sky. Ansil's broken body. Elenna's screams. "Please."

He studied me for too long, fingers never stopping their damned drumming. Finally, he dropped into an armchair and spun it to face me before he began reading.

"Status of 22nd remains unchanged. All but captain assumed dead south of Miner's Pass. Rumors of Ko receiving payment for 22nd ambush prove accurate. No motive known for Lilain's turn against 22nd. Failure to kill captain did not go unnoticed."

I squeezed my eyes shut, repeating his words like a chant in my head.

Lilain had dumped us at the goblins' mercy, knowing we never stood a chance.

"Sathos," the prince began, oddly gentle. When I didn't open my eyes, he nudged my knee with his. "What prompted this? Why would Lilain want her best squad dead?"

I ignored him, listening to the report echo in my head. It was all there. Kazen's camp smelling of fucking fresh chicken. Since when had goblins afforded *chicken*? Or new clothes strung on lines? And the crates of expensive oranges in the valley? Lilain had paid them in clothing and food. In hindsight every hint blared irrefutable, and I'd ignored them for the compulsion urging me to kill Ko.

The compulsion.

We couldn't retreat from the valley, forced to stay until one by one we died—except me.

"I don't know," I finally whispered. "Elenna and Ansil were neck deep in a rebellion, but they hadn't made moves that would out them. Besides, if Lilain caught wind of treason, she would've strung them up for the city to bear witness. She wouldn't pay off a goblin army. Too underhanded. She wanted us dead, and she wanted to hide it."

Why?

"There's more." The prince leaned forward, his knees brushing mine. The green in his eyes overtook the brilliant gold, dark and foreboding as whatever he was about to say. "Lilain knows you're here, and she wants you back."

Somehow, I paled further, heart slipping somewhere by my feet. Of course, she did. I had deserted. She would hunt me until my blood splattered the walls of her cavern. There were a dozen reasons I couldn't go back, but I could only think of how Lilain would boil my blood until I was nothing but a stain on her cavern floor.

The prince shifted closer, widening his legs to trap mine within them. I nearly kicked his shin with a warning to back up. Instead, I gulped the cloud of grounding cedar and spiced air. I wasn't in Lilain's cavern with her poisoned jasmine magic. I was in the Night Realm and for now, I was safe.

Gods, what a twist in fate.

"Morgenna won't let you go, Sathos. Whatever game the queens are playing, you're a pawn. Call it safety, call it a prison, but you're stuck in the Night Realm."

"Lilain won't back down."

"No, nor will she simply wait." He reached for another letter, handing it to me. "She's already made her first move."

I scanned the words and squinted to read again. "The rumors are true?"

"Very true. I saw the vampyres myself last night." He ran a hand through his short waves, extending his long legs and bumping mine. He frowned, as if realizing how close he'd inched toward me, but he didn't move. "They're briefly spotted nearly every night up and down the border before they vanish back into the Blackwood. No telling how many there are."

"What does this have to do with Lilain?"

He pointed at the discarded report holding Lilain's betrayal. "Spies reported vampyres in and out of her caverns. We know she's in league with them, but to what extent? She may be using them to fetch you from the Night Realm, but that suggests a far deeper scheme. It may go back further than the 22nd's ambush."

Guilt, thick and viscous, oozed over my prickled skin.

This was my fault. I was supposed to save the Night Realm from its monster and instead I'd foisted upon them not only Lilain's wrath, but a host of vampyres intent on the Mother only knew what. Not even Night Witches deserved Lilain's cruelty.

I frowned and leaned forward, mirroring the prince with elbows on knees. "It doesn't make sense. The only vampyres on Efelldor are the outcasts from Gilgador. They're a pathetic handful their kind on the continent don't want."

A knock thundered at the door.

We sprang apart and stood. A burning thread of shame wove through me, like I'd been caught with my hand in a jar of sweets.

The head of a young page poked through the door. "I'm terribly sorry to interrupt, Your Highness. The queen insists you report the latest missive at once."

"Of course, she does," the prince muttered under his breath. The mask I hadn't realized was missing slid back on. "Please, assure the queen I'm on my way."

The page nodded and dashed from the office, leaving the prince and I alone.

I sank back into the chair as memories surfaced. Lilain's constant deadly summons. Elenna and Ansil at my side for each of them. Elenna and Ansil who Lilain murdered and wiped from the world. The good and light in them—gone forever. I should've died with them—if not for Elenna's sacrifice. I was nothing compared to her light. My magicless nature, my pathetic upbringing.

I wasn't worth her sacrifice.

My throat tightened and tears swam across my vision. A whole month and my emotions chose *now* to betray me?

Dashing tear tracks from my cheeks, I cleared my throat. No, not here. Not yet. Anywhere but where the prince would see. Avoiding his gaze, I leapt up, striding for the exit, begging the sob tightening in my windpipe to wait a minute more. I reached for the doorhandle—

"Wait."

The near-silent footsteps crept closer. A warm hand gently uncurled my fingers and pressed something cold into my palm. "This opens the eastern tower overlooking the sea. It's the Onyx Palace's highest tower . . . should you need a quiet place to reflect."

The iron key in my hand was simple, but it signified something simpler—understanding. Some petty part of me wanted to fling the key back at him and pretend he hadn't taken pity on *me*. An ache crawling up my throat drove me to the eastern tower anyways.

The key opened a stairwell spiraling high into the darkening sky. A blanket of winking stars waited beyond an overhead trapdoor. Chilled wind coursed through the flat, bare tower top. Below, the Eastern Sea churned beneath in the bay, a gray foam under the moon's horizon.

Sagging against the tower top's circling parapet, I set my sobs free. Tears crested over my cheeks as I imagined each detail of the twelve faces Lilain stole. The freckles on Hecuba. Oris's wild curls. Elenna's never-fading grin. Gone because of Lilain's betrayal.

Sobs shook my frame. My tears fell hundreds of feet onto the jagged cliffside, seeping into the rocks. Lilain hadn't only stolen twelve airwitches. She'd stolen the fiery valor of Uzza, the thirst for adventure in Oris. Each of them had held infinite dreams of hope and she'd snuffed them out.

I ripped the leather cord from my braid, letting the wind tangle the long strands into a nest it'd probably take me an hour to undo. A reckless urge to feel alive prompted me to climb the parapet. A need to prove to Lilain she hadn't stolen *my* life. My feet were barely small enough to balance on the narrow stone. Wind howled in my ears, screeching for me to get down.

Gathering my trivial air magic, I directed it beneath my feet. I rose unsteadily into the sky and hovered a scant inch above the stone. I shut the foreign world out and imagined I was beneath a desert moon on my broom. I'd always preferred the sky to anywhere else in Efelldor.

It was the closest thing to home.

I could almost make out Ansil's chiding through the winds. How many times had I heard his warnings to slow down, to be less reckless? *You do realize you're one strong gust from toppling off?*

Stretching my arms to the sky, I released another gurgling sob, wishing he could chide me in person, pull me off the parapet himself. *You and Elenna are the reason for this one white hair,* he'd once whined, brushing his hair as he had ritually done each night. *It'll multiply one day, mark my words, and I'll blame you, Alys.*

But he wouldn't. Not ever.

I crashed backward onto the tower top, laying on my back and releasing every bottled sob I'd stoppered since the ambush. I would never see any of them again.

I was truly alone.

And I hated it.

The clocktower bells struck midnight when I rose, scrubbing at crusted tear tracks. I wasn't ready to return to my bleak rooms. Here amongst the wind and silence, I felt the inklings of peace. Wondering if I could get away with spending the night up here, I climbed the parapet and lay down to watch the glittering stars.

The bells struck one when the trapdoor rattled open, and the prince appeared. Hands in his pockets he stepped beside my place on the parapet but kept his gaze on the sea.

"Most witches would throw up if they tried laying there."

"Eh, if I fall, I'll bounce. Day Witch privileges."

He lifted a brow. "I'm fairly certain even Lilain couldn't land that, but I'll happily help you test your theory."

I snorted and sat up to face him. Telltale tight creases around his eyes and mouth told a familiar story of a queen's displeasure that hadn't been there before Morgenna's summons. I shifted, inexplicably uncomfortable with the crack in his mask and the witch behind it that may've been more than Morgenna's right-hand heir.

"Why did you give me a key to this tower?"

Startled, he ripped his gaze off the foaming waters. "You didn't have to accept it."

"Don't dance around my question, Prince. I'm not one of your political sycophants."

He crossed his arms and let out an unimpressed sigh. "I don't understand how such a small witch harbors so much pride. You're barely tall enough to see over this parapet."

"You would know all about the foibles of pride because you're such a paragon of humility, Crown Prince Maddox Lexsidus of the Night Realm, Commander of the Night Guard, Lord of the Magistrates. Exactly how many titles do you hold, oh humble one?"

"Which one of us oversees a realm and ensures the prosperity of its people? Some would say I've earned my pride. What do *you* do, besides get captured?"

I bit the inside of my cheek to keep from punching his perfect face. Tossing the key into the air, I gleefully watched his narrowed eyes follow it over the parapet before I snatched it. "I earned every bit of my pride through blood and sweat. Yours was handed to you on a silver platter alongside everything else."

He twisted his mouth before opening it and then promptly snapped it shut. Bracing his elbows on the parapet beside me, he wearily said, "You enjoy bickering, don't you?"

"Only because you make it easy. Besides, you're the only one who can keep up. Probably has something to do with our matching enormous prides."

I was sure the corner of his mouth lifted. Just barely. Realizing he'd out-maneuvered answering me, I attempted another question.

"Well then, why did you save me in Morgenna's challenge? We both know you could've snapped my neck."

"Yori asked me to."

"Truthful as that may be, why did you agree?"

"Because you're the only one who can keep up."

I huffed out a hoot. "You truly are incapable of answering anything directly. I should shove you off the parapet for all you're worth."

"Wouldn't put it past you. You already tried to stab me."

"Oh, please. I knew there wasn't a chance that knife would touch you. I needed a distraction, and if you recall, it worked."

He raised incredulous brows. "And yet, something tells me you wouldn't have hovered mournfully over my body if my reflexes failed you."

A laugh bubbled out, breathless and real. I clamped my mouth shut and cleared my throat. "Back to my first question then. Why give me the key? You didn't have to offer me peace. Murderous Day Witch and all that. Isn't that what I deserve? Pain and misery?"

He dragged his gaze from my face to the key in my outstretched hand. When he looked back up, his piercing, eerie eyes cracked the bravado I stamped onto my features every morning. The teasing banter faded. What remained was a stark understanding. It skewered my armor of snark to the terrified witch inside who had no idea what she was doing.

"Because I've been where you are," he finally said. "Where you bottle grief, not realizing its slowly eating you until there's nothing left but regret." He gestured to the open tower. "Up here there's nothing holding it in."

I reached for my ear, toying with an earring. It spoke of my grief, but the kind I'd resolved and made peace with. Losing the 22nd was a starved grief, one I hadn't acknowledged until then, as if holding out hope I'd wake up and discover it'd been a nightmare. Losing Ansil and Elenna. The Mother's command. My newfound fate. I wanted to wake up from this new life and fly into a morning sun.

But there was no waking up. I was living my nightmare.

Maddox caught a strand of my hair fluttering over his face. Fixed on the sea, he absently rolled the strand between his thumb and forefinger. "Grief is a double-edged sword. It's a natural process of healing for those who remain behind. But it also holds the power to drag us to uncharted depths. Sometimes deep enough we can't climb back out." He let go of my hair, watching the wind gather and fling it into the air.

Finally turning to me, he softly said, "Regardless of where we stand, Sathos, I'd never wish that drowning on you. Not when I thought you might find a way to climb out on this tower top."

The gold in his eyes had turned silver in the moonlight, slightly less peculiar than usual. I couldn't bring myself to pull away from their odd draw. Whatever he saw, I hope it reflected the same resolve I saw staring back. The sort of persistence to take one more step even while the world threw itself around our ankles.

I bit my lip and, for once, hoped I didn't sound mocking. "Who did you lose?"

The prince mask slammed down as he spun toward the sea. "My parents. It was when Melis and I returned home after our final term at Amethyst Hall. After we . . . began our separate ways." Scoffing, he braced one elbow against the parapet and peered down. "Two idiots too caught in their pathetic squabbles to notice anything beyond themselves."

When he didn't go on, I scooted closer. "What happened?"

He let out a dark laugh and tapped long, pale fingers on the stone. "In short? One died and the other couldn't handle it, so they followed the first into the Soul Lands."

I scrambled to think of an applicable reply. Nothing came to mind. Gods, no wonder he and Melisandre were such gloomy witches. That he held himself out to the world at all instead of caving to grief magnified my respect.

"You think you're to blame."

"Don't you?" He gave the sea his back, leaning on the parapet beside me. Beyond his icy disdain I recognized something new—guilt. "If we—if *I* had been more present instead of selfishly fixated on myself, I could have done *something*."

I didn't have words to lessen the familiar monster of regret leering over him, but the silence ate at me, and I blurted, "I never knew my birth parents. I was found on an orphanage doorstep with nothing except my name on a scrap of paper pinned to a scarf wrapped around me. Kazadorah's streets were preferable to that shithole, and one day I ran away and never returned."

Precariously perched, I drew my knees under my chin, wrapping arms around my legs. The pathetic story poured out like a rushing river of misery.

"I was small but quick enough I could steal to survive without getting caught. At least, not until I was fourteen. I couldn't read, but the pretty illustrations of books in a window tempted me more than any loaf of bread. It was stupid, but I stole one. The shopkeeper sent a group of thugs to retrieve the book, but I wouldn't give it up. They cornered me in an alley and pinned me to the ground to—well, I suppose they intended to prove how little power I had."

Slouching, I burrowed deeper into my knees, muffling my words. "I was certain I would die there. Five grown men against a half-starved girl. Captain Federikka Sathos stepped into that alley, lit up in fire and smoke. A month later, I was a well-fed page in the DRAS under her sponsorship where I met Elenna and Ansil. All my dreams birthed from one awful circumstance. She gave me her name, taught me to read, to think thoroughly, and she instilled in me a determination to be more than my circumstances.

"And then . . . three years ago, she was scouting the Borderlands alone. She was doing me a favor and searching for an ancient, abandoned library supposedly out there. We both harbored an unhealthy obsession with finding ancient ruins. Anyway, around this time, I'd started gaining a reputation with the 22nd and Lilain had us flying all over the realm. She wouldn't let me go search for this abandoned library rumored to be in the Blackwood, so I asked Federikka to do it. Maybe if I hadn't selfishly begged her to go looking for something so trivial, then she'd be alive. Instead, she flew right into an elf hunting party. You know how they feel about airwitches."

I shrugged and let out a self-deprecating laugh. "All that to say you're not alone. Turns out we're both equally stupid and full of guilt. It makes no sense to take that guilt on, but it rots inside us all the same. I'd say we should move on and become better people who learn from their mistakes, but we both know that'll never happen. It's what sets us apart from everyone. Keeps us alone and miserable."

Finally daring a peek in Maddox's direction, I found something in his blank stare that made me waver, like I'd exposed too much in return for too little. When he glanced away, I couldn't help the shiver rolling down my spine.

Lips twisting, he softly said, "You were easier to despise when you were nothing but an arrogant little demon who talked too much."

The wind snatched at my laugh, offering it as penitence to the sea and stars for the ugly words once between us. A peculiar calm settled over us, a knowledge that while we may not have liked one another, we understood each other. Alone and apart, we both belonged to a sky high above everyone else.

Abruptly, the wind shifted, sending my hair flying into his face.

"How did you evade Morgenna's compulsion that first day?" Any peace evaporated with the new razor-sharp edge in his voice as he flung my hair back.

I gathered it in frigid hands, blinking up at him. "I didn't evade anything. She caught me off guard. I didn't realize she could compel."

"You lied and told her you were magicless."

I leaned back, taking in the chilly indignation rolling off him.

He was serious.

An indignant giggle burst free. "I *am* magicless. I can barely fly. I can't summon light or fire. I obviously can't spellcast or inscribe runes. The little air I *can* summon is useless—exactly what I told Morgenna. What the bleeding Mother makes you think I'm lying?"

He straightened to his full height, taller than even my perch on the parapet. Bracing his arms on either side of me, he leaned forward, effectively trapping me. He was far too close. His warmth cut the wind's reach, shielding me.

I'd rather have the wind. At least it didn't scramble my brain.

"Because everywhere I go in the palace or barracks, I can smell where you've been. I can smell your fucking magic. Don't lie to me when it's all I can smell right *now*."

Just like that, my brain unscrambled.

Scoffing, I held up empty open hands. "Well, I'm clearly not summoning magic now. How do you explain what you're smelling?"

His gaze flickered across my face, searching for proof I was lying. With an irritated sigh, he snapped, "You, Alys. It's definitely you. No one else smells half as maddening. I'm going to have to summon half the palace's shadows in my office just to get the smell of you out of it."

I rolled my eyes and tried not to dwell on how my name sounded like a beautiful curse from his mouth. I shoved him backward and hopped off the parapet.

"And you accuse me of being dramatic. What does my supposed magic smell like anyway?"

He shoved his hands into his pockets and studied me for a long moment, as if weighing whether to tell me. "Like a spiced sweet."

"Well, that certainly proves you're not scenting *me*. If I had powerful magic, I guarantee you it would smell like death or something equally terrifying. What an insult to say I smell *sweet*." I started for the trapdoor but stopped to pat his arm with a simpering grin. "Try not to sniff me as I pass. Everyone knows how much the prince loves his sweets."

He made a face and jerked from my touch before dryly retorting, "No, thanks. Right now you smell like a sweaty sweet someone dropped in a damp boot."

I threw my head back and burst into genuine laughter.

He fixed back onto the sea, nearly succeeding in hiding a half-smile. The tiny movement was barely anything, but it released a torrent of fluttering in my belly. I found myself wishing it was the beginning of a stomach sickness and not traitorous butterflies.

I had to get off the tower before I did something incredibly stupid.

Shoving the tower's key at him, I made for the trap door like salvation waited on the other side.

He snagged my arm and pressed the key back into my hand.

"Keep it. You live in Morithia now. It'll be the closest you can get to flying away."

Only when I'd reached the courtyard below did I realize a weight had lifted off my shoulders. I glanced behind me at the tower and winced. My future was set in something more resolute than stone—it was set in fate. I couldn't afford to drift off my Mother-given path for anyone. Efelldor and the fate of its neglected rested in my hands. I knew with certain confidence entertaining thoughts of Morgenna's heir was a danger to all of us.

If he was half as wrapped in her compulsion as I suspected he was, then he wasn't just a hurdle. He was a weapon waiting to be used against me.

Part Two

The new Creatures born of bitter soil were not of one but two...
-from 'Duality of Witches'

19

DEALS ARE INKED IN RUNES AND HOPE

Corryn

A minute more, and I might slap the bureaucracy out of this bushy-browed fool.

"A runic instructor has no business reading portents," the divinationist droned, massive brows scrunching like caterpillars. "They are the study of prolific divinationists, witches who've spent decades unraveling the delicate web of fate's future. They certainly aren't for the eyes of an instructor who merely teaches the realm's brats."

He spun on his heel and disappeared into Amethyst Hall's library, and like the last six divinationists, took with him any hope of information. The last one, a pinched-mouthed elderly woman, had spent half the interview convinced I was her assistant. At least, she'd let slip the last recorded portents had come in a flurry twenty-eight years ago and nothing since—a horror for any aspiring divinationist, apparently.

But not for me.

At days shy of twenty-eight years old myself, that meant one of those last portents must've heralded my fate. Which meant the flurry of portents also revealed the other fated witches. At least now I knew I was searching for the last portents.

A needle in a haystack, but at least I knew which haystack.

Every divinationist agreed the only outsider allowed within their ranks was Queen Morgenna. If she'd squirreled away the portents, then she had half an inkling of what they contained. I doubted, and hoped on the Mother, she knew whom they spoke of, or she would've killed us all by then.

Unless she had—and only I remained.

Rilessa's office door was snugly shut when I arrived, reminding me I was over ten minutes late for this meeting. A quick glance through the room of perfumed and feathered courtiers suggested a terribly important meeting. I spotted empty space along the back wall and slunk through the glowering courtiers to find a place beside Yori with an apologetic wince.

The giant guard smiled and whispered, "You haven't missed much. Just a bit of bloating from courtiers demanding Rilessa provide a complete list of wards protecting their children from vampyres. Maddox refuses to allow it. He told them it negates the purpose of protecting the students if everyone knows the magic behind it. Now, your poor mother is caught between appeasing the courtiers and knowing Maddox is right."

The Night Prince leaned against Rilessa's desk, arms crossed. In a quiet voice, he ripped apart their contentions. He pointed out it took one poorly spoken word for a wildfire of rumor to begin. Who's to say that wildfire wouldn't reach the vampyres? What if they had spies amongst us? If they knew a way into the school what was the point of wards? If they wanted security, they'd have to trust the headwitch they'd appointed themselves.

The flummoxed courtiers snuck irritated glares at Rilessa, but her demure elegance never faltered. One by one the courtiers agreed with Maddox as if this was always their idea. In a cloud of scented oils, they marched from the office, heads held high, noses in the air, pretending they left with what they came for.

Power rarely equaled brains.

Yori pushed from the wall and shook my hand.

"Always a pleasure, Corryn."

I smiled but my gaze fell onto Maddox and my mother speaking in low voices. Edging for the door, a plan shaped—risky as it was. I couldn't let another Dual Witch die under my watch. The longer I waited to unite the six, the more chances Morgenna and her beast had to murder another innocent.

Pacing outside Rilessa's office, I counted the pearls on my wrist.

One. Two. Three.

The bracelet spun. Was I being hasty?

Four. Five. Six.

Surely, I could find the portents on my own. Nyx and the Mother assigned *me* this task. I was meant to find the others and unite us.

Seven. Eight. Nine.

I simply needed patience, not a mad dash of a plan that might backfire on me. Glancing back at Rilessa's door, I sucked in a deep breath through the anxiety squeezing my windpipe.

Ten. Eleven. Twelve.

Too much time had passed without answers. The bracelet spun quicker, nearly slipping from my fingertips.

Thirteen. Fourteen. Fifteen.

I needed answers and the clock was ticking. Sixteen. Seventeen—

The pearls launched from my wrist, skidding down the marble floors and halting before a pair of polished boots. Maddox stepped from the office and bent to retrieve the pearls. He pinched them between two fingers as if they were the tail of a rodent.

"Any other witch would've burned this long ago." He tossed it at me. "Gods help you if she finds out you still have it."

Heat flooded my cheeks.

I snatched the bracelet midair and slipped it over my wrist. "Not every souvenir is meant to remember pleasant times. Some are reminders of mistakes to be corrected."

His single raised brow said I was foolish. Maybe I was.

I waited for Yori to pass from earshot before whispering to Maddox, "We need to talk." Pointing toward the seclusion of a nearby white marble column, I followed him into their shadow. It didn't slip my notice he wouldn't give me his back. He didn't trust me nearly as much as he'd claimed. Few witches overpowered his magic. Being one of those few had set a target on my back and time hadn't erased it.

He ducked into the shadow of the column, neatly stepping over a crack—one he and Melis had created with a misplaced prank that had nearly brought down the dining hall.

Wringing my hands, I tossed any lingering reservations and blurted, "I'll do it. I'll find you a book on Death Runes."

His eyes narrowed.

"Out of the goodness of your squeaky-clean heart, I'm sure."

"Or because I need your connections to find me something, and I need you to do it without any fanfare."

"So a favor . . ."

"An exchange," I corrected.

"And what do you want me to find?"

I swallowed and prayed to the Mother I'd made the right choice, otherwise I was about to throw myself at the mercy of Morgenna's wolf. "Where the portents are kept."

He reared back and made a face. "How should I know where the portents are kept? Don't those belong to the divinationists who translate them from the stars?"

"According to them, their findings are the property of Queen Morgenna. I'd like to know where she keeps them."

Something dark crossed his expression so briefly, I wondered if I'd imagined it. "Answer this carefully, Corryn. What do you want with a portent?"

"Funny you should ask. I would have thought you remembered my choice of study when we were at school or what forced me to pick something else."

His mouth twisted in disgust, but whether directed at me or himself, I wasn't sure. Nor did I care. Not after he'd ruined my one chance to escape Amethyst Hall. Instead, because of foolish spite on both our parts, I remained stuck in the only place I'd ever called home as the rest of the world moved on.

"If you can find out where the portents are kept," I said, "I'll find you a Death Rune book—*if* Amethyst Hall has one."

"Fine. But on the other hand, I can guarantee if Morgenna's stashed the portents somewhere, she'll have made sure they're well-guarded. I can't imagine she'd allow any prying witch to find them. What if I can't?"

"You can. You're the second most powerful witch in the realm."

He made another face like I'd told him he was the second *smelliest* witch.

The shadows pulsed, skittering across my shoes, questioning Maddox's need. I toed the crack in the floor, glad he'd learned to control the shadows instead of letting them explode out of him. Or that he stopped using them to egg mine on, trying to determine who was stronger.

That never ended well.

"Fine," he snapped. "But I get the book now before I return to Morithia."

"Only if you swear on your mother you'll do all you can."

The glare he gave me was laced with lethal venom, but he swore.

Satisfied, I led the way to the library, avoiding curious stares along the way. Giggling students found themselves in need of help with their studies, asking pointless questions while batting their lashes. No matter how ideally shaped Maddox's features, the permanent thundercloud over him dissuaded all but the most persistent from addressing him directly. Those he sent off with a single frown.

"I almost feel sorry for you," I laughed when an older girl ran off, pink-cheeked and mortified when he couldn't recall her or her parents. We approached the massive library doors, and I tugged one open, gesturing him in. "You'll never know what it's like to blend in."

"Someone said the same thing just yesterday." He slipped inside the library with a long-suffering sigh. "I was told I was too pretty to take seriously, but I needn't worry. She had a plan to *fix me* if I handed her a knife."

I hacked a startled laugh into a cough.

The stories circulating from Morithia must've been true. Derisive, outspoken, and a nerve that rivaled the princess general's, Captain Sathos would make an incredible interview for her insights into the Day Realm.

I didn't dare voice that aloud.

Instead, I diplomatically said, "Perhaps loneliness prompts her prickly attitude? Her entire life has been upended after all. She's a witch captive to her enemy."

"Or she's a witch who straddles a line between absurdity and arrogance." He looked up to inspect the library's rotunda of violet stained-glass. "I thought Melis had the worst sense of provocation. Sathos opens her mouth and *all* that comes out is provocation."

We entered the rotunda, and its regulated silence cut off need for reply. The familiar scent of old parchment and ink gave the sense of returning home. Built long before the school, the enormous library tower once served as a learning center. Legend claimed even Day Witches once traveled to study here, but there was no evidence of that. Or if there was, it was destroyed in the Lost Five Hundred Years.

I glanced down at my arms and wondered which one I'd happily snap in exchange for a book from the missing years. Flexing each of them, I decided both.

Maddox raised a single brow in question, and I dropped my arms with flaming cheeks.

Along the northern wall, an iron door led to the stone maze of rooms below. Students weren't allowed beneath the rotunda. Even instructors required special permission to reach the lower levels and their dark magic books. The moment courtiers appointed Rilessa as headwitch, I'd applied for permission. Rilessa's sway proved pivotal, nepotism be damned. The day I applied my blood to the iron door's lock proved the proudest of my academic career.

Then I'd gone below and quickly realized dark magic should be left in the dark. Even Rilessa couldn't enter certain warded rooms below, forbidden by the queen herself.

Death Runes might well be among those.

The lower we descended the stairs behind the iron door, the colder it grew. Our breaths became crystallized clouds. Dust puffed up around our ankles where we walked. A few lanterns hung from the stone walls, lighting the way to rooms of forbidden magic.

"I take it Captain Sathos is settling in, then?" Anything to break the tense atmosphere. Smiling when Maddox's scowl returned, I explained, "I hear my students' stories passed from their parents. You can't fault her for provoking you. You're the one who caught her."

"A point she never lets me forget."

"I intend to meet her one day. Imagine what she could explain about the Day Realm and its magic and history. They've held onto witch roots more than the Night Realm, you know."

"She'd eat you alive."

I scoffed, recalling the dark-haired witch I'd seen in Grelgesco. Small and impish with large eyes glittering with mischief, she didn't seem capable of the violence the stories claimed.

"You're only saying that because everyone knows she's not afraid of you."

"I'm saying that because she's dangerous. Morgenna compelled Sathos within an inch of her life to keep her loyal to the Night Realm, but she's too shrewd to stay trapped forever. Whatever foolish gossip you've heard, remember she's killed hundreds of us, and she wouldn't hesitate to add another if she could get away with it."

Refusing to shudder, I peered into the nearest room. A ward gently shuffled me backward. Well, I'd found my first inaccessible room that even my ranked status as the headwitch's daughter wouldn't make a difference to. It didn't matter—I'd caught a glimpse inside. Poisons and their use in potions.

I continued to the next room. And then the next.

For the next few hours, I searched the rooms, descending lower than I'd ever gone. From the deep dust, I suspected no one had been this low in decades. Sometimes I'd walk into a room and lift the books from their shelves. At other times, I'd barely gain a peek before a ward pushed me back. Then there were the wards that flung me onto my rear, violent and nasty. On those occasions, Maddox pursed his lips and sent shadows to haul me up. His annoyance only grew with each room and failure. After the last irritated sigh, I was ready to burst into tears.

Perhaps I'd find those miserable portents on my own after all.

Taking a deep breath, I stuck the toe of one boot over the next threshold. Nothing. The room was smaller than the others, more of an alcove than a room. A single bookcase waited in the center with empty shelves.

No, not empty.

A single leather-bound book lay crookedly on its back as if someone had tossed it onto the bottom shelf in haste.

Or revulsion.

I took another step forward and the air crackled.

"Shit," Maddox hissed before lunging.

Air sizzled over the threshold just as Maddox ripped me from the alcove, throwing me onto my rear in the corridor's safety. I stared open-mouthed at the threshold where blue flames crisscrossed the entry.

"Is that—"

"Day magic," Maddox finished, examining the dying flames. "A Day Witch warded this room."

"Then the legends are true? They truly studied here."

He shrugged. "It's not a wild belief. The realms weren't always at odds. It's likely they worked together to build up the library's collection." He frowned and toed the evaporating smoke. "What was in there?"

Wincing, I rose from the floor, slapping dust from my skirts. "A single book. I couldn't see the entirety of the title, but I caught one word—'*Signum.*'"

Rune.

Oh, I'd already found hundreds of rune books down here. Some I'd read before. This one was ancient. Abandoned in haste and heavily warded—certainly worth another peek.

Maddox groaned and shoved his hands into his pockets.

"Listen, I'm going to tell you a story of how Melis discovered a way through our mother's locked wards on her jewels. What you do with that story is up to you. I'm going to tell you with my back turned. Do you understand?"

Eyes wide, I nodded. I'd never seen a compulsion loophole at work. Was it all a matter of semantics? I hurried back to the threshold as he began.

"Melis discovered each ward has a weak point. A place where shadow can seep through. We could only guess it has to do with ranking power. If the thieving witch is stronger, they can force the locked ward's weakest point. It's no more than a pinprick."

Summoning shadows, I slid them across the threshold and hoped I was stronger than some long dead ancient witch. Blue flames sprung forward and swallowed them with a hiss. I continued summoning, searching for a weak point. Toward the bottom, a sliver of shadow snaked its way through a hole in the flames, no bigger than my thumbnail. I nearly yipped but turned it into an odd gurgle. I wasn't sure if it would trigger Maddox's compulsion. We didn't need him leading me out in binds for stealing a warded book.

Sweat beaded along my spine. When had it become a furnace in here?

My thread of shadow slithered up the bookcase to the bottom shelf.

"From there," Maddox continued, "Melis realized our mother's lock wards only kept us out, not in. Melis could use her shadows to steal the jewels and pass them through the wards untriggered."

I nodded to myself. If I could grab the book with shadow, I could pass it back. My shadow inch wormed up the bookcase and wrapped around the lone book, careful not to crush the withered cover. It appeared made of ancient leather—probably easily damaged if I wasn't careful. The real test would be passing it through without triggering the flames and destroying it.

A restless tapping broke my concentration.

I fumbled the book.

My shadows dove, barley catching it before it smashed into the ward.

I resisted the urge to snap at Maddox and his impatient fingers. Slowly, I guided the coiled shadow toward me. Breath held, I pulled it inch by inch through the ward. No flames. The crackling air hissed, but the ward held. A moment later the book cleared the crackling air.

"Yes!"

Seizing the book, I flipped it over and examined the cover.

But it was all wrong.

Crying out, I stumbled back, letting the book drop in a cloud of dust.

"It's bound in *goblin skin*."

Maddox whirled and leapt for the awful green leather book. He flipped it open.

"Better than witch skin, I suppose."

He tapped the cover page triumphantly before flipping through the pages. Shadows flitted around his head, sharpening the planes of his features. "This is it. We found one, probably the last one of its kind. *Mortem Signum*. Death Runes."

He laughed, low and breathless. The sound was a dark elegance, like the curling shadows reverently stroking the book. It sank a cold dread deep into my bones, reminding me too much of Morgenna. He ripped frantically through the pages, searching for something.

"This will take months to translate. But—"

"Put it back, Maddox."

My voice trembled and the remaining corridor shadows raced for me, curling over my skirts in fawning claws. "That book is evil. Can't you feel it? Death Rune practice was outlawed for a reason. They go against the Mother's natural order. It's bound in goblin skin, for gods' sake. No good can come of it. Put it back."

"Don't be so naïve. Good is relative. Besides, I can't put it back without burning it." He tore his hungry gaze from the yellowing pages and snapped the book shut, tucking it under his arm. "A deal's a deal. When I find the portents, I'll let you know."

"Wait—" I sprang forward, hurling my shadows for the book.

Not all shadows answered to me. I caught a glimpse of Maddox's cruel smirk before darkness swallowed him, and my shadows grasped nothing but air.

Gripping my bracelet, I let loose a shallow exhale.

What had I done?

20

THE SHARP BITE OF A DAGGER

Alys

F ew things ruined breakfast like an old woman dragging a body behind her. When Matilda limped through the Dueling Dragons door. I blinked five times before my brain made sense of what I saw.

I shot from my place at the rickety table, nearly overturning a breakfast of porridge and tea onto Rugard and Simone's laps.

Months had passed since I asked Matilda for proof of her commitment to overthrowing Osrin Atercruor. Months of befriending her widowed son-in-law and granddaughter, of growing a grudging mutual respect for the people of the Water Wheel. In this bleak district I'd found familiarity where the palace offered nothing but prejudice. I'd even celebrated my twenty-eighth birthday with them—or the day I pretended was mine. Foundling difficulties. Rugard had baked a delicious apple tart I nearly finished by myself. Much better than the absinthe disaster of a night Yori, Nik, and Sylinia had pushed on me.

No, I'd begun to believe the subject of Osrin dead and dropped.

The body smashing into chairs behind her proved otherwise.

Brows furrowed into a silvery line, the older woman didn't acknowledge the startled offers of help from the early morning tavern patrons. Ervik prowled behind her. He trailed the body like a cat who'd finally caught the rodent eluding him.

Rugard ordered a wide-eyed Simone to go upstairs and mop the floors. In the same growl, he cleared the tavern. Once the girl and curious onlookers vanished, Rugard hurried to his mother-in-law and hoisted the body onto the table, scattering our bowls to the floor.

"Is he . . ." I poked the unmoving body, holding my breath against the reek of sweat and piss. The icy hand in my head I'd accepted as part of my new life thankfully didn't stir.

"Dead? No." Matilda sat in a chair Ervik offered, wiping her weathered brown forehead with a trembling hand. "Ervik and I caught this one peeking into that pathetic excuse for a girls' orphanage. Figured he might know some things. Ervik says he's one of Osrin's grabbers. Ruined dozens of young girls' lives, hoisting them off to gods know where."

Ervik leaned over the body, inhaling the stench with shuttering eyes. "Not anymore."

"You wanted proof, Sathos. Here it is. Proof of my damned commitment. I snatched him myself with a dozen onlookers. If I'm in this, bet the rest of the Water Wheel stands behind me. No one outside of Osrin's thugs would dare rat us out."

I didn't doubt her.

"Ma," Rugard whispered, clenching the old woman's shoulder, "last chance. Are you sure?"

Matilda grasped his hand in her withered one. "The day you lost a wife to Osrin's thugs, I lost a daughter. I won't lose a granddaughter too. I want a different world for Simone. One where she can watch the stars without worrying what waits in the dark. For our sweet Simone, I'd defile my soul and sell it for justice. Over my blood and body will this continue." She turned her steely gaze onto me. "With or without you, Sathos."

The icy claw twitched, unpleasantly scratching my will.

This walked a fine line.

Sensing my unease, Matilda rose and offered me her chair, spinning it to face away from the table. She pointed to it and said, "What we do is beyond your control, right? You haven't seen anything unlawful. We haven't told you how he came to be in our hands. We've broken no law."

Twin sapphire flames burned in her glare—a light against the roaring darkness of the Water Wheel, ready to illuminate the world and expose the monsters in the dark. She pulled out an unadorned iron blade and flipped it in her hand, studying it with deep-rooted loathing.

"Tell us how to get Osrin's weaknesses out of this shitbag. For curiosity's sake, tell us how to make a man hurt."

I could almost see my fated path glowing before me. A step in destroying the monsters plaguing this realm. One step at a time until I reached the final evil that sat on the golden dragon throne.

Until then, the witch on the table would do.

"Have you heard of a penile fracture?" I asked, throwing myself into the deep end of a pond, hoping my swimming reflexes kicked in before the weighted rope of compulsion tied to my foot tightened and dragged us all down.

In the end, the peeping witch had little to offer. He ended up being nothing; a low-level thug, grabbing women and children off the streets as fodder for Osrin's trafficking. He knew little of the inner workings of his operation. Although, amongst Ervik's giggles and Rugard's retching, Matilda forced him to admit the name of a tiny tavern Osrin and his men frequented in a dusty, overlooked corner of the Water Wheel—The Villager's Egg.

A poor start, but a start, nevertheless.

I'd wandered off back to the Onyx Palace to begin a day of sparring, but I'd never managed to eat a breakfast before Matilda interrupted.

The barracks dining hall buzzed with chatter. Each unit of Guard huddled together over breakfast as they prepared for the day. An ache prickled inside, despite my efforts to shove it down. Whatever truce momentarily sprung between us on the tower top, Maddox continued refusing to assign me a unit, and Morgenna had made no motion to care whether I sat on my ass or not.

Not that I blamed Maddox. A Night Guard unit and the trust it required between captain and soldiers was out of the question. For now, I was content to spar and occasionally train pages.

I spotted Yori's familiar warm smile and beamed back. Across from him, sat the Night Prince, sifting through a stack of books with twisted lips like they'd personally offended him by obscuring whatever he searched for. As always, he was fastidiously dressed. His simple lamb's wool pants and tunic were pressed and unwrinkled, his boots polished to a mirror shine.

The perfect portrait of a prince, except . . . Dark stains under his eyes didn't match his clothes. His hair had grown long enough he probably sent the courtiers into a horrified tizzy. While it didn't compare to a Day Witch's, it hung well below his ears, in danger of grazing his shoulders.

Naturally, it only served to make him appear that much more deliciously unapproachable—which never quite worked on me.

I slid onto the bench beside him, knocking my knee into his hip. Only a ticking muscle in his jaw acknowledged me. Few things gave me greater satisfaction than winding him up. The fact he knew it made our twisted game more thrilling.

Humming one of Nik's favorite lewd songs, I squinted and held a fist to Maddox's head.

He shut one book and side-eyed me before opening a crimson-covered one. "Whatever you're doing, go do it somewhere else."

"I can't measure your hair from somewhere else."

"Do I dare ask why you're measuring?"

"Just wondering how easy it would be to pull."

He didn't bother looking up. "About as easy as yours would be, I imagine."

"Is that something you imagine often?"

Bits of bacon exploded from Yori's mouth, raining over his plate and down the table. He thumped a fist against his chest, wheezing something that sounded like, "Can you not? I'm eating."

Maddox yanked his books back from Yori's bacon rapid fire and passed the gasping giant a linen napkin. Ignoring my attempt to spark an argument, he reopened his book. I blew out a frustrated huff, and the subtlest of smirks broke through the mask before his precious book took precedence.

Stradling the bench, I scowled and leaned closer, attempting a peek at the crimson book's contents. I managed a glimpse of what looked like runic translations before he snapped it shut and tossed it onto the bench on his opposite side.

Why was he reading up on runes?

I tried peering over him, stretching across his lap to catch the book's title.

His hand stole around my throat in a rough grip that sent flurries spiraling low into my belly. Squeezing softly, he hissed, "I have zero desire to smell you on me for the rest of the day, Sathos. Go sit *anywhere* else."

Jaw clenched tight enough to break a tooth, he shoved me back.

I let loose a triumphant snicker and scooted back to my spot before pouring myself a cup of tea. The arrogant git doggedly continued insisting he smelled my magic. Nothing I said dissuaded him, and he remained convinced I'd somehow circumvented Morgenna's compulsion.

Across the table, Yori cleared his throat and broke into familiar recitation of Maddox's daily schedule. Maddox reached for the last apple, scowling as he argued with Yori over his morning.

I blocked them out and scanned the table for more fruit, hoping for another apple. They were the last of the season and I'd have to wait ages for another fresh one—*if* I survived until the next harvest.

Without breaking from his conversation, Maddox extended the last apple to me. He didn't turn, deep in an argument about a meeting with a handsy Second Order priestess. I stared at the fruit like it might strike like an adder. He gave it an impatient shake, and, before I changed my mind, I snatched it and took an enormous bite. I didn't know which was odder—the prince who forgot he was a prick or the prince who knew my fixation with apples.

Munching contently, I hooked my toes onto the bench across and leaned back to catch a glimpse of Maddox's books from behind. The crimson one hung partially off the bench and if I leaned a bit further . . . I caught *Translating Runic* something before Maddox slid them from view.

"If you were any more nosy—"

He snapped his mouth shut, and cocked his head to the side as if listening.

Books forgotten, I straightened and searched Maddox for a clue. Across the table, Yori did the same.

The Night Princess kept mostly to the border outposts, returning to the city only when Morgenna summoned her; a choice I didn't mind. The less I saw of the blunt-haired bitch, the better, but if she was willing to reach out to Maddox over their twin bond, her news wasn't good.

Maddox swiveled to me and his lips thinned.

Bells went off in my head, and the soldier in me went numb. One of the first things pages learned was how to disassociate to prepare for whatever came.

He stood and the table of officers went silent.

"We have a situation at the border. All officers to my office, now."

The scraping of all the benches at once nearly drowned summons for pages. Officers rushed for the doors and the rest of the Guard made for the armory.

"You too, Sathos." Maddox grabbed my wrist and hauled me through a river of wide-eyed pages, ignoring my grumblings over my forgotten apple. Of all times to be included . . .

Half an hour later, I perched on Yori's armrest. The vampyres had finally made their move. Melisandre had answered a late-night call for aid from a village in the Blackwood, but by the time her legion reached the village, nothing but drained bodies remained. The vampyres had vanished.

"A whole village dead! The Night Realm's known for months this was coming and did nothing," a haggard captain growled.

"How were we supposed to suspect they'd *drink a village dry*?" Yori said. "Aren't they supposed to prefer humans?"

"Supposedly, according to what we learned at Amethyst Hall, but clearly not true. Fat lot of good school did us and those villagers." The captain banged his fist on the table. Agreement sounded through the office.

I swished my leg back and forth, leather pants against leather chair, building friction—and my growing irritation. I hadn't realized how little the Night Realm knew of vampyres. Like Lilain, Morgenna wanted nothing to do with the continent that exiled witchkind. But unlike the Night Realm's soldiers, the DRAS couldn't ignore the stray vampyres in the Day Realm's Sorrelikah Jungle.

Nik stepped from behind Maddox's chair, determination furrowing his brows. The young guard caught the attention of each officer when he said, "Let's not be rash. What exactly do we know of vampyres?"

Silence reigned until Yori answered, "Not much. They haven't been this far north since—well, not since the fall of the elves. Turn of the millennia, I guess. They don't cross into the Borderlands, certainly not this far north. There aren't any humans in the Night Realm."

"We know they hunt at night. Cursed by the gods to stay out of the sunlight or they'll burn," someone added.

Nodding, Nik rubbed his chin and said, "They prefer human blood to any other Creature. Most remain on Gilgador—few make it to Efelldor. We aren't taught much about them at Amethyst Hall. They remain a part of Gilgadorian history and"—he tossed a wary glance to Maddox—"Queen Morgenna sees no need to learn much about those who exiled us."

They didn't know the vampyres were after *me*. That Lilain sent them in whatever twisted allegiance she gained from them in exchange for my neck she hadn't managed to snap in the goblin ambush. They only knew the sightings at the border had become attacks—a definite provocation.

Witchkind as a whole knew too little of vampyres. Efelldor had been meant for the witches' exile. A few goblin clans and the Nordith elves had been exiled from the continent alongside us for their part in the attempted human genocide. But vampyres? The small part they'd played had cursed them to the night. They remained on Gilgador, save for the few who chased stray humans to the dark jungles of Efelldor, lazy and content to hunt there.

I waited for Maddox to intercede and sprout some plan I'd probably hate, but he'd been oddly silent the majority of the meeting. Most likely stuck in bitter conversation with Melis.

Sensing my gaze, he looked up and grimaced. His drumming fingers paused their staccato beat, flattening on the table. Not for the first time, I wished I read him half as easily as he read me.

Well, if *he* couldn't lead this meeting . . .

"Vampyres prefer human blood because it lacks magic." My feminine voice cut through the male growls, and the room went silent. Every eye found me, daring me to continue. I'd had enough of their puzzling out what should've been obvious. A DRAS airwitch sat amongst them—a cheat sheet to their questions.

I slid from Yori's armchair and stood.

"The higher the being on Creational Order, the more potent our blood. Normally, a vampyr would never touch a witch or elf. Too much magic. It's certain death for them. Think of it like getting high. They overdose on our potent magic and die. Which means"—I pursed my lips and again glanced at Maddox, irritated when he wouldn't look up—"somewhere in the Black-wood there's a heap of dead vampyres. If they drained an entire village of witches—"

"But why?" Nik blurted. "If it means death, why attack at all?"

I tried Maddox again, but this time he was scowling down at the table as if the polished wood spelled out an insult. Oh, to be a fly on the wall of his head and hear what Melis said.

Answering Nik, I waved a hand at the room of powerful Night Witches. "Because before the overdose, they briefly take on the magic of their victim. If you wield shadows, for a short while before they die, they can too. You can veil? So do they. It's a suicidal attack, but it can yield deadly consequences."

Unsurprisingly, the room erupted into howls and more fist banging. These were sons of courtiers, after all. They were used to browbeating their way through anything: goblins, lower Night Witches, each other.

Until now.

"How do *you* know this, Sathos?" someone called out.

I rolled my eyes, begging the Mother to gift powerful witches brains to match. "The Sorrelikah Jungle is in the *Day Realm*. Did you lot think the DRAS never came across a vampyr?"

"You've fought one? *Killed* one?" Nik asked, leaning forward, brows dipping in concern. "Tell us what you know."

"Of course, I have. My first squad was assigned the Sorrelikah Jungle."

Again, the room fell silent, waiting on my next words. This was my chance to convince them I was on their side, that I wanted to help.

Forcing my way through a block in my throat, I paced the stone floors and hoped the movement settled the building storm. "A vampyr's magic is parasitic. They're one step below us in Creational Order which means, yes, they're born less powerful, but only until they've fed on a magical Creature and stolen their magic. Goblins are the easiest targets since their magic isn't potent. They don't have much of it, but a vampyr can build up their magic stores by feeding on dozens of them. And it doesn't fade. Once they retain goblin magic, they keep it."

The outcry threatened to drown my next words, but I held up a hand and to my surprise, they quieted, leaning toward me. "You just need to know they're faster than a nymph, and they *will* outrun you. You'll need every advantage against their speed, like lighter weapons and armor."

More scoffing. I shrugged. The truth didn't change regardless of pride.

"What I don't understand—" I said, more to myself, disregarding the quiet immediately falling at my words. I sank into the empty chair beside Maddox, squinting out the window behind him as I gathered the gale of thoughts storming my head. "Where did they get the numbers to pull off an attack this large?"

Maddox finally spoke. "According to the tracks left behind, they number close to a thousand—a legion."

No one uttered a word. We stared at him in open-mouthed horror.

"There can't be that many in Efelldor," I protested. "Let alone enough to hunt the Night Realm villages. Vampyres in Efelldor are solitary. They're the scum of their Gilgadorian kind. Lazy, idiotic Creatures. Nothing like their brethren on the continent who the humans claim hunt in organized legions."

Blood whooshed from my face, and I jerked to meet Maddox's equally pale stare.

The meetings Lilain had had with vampyres in her cavern.

They weren't vampyres from the jungle. Somehow the Day Queen had brought a legion of Gilgadorian vampyres to Efelldor and hid them in the Blackwood.

"What did she promise them?" Maddox said, quiet enough the officers leaned closer to hear, but I heard the words in between. *In return for finding you, what did Lilain promise?*

It didn't matter. Not yet anyways. I inched closer.

"How does an entire legion disappear? They're faster than us, yes, but not so fast they vanish. Why not stay to finish off the Night Army?"

"It's a message." Maddox sat back, pinching the bridge of his nose. "They're taunting us."

Searching the Guard shifting in their seats, I frowned, wishing I could give better news. For once, I wasn't the villain. "In that case, they will strike again and soon. We need to be prepared. If we split the Night Army among the Blackwood's villages—"

"The general thinks they'll attack tonight," Maddox interrupted. "Her scouts followed tracks to the neighboring village, Nyxinthi, before they lost them. She's requesting several Guard units umbranate to the village at nightfall. Nyxinthi is a large town of children and elderly—we can't risk losing more innocents. And"—he narrowed his eyes on me, fingers once again drumming wildly—"she wants you there, Sathos."

I nodded absently, returning to the window and its clouds. An airwitch who'd fought vampyres before would be instrumental in holding them off. It also played right into the vampyres' hands—and therefore, Lilain's. The brewing storm crackled within, lightning shining on another facet of my predicament. How did I balance the new threat with the Mother's fate?

Or was this fate too?

A little guidance from the gods would have been nice. *Don't fuck up your path, but we can't tell you exactly what's on that path.*

Utterly worthless.

Orders in hand, the officers rushed from the office, calling for their units and pages.

"You realize it's a trap, right?" I called to Maddox when the room had emptied. I couldn't put any bite into my words. "It's an obvious way to draw me in. If we're not careful, we'll play into their hands."

He didn't bother turning from his desk, searching through stacks of paper. "Should I leave Nyxinthi unprotected and hope nothing befalls their innocents? You alone understand what we're up against. Would you prefer to sit back, safe and sound, while others die in your stead?"

The cruel words stung; a sign, perhaps he didn't read me as well as I believed.

Sighing, I folded my arms across the table. I rested my chin on them and watched clouds drift across the cornflower sky in the window. Wispy and quick moving, they would've been a dream to fly through. The autumn-laced air of the Night Realm would send my blood racing, amplifying my fall through the puffy clouds.

"If I could, I would've already died for them," I finally said in a barely audible whisper.

I didn't want to sacrifice myself for a people who would rather choke on glass then touch me. But for the few, like those in the Water Wheel who deserved much more than their own people offered, I would give everything to save the little girls in the proverbial alleys from *all* the monsters coming for them.

"I'm a soldier, Maddox. That was always my purpose—to die for the innocent. *Death* is what I was made for." He had no idea how deeply my words resounded with my fate. Or that I should've been looking for any excuse to stay *away* from battle, if only to live long enough to see my damned fated path through.

Knees slamming into the table's underside, I shot up.

Fated path be damned.

What was the point of saving a realm from a mad queen if there wasn't a realm left to save?

"I was ready to go to Nyxinthi, and I'll yet go on your promise to never question my morality again."

"Alys—"

"Whatever you think of me, correct it now. I'm not going to turn against the Night Realm's innocents." I spun, voice catching. I met his wary gaze evenly, refusing to blink. "I'm not the monster you make me out to be. I would *never* put my life above an innocent's. Don't *ever* question that again."

I carried myself from the office on a torrent of fury and pride. Life had offered little at my birth. Pride and stubborn will were precious, but above even those, I had morality—a rare treasure born from Lilain's cavern of horrors. My conscience wouldn't crumble, not before queens, not before death. Not even before fate.

If I was needed at death's altar, then I would kneel before it with my head high and my sword higher.

21

ALL WITCHES BLEED RED

Alys

S omething about umbranating unsettled me. Long curling swaths of darkness beckoned the Night Guard in the deepening shadows of the barracks courtyard. One by one the witches gathered the abyss and vanished into a sucking whirlwind of black.

I'd spent the last ten minutes gaping at the devouring shadows. Sylinia had explained Night Witches could umbranate across short spaces in daylight, using shallow shadows. But longer distances—such as umbranating to the Blackwood—needed deeper, darker shadows. Like those of nightfall. The darker the shadow, the easier navigation was through them.

I listened for the clocktower's chimes, waiting for Yori or Nik to umbranate me to Nyxinthi, hurrying them on. Each moment waiting churned the roil in my stomach. I paced back and forth, twisting an earring around and around in my lobe. Stealing glances at the snatching shadows didn't quell my apprehension, nor did a quick glance at the tempting sky.

But a snide quip from the prick of a prince at least broke my anxiety-ridden gloom.

"Does it help if I assure you umbranating is better than flying?"

Snorting, I glanced over my shoulder to an approaching Maddox. "Considering you've never flown, you'll understand if I don't take your word for it."

"Shadows versus balancing on a strip of wood a thousand paces in the air? Even a thick-headed witch would recognize which is better."

A grin tugged my lips, but I turned away, searching the courtyard for Nik who'd promised he'd be here soon. My chest remained raw from Maddox's earlier accusation. I wasn't in a mood to tangle with him. Nor admit his earlier words had stung.

"Don't sulk, Sathos." He tugged my arm through his and dragged me to the nearest deep shadow. "Someone might think you're capable of getting your feelings hurt."

"I don't have feelings. Savage Day Witch, remember?" I eyed the approaching shadows and attempted to pry my arm back, but he only pulled harder. "I'm not umbranating with *you*. You're supposed to be the terrifying Night Prince, bearer of awful power, most mysterious and terrible, blah, blah, blah. You might umbranate somewhere secluded and eat me."

He abruptly halted and whirled.

I lurched into the solid wall of his chest, seizing his arms for balance. Righting me, he gripped my shoulders, nose inches from mine. Wide-eyed, I froze. I could've counted each faint freckle scattered across his cheek bones. How had I never noticed those before?

A grin spread over his features, self-satisfied and wicked.

"I might *eat* you?"

Heat exploded through every capillary across my cheeks and into my ears. "That's not what I meant," I tried to hiss.

His distraction worked. Darkness flooded us, ripping the words from my mouth. Vined shadows ensnared our bodies in a paralyzing hold. From the darkness, a thousand screams erupted, shrill and unending in a sound that rattled my brain—the sound a Creature makes before their soul is ripped from their body. Vining shadows grabbed onto my mouth and nose.

I couldn't breathe.

Couldn't scream.

We were falling, careening through everything and nothing.

Panicking, I grappled for the hands clenched around my shoulders. Maddox wouldn't let go. He wouldn't give me to this screaming void, would he?

And then we were in the Blackwood.

I choked out a whimper and wrenched from Maddox. The sound of a village gate screeched close by. Delicious, humid air surged into my lungs. Stumbling onto my knees, I plunged my fingers into the mossy, forest dirt—solid and real.

"What the bleeding Mother was that?" I snapped to the grinning prince. Hands in his pockets, he looked far too pleased with himself. "Did you make it worse on purpose?"

"If only I could."

"It's *always* like that? What's in there?"

He shrugged, glancing toward the village peeking through the trees. "Lost souls? Demons? The Crone herself? No one knows. Anyone foolish enough to wander the shadow plane never returns."

Ears ringing, I shut my eyes and flopped onto my back, willing away the unsteady blur of the world. Shortened travel wasn't worth the horror. Evil waited in the shadow plane, and if I could help it, I wanted nothing to do with what lay in wait.

Something lifted my braid from the ground, raising it high before letting it fall onto my face. I pried one eye open to find my dimachairi hilt inches above me. I slumped back to the ground, groaning with one arm tossed over my head.

"Now what? You haven't toyed with me enough?"

He laughed. The rare, satiny sound made every hair stand on end.

"Get up, Alys. We need to get going."

I hated the way he said my name. Soft and velvety, but with an edge that bordered on a threat. I'd heard it a thousand times from many mouths, but they'd never conjured wild fantasies involving long fingers.

Hating myself, I rose and eyed Maddox. The broadsword hanging off my hip was a behemoth and liable to get me killed. Too heavy and slow, it stole precious time and energy to stave off quicker vampyr attacks.

"What do you want in exchange?" I asked slowly.

His crooked grin evaporated, and he clenched his jaw. He extended the swords again, closing the gap between us. "Nothing. They're a promise."

My words from that morning flooded back. *Promise you'll never question my morality again.* I snatched the swords and pressed them to my chest, savoring the feel of cold steel against my cheek—the feeling of *trust*.

Motioning for me to spin, he unclipped my plain cloak from my shoulders. Before I could protest the cold, he'd tugged something from his bag and tossed it over me. "You make an easy enough target with your long hair. With a Night Guard cloak, you'll blend in better."

The golden embroidery on midnight wool hung heavy around my shoulders. Even more so when I realized two openings in the back had been customized for my dimachairi to slide through.

Turning around, I opened my mouth, but nothing came out. What was I supposed to say to the witch who'd captured me, forced me before his mad queen, and then proceeded to show me a hint of regret?

"Thank you," I managed, my gaze glued to my feet. Two words I'd never thought I'd say to *him*. Maddox shifted his weight and glanced toward the village, as uncomfortable as I was. Eager to dispel the awkwardness, I offered a mocking salute. "I promise to be on my best behavior and not behave like a murderous little demon."

His evident relief washed away the tension between us. The tiniest grin tugged one corner of his mouth. He leaned down, nearly nose to nose. His magic swirled over me in a spicy, delicious wave that had no businesses being that addictive. "You're about to go head-to-head with my *benevolent* sister. Watch what you promise."

"I suppose since you returned my dimachairi, I'll promise not to lop off your sister's head with them." I scrunched my nose like I'd smelled something awful. "Even if justice demands it."

He gently spun me again and helped me into my dimachairi harness beneath the cloak. "You and your morals are undeniably odd, Sathos. I'd say it's because you're a Day Witch, but I think even amongst them you're entirely your own witch."

The elegant clip of his deep voice sank deep into my skin like a warm bath. One day I would get him to read aloud a book, and I already had one in mind—an absolutely filthy one.

I tried refocusing on his words as he strapped the dimachairi harness beneath the Guard cloak, but his touch and his scent were a heady combination. His hands were firm and confident, moving quickly through the buckles. Long fingers skimmed my sides as he worked, sending electric waves with each contact. I swallowed any telltale fantasy threatening to rise and stood utterly still.

Umbranating must've scrambled more than my head.

Over my shoulder, I said, "I've long given up pretending to be something I'm not. I don't give a rat's ass what others think. Unfortunately, that includes you, Prince."

A soft laugh escaped him, and an even rarer full smile followed. Gently, he tucked my braid into the cloak, but a few hairs at the nape of my neck became caught in the hood. Warm fingers pulled them free, brushing against my bare skin. He froze, eyes darting to meet mine over my shoulder.

Mother damn me.

Of all the obstacles to fall in my path, *he* was the worst one. Flirting and bantering was one thing. But I couldn't let *anything* come of it. No, I was fated to a life of secrecy, solitude, and a Mother-fated path he was *not* a part of.

Alone was better.

Focusing on the rotting scent of the Blackwood, I eased from his reach and finished my harness's buckles. I didn't dare meet his eyes, terrified he'd read my emotions like a book. His unsteady exhale said I'd made the right choice. Not for the first time in months, I wondered how much he hid behind his prince's mask.

We entered the village and passed cottages of whitewashed clay, thatched and trimmed like those in Grelgesco. Ghostly silence swallowed the noise of what should've been a bustling village. Children's toys dotted the empty dirt streets lined with abandoned carriages and wagons. The few villagers in the streets shrank away before veering in the opposite direction.

Melisandre and her legion had converted Nyxinthi's only inn into temporary headquarters and its main floor burst with activity. Clanging soldiers in heavy steel armor rattled the clay walls. Pages darted through the chaos, burdened with armor or drink. All of them pinch-faced and scrutinizing me like a worm in their apple.

"I never thought I'd see the day an airwitch was a welcome sight."

I followed the familiar voice to find Melisandre in her Night Army uniform bedecked with the stars of her rank. She cocked her head in a mocking salute, short blonde hair grazing her chin.

"I don't know why," I replied. "You need a superior witch to clean up your mess. Here I am."

Snorting, she waved us into the room behind her. She dropped into a chair behind an ancient desk laden with maps and reports. Bottles of liquor littered the desktop, most empty. A long-stemmed wooden pipe rested in a porcelain tray beside a plate of uneaten fruit. Summoned shadows on a wave of citrus-scented magic pulled out two chairs.

"I hope you have something better than village rumor, Sathos."

Quickly, I explained everything I'd told the Guard, including how to kill them. "Vampyres are easy enough to kill. They need copious amounts of blood pumping through their system to survive. One good slash and they'll bleed out in seconds. Doesn't have to be an artery. If you're fast enough, they're easier to kill than a witch or goblin."

Recalling the jungle witches slaughtered by stray vampyres for pure entertainment, I winced and added, "The trick is getting to them first. Even if they don't feed, one bite carries enough venom to paralyze a witch long enough to finish you off."

"Mother damn me." The princess general rubbed her temples, pulling the skin painfully taut. With a mutter and a flick of her wrist, she spellcasted an iridescent bubble over us, blocking any listeners.

"The tracks indicate one legion's worth, and they lead here to Nyxinthi." She pointed a black-varnished fingernail at her twin. "If his spies are right, then the vampyres are here for our pretty little Day Witch. Luckily for you, Sathos, the queen's made sure we can't give you up."

She grinned and leaned across the desk, dark green eyes roving my new cloak. "Maybe that's not such a bad thing. You're rather fetching in black and gold."

Maddox shifted in his chair, and Melisandre's gaze finally flicked to him. She gave him a cruel smile loaded with a thousand unsaid words only they understood.

"If I can see it, the Night Queen can too. At the first chance, she'll use—"

"What do you want from the Guard?" Maddox cut off her odd warning.

The blonde princess relaxed in her chair, studying me in a calculating manner, like wondering where to start skinning me. "Brief the men, Sathos. Tell them what you've told me. How to kill them, what to watch for, how to avoid another massacre. Then sit around and wait for the axe to fall and hope between you, the army, and the Guard we're enough to block its swing."

She huffed a sigh through her nose, wrinkling her most delicate feature. "What did the queen say about the impending attack?"

Maddox and I exchanged a grimace, recalling the horrified silence that fell over the magistrates at Morgenna's flippant words that afternoon.

"That vampyres are harmless," Maddox said drily. He reached for an apple on Melis's desk, tossing it back and forth between his hands. "Because they're below us in Creational Order, they're no more a bother than an ant beneath our boot. The realm will be fine as long as we do our job and destroy them. Then she went back to playing cards. She's more intrigued to see what Lilain will do next. The vampyres are pawns in whatever game the queens are playing, but I think Lilain plays for far higher stakes than Morgenna realizes."

Melis shrugged. "Politics are a problem for another night."

Shadows leapt over the desk, forming maps midair with icons of troops and villages. More shadows tallied the ratio of troops to the nearby villages facing attacks against the legion of a thousand vampyres.

"We have too many unknowns," Melis muttered, more to herself than Maddox and me. "Why drain the villagers if it means death? Where did they go? How do you hide an entire legion? You can't move that many soldiers and hide their trail."

I frowned at the growing probabilities against us. "If they fed on a village of Night Witches and took their magic—"

"Umbranating is a rare magic outside the most powerful of the Night courtiers," Maddox cut in, scowling at the apple. "I doubt a single witch amongst that village could umbranate. Let alone wield enough magic for an entire legion of vampyres to steal for themselves."

I scrubbed a hand down my face, thinking fast, but the shadowy numbers spun faster, ticking down to certain violence. "To drain a village of witches, a great number of vampyres died. So, where are the bodies?"

"We found nothing, Sathos. I inspected every inch of their tracks myself. Just a line of marching soldiers and then—poof. Nothing."

Maddox tossed me the apple. "Since you didn't eat the other one."

My stomach did a double take.

He settled a frosty glare at the spinning numbers behind a cock-browed Melisandre. "Now, we set a perimeter around Nyxinthi and wait."

N ight came and went. Nothing broke but the soft grumbling of Melisandre's legion and the Guard passing time. At dawn, a frustrated Melisandre left for another village, taking her legion with her but requesting the Night Guard remain.

The twins agreed to split Melisandre's legion amongst the villages in the area. If the vampyres attacked elsewhere, the Night Army was ready. Unless of course, the vampyres waited for Nyxinthi to empty of most of its protectors. All that remained to protect the village were two units of elite Night Guard, but if the legion of vampyres proved to be a trained Gilgadorian army, there wasn't a witch alive who knew if the Guard was enough.

When I told Maddox my suspicions, he shook his head. "It's a risk we take. We can't leave the surrounding villagers exposed either."

"It's another message, a taunt. They're trying to rattle us."

"Then don't let it rattle you, Sathos."

I spent most of the day dozing in a cot or chatting with Yori who'd stuck to my side amidst the growing animosity of frustrated Guard. By evening, I couldn't take anymore sneering or lewd remarks. I left the inn to wander the village, assuring a worried Yori I'd be fine on my own. Villagers stopped and stared when I passed. Sometimes I smiled or waved, but I never received more than a glare in response.

Rude.

Miraculously, Nyxinthi had a tiny bookshop. Most of the books were agricultural but a shelf of fiction caught my eye. Agria Grafeas's romance novels were hard enough to find in Morithia's bookshops, but finding one in the middle of the Blackwood was a treasure I couldn't leave behind.

I climbed to the back balcony of the inn and settled into a poorly sprung chair. My new cloak proved to be warm and indulgent—more so when I swore I caught a whiff of cedar. By the dying light, I read of Mavis and her detailed escapades with a handsome and heavily bestowed sailor. Enthralled with how long Mavis could hold her breath underwater while enjoying her sailor, I didn't hear the door open nor the silent footsteps of the prince who snuck to my side.

"What are you reading?"

Horror punched my gut, forcing out a yelp.

I slammed the book shut and shoved it beneath my legs.

"Nothing. Just an account of . . . aquatic adventures."

He narrowed his gaze onto my hands firmly tucked beneath my legs. I shrank into the rickety chair, heat inching up my neck. It wasn't as if I were ashamed of my reading preferences, but I wasn't foolish enough to give him months' worth of teasing ammunition.

That and I tended to imagine all the main male characters as him.

Maddox as a sailor did strange things to me.

Lifting a single brow, he leaned down and braced his hands on either side of my chair. Shadows brewed from the balcony's corners, slithering to find their summoner. They rose and encased us in a thin, dim bubble of bad ideas and delicious cedar.

"Then why are you hiding it?" His low clipped voice ignited sparks across my skin, setting me on fire inch by inch.

"It's mine. I—I can do what I want."

He leaned impossibly close, his breath brushing my skin. "Are you sure?"

The indifference he wore couldn't hide the black pupils devouring gold-flecked irises. They beckoned, tempting me to close the gap between us. From the way his gaze dipped, I wasn't the only one.

It would be easy. Quick. Then I'd finally know if he tasted like his magic.

In a swift jerk, he angled the chair onto its back legs.

I shrieked, flinging my arms out to the sides to catch myself. The book slid out from my legs and a waiting shadow seized it.

Maddox straightened, dropping the chair onto all fours with a crash. The rickety thing splintered into a dozen pieces, dumping me to the floor. He snatched the book from his faithful shadow and opened it with a crooked, gleeful grin.

I scrambled from the broken chair, but Maddox spun away, flipping to the center of the book where I'd buried my nose. Cursing wildly, I grabbed his waist, swinging around him to lunge for the book. My fingertips had barely reached the edges when he lurched it higher, raising it above his head to read.

"This is absolutely filthy. Although I have to give this Mavis credit for her creativity and stamina." He shot me a grin, taunting and ridiculous, any pretense of indifference long gone. Unfortunately, it didn't do me any favors.

"All right, Prince. What do you want for it?"

His answering lazy smirk released a horde of butterflies, but the book lowered an inch. "What could I possibly want from *you*?"

Stepping close enough to sense his warmth, I raised my chin and softly said, "Whatever you're thinking when you look at me like that."

His eyes widened, and the book lowered another inch.

I summoned the tiny seed of air magic inside me and leapt, seizing the book from his slackened hands. I'd barely let out a shriek of glee when he tackled me. Before I could twist out of reach, he pinned me to his side while reaching for the book with his free hand.

I must have looked utterly ridiculous, screeching and dangling with my feet barely skimming the floor, but I didn't have it in me to care.

His laughter reverberated from his chest pressed against my side, sending the butterflies into disorder. I was drowning in him. His scent. His warmth. Everywhere we touched, the skin beneath layers of clothes fizzed. Something foggy warned this was dangerous. I barely heard it past the energy buzzing through my veins.

Gasping with laughter, I swatted his hand and curled around the novel. "Rather desperate for this book, Prince. Need some help thinking filthy thoughts?"

He laughed again, the kind that made me think of silk whispering across my bare skin. Letting me down, he spun me to face him, but his hands remained very much on my waist. "Careful, Alys. That sounds awfully like a proposition." He leaned down, the gold in his eyes reinviting fantasies I'd been imagining moments before he startled me. "I don't need help thinking explicit thoughts. Trust me when I say they come naturally."

Flushed and warm, I blinked furiously up at him. A dozen retorts died on my tongue. All I could think about was getting trapped somewhere with him and finding out exactly what came naturally. The air felt unusually light. Like I could breathe in a lungful and float into the gold-tinged clouds. Vampyres and fated paths didn't exist there.

But they *did* exist *here,* and the entirety of witchkind depended on me not sabotaging my path over a prince who messed with more than my head.

"I—I should go."

The words extinguished any spark between us.

I jerked from his hands and tugged my cloak tighter, pulling it shut like it might hold me together. "I have the first night watch shift."

Maddox slowly straightened, never pulling his gaze off me. A dark curiosity lingered there, as if he was trying to unravel what was inside me and pull it out for examination. It left me feeling naked and raw, and not in a good way.

"Don't eat anything heavy before your shift. Keep your cloak on and stay near a fire."

Familiar, safe annoyance crept in.

I yanked open the door and scowled back at him. "I've taken night shifts before. I'm well aware of what I should and shouldn't do."

Crossing his arms and leaning against the balcony railing, he smirked and mockingly repeated, "Are you sure?"

No, I wasn't. Not one bit.

The sound of a thousand boots striking the Blackwood shattered the night. At the village gate, I shot to my feet beside Yori, Nik, and Sylinia, our game of cards scattered and forgotten.

I'd been right.

The vampyres had merely waited for Melisandre's legion to clear.

"Alert Prince Maddox so he can summon the general," I commanded Sylinia, careful to keep my voice low and even. I unsheathed my dimachairi with a near-silent ring. "Then find somewhere to hide."

"I can fight," the young page insisted, shoulders back, her hair fiery even in the moonlight. "I've seen battle before. Let me help."

"*No*." I gritted my teeth and tried again. "This is different. Find Maddox, then get the pages to rouse the villagers. Please, Sylinia."

Throwing a final glower toward the tree line, she gathered the darkness and vanished.

I tucked my braid into my tunic and shook out my Night Guard cloak. If the vampyres were hunting me, I wouldn't make their search easy. For this one night, I'd become a Night Witch.

Yori struck a match and lit the lantern hanging above the portcullis—the signal to the Guard and watching villagers. On my mark, Nik released the lever and opened the portcullis to the waiting Blackwood. A spring of spiced cedar swept around me, and Maddox materialized with two captains. He stole a hesitant glance at me with an expression I couldn't decipher before drawing his sword.

As one, the Guard stepped through the gate in ranks. Two units of less than a hundred witches against a thousand vampyres of unknown capabilities. The gate shut behind us in a clatter of iron and steel—the first death knell that would echo into morning.

Guilt twisted like a dagger through my gut. This was my fault. They didn't realize they would die in Lilain's vengeful rampage because of *me*. Not even a Night Witch deserved to die for me.

Cold, granite-white Creatures broke through the soaring pines. The rhythmic thud of their boots echoed against Nyxinthi's walls. As stony as unfeeling marble, they ran in perfect formation without fear or passion—soldiers centered on their objective.

Witchkind once proved to the world why we were held apart from the rest of Creation. Our passion produced both good and evil. The tempest of the Mother's mirrored Creation rose in us, an inferno and storm all at once—we commanded the best and worst of nature's wrath. We would prove it again in the Blackwood.

Our silence rose on a wave of black shadow and broke. As one we launched at the invaders. I took a deep breath, cleared out the world and focused on the battle. Raising my dimachairi, I soared into the clashing bodies. The black wave above us exploded into a thousand strands, striking white marble. My blades sliced into pale flesh, alternating between calling death and guarding it against fanged teeth.

Any doubt of their origins died. These were not the rogue vampyres exiled to Efelldor. Impressive formations and steady ranks cried the might of Gilgador.

Fighting alongside Night Witches became a new madness. I was surrounded by death on shadow and water. Steam hissed in a blood curdling song. Shadow blades splattered gore until we were drenched in inky-black viscera. A lanky guard at my flank summoned a wall of ice and dropped it onto a vampyr with a squelch.

I pushed deeper into the mass, taking unnecessary risks in my vain attempts to stave off witch deaths. But I couldn't be in more than one place at once. I wasn't enough. Panting, I dove between a guard and a stolen vampyr shadow, hacking at black mist. A wavering shadow sliced my neck, narrowly missing my jugular as it split open my cheek.

I couldn't kill, couldn't *protect* fast enough. My arms throbbed in agony; my legs threatened to collapse. A well of vampyres shot from the trees in an endless crush of bodies. Two replaced each one I cut down. Each brimmed with energy I couldn't have matched at the beginning of the night, let alone after a few hours.

Heaving a grunt, I split a vampyr down the middle. A movement behind me forced me to twist and parry. The impact shot pain up my radius and a cry ripped through my throat. Diving, I narrowly avoided the snap of fangs.

A water blade arced into the neck of my attacker, forcing head from body. I nodded thanks to my savior.

The young guard grinned with a little salute. He never saw the sword. His head slid to the side, grin frozen in place.

Bright red vampyr irises met mine behind the headless body.

Great, gasping breaths seized my lungs.

I couldn't scream—but I could charge.

The dimachairi scissored and sliced through vampyr neck. Blood sprayed. More bodies fell in a bloody haze. I kept hacking, haunted by the young guard's frozen smile.

White marble vampyres surrounded me, lunging in the slick mud. I'd pushed too deep into the trees. I needed to retreat. Find someone to guard my back. I'd lost everyone in the fray.

Where was Yori? Nik? Maddox?

No, they were powerful witches who had fought before. They'd be fine.

I couldn't lose focus.

Squinting against stinging sweat and blood, I darted through the fallen bodies and magic. Everywhere I looked, vampyres feasted on witches, their motionless bodies slumped in vampyr arms. I couldn't differentiate stolen magic from witch.

But the vampyres weren't dying.

Lips and chins painted red, they gorged on blood without consequence. Pilfered magic pushed us aside like flowers in a field. Our lines began falling to the blood-empowered vampyres. It didn't take long to realize we were being corralled to the village gate.

At least there we stood a better chance with the wall at our backs.

I screamed for the Guard to fall back—my voice hoarse as I called to re-group at the gates. In the Blackwood, we were easy prey, picked off amongst the darkened trees.

Swallowing nausea from both pain and horror, I forced my way through carnage until the gate came into view. Only a few trees littered with bodies at the base of their trunks remained in my way.

I could make it.

A body caught my foot, and my windmilling arms barely saved my balance. The lifeless, dark-haired witch was propped against a tree, facing away from me to reveal a neck ripped open.

My soul wretched from my body in an awful agony.

Not like this.

My every nerve screaming in protest and horror, I dropped to my knees and flipped the head toward me.

I nearly vomited.

It wasn't Maddox.

I scrambled upright and ran for the gate.

As I hurtled through the thinning forest, I searched every lifeless face along the way. There weren't enough guards. We were going to die, and the village would fall. I ducked beneath swords, sinking dimachairi into flesh when I couldn't dodge fast enough.

Feeling as if I crawled through time, I searched for the prince, for the familiar shadows darker than any others.

We needed help.

With draining magic, it wouldn't be long until only our heavy weaponry faced a nimbler enemy. The plan was always for Maddox to call for Melisandre should the vampyres attack. We had to hold long enough for her legion to gather and return, but without the Guard's umbranation magic, the weaker Night Army could take hours. If the vampyres smashed through the village gates before Melisandre arrived . . .

I urged my legs to run faster.

His midnight hair was impossible to spot in the darkness, but I followed the black waves of power thicker than anyone else's until I found the prince.

Maddox met my eyes over the falling head of a vampyr, black blood heavily smeared down one side of his face. My heart stuttered in recognition of how fragile his life was. Power didn't mean anything if you were dead.

Eyes narrowed, he swooped his gaze over my body, slowing over the bleeding gash at my neck.

Scrambling to his side, I shouted, "Call for retreat! We're outnumbered in the trees. Call them back to the gate!" A pair of fangs snapped inches from my neck. I leapt sideways and sliced. "The entire vampyr legion will be at the gate within half an hour. The Guard's magic won't hold until dawn. We need Melis *now*."

He ducked beneath a strike, parried another before swinging his broadsword high in the air. Face tight, he ripped through a spine with the blade and tore the head from another with a spiked net of shadow. He signaled a waiting page beyond the gate, and the boy scampered.

Seconds later, the horn of retreat blared through the striking steel and screams.

A line of vampyres rushed the gap left by those Maddox killed.

I lunged and took down two, narrowly avoiding his arcing shadow slicing through another.

The look he threw me could've flayed every vampyr in the Blackwood.

"We *have* to hold out," he snapped, shoving a slumped corpse off him. He wiped a new trickle of blood from his forehead, jaw gritted tight. "Melis says she needs an hour."

I shook my head and buried a blade into a vampyr mouth, ripping sideways through his skull. My sword clashed against Maddox's as we struck toward the same target. He narrowly avoided striking me instead.

Snarling a curse, he grabbed my arm and wrenched me behind him. Shadows exploded from the ground and ripped apart our target.

Hands on my knees, I gulped in heaving breaths. "We don't *have* a fucking hour."

Another horn, this one deep in the forest like a banshee's wail, sent the remaining vampyres whirling back into the trees where they began regrouping. Their retreat meant we were trapped between the closed gates and a legion of magic infected vampyres, waiting for the final falling axe.

A few staggering guards pushed past them, running for the village.

Nik and Yori appeared among the stragglers, racing across the slick grass on wobbling legs. The younger guard skidded to a stop and asked me through labored panting, "Sylinia's behind the gate?"

I'd barely nodded when I spotted a massive limping guard supporting two sagging others. It was the blond giant I'd fought in Morgenna's challenge. Ivory bone gleamed at his knee.

"Open the gate," he roared. "We have wounded."

"No!" I snarled back.

Bad enough I bore the blood of dead guards, I wouldn't sentence innocents to die.

Angling myself between the blond giant and the gate, I bared my teeth. "If we go in, we leave the wall and gate open to attack, and there are *children* inside." I gestured to the splintering lumber, held up by runes alone. It wouldn't last long against stolen magic. "That gate is the final line. It *cannot* fall. We hold out and draw their attack until the general arrives."

The blond growled and made to shove past me, but Maddox's shadow reared and forced him to halt.

"The gate stays shut." Maddox gestured for someone to heal the blond giant before moving to inspect the sorry remains of the Guard surrounding him. "We hold out as long as we can. When the general arrives, we retreat inside. Until then, we are all that stands between the innocents and the threat to our realm."

Sylinia peered from the other side of the portcullis, ashen but steely-eyed. Without breaking his usual calm, Maddox instructed her, "Make the villagers aware a breach *may* be imminent. *Do not* alarm them."

The page nodded once and took off into Nyxinthi.

Like another banshee screech, a high-pitched horn sounded from the forest, and in a swarm, the vampyres poured from the trees.

The remaining Night Guard stiffened, but as one we raised swords on shaking arms and looked the incoming horde dead on. If this was the end, then at least we'd make it one worth remembering.

I hoped the Mother's other fated five knew what they were doing.

From this point on, they were on their own.

Magic fell upon us in a punishing sheet of stolen magic. Biting shadows ripped flesh, water held us down and drowned. Chaos and screams became a dull roar through the constant shrill of swords.

Up, down. Slash, parry.

Again and again.

My aching wrists could barely hold up my swords, my arms begging me to let go. I tried to parry the flying sword aimed at my side. Steel buried past skin and muscle. The burning in my throat when I screamed was nothing to the fire coursing hot and bright in my side.

I ripped out the blade and slashed. On shaky legs, I fought past the burn, past the dizziness.

Focus. Stay alive a bit longer, I chanted with each sword thrust and parry.

And then a pink ray of dawn appeared.

The soft light sliced deeper than any blade through the treetops. As one, the vampyres shrieked and dropped their attack. They took off deep into the Blackwood in a hailstorm of stolen magic and defeat.

A far-off horn of reinforcement broke with the morning light, but Melisandre was too late and the vampyres were gone.

22

HOW MUCH IS A DAY WITCH WORTH

Alys

At the night's start, a hundred men stepped through the village gates. Less than half returned. For what? We hadn't wiped the vampyr threat. They snuck through the realm with newly stolen magic, lost and loosed upon the innocents. Sure, now we knew what they were capable of, of their continental origins, but fat lot of good that did if we remained blind to their next attack.

Desperate for designated healers arriving from Morithia and the promise of a warm bath, the Night Guard hobbled into a bleary Nyxinthi. Bleeding gashes crisscrossed every exposed inch of me. My red blood merged with black in morbid art across my armor. Refusing Nik and Yori's offers to carry me, I limped into the healer tent with a kidney threatening to fall out. At least I'd avoided the vampyr bites ringing the necks of too many Guard.

Healed and bathed, I hurried to find Yori amongst the inn of exhausted witches. Melisandre's office was a hothouse of angry witches venting their frustrations. I squeezed between a burly guard and a scowling Nik and listened.

The Night Army's trackers were sent to follow vampyr trails northward but like before, they ended in a sudden stop. We were back where we'd been the night before, waiting for the next attack. Through an angry tirade of shattered liquor bottles and curses, Melisandre commanded her army's more powerful officers to split up and patrol villages between here and Morithia, with hope of at least one umbranating for reinforcements should an attack occur.

I understood Melisandre's frustration. The pathetic plan wasn't much, like holding a stab wound shut with bare hands, knowing we only prevented the inevitable.

"Godsdamned pointless," Melisandre muttered. She began pacing and caught my frown. Mirroring my dark expression, she waved everyone from the office, save for Maddox and Yori. Throwing a sound encasing bubble around us, she demanded, "How would Lilain have contact with Gilgador? What are you hiding?"

Well, that hadn't taken long. Who better to use as scapegoat than a Day Witch?

I folded my arms tightly over my chest. "The last I knew, she wanted nothing to do with Gilgador. It's not as if I was privy to her schemes."

"Lilain physically *can't* step foot on Gilgador," Yori broke in, taking place beside me, a calming balance to Melisandre's ire. "No witch can, or we'd have left this godsforsaken island centuries ago."

From his place against the wall, Maddox shook his head, strands of damp hair curling beneath his ears. "That doesn't mean those from the continent can't reach Efelldor. Think of how easy it is for humans or stray vampyres to reach our shores. If the vampyres reached out to Lilain first—"

"She'd seize the opportunity to manipulate them," I finished with a groan.

Melisandre rubbed her temples and released a curse even I raised brows at. "Then is this truly Lilain's war against the Night Queen or do the vampyres have their own agenda? Are you the target or not, Sathos?"

Maddox interrupted the fight he no doubt sensed brewing between his sister and me with a terse, "We're not solving anything this way. Go rest before umbranating to Morithia. Gods know what mood we'll find Morgenna in."

When evening arrived, I looped my arm through Sylinia's and tried not to vomit through the shadow plane. She landed us in the only wardless area in the palace—the barracks courtyard. Protective wards provided a shield to the rest of the palace save for this one space. Even the city had wards to prevent invasions. None as powerful as Morgenna's wards on the Onyx Palace.

Declining Sylinia's attempts to cheer me with a trip to the tavern, I found my way to the barracks' dining hall instead. In the empty hall, I poured myself a steaming cup of tea, wondering how I'd lived this long without the brew. Downing the whole cup, I relished its burning trail. I considered pouring Maddox's not-so-secret stash of whiskey into the next cup when quick footsteps broke my lonely gloom.

Melisandre loomed over my table, for once stone-cold sober and without a nasty quip. Her catlike eyes pinched at the corners, she stood as if a board had been nailed to her spine. "The queen summons all officers who were at Nyxinthi, including you, Sathos."

I should've started with liquor in the first cup.

As we walked to the domed throne room, Melisandre cleared her throat. "I've heard what you did for Nyxinthi, how you refused to let them open the gate. For what it's worth, thank you. I still think we should toss you to Lilain." She offered me a half-grin before sobering. "But I'm grateful for your help. We'd be dead without your guidance. Although, it may not mean anything when the queen's done with us. You're about to discover what lies behind her smiles."

We entered the throne room to a heavy silence. The usual crowd of simpering courtiers had gone. Only the magistrates, the highest of Night lords remained. Each of them hovered beside Morgenna's throne, wary of her reach. One of them, a sharp-nosed fellow with keen eyes, almost looked remorseful.

Gods, if a magistrate felt sorry for me, this evening didn't bode well.

The moment my boot found the golden rug, Morgenna's fury swept over me in a blast of Night power, its awful scent of roses, cloying and pungent. Her shadows dove, only to split around me and slam the doors shut.

I kept my face blank. I'd endured Lilain's wrath for years. I could handle one night of Morgenna's.

The Night Queen sat balanced on the edge of her throne, pink-varnished nails clicking against a golden dragon armrest. Behind her, the stars peered through glass walls. Their twinkling lights seemed eager to witness whatever was unfolding—a show Lilain deprived them of in her underground cavern. In this glass cage, Morgenna hid nothing.

Maddox and two captains waited before the throne, Yori not far behind. The gentle giant's wide amber eyes mirrored my rising panic. Maddox hadn't pulled his gaze from the queen, utterly blank without even his typical indifference—which was perhaps the most terrifying foreshadowing of the evening.

"Tell me, General," Morgenna began without preamble, sliding one thin finger down the dragon's snout. "Did you succeed in vanquishing every last vampyr?"

Melisandre clenched a trembling hand into a fist. The corners of the throne room pulsed, begging their princess to summon them. Maddox's shadow turned to her. A finger of darkness snaked for her before halting at her feet.

The act of rare solidarity didn't reassure her—nor me.

"No, My Queen," she whispered to the rug. "Unforeseen circumstances prevented—"

"I do not want excuses, Melisandre. Did you or did you not slaughter the vampyres?"

The shadow at her feet circled, as if ready to catch her.

"We did not."

"And you, Commander of the Guard," the queen purred to Maddox. The shadow snapped back to mirror his ramrod straight posture. "Do you bear some sad tale of an excuse for your failure?"

"No."

More ice frosted the single word than compulsion itself.

Morgenna smiled, unbothered. "Are you aware of Creational Order?"

Maddox jerked a nod.

"You understand we witches are *above* vampyres? More powerful, more blessed by the Creationist herself. Yes? Then you *must* understand my disappointment in your failure to rid my realm of them. How weak we must appear to the might of the DRAS who do not fail *their* queen to be rid of these pests."

I stiffened into stone. Beside me, Yori did the same.

We were pawns who'd spoiled her game with Lilain. She didn't care about lives lost, or the nearly obliterated village. She didn't care vampyres roamed her realm, risking more innocents. Our failure to drive them out made her look weak against Lilain. Only her crushed pride rankled her, not guilt.

"We were not prepared for their efficiency nor their unusual nature in siphoning our magic without consequence," Maddox said. Each slow, measured word spoke of years stepping around her vacillating moods. "While we are superior in combat and sword, they proved too swift. Advanced strategy and magic doesn't make up for our lack of speed. With planning, the next time—"

"The *next* time?" Morgenna threw her head back and laughed. "Oh, Prince Maddox. You do not understand." Quicker than I could follow, she shot in front of Maddox, baring her teeth inches from him in a savage smile. "There never should have been a *next time*, boy."

Maddox may have towered over her, but drumming fingers spoke to the great effort of remaining frozen.

Neither of them blinked.

Clenching my hands, I willed myself to remain in place. He knew how to ride out her swinging moods. Surely, this wasn't the first time he'd suffered her anger.

He would be fine.

In a low measured tone, he finally said, "For that I am most sorry, My Queen. I cannot atone for my mistakes and failures."

"No? But could another atone for them?"

Every long line of his body went motionless, and something cracked in his expressionless façade—no more than a blink's worth of telltale panic.

"Fear not." She patted his cheek. "Atonement is within reach. Perhaps we should follow Queen Lilain's example. Using one witch to punish another has proven effective for her. Shall we watch my favorite drama open to the second act?"

His shadow lurched almost as quickly as he did, but Morgenna's shadowy eels were ready. One wrapped around his chest and restrained his arms to his sides. Another wrenched shut his mouth, silencing whatever warning he'd been about to call out. A third pinned down the shadow racing across the golden carpet, wrestling it motionless at my feet.

Dread pooled in my lungs.

Black eyes glowing silver, Morgenna pointed to the twins. "*Neither of you will move from your positions. Nor will you speak. You will only watch.*" She smiled prettily, releasing shadows from a frozen Maddox. "And perhaps last night's mistakes need not repeat."

Compulsion's silver glow faded from the depthless black pools and latched onto me.

Who better to be the whipping girl than the Day Witch?

"Captain Sathos," Morgenna called, sweet and mild. She could've been ordering tea. "Please, come closer. No, closer still, to the edge of the dais for a better view."

Sluggish blood forced its way through my body, heart churning fear through every vein.

With poisoned sweetness, Morgenna asked Yori to step forward. Glowing eyes forced him to hand over his dagger. The massive trembling hand twitched, but Morgenna wrapped dainty fingers around the hilt.

You can handle whatever she throws at you, I pleaded with myself. *It can't be worse than a blood boil spellcast.*

"Closer, please, Captain Sathos," the queen called. Dark lashes fluttered against pale cheeks, shadow against light. Night against Day.

"*You will take this dagger and plunge it into your heart.*"

No amount of stubborn will could fight the tundra washing over me.

I may have been a temporary pawn between Lilain and Morgenna, but I remained a magicless Day Witch. Disposable and pointless. Nothing more than a lesson served for more powerful witches. They didn't care if I died, I was merely Morgenna's example.

You want the dagger, the icy voice crooned, destroying rationality.

I reached for it, mind hazy, trying to push through the block of ice. This was wrong—wasn't it? Curling my hand over the hilt, I stared at the razor thin edge. I didn't want to die. I had a fated path, but what was it? My trembling hand rose higher. The onyx hilt caught the candlelight, gleaming like the night sky behind it.

You want to die, the cold chanted.

I plunged the dagger down.

A wet crunch splintered bone and flesh. Breathing morphed into fire. My skin, my lungs—everything burned in the blaze radiating from the dagger. I tried to gasp but the sound wouldn't come. Swaying, I watched a gush of blood swarm the onyx hilt, down the black and gold of my cloak and onto the floors. Red spilling onto black, matching the specks dotting my vision.

I sank into a kneel before slumping into a growing crimson puddle. I wasn't a whipping girl—I was a threat.

A dead reminder to those who would cross Morgenna.

Silver light flashed behind the queen, and a black hole began forming from the light's center. Shimmering silver flames engulfed the figure of a woman stepping from the abyss. Skeletal and ancient, the goddess of death strode into our world. Silver hair peeked from her dingy hooded robe. Nearly white irises threatened to disappear into the whites of her eyes, as colorless as the rest of her.

My wet laugh rattled my bones in a defiant gasp.

The Crone—the Mother's sister and ruler of the Soul Lands—peered down, a curious frown creasing a face more bone than flesh.

On the dais, Morgenna taunted the twins, her words lost to the fog swallowing my senses. I tried to look back, to find Maddox or Yori. Even a magistrate would've been welcome. Anyone to prove I wasn't imagining the Crone.

Of course, only I could see her.

She'd come to collect *my* dying soul.

In a coarse voice of bone against bone, she said, "Together, we shall see if your soul is mine to reap. This next thread in the tapestry of your fate is not yours to weave. You must hope another weaver chooses the right thread. It is the bane of life to understand our fate does not belong entirely to us."

She twisted her spindly neck to watch Morgenna. An eerie smirk that belonged on a much younger face stretched bloodless lips. Whatever intention she read in Morgenna drew a raspy snicker. Without warning she bloomed into a silver flame. Another black hole appeared behind her and sucked in the flame, leaving nothing behind but the scent of musty waters.

Wait, was I going to live or not?

The haze of losing too much blood thickened. The puddle beneath became a river, spilling my life onto the floors. My eyelids became too much of a burden to hold open.

Life wasn't up to me. I was dying, and I couldn't do anything about it.

I'd failed my path, and it had passed to another.

"I warned you," Morgenna was softly saying. "You know how this ends. *You are released.*"

Something slid beside me, splashing blood onto my jaw. A hand flattened against my stomach. Another pulled at the dagger.

The dam burst and blood filled my lungs. Eyes flying open, I gasped for air.

Choking. Gasping. Gagging.

Blood spilled from my mouth, my nose.

I was drowning.

Spiced cedar, stark against the rich taste of iron, filled my body. Maddox was saying something—no—yelling for Morgenna to release Melisandre. Dimly, I recognized I'd never heard him yell.

A painful ache erupted in my chest. He'd shoved his fingers into the jagged cavity. More magic blazed into me. I could feel him *in* my soul, a strange warmth both soothing and wholly foreign.

It wasn't enough.

Oblivion glittered beyond reach, holding out arms and promising rest. I wanted to snatch it and never wake up weary again.

"No, no, no. Don't you dare let go, Sathos," Maddox hissed. His unfamiliar panic spilled into his magic, sharp and broken. A sticky hand cupped my face. The smooth voice I'd come to known as unflappable, fractured on a whispered plea. "Open your eyes. Do not let her win. Please."

But I already had.

23

OBLIVION'S CALL

Alys

I lingered on a strange precipice of living and dead, teetering toward one side and then the other. I had no body, only a curious sphere of writhing fog. The sphere was threaded with silver and gold, catching light I couldn't pinpoint. Images shimmered within the fog. A barefoot girl running through sandy streets. The same wide-eyed girl, a little older in an alley clutching a book. A woman kneeling on a golden carpet—the same golden carpet below the sphere.

No, not a sphere—my soul.

I peered down at the scene unfolding below.

Morgenna sat on her throne, one leg crossed over the other, dainty slipper swinging back and forth.

Again, the prince stuck his fingers into that rip in what remained of my mortal body. He wasn't doing a good job healing me. But then, he'd once told me he couldn't heal much beyond broken bones—his magic's one weakness—yet he wouldn't let me die.

Connected by a cedar-scented tether from his healing spellcast, my soul barely held onto my body. The tether had begun fraying, releasing my soul one wispy strand at a time. Oblivion's call grew louder with each torn strand.

What did it matter if I died? Didn't I deserve rest? Wasn't that a soldier's final compensation for a life of sacrifice?

Tittering laughter flung me toward the living side, once again balanced on a precipice. The flimsy sound tugged at something pointed within—a memory of an onyx hilt held high.

Morgenna pointed to Melisandre with silvery glowing eyes and the blonde princess jolted from her compelled stillness to scramble on all fours to my side. Slipping in my blood, she grasped her twin's hand and plunged their joined fingers into my broken body.

The tang of citrus anchored onto the cedar tether. Together, the two magics wove a delicate chain, threading in and out of the rip in my mortal body.

I dared a glance at Morgenna, and the pointed thing inside me sharpened. Greed curled the edges of her mouth, a preening sneer over the incredible power she controlled with mere words. She alone commanded the greatest threat to her throne.

With a crack, my soul whizzed down the solid tether and faded into my body. Darkness blinded me for a split second, and then my senses burst from within.

The light of the stars beyond the glass became blinding. Dozens of magics rushed up my nostrils. Every nerve tingled with pent-up energy, blaring to erupt.

I was going to live.

Live and destroy the hungry animal sitting on the throne.

Destroy the domed cage above.

A weak laugh burst from me in a greedy attempt for life-giving air. The arms holding me shifted into a painful crush, and I found Maddox's terrified gaze.

How had I ever thought he was cold? Only warmth like a fireplace after a frigid, long flight beamed from the sparkling gold lights, brighter than even the stars beyond him.

Something lifted its head inside me, a hopeful sort of curiosity. Before I could pinpoint what waited in that lovely warmth, my exhausted body took over and darkness flooded everything.

24

WHAT HIDES IN THE DARK

Alys

Waking up in my bed to a new scar wasn't shocking. For a Day Witch under Lilain's bloodthirsty court, it was simply another morning. I was the disposable Day Witch used as a reminder of the Night Realm's true power. Of course, I'd been the scapegoat.

Hardly surprising.

What *was* surprising was the gaggle of Night Witches fluttering over my bed like I might keel over any moment. Yori and Sylinia were the worst. They fussed and mothered me, bringing me meals, begging me to open up about how I felt. *Nothing* wasn't an acceptable answer—no matter how true.

Even Nik showed up with a small stack of books. "Something to pass the time. Wouldn't want you turning on Yori or Syl in boredom." He'd tried to it play off as nothing more than an errand, but I didn't fail to notice he'd brought me books by my favorite novelist, Agria Grafeas.

Or that Sylinia's cheeks went pink at the new pet name.

On the second day, Melisandre briefly stopped by with Yori. I spent the entire time gaping before demanding to know if she'd come to finish me off. She'd snorted, then drawled, "I saved your life, Sathos. You owe me, and you can guarantee I'm going to call my favor in when you least expect it."

Maddox never stopped in.

Not that I was shocked. As if the Night Prince had time for his captive who had a hard time staying alive, but he *had* helped save me. Again. I should've been satisfied. Against my better judgment, the foolish hope he'd appear never quite vanished. Another pointless fantasy.

By the third day, I was beyond bored and bordering on trapped. I felt fine, mentally and physically. Gratitude toward my two nurses—or captors—had fled. Threatening to dump the next bowl of tasteless broth over their heads, I shooed them from my rooms. I dressed in a soft woolen tunic and threw on a plain black cloak, immediately feeling more like myself.

Hurrying down to the city below, I thought through the one thing that *had* bothered me about Morgenna's compulsion to kill myself—the compulsion itself.

In my arrogance, I'd come to rely on wit to outmaneuver Morgenna's compulsion. If I could heal her city, perhaps I'd turn them against her without lifting a compelled finger myself. Compulsion loopholes wouldn't be enough. I had to correct the power dynamic and find something to destroy Morgenna *and* her compulsion.

The Mother claimed I'd find power.

Maybe she *hadn't* meant metaphorically. But that would have to wait. For now, the Water Wheel and its people took precedence.

The Quies River smelled unusually foul, like an entire wagon of dirty baby nappies had been dumped into the water. Holding my nose, I angled from the river, ready to sprint for the Dueling Dragons tavern, but a tempting alley caught my eye. Weighing prolonged shitty air over the dangerous shortcut, I chose the shortcut.

The narrow alley was empty save for an old man passed out in a puddle of gods-knew-what. Stepping over him, I scurried between crates and broken glass, anxious to pass before someone stepped into the alley.

I'd nearly made it through when a door ahead of me opened. A hooded figure stepped out. Inwardly cursing my bad luck, I halted. The witch hadn't yet seen me. Without glancing backward, they hurried toward the alley's exit.

Relieved, I followed. We'd made it all of two paces before they straightened and whirled. I had a second to leap back, crashing into a barrel of mead. I caught sight of the face beneath the hood and relaxed against the foul-smelling barrel.

"Gods, you startled me," I snapped at Maddox, peeling from the barrel.

"*You* were sneaking up on *me*."

"No, *I* was here first. You stepped in front of me."

He flicked his hood back, releasing a surge of spiced cedar with his thick sooty waves. Shaking his head with a small grin, he took a step toward me then hesitated.

Features tightening, he leaned back with a faint sneer.

What had he been doing down here?

Cloaked and hooded, he'd stepped from a tannery owned by Hectir Albanox, a lethal crony of Ervik's. I studied him, wishing for the thousandth time I knew what ran through his head.

Reaching up to adjust an earring with a tentative smile, I said, "Yori claims you carried me to my rooms the other night. At this point thanking you for saving my life is going to become annoyingly commonplace. One of these times you should just let me die."

From his scowl and the quick step he took backward, I would've thought I'd told him he smelled worse than the river. He took another step back, icy disinterest firmly in place. My smile faded.

Did *I* smell worse than the river?

Any trace of his panic I'd seen in Morgenna's throne room had vanished, which meant I'd probably imagined it—to be fair, I'd been half-dead. Instead, icy disinterest, more rigid than ever, frosted his expression.

He shoved his hands into his pockets and snapped, "I'm in a hurry for something important, Sathos. Is there a point to this?"

I blinked.

Something important.

Clearly not me.

How foolish I'd been to think I was anything more than a thorn in his side he was forced to bear. Everything between us was in my head, and maybe that was better. After all, I had the Mother pounding at my door, urging me onto my path. *He* wasn't on it.

Forcing a grin—a damned shield against the prickling hurt I couldn't altogether block—I dryly said, "Forgive me for keeping you, *Your Highness*."

I bent into a dramatic bow Elenna would've been proud of. He didn't move, icy scorn permanently etched over his stupid, perfect face. Scoffing, I shoved past him onto the dingy district square.

Idiot.

Every head in the Dueling Dragons snapped to attention when I slammed the door. Wary stares followed me as I stomped toward the bar where Simone and another young girl were washing tankards. "You two. Upstairs."

The compulsion swimming in the glacial waters of my head slept on. Unaware and untriggered. I wasn't fighting Osrin, after all. I was serving the Night Realm's most vulnerable subjects. Holding tight to that thought, I slipped between Morgenna's words.

Matilda rose from a table, sweeping coins into a leather pouch. "Simone," she called to her granddaughter. Determination rivaling the fiercest guard in battle crept over her. "Pay attention to Sathos like your life depends on it."

Simone followed me to an empty room. She'd barely shut the door when I lunged and yanked her head backward by her hair. She screamed and clawed at my grip. Terror became mewling whimpers. Her hair began ripping in her efforts to free herself.

"What now, Simone?" I growled into her ear. "How do you make me let go?"

Her nails dug into the thin skin at my wrist, but I tightened my hold. Whimpering, she tried stomping on my feet, but I barely felt it. I pulled harder, twisting her neck into a painful angle.

"Grab my wrist and force your elbow over mine. Good, now drop to a crouch."

She did as I asked, hissing when the motion ripped more strands from her scalp. I let her pull me down, loosening my grip when her elbow strained my tendons.

"Pull my arm up. Hard."

The painful crack forced a grunt from me, but it was enough to fade her fear. The small sound offered a new power she'd never held. Through her sniffles, a new hunger blossomed. One that wanted to hold her newly discovered power high like a severed head and show the world *she* was the one to be feared.

Stretching the kink out of my shoulder, I rose and pointed to the other girl, a trembling blonde thing with huge watery eyes. "Now you, Jorlenne."

"**J**orlenne's mother says another family was found dead in the Blackwood."

I frowned at Matilda sitting across a worn tavern table as she read from the delivered letter.

"*Another* family?"

Beside Matilda, Rugard watched Ervik teach Simone how to spellcast simple healing onto her battered friend. Each girl shone bright with purple bruises and triumph, ready for more.

Rugard's pride was tangible in the musty air, even as he said, "Happens every so often. Rumor has it Night Witches shack up with a mistress or some forbidden love and hide out in the Blackwood. They raise their bastards there, away from judgment. Years might go by, but eventually they turn up dead, killed by a nymph. Whole family dies. That's why living alone in the Blackwood is damned foolish."

Matilda folded the letter into neat square and tucked it into her apron. "The Blackwood beast is no nymph. Kills too cleanly. And it's no accident. Whatever it is, I think Morgenna commands it. She can't fathom the idea of a Night Witch living beyond her control. The beast is just another Osrin Atercruor, a weapon to control her people. But we aim to change that."

Ervik swaggered to the table and dropped into a rickety chair. "With Sathos's help we'll scope out that tavern the perv gave us, the Villager's Egg, and find another creep there. We—ahem—*question* him on Osrin's schedule and plan our next move."

"Careful," Rugard rumbled. He rubbed the stubble on his chin with a beefy hand as he watched Simone. If anyone had something to lose, it was him. "We have one chance. If we fail, he'll turn on us quicker than the slippery adder he is."

"Then we take every precaution," I said, wary of the ice stirring in my head. "We plan carefully and don't take unnecessary risks. We learn everything about his routine and from there . . ." I let the meaning dangle in the air.

"I'll do it," Ervik said, teeth glinting too white. "I'll *finish* the plan. I know about a hundred men eager to *finish* Osrin's goons apart the moment he's gone, too."

"No." Matilda pulled a knife from beneath her apron. She set her trusty unadorned iron blade on the table, studying it as if it were a rat in her tavern. "Not you, Ervik. There are too many women in this district diseased by injustice. We learn his routine and *I'll* take care of the rest. No one will ever know of Sathos's involvement. We women hold secrets tighter than any adder's grip. Let the rest of the city think she's simply teaching the women to defend themselves."

And so it went; I taught the girls and, one by one, the girls' bourgeoning confidence lured in the city's worst monsters, prime fodder for Matilda's *questions* while I turned a literal blind eye. Perhaps that's how I found myself squinting at the Quies River as I did my best not to question the origins of the screams behind me.

Maybe the screams came from the man under Matilda's knife. Maybe not. Or perhaps they were a product of Rugard's insistent growls for Osrin Atercruor's weaknesses. Perhaps I misinterpreted the screams altogether and they weren't the tortured sounds of one of Osrin's cronies. Maybe they were screams of twisted pleasure. Mother only knew what was happening behind me.

It wasn't as if I could see.

The icy tendril curling around my will hesitated, unable to make sense of my thoughts and what I saw—the mouth of the Quies River as it entered the city through the wall's massive grate. Nothing criminal there. The screams could've meant anything. Perhaps evil and justice blurring in revenge's brushstroke. Maybe not.

The screams fell silent, and Matilda appeared in my periphery, wiping her hands against a black linen apron. "You know that nervous little thing Simone runs with? The blonde one? Jorlenne?"

I nodded. Quicker than the rest, Jorlenne had picked up a dagger first and thrown it with an ease Ervik envied. But the quivering lower lip never stopped—a result of being her mother's only surviving child after losing three sisters to Osrin.

"Osrin wants her. Been eyeballing her for weeks now, but her mother only lets her out under her careful eye. Or mine."

"She's *sixteen*," I hissed, horror roiling my gut. Understanding where Matilda's thoughts headed, I spun and seized her arms. "No. We're not using the girl as bait. It's dangerous and goes against the very principle of who we're protecting."

"It's exactly in line with our principle." Matilda eyed something behind me and tugged me from the river's view. "Save many with one. Besides, we're not sacrificing Jorlenne."

Something splashed into the Quies and Ervik materialized. "Jorlenne could take care of Osin herself. She's got a vendetta deeper than any girl in the Water Wheel. If only Matilda didn't want a piece of the pie herself."

The old woman snorted and rolled her neck. Age didn't deter vengeance, and Matilda would undoubtedly seize the *pie* and swallow it whole. "We're doing this with or without you, Sathos," she reminded, "but our chances of success rise with you helping us."

Growling at the river and the new bobbing shape beneath the frothy surface, I threw my hands into the air and agreed.

And Maddox accused *me* of strange morals.

25

DON'T QUESTION THE PORTENTS

Corryn

I hated the shadow plane. If I had time and audacity, I would've ridden a carriage to Morithia. Still, a few moments amongst the shadows threatening to suffocate me were preferable to wasting days on the road. Besides, I was eager for answers.

Maddox's note had arrived that morning, insisting I see him after my classes finished. If he had news on the portents' location, I'd venture into the heart of the Soul Lands for them.

Spinning the pearls around my wrist exactly five times, I sucked in a deep breath and hurtled through the shadow plane toward Morithia. I imagined a map of northern Efelldor as I dodged the shadowy hands. Time and space folded around me in a mass of darkness, each blurry shadow connected to the next and the next, writhing together in the shadow plane connected to the world. I passed through it all—villages, forests, the pits of the sea—focusing on Morithia and the Onyx Palace barracks in my head.

The shadows mercifully spat me into streaming sunlight. I stepped into the barracks courtyard, pleasantly surprised by the warmth infiltrating an otherwise plain space. I'd expected the home of the Night Guard to display their commander's wealth in a barrage of onyx and gold. Instead, I found a simple gray-stone courtyard with a single oak tree at its center, stretching for the open sky above. Beneath the oak waited a familiar giant.

Yori waved and hurried forward. "You're early, but no matter. Maddox is waiting for you. It's truly good to see you again, Corryn. Welcome to Morithia and the Onyx Palace."

Threading my arm through his, he guided me through the maze of corridors and countless guards. Each black-and-gold cloaked guard threw me a curious glance, some eyeing my skirts with thinly veiled contempt.

I kept close to Yori, head down, trying to shrink into the shadows. Sensing my unease, he kept up a steady stream of chattering. He asked about my mother, my students, if I enjoyed the Vinnith Mountains during autumn. The soft creases around his eyes never faded, his smile never dimmed. How did someone living close to Morgenna remain untouched by her evil?

We crossed through a dining hall and Yori's smile finally faded. "Are you happy then?"

I considered lying, but he didn't deserve that. "I think I'm as happy as I can be. I'm where I need to be and in that I have a certain serenity that cannot be stolen."

He nodded, pleased enough with my wordy answer. He opened a door to yet another corridor and pointed me through. I took a step forward and slammed into a warm, hard body. Papers flew into the air and my sharp gasp followed. Thrown backward, I landed on my rear, blinking back tears as sharp pain radiated up my spine.

"Shit," a low feminine voice hissed above me. "Sorry. I wasn't watching where I was going." Papers littered the floor, but a shadow reared to reorganize them into a neat stack. The lovely scent of a hothouse orangery wafted over me as the shadow worked.

With it, a thousand memories I would've rather kept buried.

Pretending I didn't see the black-tipped hand she held out, I looked up at Melis and winced. Physically, she hadn't changed since our school days, as regally beautiful as she had been on the day she'd slid beside me on the bench at Amethyst Hall and asked why I always sat alone. Angular, sharp-cornered eyes had studied the odd little witch who counted things to keep her fear under control. Forty-seven gold flecks had burrowed into my shell and delved to understand what lay beneath the shy, lonely girl. She'd even let me count the golden flecks on days anxiety threatened to eat me.

But the woman above me held none of that girl's tenderness.

Our gazes collided, and her grin vanished. She snatched her hand to her stomach and breathed in sharply. Seizing the papers from the waiting shadows, she demanded, "Why are *you* here? What business do you have amongst the Night Guard?"

I fumbled for an answer, but the ability to form words slipped from my mushy brain. "I—that is—I'm searching—"

"She's here in an official capacity for research," Yori broke in, taking pity. He helped me up, throwing Melis a reproachful look. "I'm afraid it's not your business, Your Highness."

I stared at the stone beneath my feet, my skin itchy and hot. Begging the Mother to open a hole beneath me, I slipped my hands into my pocket. Gods, I hoped Melis hadn't seen the bracelet.

"It *is* my business if she's sticking her nose where she ought not," Melis snarled. She opened her mouth to spew something else, but her shoulders sagged, and the furious gleam in her eyes winked out. She spun and sped through the door. I dared a peek, watching her go with mingled relief and disappointment.

Melis paused at the doorway and glanced over her shoulder, catching my stare.

My stomach exploded into a thousand flittering insects, each vying to crawl up my throat.

Swallowing, I said, "I swear I didn't know you were here."

"Oh, I believe you. I always seem to pop up at the worst times, don't I?"

"Melis, wait." My feet moved on their own accord, finding a path my mind hadn't caught up to. "It's been ten years. Much has changed and we're not the same witches. Surely as adults now, it's time to mend this rift. If not for me, then for you and—"

"No, you're exactly the same. Trying to please everyone. Trying to find the light in the middle of the Mother bleeding night. Save your energy for your precious research. It's all that ever mattered to you anyway. And look where it got you."

Then she was gone in a ripple of shadow and oranges.

Yori and I climbed a set of stairs to the top of a turret to Maddox's office. The gentle giant pretended to be entranced with something out the window while I rubbed tear stains from my cheeks. With a final loud sniff, I clenched my jaw and straightened my shoulders.

Rounding the final stair, Yori and I jolted as a loud shriek erupted from the shut office door, followed by, "I don't give a flying fuck what you think is appropriate."

Yori scratched his neck and smiled wanly.

"Seems Maddox is preoccupied. This may take a minute."

The shriek was followed by a crash of what sounded like a falling chair. Or table. Possibly both. It didn't take much imagination to wonder who'd dare speak to the Night Prince like that. Clearing my throat, I folded my hands and rocked on my heels. I shouldn't be pleased, but I *had* been looking forward to meeting Captain Sathos. Perhaps the gods thought I deserved a boon after my run-in with Melis.

I couldn't hear Maddox's low answer, but the Day Witch's response was clear. "No! Why are you punishing me like this? Give me a unit and let me hunt the vampyres down."

Yori rubbed a hand over his beard, muttering, "Godsdamn it, Alys. This again?"

The door flew open, and a woman staggered from the office, shoved out by a thundering storm cloud of shadow. "You *arrogant,* whiplashing, hypocritical, prick of a prince," she seethed, clawing at the shadows, trying to find a way into the office. The black waves wouldn't budge.

"Give it up, Alys," Yori gently called, stepping between the cursing witch and me. "You know he won't change his mind."

I peered around Yori and smiled hesitantly at the woman, marveling at the long black braid swishing past her hips. If it wasn't for the waiting portent information, I'd have tossed Maddox over to pepper this peculiar witch with questions. She didn't spare me a glance, glaring at Yori with a fury of a wood nymph protecting its kill.

"He knows my value," she fumed, unable to hide the melodic slur of her accent. "It's not sitting on my ass waiting for another vampyr attack. Tell him to get over himself and *use me*." Giving up against the wall of shadows, she threw her hands in the air and loudly declared, "And to stop pretending I don't exist. I thought we were past this petulant behavior."

She took off down the stairs, back impossibly straight as her braid swung.

Cursing Maddox under his breath, Yori gestured for me to pass through the fading shadows. He stole one more glance at the stairs and a crease formed between his black brows. Entering the office, he said to Maddox, "You're going to force her to do something stupid to get your attention."

The Night Prince slumped in a chair behind his desk, glaring at an over-turned chair in front of him as if he couldn't decide whether to tear its legs off or go and carefully right it. "She'll get over it."

Dark circles stained the pale skin beneath his eyes. His hair had grown far too long for a respectable Night Witch, giving him a slightly unhinged air. The drumming fingers never stopped, like he was a string pulled tight enough to snap.

I shouldn't have added anything to what was certainly none of my business, but I said, "You're underestimating how alone she feels." If anyone was pulled tighter than Maddox, it was the Day Witch trapped in a palace she couldn't avoid, surrounded by witches who didn't understand her—something I resonated with.

Maddox dragged his gaze from the chair and blinked at me, as if questioning why I was there.

I pulled his note from my reticule and tossed it onto his desk. Righting the fallen chair, I sat and examined his office. I hadn't forgotten the last time I'd seen him and the eeriness he left with. Nor had I forgotten the Death Runes book. But a quick glance about the office didn't offer any clues to its whereabouts. I wasn't about to bring it up. I'd deal with whatever dark magic he was playing with later.

"Thank you for escorting Instructor Stellanati," Maddox said to Yori, recognition clearing his glazed expression as he picked up his note of neat, tight spikes. "I'll return her to the courtyard whenever we've finished our discussion."

Yori gave a short bow and left the office, dismissed. How he put up with Maddox, I never understood. Clearly their friendship was built on far more solid ground than I realized.

The moment the door shut, Maddox wasted no time and spellcasted a sound-trapping bubble. "The portents are kept here in Morithia in the Jansk District. Specifically in the Mother's temple under the watch of the Second Order Priestesshood."

Searching through a towering stack of leather-bound notebooks, he pulled one toward him and flipped through it. I peered across the desk in shameless curiosity. Time stamps noted each entry, and I realized the journals were records of his daily activities. Even his massive memory couldn't keep up with the realm's every detail.

"One simply can't walk in and tour them," he continued, reading from an entry. "Besides guarded by the priestesses, the portents are surrounded by wards. No mere instructor—no offense—could walk in and demand to see them."

I sat back in my chair, spinning my bracelet and thinking fast. This couldn't be the end. I *had* to get to the portents. Mother curse me, I'd steal them if I had too.

"Help me get into the temple. I helped you get that awful book, didn't I?"

Maddox lifted a brow and leaned his forearms against the desk. "I can't help you break the law code, Stellanati. I told you. I'm compelled to uphold it."

"I'm not asking you to break it. Only to find me a way to get a glimpse of the portents. It's not as if I can translate them. I'm not a divinationist." A lie of sorts. I had faith I could *eventually* translate them. But he didn't know that. "No harm in a little peek. Especially if you take me on the tour yourself. Surely if the Night Prince and his companion ask for a tour, the Second Order will grant it?"

He studied me, eyes all wrong. They had too many gold flecks. Not enough of the fern-colored green.

"Fine." He held up a finger. "But on one condition."

"Name it."

"Any ill-will between us is erased."

My heart skittered to a stop. Nothing in this office spoke of a witch who'd once had a close family—and a twin who'd rarely left his side. Everything was neat and placid, devoid of any character. My own desk in my classroom was littered with portraits of my favorite students and my mother. I was a lonely nobody and even I had more personality than this room. But wasn't that partly my fault? Hadn't I told Melis it was time to mend rifts?

I shook my head slowly and sat back. "Is it that easy?"

"I hope so. I don't have energy to hold onto grudges."

Neither did I. "All right. Help me and all ill-will is erased."

Relief, awkward as it was, settled onto me. The first step toward something new. Maddox's shoulders sagged an inch, and I wondered how much weight his conscience held. Admittedly, they probably held less than mine.

"When I'm granted access to the portents, I'll send for you," he said, shoulders straight again, voice low and smooth as if nothing had changed. "But it will take time."

"I'll await your note." I followed him to the door, unsettled by our newfound direction. Ten years of hating someone, only to abruptly stop was . . . odd. But I was willing to try.

In the stairwell, I paused. "May I offer you a piece of advice as a token of new goodwill?"

He tossed his cloak over shoulders and ducked his chin to button it. "Why not?"

"I don't know Alys Sathos." His fingers stumbled over a button, but he didn't look up. "But I do know capable women won't be held down. They always find a way to prove their value, if only to themselves."

His granite features didn't so as much shift.

I shrugged one shoulder and said, "If you continue holding her down, you may not like how she proves herself."

26

KNOWLEDGE IS A POWERFUL KEY

Alys

T he library tower on the cliffside was more tempting than an apple tart laden with heaps of frozen cream. Albulus Tower held the key to every secret—Morgenna's compulsion, the Lost Five Hundred Years, my supposed power—I was sure of it—if I could find a way to get in.

Sylinia had the gall to laugh when I asked how to get inside. "Even a courtier needs permission from either the queen or the literary magistrate to enter. I'm sorry, Alys, but without permission, you're not allowed."

If I was going to solve any of my problems—whether Morgenna or the vampyres—I needed more information. Knowledge may've been power, but it was also a key to unlocking a cage.

With that in mind, I hurried to the barracks and the officers' meeting I'd begun forcing my way into. No one paid me any attention when I slid to the back and perched on Nik's armrest. No one except Maddox. His gaze flicked to me the moment I entered before doggedly returning his attention to the speaker.

He still wasn't speaking to me then.

Petty baby.

The officers droned on about Nyxinthi; what they could've done better, where they succeeded, things we'd already discussed a dozen other times.

At this point, they were talking to hear themselves speak. This time, they kept circling the Night Guard's one glaring weakness.

"We know shit," a bushy-bearded captain barked. "We don't know how they're stealing our magic without dying. Don't know how to stop their speed. Don't know how they vanish. Mother curse us, we don't even know if they *can* be stopped. What do we know about them besides they're faster and more powerful? Weaknesses? None I can think of."

The guards shifted in their chairs, avoiding making eye contact with one another. Testing my luck, I dipped a toe in the water and hoped they'd at least hear me out.

"If you want a chance against their speed, you need to change the way you're fighting."

Every head snapped to me like I'd grown another head.

Nik looked up and grinned. Patting my leg, he urged me on.

"Look at it this way. I'm magicless, and I held my own just fine in Nyx-inthi. Why? The dimachairi doesn't weigh half as much as a broadsword. Heavy attacks might work fine against another witch or a goblin. But against the speed of a vampyr, you need lighter steel and quicker reflexes."

I waited for the outrage, but it didn't come. The officers peered as if seeing me for the first time. Nik squeezed my leg in assurance. Borrowing a bit of his confidence, I said, "Think of the magic you drain trying to keep up with them. You could halve your magic usage if you wielded a blade more efficiently."

"Are you suggesting we fight like the DRAS and use dimachairi?" the bushy-bearded captain growled. "How dare you? We are sons of courtiers—"

"I'm *suggesting* if you want a chance at defeating them, you need to fight more efficiently. Create a new name for your lighter blades if it pleases you. Change their design and call them shadow cocks for all I care. Just make them lighter."

Snickers and grins lit up the room. A warm glow of acceptance shamefully filled me. I'd missed leading a meeting. Or having others look to me for guidance.

I dared a glance at Maddox. A pathetic piece of me hoped to find a glimmer of acceptance. But of course, he narrowed his eyes because that was the only way he'd look at me now. The icy stare fell onto Nik's hand on my leg.

"As for the rest"—I pointed out the window where Albulus Tower sparkled on the clifftop. Two birds. One stone—"we do what soldiers seem to forget we're capable of and research our enemy."

Here, I lost the officers.

They exploded into moans of horror. Read? They would rather wield dimachairi and try to fly on a broom than lower themselves to *reading*. I rolled my eyes to the wooden rafters, begging the Mother to save me from the stupidity of a self-inflated man.

"Enough," Maddox's low voice cut across the grumbles. The officers immediately quieted and turned to him. "Sathos proves a point. We need to change the way we're looking at this, and we can't change if we don't know what we're up against."

Barely above a whisper, his elegant voice exuded power and brokered no arguments. A voice I *really* shouldn't have been imagining telling me to bend over. I crossed my legs, trying to disguise a shiver inching down my spine. Nik shot me a knowing grin I rewarded with a heated scowl. Silently laughing, he gave an exaggerated shiver, like a writhing worm on a hook.

Maddox continued. "I'll assign a select few to search the library tower's archives with the queen's permission. In the meantime, we begin training with lighter weaponry."

My brows shot up. He'd given into my suggestions without any resistance. I waited for the other shoe to drop, but nothing came. He dismissed the Guard and, without a backward glance, strode to his desk, searching through the stacks of leather-bound notebooks before selecting one.

"Oh, to be a beautiful witch no one can say no to," Nik muttered in my ear, snatching my attention with his snicker. He took a scone from the refreshments laid out on the table and rose, cramming the entire pastry into his mouth.

I made a face and handed him a napkin as he scarfed down the pastry. I tried not to think about how much the young guard reminded me of Elenna.

I couldn't open that wound again. But my throat tightened anyway. I looked sharply toward the window and its floating clouds, blinking away sudden moisture.

Sensing my mood's nosedive, Nik's grin gentled. He wrapped an arm around me and rested his chin atop my head. "Next time, you can have the last apple scone," he teased, trying to draw a smile out of me, and it worked.

He abruptly straightened. A wide, mischievous smile stretched his dark cheeks, as he proclaimed, "You're pretty. I'm pretty. Let's get married and have pretty babies."

Snorting a laugh, I leaned into his side, grateful for the easy way he always managed to erase my gloom. "Yes, let's conveniently forget I'm a captured Day Witch seven years older than you and get married."

He glanced over my shoulder before winking and tugging my braid. "I'll marriage bond with you if it means getting to see my favorite hair spread out on my pillow each night."

I grinned and flicked his nose. "Nice try, Nik." With a conspiratorial whisper, I added, "But I don't have red hair."

The smug smirk fell into wary search of the emptying room for a certain page.

"Who said anything about red hair?" He aimed for a careless shrug before leaving with another scone crammed into his mouth.

"You can't marriage bond a Night Witch. You're not one of us." Maddox hadn't bothered to turn from his notebook, scribbling something in his freakishly neat writing as he stood over his desk.

"Why not? If I'm stuck here for the rest of my life, I might as well find someone—"

"Morgenna would never allow it."

Well, I would either die long before I considered bonding *any* witch, or I would tear Morgenna off her throne and it wouldn't matter what she thought. Striding past him, I flopped into his desk chair, giving him no choice but to scowl from across the desk.

I offered a smug grin.

"Unfortunately for Nik, marriage bonding was never high on my list of goals. Being alone is far better than magically attaching one's soul to another." Some nights I still heard Uzza's scream as Rami fell to the goblin tents.

"Besides," I continued, picking up a leather notebook and opening it to find pages of intricately sketched runes. Beneath them, pointed handwriting in the Mother tongue outlined and measured each of the rune's swirls and lines. "It's not as if anyone would want me. I don't even know if I have enough magic to bind another's soul to mine. Makes for a poor match." I ran a finger down the paper, tracing his lines. "These runes are beautiful. Who knew talent lay beneath the brooding."

A shadow snatched the notebook from my hands, throwing it to an icy prince.

"What do you want, Sathos?"

Ignoring the prickly hurt threatening to rise, I wandered to the long meeting table. Tossing a prayer to Fortuna for luck, I said, "Permission to enter Albulus Tower with your *selected few*."

Maddox let out a wry laugh. "As if Morgenna would allow that."

I seized a scone from the table, desperate for my hands to do something or they'd find their way around his neck. "You *can* get me permission. But you won't because I've done something new to offend you. Let me help. I'm the cause of the vampyr mess anyway. Let me fix it."

Without turning, he searched through his stack of reports and snapped, "I'm not having this conversation again, Sathos. *Leave* before I throw you out on your ass again."

He couldn't even be bothered to use my name anymore? I wasn't Alys who knew the poisonous combination of guilt and grief. Who could argue with him for hours about the proper use of vitricus mushrooms or the properties nymph venom. I wasn't *Alys* who he could tease and laugh with.

No, I was back to *Sathos*, the ungrateful Day Witch he was dying to wash his hands of. Whatever I'd done to upset the precarious balance, I refused to resolve. I'd given everything to this godsforsaken realm and its prince. And what did I get in return? An icy, unfeeling mask.

Leave.

Inhaling deeply, I breathed through the hurt burning into something more vicious. Its little claws dug deeper into my already tender sensibilities. It took over any logic and without thinking of the repercussions, I flung the scone.

The pastry shattered on impact, raining crumbs down his back.

One hand to his head, he whirled. "You didn't."

A rational witch would have sank to their knees in apology to the Night Prince, but I had never claimed to be rational—not around him.

Naturally, I aimed my fist for his perfect face.

He snatched my wrist midair and spun my back into his chest. I tried to twist from his grip, but he yanked my trapped hand to the desk. My tiny snarl melded into a yelp as he grabbed my other arm and trapped it between us. I swung my foot back into his shin with every raging cell I could muster. His hiss was music to my ears, but it wasn't enough.

I threw my head back and aimed for his long aristocratic nose. Swerving, he dodged, and my head fell harmlessly to his shoulder. I inhaled a shuddering breath, ready to pop my shoulder out of socket and slip from his hold. I would slam that smug, arrogant, whiplashing face into the desk.

Instead, I looked up and froze.

His narrowed eyes widened inches from mine, and his grip tightened.

I'd forgotten how utterly bright his eyes were. The dark forest green would have been beautiful on its own, but I could've lost myself to the shimmering gold; like every fleck held an infinite galaxy, waiting to be explored.

I couldn't think past anything but touching more of him. Like the need for him burned me from the inside out. I could forget our bickering or his new vexation. I would forgive it all if he gave into me.

Inch by inch, I relaxed against him, slipping my arm from between us to slip my hand into his loosened one. From shoulder to hips, I drank in his warmth like I'd been stranded in the rain and had made it before a fire.

The hand holding my wrist to the desk slowly relaxed. It trailed up my arm, past my elbow until it floated over the top of my shoulder. His heart raced against my spine, his breath on my neck. I couldn't make myself breathe when he reached my throat, splaying his hand. One long finger slid up my neck to the side of my jaw and pushed my head to the side.

He lowered his head and inhaled as he skimmed the sensitive skin below my ear with the tip of his nose. My eyes fluttered shut, every nerve injected with lightning. His fingers at my throat lightly squeezed and everything below my navel tightened.

Without warning, he shoved me.

Like he'd thrown me from the tallest tower, I floundered and tripped into a nearby chair.

Maddox walked around his desk and sat down with a long sigh. As if I hadn't felt his haggard breathing against my neck or watched the black dot in the center of his eyes devour his irises, he pulled out a book on runes and flipped through it like nothing had happened.

I had never wanted to die more.

A fog thicker than butter clouded my head as I stumbled to my feet.

What was I thinking? *Of course*, he'd pushed me away. Why would I think he wanted *me*? *It's better to be alone*, I reminded myself. *You can trust no one better than yourself.* Somewhere in Morithia I'd lost focus of that. Or rather somewhere in a cruel prince's golden eyes.

Willing my heart to slow and my skin to cool, I made for the door, hoping to the Mother he wouldn't say anything, and we could pretend it hadn't happened.

"Sathos."

Shit.

Maddox was lazily tipped onto his chair's back two legs, the picture of easy grace. "That wasn't supposed to happen, and it will never happen again."

A mocking laugh burst out, jagged like the humiliation spearing me. As if I didn't know one small lapse in judgment wouldn't change what he thought of me. I was a fucking Day Witch stuck amongst those who would always be better than me.

"Not with you, it won't."

The delicious crash of all four chair legs finding the stone floor echoed through the stairwell.

I threw myself into training the Guard with lighter swords, pouring effort into ensuring they'd survive the next vampyr attack—my conscience demanded it. Each night I fell asleep before I hit the pillow, too tired to even dream. Between training the Guard and the young women of the Water Wheel, I was running ragged.

By the end of the week, Sylinia soundly sent me to the sparring ring floor, her new light sword at my throat.

I let out a cackle and proudly smacked the wooden floor in submission.

"You'd have made a formidable airwitch. Gods, if I'd a witch like you on my squad, we could have terrorized the entire island. You and Nik both."

Sylinia snorted and dropped to the floor to join me in catching my breath. "Don't tell the prick that. He doesn't need a bigger head. He's already smugger than a rodent in a chef's garbage that Prince Maddox chose him as one of the few allowed into Albulus Tower." We each mimed a gag before bursting into laughter.

She pushed up onto one elbow. Her grin dimmed as she lifted the end of my braid.

"Do you miss being an airwitch? The flying, the desert—everything that made you a Day Witch?

Did I? I thought about what it meant to be a Day Witch and to my surprise I couldn't pinpoint an idea. It wasn't my hair or my piercings. Not my accent or swords. Any Night Witch could pick those up and become one of us. So, what was the essence of a Day Witch beyond magic I couldn't even summon?

"I miss flying and the feeling of being unrestrained from everything be-low." The pink sky above almost seemed contrived to me, mocking me with its beauty. "I certainly don't miss the desert. Or the unrelenting fight to stay on top of the DRAS hierarchy. What I miss I can never have again, even if I returned."

Yori's cheerful bearded face broke our view and my melancholy ponder-ings. He wore an impossibly wide grin. "You're needed at Albulus Tower, Captain Sathos, on request of Prince Maddox. He's changed his mind. You've been given permission."

I threw my hands into the sky and let loose a nasty curse. "One day, one of us is going to kill the other. Either I'll strangle him, or he'll snap my neck with his whiplash."

"Threaten all you'd like but admit you're bursting with satisfaction," Yori replied. He heaved me up and nudged me to the ring's stairs, waving goodbye to a snickering Sylinia. "Think of it this way, everything you ask of him, he gives you. Begrudgingly, looking for a way out, and cursing the Mother as he does it, but he does *do it*."

"Not everything. And he only partially gives in because he's ready to be rid of me."

"That's not—"

"Yori, I appreciate you defending him. You're a good friend. The best any witch could hope for, but he doesn't like me. Trust me." My cheeks burned, remembering Maddox's rejection in his office. "He can barely stand to look at me. I suspect the only reason he's allowing me into Albulus Tower is you *approved* lot haven't had luck finding anything on vampyres."

Yori studied me for a long while, and I withered under his too-know-ing stare. "I'm his closest friend, Alys. *Trust me* when I say you're *both* incapable of seeing the good in yourselves. For two people so intelligent you're also fucking clueless. Look, just be thankful he got you in. The queen wasn't pleased, and he had to maneuver through"—he bit his lip and frowned—"*political hoops* to gain you access."

I pursed my lips, but the howling clifftop winds swallowed my response.

We hurried through the bitter cold to the library tower. The pinched-mouth literary magistrate waited inside the door, checking an enormous pocket watch I swore was carved from a diamond the way it sparkled. To get through the library's wards he'd have to key my blood to the runed magic. Pricking the tip of my finger, he smeared my blood in the shape of a pennant onto the tower's exterior. Glaring at me, he smeared his own blood over it and muttered the accompanying spellcast. The warded tower shimmered opalescent in pale violets and blues. A buzz like a bee trapped inside me accompanied it.

I scratched my chest with a frown but followed Yori inside.

Pristine white marble blinded any witch who entered Albulus Tower. Everything but the books was white—the floors, the walls, even the book-shelves. Spiraling levels of open balconies above displayed thousands of books. Alcoves and doors dotted the landings off the spiral staircase at the tower's center, hiding gods only knew how many more books.

Inhaling deeply, I groaned and clutched my chest. The smell of parchment, ink, and glue was a musty perfume I'd gladly wear. Yori laughed and threaded my arm through his. He guided me toward the spiral staircase, pausing every few paces to allow me to gape at cases of ancient books. Guards patrolled the maze of bookshelves and academics nose-deep in books. A few called out greetings. Others narrowed their eyes, their glares burning into my back.

Some things would never change.

Wards shimmered at every landing as we climbed up the stairs, smelling of Morgenna's sickly rose magic. Up here, the wards refused admittance to even the most acclaimed academic. Behind them, empty corridors of hundreds of books waited, dusty and begging to be touched.

We stopped at the final landing before a solid oak door. Hand on the golden doorknob, Yori paused. "This is the royal family's reading room. Only the twins and the queen are supposed to be allowed inside, but Maddox is the only one who uses it, so, he decides who enters. Before we go in . . ." He bit his lip and ran a massive hand through his beard. "He's on edge tonight.

Morgenna does that to him and getting you permission this afternoon put him in a foul mood. Try not to take anything he says too personal."

"I'm not going to coddle him. If he behaves like an ass, I'll tell him so."

"Alys—"

I pushed past Yori and opened the door.

The large reading room looked like an extension of Maddox's office. Panels of inviting wood covered the walls, hiding the cold marble in favor of rich maple. Three reading areas scattered the plush, blue-and-green rugs, each with their own circle of leather sofas and stuffed emerald-green velvet armchairs. A glass door in the back corner led to a balcony overlooking the bay and the Eastern Sea—the perfect view for a royal family.

On one side of the room, Nik and a few guards sat around a low table stacked dangerously high with books. They spared a glance from their rigorous conversation on vampyr females to wave at us before returning to their argument.

Nudging my shoulder, Yori tilted his head toward the opposite corner of the room and said, "Maddox will explain our research process to you. And for the love of the Mother, please don't piss him off."

He joined Nik and the others, giving me a heavy stare over his shoulder before tipping his chin toward corner.

Muttering a curse under my breath, I straightened my shoulders and made for the corner where the Night Prince sat alone on a sofa, back to me and nose in *Vampyric Organ Functionality*. He ran a long finger down the torn seam and frowned.

Hanging over the sofa's back, I asked, "Organ functionality? No wonder you haven't found anything useful if you're reading books like that."

He snapped the book shut and spun, eyes wide. Then in usual Maddox fashion, they iced over. He twisted back around, muttering something no doubt foul under his breath. I strode to the sofa's front and found a streak of pink creeping from his collar. An inkling of gratification *almost* blotted out my mortification from our last encounter, but I was fully prepared to square my shoulders and look him in the eye, no matter what.

"This book is better than some of the others we've been given."

Noting my frown, Maddox sighed and pointed to the high-backed chair opposite him. I ignored him and plopped onto the far more comfortable looking sofa beside him. His lips thinned, but he continued. "We're not allowed to pull books ourselves. The literary magistrate finds and brings up what Morgenna believes are appropriate materials."

Up close I realized Yori was wrong. Maddox's wasn't angry, he was exhausted. Faint marks shadowed his eyes. Tight lines pinched the corners of his eyes and lips, harboring more tension than any witch should carry—tension brought on by Morgenna. If I dealt with her daily, I would've snapped long ago.

No wonder he was always in foul mood.

He waved a hand toward dozens of stacked books on a table. "We've been at this a week and found nothing useful. Nothing to combat the venom of their bite or how they vanish. Some books have entire chunks ripped out. I don't know why Morgenna bothered allowing us to research if she doesn't want us to know more about them. She's"—he hesitated, fingers drumming on the cover of *Vampyric Organ Functionality*—"she's not entirely forthcoming."

I snorted. "Obviously." The question was—what was she hiding? Grabbing a book from a stack on the table, I curled into a comfortable position. "Why call for me? Needed a brain in this endeavor?"

"A mouthy pain in the ass, more like," he muttered, busying himself with another book and refusing to look at me. "You wanted in. Here you are. Remember—books stay in the room and don't bother copying anything. Someone will always search you when you leave the tower. Work your way through the stacks up here and find *something* we can use against vampyres in battle. A haphazard way of researching, I know. But it's the best we're allowed."

This back-and-forth, push and pull between us, the teasing and banter—I'd missed this—missed *him*. Maybe I couldn't have everything I wanted-ed. He wasn't a part of my fated path. But maybe I could banish my aching loneliness with the pretense of his friendship and believe I wasn't entirely unseen.

I sat back against the sofa with *Methodology of Vampyric Worship,* feeling light for the first time in weeks. But I found nothing of use in the worship book, nor in *Creational Birth of the Vampyr.* Entire swaths had been ripped from that one. More empty binding than information, especially the bit on witches.

Tossing the useless book onto the table, I turned my attention to Maddox. Sensing my stare, he looked up and frowned.

"Does this mean you've forgiven me for whatever I did to upset you?" I'd meant for the words to come out flippant, not hesitating and soft. "Was it for failing in Nyxinthi or forcing Morgenna's hand in front of the court? I should've seen it coming. In Lilain's court—"

"Stop," he hissed, clutching his book tight enough to turn his knuckles white. He took a deep breath and slumped back into the sofa, looking at me as if I'd admitted I sacrificed baby goats at the Crone's altar. "Don't *ever* blame yourself for what happened. I should've . . ." His fingers began a wild rhythm on the already battered book.

"I'm not upset with you," he finally said, quietly, not meeting my eyes. "Perhaps upset at a thousand other things beyond my control but not you."

"Even if I'm also beyond your control?" I shot back with a wobbly grin. His soft admission made something crawl in my stomach. I preferred his haughty arrogance. Or even the frigid contempt. Anything but the misery Morgenna had unleashed on him because I'd pushed for permission to the tower to find a way to undermine his realm.

He rewarded me with a crooked smile and shifted closer. His knee knocked against mine, but he didn't pull back. Spicy cedar swirled, and I sucked it in, fueling dangerous thoughts as his gaze roved my face. "You're here, aren't you?"

I burst into relieved laughter.

Gods, I'd missed this side of him.

"Thank you." I offered a rare, true smile and fiddled with an earring. Concentrating on my words and not the thudding tempo of my heart, I whispered, "For believing in my wild ideas, for securing me permission to be up here. I—I want to protect this realm as much as you do, as implausible as that sounds. You didn't have to take a chance on me, but you did, and I'm grateful."

A tiny divot appeared between his dark brows. He breathed in deeply and swept that eerily bright gaze over my cheekbones, my mouth, and down my throat. I had the uncanny feeling he was memorizing me, burning this moment into his head.

Without warning, he jolted to his feet and sent the books thudding to the floor. I tried gathering them, but he shoved past me and snapped, "Just leave them."

I gaped at his back as he prowled for the door. When the door slammed shut, I flopped against the sofa cushions and winced.

Maybe he hadn't been memorizing.

More like trying to restrain himself from reaching out and strangling me.

A nagging voice reminded me I shouldn't have thanked him. I'd already pushed him for more, and he'd made it clear how he felt about me. I shouldn't have tried to be more than the irreverent, ridiculous witch who wanted ridiculous things she could never have.

Picking up the dumped books, I carefully straightened them back into stacks on the table. They shouldn't have been discarded like trash. They were precious. Valuable. Worth something to someone. Worth more than the turbulence they'd endured.

Not for the first time in months, I found myself alone with only books for company and a ball in my throat threatening to become a sob.

27

SPARKING LIGHT WITH HOPE

Alys

I hated the Night Realm with the fury of a rabid nymph—most days—but even I had to admit they had lovely clothes. I eyed Albulus Tower's desks with their hunched academics and smoothed down my lamb-wool skirt. Intent on finding answers to my fate, I adjusted my lace blouse for the thousandth time and tightened the ivory ribbon holding back my hair.

It didn't take me long to realize I had no idea what I was doing. My original plan had been to seek books on magical amplification. If I could figure out how to boost my pathetic magic in the same way a broom boosted air magic maybe I'd give myself a chance against Morgenna. A pitiful chance, maybe, but better than what I had.

Except I had no idea how to find such books.

The tower's shelving system was a baffling mess of numbers and coordinates I didn't understand. I was bent over a shelf on poisonous firebushes when someone cleared their throat.

I shot up and found one of the magistrates peering over his spectacles at me. Slight and thin with a nose like a blade, he stood barely taller than me. Graying chestnut curls were swept away from brilliant blue eyes behind black wire halfmoons.

"While I applaud your efforts to better yourself through literary pursuits, I must insist on accompanying you back to His Highness's reading room."

Shoving a book on the firebush's herbal properties back into the bookshelf, I blurted, "I have permission to enter the tower."

The magistrate offered a nearly genuine smile.

I finally recognized him as Morithia's city magistrate, Lord Felumbra, the only one who'd looked sorry when Morgenna punished me. "You have permission to read whatever the literary magistrate recommends *in Prince Maddox's reading room*. I'm afraid you do not have permission to roam the tower."

His smile went slightly crooked. Felumbra may have been more soft spoken than the other magistrates, but an easy-going shark still has plenty of teeth. "Perhaps this tidbit slipped your mind. Come, Captain. I'll escort you up, and this little memory blunder shall remain between us."

I bit down on a curse that didn't match my outfit and wound my arm around his offered one. He escorted me to the tower's highest level and shut the door behind me with a click and that shark-like smile. Penned up where I belonged, I threw my hands up and released a silent scream to an empty room.

Failure, again. So much for two birds and one stone. If Morgenna was having me watched in the library tower, it didn't bode well for my plans. I would have to think of something else.

At least this late in the afternoon, I'd have the reading room to myself for hours. Solitude suited my foul mood nicely. I might as well do something worthwhile and tackle the approved books of vampyr information. I heaved all the blankets in the room onto the floor, muttering curses on the Mother and all the gods who had meddled with my fate as I worked. The fireplace was well and roaring when I crawled into my nest of books and blankets.

Immersed in the vampire kings of Gilgador and their lives after they were cursed to remain beneath the moon, I didn't notice the pink and oranges of evening creep across the windows. When the door creaked open, I barely heard it, engrossed in vampyr lore and their obsession with finding a cure.

Pulling my mind from a fable of a king attempting to exchange his first-born for a cure, I raised my head. Maddox strode into the room, flicking through one of his leather journals and scowling down at the heavily inked pages.

Lovely.

Fate knew I needed a whiplashing prince to improve my mood.

When I snapped my book shut, he jerked his head up and blinked down at me on the floor.

"Why are you dressed like that?"

After ignoring me for a solid week, after he walked out on me—*this* is what he said?

"I've wondered why you aren't marriage bonded, Prince—catch that you must be. Turns out, not even that face is enough to get past your sullen, dreadful persona." Ignoring his startled chuckle, I smoothed out my crinkled skirts. "It's my leave day. I'm allowed to be soft and delicate every once in a while, you know."

The strangest expression passed over him, like I'd said the damnedest thing. Clearing his throat, he pointed to the darkened window. "Well, your leave day is nearly over."

I squinted at the night sky and realized that was probably why every joint was screaming. Folding the blankets, I straightened my nest, feeling Maddox's burning stare rove over me. I instantly regretted the silly skirt and blouse.

The awkward silence looped around my neck, and I found myself blurting, "The literary magistrate brought up fictional works this afternoon. Mostly fables. I don't think there's much to be gleaned from them, honestly. There's even a book by Agria Grafeas amongst them, but I've already read that one. I've already read all of her books actually. She has a long back list—"

An idea slammed into me.

Of course.

Spinning on my heel, I sprinted for the door.

"Wait—you don't have to leave."

In two long steps, he was between me and the door.

I seized his hands, barely containing my delight. "That book I was found with? *Hot Blooded Love*? Agria Grafeas is the only novelist who has written vampyr romance novels. How does a witch know what a vampyr bite does? How does she know they have incredible speed?"

"You knew all those things," he argued, glancing at our hands with dipped brows.

I yanked them back. "Yes, but I was an airwitch stationed in the Sorre-likah. Vampyres don't normally hunt witches, remember? So how does a *novelist* know so much about them? If we could speak to someone who's been around them long enough to write a story about them, she may know their weaknesses. Wait here. I'll grab it."

Dashing through the palace for my rooms, I snatched *Hot Blooded Love* from my bookshelf. I flipped the worn pages and found what I was looking for. Each page recounting vampyr bites proved me right. The woman on the cover falling into the vampyr's arms wasn't swooning with desire, she was *paralyzed* from his bite. Well, admittedly, there may have been some swooning. It was a romance novel after all.

Grinning wide with a madly thumping heart, I hurried back to Albulus Tower, but the reading room was empty.

Naturally.

Once again, I had to put too much faith in him.

"Back here."

I whirled onto the open balcony door. Maddox stood just outside, half-concealed by shadows. He stepped into the firelight, angling his head. "You don't think much of me, do you?"

How was I supposed to answer that? "Do you blame me? You're ... fickle."

He twisted his mouth into a grimace and almost seemed to sag. With an exasperated sigh, he crooked his finger to join him.

I made a split-second decision and followed him into the open air. Chilled winds swooping off the sea gutted the fireplace's warmth. I shivered and wished I'd worn my wool Guard uniform instead of this flimsy blouse, pretty as it was. As if hearing me, the balcony's shadows rose and dove back into the room, returning with the blanket I'd discarded and throwing it over my shoulders.

Fickle.

"Look," I began, shoving the romance novel into his hands, but he didn't open it. "If you read it, you'll realize Agria Grafeas has knowledge no one but a veteran airwitch would know."

"How do you know she isn't one?"

I shook my head. "Her writing career spans a lifetime. She's also written elf romances and her acknowledgments in the back of those books make it out like she's lived in Nordith. Airwitches aren't allowed there."

Rattling off more scenes, I proved the novelist had been amongst the vampyres; their bite, the ensuing paralysis, the way they moved, their speed, even the sound of their high-pitched voice. All led me to believe Agria Grafeas might know what no other witch could—how to stop a vampyr legion. Pacing, I urged Maddox not to dismiss the novelist's knowledge. If we could find and speak with her, we had a chance the tower's books hadn't given. He leaned his arms onto the balcony's railing, peering down at the sea.

Huffing, I threw my hands into the air.

"Are you even listening to me?"

His eyes finally snapped to mine. "To your ridiculous goose-chase of a plan? Unfortunately, yes."

"It's not ridiculous. As of now, we have nothing to go on. We sit waiting for the next attack with no preemptive solution. Tell me searching through hundreds of worthless books in Albulus Tower will save innocent lives. Tell me you trust your queen to save her people."

His silence was an answer I suspected compulsion wouldn't let him speak aloud.

I tried again. "We both know Morgenna is hiding something. The Lost Five Hundred Years of history, the forbidden books, the refusal to let us search more. She'll be the death of hundreds of innocents. We need to try something else."

"You're grasping at straws."

"Straws are all we have," I cried, clamping my fists in the soft wool of my skirts. "We have to try *something*."

Maddox scowled and raked his hand through his dark hair. "Even if your plan held merit—and I'm not convinced it does—who could we trust to seek the novelist? By the sound of her name, she's probably a Day Witch living in the Day Realm. You can't expect Morgenna will allow you to return home. Will compulsion even let you leave the Night Realm?"

I bit my lip and thought about crossing the Borderlands. An icy claw raked down my will, but it didn't tighten. "I would go to save Night Witches," I said slowly. "As a guard I'm compelled to *protect* them. I would *return* to protect them." The ice slithered away, content with my intentions.

Shivering, I tightened the blanket around me and rested against the railing beside him, leaving little room between us. I wanted to lean into him and chase his warmth, to cleanse the chill compulsion left behind.

I'd already pushed him too far, and I had too much pride to try again.

"It has to be us who find her, Maddox. You're one of the few who can umbranate that far and as a Day Witch, I can convince Agria to help us. Together, we can do this in a few days and be back before Morgenna realizes. We can save the realm." I huddled deeper into my blanket, already regretting my next words. "I know I'm difficult to get along with, but I'm asking you to put aside whatever revulsion you have for me. Maybe it's time we become allies."

He ripped his glare from the sea and drew back as if I'd slapped him. Anger, abrupt and biting, rippled off him. This wasn't masked contempt. This was genuine frustration, and it hit me he'd never been truly angry with me until then.

"We *are* allies. How many times have I saved you? How many times have I chosen you over Morgenna against common sense? Why would you think I'm on *her* side and not yours? I can't even think badly of her without feeling like something's ripping open my head. Look around, Alys. You're a Day Witch in Albulus Tower. An airwitch turned Night Guard protected in the royal apartments with far more freedom than any captive. Who do you think made sure you had those things? Your *enemy*?"

Guilt stung like the biting wind, but I gave into my own pent-up frustra-tion and snapped, "Then why do you keep pushing me away? When you do manage to look me in the eye, it's like I'm shit beneath your feet. How could I *not* think you hate me? If you don't want to come with me, then say so. Don't tear me down to do it. I *will* figure out a way to find the novelist. I'll—I'll go with Nik. It'll take more umbranation trips, but he'll find a way."

He clenched twitching hands, somehow becoming colder. "Don't manip-ulate me."

"I'm not—" I choked on my tightening throat and shut my eyes. This was all wrong. Opening my eyes, I whispered, "I don't want to go with Nik or Yori or anyone else. But I won't make a fool of myself and beg you to come. You've made it clear you don't want me, and I have more self-respect than to fight for something that isn't there."

His face went blank.

Releasing an uneven breath, he launched into a frenzied speech, as if ter-rified the words might fester if he didn't get them out. "You were supposed to realize what a bad idea this was. I would make sure you didn't want anything to do with me and then everything could go back to the way it should be. But then the other night—when you first came to Albulus Tower . . . Gods, Alys. You never do anything I predict, and it's going to get one of us killed. I never counted on you internalizing everything and taking blame for something I should've protected you from."

An unfamiliar spark of hope ignited inside me. "What are you talking about?"

The mask vanished.

In its place, something frantic and untamed took control.

Snarling softly, he seized my face between his hands. "This, right here—this feeling of being torn in half between wanting you and wanting you *safe*. But—godsdamn it, Alys. You can't begin to fathom how much I want you. I feel as if I'm suffocating without you. The moment you enter a room I can't think clearly. You're barely in my periphery, and I'm instantly fixated on the way you breathe, the way you smell, or speak. I'm entertaining a thousand scenarios on how to get closer. If you had any idea how many times I think about you on any given day, you'd run. You are an obsession I crave and everything I shouldn't."

A full second ticked before I comprehended his words, but when I did, the world tilted, and nothing was as I thought. I dropped the blanket and lunged for his tunic collar. "You stupid, over-thinking *idiot*. Why would you hide this from me?"

"Because you nearly *died* in my arms. Morgenna saw what you were becoming to me and used you as punishment. Your blood was *everywhere*, Alys. How could I risk that again? I couldn't let her believe there was something more between us. It was either push you away or risk shackling you to Morgenna more than you already are. I couldn't do that. Not to you."

I shook my head, battling between a curse and a frustrated scream. Maddox swept his thumb over my lower lip, a whisper of pressure. Too soft. Too gentle. I wanted—*needed*—more.

"What if the outcome of our story doesn't matter?" I whispered. "What if we stole a single page of happiness for ourselves?"

His dark smile didn't hold any hope. "Morgenna won't let either of us *ever* be happy, especially not together. She needs control and she can't have that if she thinks there's someone else who supersedes her. If she discovered we went behind her back . . . You don't understand what she's capable of."

I raised onto tiptoes and tugged him closer until we were chest to chest, galloping heart to galloping heart. "Don't patronize me. I know this doesn't have a happy ending, but I know what I want and so do you."

His grip tightened, delicious pressure confirming I'd nearly broken his final wall. He dropped his gaze to my lips, and the air hummed. Biting winds sliced through my thin clothes, but for once, I didn't feel the frigid night.

"Alys—"

I cut off his warning and whispered, "Did she compel you not to kiss me?"

Again, his gaze dove low before flying back up, searching, giving me one last out I wouldn't take. Tension crested with each flex of his hands on my cheeks, swaying us on the edge of a proverbial cliff.

He closed the gap.

Maddox's lips collided with mine and time blinked. The storm building for months between us finally broke, obliterating every frustration. There was nothing delicate about the way he kissed me; no hesitation in his lips or tongue meeting mine. Every feeling I'd denied for months gave into a heady desire to claim him. I'd been right—he tasted like his magic—a scorching cedar forest of familiarity and secrets.

Hauling me flush against his body, we burned together beneath wool and fingertips. It wasn't enough. I wanted to burst into flames. Skin on skin. To feel like I danced amongst flames. His hands never lingered in one place, as desperate as mine to map the other's body. I buried my fingers in his soft hair, gripping tight.

Someone groaned, but I was too far gone to recognize who.

He abruptly ducked and seized my hips. Hoisting me into the air, he brought us level.

"You're giving me a neck cramp."

"I am not. You are not that tall."

Maddox grinned and seated me on the balcony railing. "No, you're just that short."

Then he was on me again, undoing the top buttons of my blouse without breaking us apart. His tunic came untucked, and I giggled into his hiss as my cold hand slid up the hard planes of his stomach. We were a cocoon of wandering hands and swallowed gasps, each egging the other on. Somewhere in my foggy head, I knew this balcony didn't offer much privacy, but as long as he was touching me, it didn't matter.

I reached for his belt and tugged him closer between my legs. Electric fire slithered down my spine and sank lower. Hearing he wanted me made my head spin. But feeling it pressed between my thighs was enough to eddy every caution from my head with a whimper.

He broke the kiss, his hooded gaze even with mine. Each golden fleck was in danger of succumbing to black. "Take down your hair."

The low razor edge in his command sent a new curl of heat unraveling low in my belly.

I reached for the ivory ribbon holding my hair and pulled. Sable sheets of hair tumbled down between us.

Maddox gathered it with one hand, a muscle ticking in his jaw. Breathing harshly, he wound his fist around it and slowly pulled, forcing my chin skyward. My eyes fluttered shut. I pushed everything out from my crowded head but him. The tingle in my scalp. Where he had an arm wrapped around my waist. His smooth lips on my skin at odds with the scrape of his stubble.

He made his way down my jaw, nipping, then soothing my skin with his tongue.

"You're going to ruin me for anyone else, aren't you?" he whispered into my throat. "You and your honey-sweet, soft skin I could spend a solid week exploring."

I struggled to process his words as he traced my collarbone with his mouth. He dipped lower to skim the silky trim of my brassiere. Rushing blood in my ears drowned out my panting. I was languid. Boneless. Slowly coming undone. And he had barely started touching me.

"A week is a very long—" I gasped. He'd yanked my head further back, my neck exposed to the Night Realm air and its prince. I leaned backward over the railing, barely grasping his arms. If he let me go, I'd fall. My oxygen-deprived brain didn't mind as long as his mouth was on me.

"I've spent months imagining all the things I'd do with this soft skin, how I'd draw your little gasps, and they would take a solid *week*."

Shivers stole down my body, releasing a wash of prickled skin that had nothing to do with the sea breeze. A triumphant smile moved against my pulse. Surrender was nothing to what I'd happily give to keep his lips wandering down my body.

He pulled away. "Maybe two weeks."

I raised a brow and wound my arms behind his head, drawing him back. "What makes you think I'd have the patience for that?"

"Shall I prove it to you?" He explored my mouth at a more leisurely pace than before, dragging my skirts up, unbearably slow. Inch by inch, the sharp breeze bit into my bare knee, then my thigh. A warm hand followed, smoothing the icy sting in indolent circles. I couldn't bring myself to care about the pathetic noises I was making, squirming shamelessly closer. I needed his long fingers higher. I needed him to sink into me and bring to life every repressed fantasy I'd had for months.

A familiar sound prodded the back of my mind.

Footsteps. Distant voices.

A door opened, and the voices grew louder. I'd barely registered the danger when a shadow swept us into a darkened corner of the balcony.

Heavy, thrumming shadows pressed me into Maddox. His erratic pulse thundered beneath my ear. He'd pushed me into a corner between the balcony railing and the wall, shielding me with his body.

Nik's drawl called from the reading room, and Yori answered with a booming chuckle. They began ribbing one another over a drunken disaster involving a horse and carriage, oblivious to the open balcony door.

Thick shadows obscured the balcony, but I blindly took Maddox's face between my hands, brushing my thumbs beneath his cheekbones. "We're safe. It's only Nik and Yori. They didn't see us. And even if they did, they'd never betray us." I softened my whisper. "I'm safe, Maddox."

We were unnaturally still for another moment before the shadows withdrew.

He buttoned my blouse as I retied my hair, murmuring, "We can't do that again. It's too easy to get caught. Don't look at me like that. That was the *last time*."

"Of course. It's out of our systems now. No need for a week."

He made a face that said he certainly didn't agree but he wasn't going to argue.

Shrugging, I pulled from his arms. I hid my grin as I aimed for the balcony door and flipped my gathered hair over my shoulder.

"That's not fair, and you know it," he hissed. "Forget a measly week. I'm going to need years to get you out of my system. Decades." Reaching for my wrist, he spun me into the wall. With his long, lean body covering mine, he pressed me into the frigid stone. My gleeful laugh disappeared into his mouth.

The push and pull between us delved into something frantic, devoid of any logic. An irresistible recklessness beyond reason. Certain doom lay ahead, but surely, I could hold onto a few snippets of happiness?

Breaking apart, I threw Maddox one last self-satisfied grin.

Nik and Yori were settled before the fireplace, roaring with laughter, books forgotten. At our entrance, they abruptly straightened.

I smoothed my skirts and joined them with what was probably an overtly cheerful smile. Nik crinkled his nose and looked me up and down. Yori was more discerning. His arched-brow gaze took in my creased skirts and stubble-rasped throat, no doubt cataloguing how Maddox carefully avoided looking in my direction. A telltale smirk said our secret was safe.

Any tension in the room evaporated when Nik asked, "What the fuck are you wearing?"

28

HISTORY IS STAINED BY MORE THAN BLOOD

Alys

T he tiny Amethyst Hall instructor stood ramrod straight like a rabbit staring down a wolf, somehow expecting to win. Maddox's familiar expression of poorly restrained patience said she didn't stand a chance. Still, I respected her sneer as she waggled a finger. He probably deserved it.

The Harkening Ball had transformed Morgenna's glass court into an unrecognizable festival of decadence and dancing. While the ball originated as an evening of pleading courtier cases before the queen, it had evolved into an opportunity to preen for her favor. Courtiers in their finest silks and house jewels danced before her, hoping to catch her eye. I certainly wouldn't. Not in the formal uniform of the Guard.

I scratched at the stiff wool of my jacket and huffed. At least it bore a captain's golden insignia on the breast pocket. An intricately embroidered golden ribbon tying my braid back made me feel a smidge less drab, but a matching silk dress and robe would've been a nice change.

Seeking shelter from the hordes of drunken courtiers behind a dragon ice sculpture, I fixed my attention on the figures arguing against the glass wall. Maddox was barely paying attention, and the little instructor—Corryn, Yori called her—noticed. Her round features hardened, and she drew her arms tight over navy-blue robes and dress. Something spun at her wrist. The more agitated she became the faster it twirled.

"How does a Day Witch tolerate this frippery without puking?"

I whirled toward the snide remark, smacking into Melisandre and nearly knocking her wine goblet to the floor.

Dressed in bold crimson robes and smelling like she'd found the wine cellar, the Night Princess nodded at the dancing courtiers. "Your first venture into courtier politics and it's the Harkening Ball. Nothing but primping and plotting. A single one of them could feed a village for a year with the jewels around their neck, but they could never be so concerned. Have any of them bothered to thank you for Nyxinthi? Risking your life for their realm?"

Snorting, I began ticking off the braver—or more drunken—courtier requests. "More like—do Day Witches eat their dead? Is it true Lilain keeps river nymphs in glass tanks? Oh, and my personal favorite—are our women generous with their sexual favors, and if not, was I? Turns out bedding a Day Witch is high on their lists of things to do before they die."

Melisandre ran an assessing scan over me. Then made a face and gagged. "Not even if I shut my eyes and imagined someone else."

I rolled my eyes before going back to lazily skimming the crowd, floating past the small orchestra to the figures by the glass wall.

One week had passed since that night on the balcony, and Maddox and I hadn't spoken once. He was avoiding me, probably brooding in twisted guilt, but I wasn't going to break the silence first. If he meant anything he'd said, he wouldn't stay away forever.

"You know," Melis slurred, steadying herself on my shoulder. "We spent years clashing swords in the Borderlands, determined to kill one another. But I would've never guessed I'd feel sorry for you. Everyone raves about how clever you are. How you outwitted every witch between here and Kazadorah, and that's how you became captain of the 22nd. But I think you're rather stupid. You have to be if you think you can bag Maddox."

The wine I'd been sipping suddenly went sour.

"Is this your attempt at sage advice? I liked you better when you were trying to kill me."

"I could kill you *now*, save you the misery you seem bent on chasing."

She took a deep pull from her crystal goblet and wiped her mouth with the back of her hand. Tipping her chin to the glass wall, a sliver of clarity entered her eyes. "You correctly assumed it was a girl who came between us. Well, there she is. With him. Tiny little mouse and she somehow ruined a bond I used to think was unbreakable."

Melisandre laughed, swaying to the bitter sound. Wine sloshed over the goblet's crystal rim and onto her already stained fingers. With a sigh, she threw back the goblet and downed the rest.

I tried to see through Melisandre's eyes, but a flash of memory played over the glass wall. I could almost imagine Ansil's imperious scowl on Corryn's rounded features as he scolded Elenna yet again for another raucous night. Elenna's huffs and growls were little different from the contempt twisted on Maddox's face. The goading words Maddox and Corryn exchanged reminded me too much of siblings to think there was anything romantic there. One was more likely to punch than kiss the other.

"What happened?" I finally asked.

"Ask Maddox. He can't seem to say no to you, no matter what it costs him." She flagged a servant and grabbed another goblet. "Tell me, Sathos—do you honestly think a street urchin like you has a place in this court? Can you keep up with the backstabbers here? Forget the Night Queen. Her plumed vipers would tear you apart for thinking you had a chance. *You?* A princess consort to their precious Prince Maddox?"

As if he heard his name, Maddox turned and found me. But Melisandre's wine-sticky fingers wrenched my chin to face her. "See? *Stupid.* Don't you get it? That's what emotions do to even the most lethal of witches like you and me. They *blind* us to the backstabbers. So, open your eyes, Sathos. You don't know what monsters he and Morgenna hide in the dark. He will *always* belong to her first. No matter what he feels for you, he *will* betray you. You're a Day Witch, after all. You don't belong."

Inhaling sharply, I yanked from her hold and stumbled into a woman with canary-yellow robes. Her high-pitched laughter pierced my ears. The music became grating. Perfume and sweat toxic. Too many warm bodies. All of it rushed in a blur.

How had I got here—this throne room of witches with more power in their smallest finger than I could ever touch? *You don't belong.* Why had fate deemed *me* worthy? I was nothing. Useless. I was pathetic and in over my head, chasing after the wrong things. I should've been searching for a way to bring down Morgenna. Not dallying with a prince. What had I done to free the hungry and oppressed? Ate palace food? Slept under silk sheets?

See? Stupid.

Fate chose wrong.

Open your eyes, Sathos.

Melis was right. I was an airwitch, the captain of the dead 22nd DRAS squad. A magicless soldier who'd connived her way to the top. I wasn't a princess. I was a murderer and a thief and a liar.

A pitiful liar who was lying to herself.

I barreled past a laughing Melis. Past the courtiers, ignoring their protests and shrieks as I heaved through the crowd. *Find the sky and wind and the clouds and clean air,* I told myself. Far from the sticky throne room and everything it signified—everything I'd failed. Myself. The Mother. Every starving witch trapped on this miserable island because I was becoming lax.

In the corridor outside, Yori frowned and reached for me, but I ducked under his arm.

"I'm fine. Just need air."

I tugged open the doors and gulped a blast of frozen wind, but it didn't settle the rising panic. Ignoring Yori's calls to wait, I dashed for the cliffs and the salted skies. Past the palace, past Albulus Tower and its secrets I'd failed to find.

Beyond the palace's thrum, the air lifted. Far from the stench of failure, I could breathe.

By the time I reached the cliff drop, my teeth were chattering. The winter-tinged sea air blew in frigid gusts, penetrating my wool jacket. Shivering, I dropped to the cliff's edge, dangling my legs over the crashing water below. Snow drifted in small bursts from the gray thunderheads. Fluffy flakes dropped into my lap, dotting my pants with wet pinpricks. They floated into my open palm and melted into nothing. Like me. Nothing against the might of the Night Realm.

A soft crunch on stone warned of an intruder, but the wind drifted a familiar scent of forest and spice as a token apology for my shit evening. Of all his infuriating qualities, Maddox's most annoying was his unfathomable ability to read my intentions—and apparently, predict where I'd run.

He lowered beside me, unfolding long legs over the cliffside. A true witch of the north, *he* hadn't forgotten his cloak. The wind that only a moment ago offered an apology, now bit at exposed skin at my hands and throat, forcing another shiver.

"Someday you'll remember you no longer live in the desert."

I threw him a glare as he unclasped his cloak, but my nasty retort died on my tongue. He tucked the black, fur-lined cloak around my shoulders, leaving him in silk. Dressed in perfectly tailored midnight robes that skimmed the tops of his knees, he was the perfect prince. A fine golden thread wove faint stars and dragons through the silk fabric. Any other witch would've salivated over the rich way it cut across his broad shoulders and narrow hips. I hated the silk. It hid the true witch within. The one I'd come to see as both my rival and friend—my equal in everything that mattered.

"You shouldn't," I whispered, but I drew the fur closer. It still held his warmth. "What if someone sees?"

"Out here on the cliffs? Right before the first snowstorm of the season? Only an idiot would risk getting caught out in this tempest." He grinned, but a hesitancy lingered behind the teasing smile. It fell when I didn't return it. "What did Melis say?"

I shrugged and sank my fingers into the plush cloak, breathing in his lingering spicy scent. "Her usual poison that manages to strike everyone where it hurts most. In this case, a reminder I don't belong in this court. Coupled with too many glasses of wine and seeing you with Corryn—she went for my jugular."

Maddox's expression offered no insight into his thoughts. He studied the swelling white waves growing on the horizon, following their doomed path to crash onto the cliffside beneath us.

"She wasn't always bitter," he finally said with a note of surrender. "Once, she was perpetually neck deep in mischief. Anything for a laugh. She drew us both into enough trouble for a lifetime. Especially at Amethyst Hall. In the beginning, everyone adored her. She could make anyone laugh or put them at ease."

He squinted at the snow-laden clouds. "When we turned sixteen something changed. I suspect that's when Morgenna first compelled her. Up until then, compulsion was something our parents only warned us about. I could never get Melis to explain what Morgenna forced her to do. Only that Morgenna would call her from Amethyst Hall for days at a time. Then send her back a lifeless shell.

"Afterward, Melis leapt for control however she could—usually at the end of a bottle or—later on—in someone's bed. Yori and I begged her to be careful, taking turns healing her from drunken stupors each morning so she wouldn't get caught by our instructors. She rarely listened. Her need for control eventually extended to others and more than once she put other students in danger. Had she been anyone but a royal, she would've been expelled."

Maddox shivered, blinking at a speck of memory on the sea. I scooted closer until I was pressed against him and tossed the cloak around us like a blanket. He jolted and started to protest, but I drew my arm through his beneath the cloak and motioned for him to continue.

"At first, Corryn didn't mean anything to Melis. She was the quiet daughter of an instructor, surely only at Amethyst Hall because of her mother's influence. Not because of any great natural power—so, I thought. It was because of her I discovered what it was to fight to be on top. I was no longer the cleverest witch, nor the most magically powerful. I fought tooth and nail to best Corryn, and oftentimes I didn't. It takes a toll on an arrogant little shit," he said drily, grinning at my laugh. "Our rivalry lasted years; a grudging respect came from it but nothing more.

"In the beginning, Corryn was only a curious little know-it-all to Melis. Barely friends. Melis didn't care about academia. She was slated to be general; she was there to hone her magic. At least until Morgenna. She fell deeper into addiction and then didn't care about anything. I wasn't getting through to her. No one was. Until Corryn. To this day I don't know how she did it, but she pulled Melis from a terrifying place. She befriended her and helped her find self-control in something as simple as falling in love.

"They were inseparable during year eight, our final year at school. Head over heels, one never far from the other. I'm ashamed to admit I was jealous of how easily Corryn understood Melis and helped her conquer her addictions. But I wasn't so proud I would've come between them, not when I saw how alive Melis was. Almost back to her usual self."

Beneath the cloak, his fingers began a harsh rhythm against his thigh. I laid my hand over them and gently pressed them to be still. Shutting his eyes, he laced our fingers. Perhaps I shouldn't have, but I pulled our joined hands into my lap and savored the feeling of his rough callouses sweeping over a crooked scar on my wrist.

"Morgenna ruined them," he continued softly. "Oh, I had a part, you'll see. But Morgenna must've begun to suspect she was losing control of Melis. She called her back to Morithia to do gods knew what. When Melis returned she was an entirely different witch. Cold, empty, and drinking more heavily than ever. Corryn tried her best to bring her back, but this time she couldn't. They began fighting over everything. I think Melis was *trying* to hurt her, but Corryn was too stubborn to let go. Their bickering turned into hours-long screaming matches everyone in our dormitory tower could hear.

"One night right before the final term ended, the fighting turned violent. While Melis had refused to let me into her head for months, I could sense her emotions when she was drunk. That night she was livid. I was set on staying out of their fights, but drunk and unstable, Melis's magic exploded out of her. It rattled the tower and for a moment, I thought she'd bring it down.

"I ran up the stairs and found Corryn outside Melis's room, on her knees, sobbing, and pounding on a door, screaming obscenities at Melis. I couldn't leave her there, crawling on all fours, half out of her mind. You have to un-derstand—Corryn Stellanati is a rigid as they come. She never cursed. Didn't drink. Never lied, never cheated. She was a perfect model of a levelheaded young witch who never broke the rules. I didn't know what to do, but I sat with her on the floor, letting her cry on me, trying to understand what happened." Maddox shook his head, fingers tightening.

"She was never one for pettiness, but I suppose whatever Melis did to her that night twisted her natural instincts, because when we heard Melis's door open, Corryn kissed me. I'm sure you can guess Melis's reaction. I was sure for a half a moment, she would kill us both."

Tracing the embroidery on his sleeve, I weighed my words carefully, un-derstanding the precious value of his trust. "She was hurt. They both were. You were caught in their crossfire. But was this really enough to break a twin bond? It seems spiteful, even for Melis. Like a smokescreen for deeper resentment that she used as an excuse."

Maddox laughed, a mocking, depreciating sound. "You think too much like me. I don't know. But I *do* know Melis felt betrayed by the two she thought loved her most. That if I was willing to go behind her back with a girl, what else was I capable of? She swore our bond from then on was only a physical manifestation of being born together and nothing else. She moved on quicker than Corryn or I did, settling into the role as future general of the Night Realm's armies. Maybe that's what she wanted all along and she used that awful night to cut us both out of her life."

Flurries of snow drifted into our tiny makeshift tent, crusting his dark hair with a silver crown he'd never wear with Morgenna on the throne. He caught my stare and shifted closer. Dabbing my cheek with a featherlight touch, he pulled away with a balanced snowflake on his fingertip. But he wasn't looking at it.

I couldn't think. Didn't dare breathe. Utterly entranced by the awe-struck way he stared at me.

The snowflake melted into his skin and whatever spell was between us melted with it.

"What happened outside Melis's rooms wasn't my fault. My conscience was clear, even if Melis never saw it that way. What I did to Corryn in retaliation, however, was unforgivable. Her pettiness had fractured my bond with my twin, and I couldn't let it go. Never mind the bond was already broken beyond repair. Corryn was an easy target of blame. By that point, her brilliance had attracted the academic world. A noted divinationist offered her an apprenticeship and a shiny new career. With it, freedom without obligation—something I'd never have as Morgenna's heir.

"I suppose a fair bit of envy fueled my revenge when I spread a rumor she'd cheated her way through school. Anyone who knew her would recognize it as cheap gossip, but the damage was done, and Corryn lost her apprenticeship. By the time she was cleared of any wrongdoing, no academic would associate with her."

"Do you regret it?" I asked. "Ruining her life?"

He threw me a sharp glance. "Do you still think so little of me you think I don't?"

"Answer me."

His shoulders sagged, and his hand went limp beneath mine. "Yes, Alys. So much so that I blackmailed and cajoled the school's ruling courtiers to vote her in as an instructor when no one would employ her. Amongst many things, I regret what I did to Corryn Stellanati."

I raised a hesitant hand and traced the scar running alongside his cheek. "Then forgive *yourself*. You were barely adults, learning to navigate a harsh, new world. Mistakes are meant to be made. It's how we grow, how we learn to forgive. You like to punish yourself with guilt, but at some point, it becomes more of a shield from moving forward. Let it go."

He pulled my hand away and pressed his lips to my palm. Warm waves radiated from the contact, shooting straight into my soul. "You have a rare gift for making anything sound possible. Don't lose that."

I smiled up at him, wondering how Melis didn't see his need for reconciliation as clearly as I did. How she didn't see he missed her. "One day you'll fix it. Melis will remember what's important and realize she needs you. Don't let it be too late. I'd give anything for a bond like yours."

"I think it's already too late. Neither of us are worthy of a twin bond, anyway."

"Why do you say that?"

He didn't answer. The cliffs howled and dusted us with snow, but not even the warmth of the Harkening Ball was tempting enough to leave the sea's seclusion. The panic from before had melted away and what remained was a steady calm in Maddox's unwavering presence.

Maybe I could hold fate in one hand and him in the other.

"Alys," he began, dragging a slightly glazed expression from the sea. Hunger bloomed there as heavy as the dark clouds above us. "If I asked you to go inside before I did something stupid—like kiss you—would you?"

"Don't ask questions when you already know the answer, Prince."

"How about this one? Has anyone ever accused you of being reckless?" His hungry stare fell to my mouth, and for once, I knew every thought passing through his head. "That maybe not everything is worth making a stand for?"

"You don't decide what I choose to stand for." I shifted closer, peering up at him through lashes and snow. "Maybe I choose you."

He took my hand and tugged me closer still, until I was pressed against him from pounding chest to trembling knee. The winter storm howled louder around us, threatening to dump ice and sleet.

Like I was starved for touch, I leaned further into him and drank in his intensity.

Like he and I were all that existed in this storm.

The sky boomed.

We would have to go inside soon. But I could wait a little longer.

"This thing between us isn't going to end well," he whispered, running a finger down my jaw and back up to my lips. "She's going to find out."

I traced the contours of his face as if I could memorize this moment—the dip below his lips, the straight line of his nose, the symmetrical balance from one side to the other nearly down to the last faint freckle. There was a new softness in his gaze. A sort of reverent awe I wanted to bask in.

"I know," I whispered back. "Kiss me anyways."

So, he did.

29

THE WORLD BLOOMS IN TWOS

Corryn

D ozens of courtiers glided past, but I'd never felt more alone. In the center of the dancing floor, Melis whirled to a dizzying beat, a dark-haired beauty on her arm. Their intoxicated laughter blended into the worsening courtier antics. The Harkening Ball always ended in a tumult of drunken revelry and remorse.

Tonight was no different.

Nothing forced me to remain. I'd done my duty, shaken the right hands, and acted the perfect stand-in for Rilessa who'd played off a headache to avoid coming. I didn't blame her, but for once I wished I hadn't been the dutiful daughter.

Melis's drunken flirting with woman after woman didn't ease the scar itching to rip open. I found myself wishing she'd grown uglier with age instead of more lovely. Skintight black pants encased her long legs, barely hidden by a scarlet robe that didn't even hit mid-thigh. Her burnished gold hair was severely disheveled. I'd lost count of how many women had run their hands through it.

Tears pricked the back of my throat, and I lunged for the hidden pearls in my pocket.

We were never meant to last. We both saw to that. We'd taken turns smashing the beautiful glass creation we'd fired from our loneliness and misery. Bitterness wrecked us until nothing remained but jagged edges of words we couldn't take back. When that wasn't enough, I'd dragged Maddox into our mess and ripped away the last witch Melis trusted.

If she was a poison, then I was the toxic aftermath.

Deciding I'd had enough self-inflicted pain, I weaved through the revelry for the door. I'd almost made it when the golden hammered doors cracked open.

Captain Sathos slipped in and headed for a gaggle of guards. Pink tinged her cheeks and nose in a pretty flush against her golden skin. A snowstorm wouldn't have been my preference to take in the beauty of snowfall.

To each their own.

I made for the door again, but this time Maddox rounded the door.

Instant annoyance flooded. I'd only agreed to the Harkening Ball to question Maddox on his success with the Second Order and the portents, but the git's head had been somewhere else.

Stone-faced, he flicked his wrist. Snow rose from his cloak and flew back into the elements. As he shut the door, I stifled the urge to corner him again. Handing his cloak over, he hurried for the archway and throne room. His gaze slid to the cluster of guards, lingering on the pink-cheeked Day Witch—cheeks, perhaps, not solely flushed from the cold.

How did anyone claim he was clever with a straight face? Those two were a political explosive waiting to go off—and none of my business.

I thanked the cloak attendant and threw my plain cloak over my shoulders. I pulled open the door and tossed one more curious glance over my shoulder at the laughing Day Witch. She had an arm around a redhead, in a far better mood than the last time I'd seen her.

Did Day Witches know about Dual Witches and Morgenna's hunt? Did they know the danger of lying with a Night Witch?

Mother curse me, I couldn't just leave and not warn her. Not that I had a clue what to say. *Don't give your heart to him. He may or may not be a murderous psychopath, but he's definitely a Night Witch capable of putting a dangerous child in you the queen will kill you for.*

Mind scrambling, I made a beeline for the guards. Yori saw me first. He waved and took over my awkward efforts by introducing me to Captain Sathos.

Something about her made me pause. She smiled and greeted me politely, but a restless energy kept her in constant motion. As if without a sword, she wasn't whole.

Ignoring any misgivings, I took her offered hand and shook it.

In a rush of fire, my magic hurtled to meet the hand in mine.

Electric sparks burst between us. Heat forked between our palms. I wrenched my hand back, heart racing. The magic didn't break. It streamed between us in a river of unseen power.

Captain Sathos yelped, shaking her hand like I'd burned her.

"You *did* burn me," she hissed. "What did you do?"

"I didn't—"

I stared at eyes the same brown as mine—like milky tea, fresh from a pot. Fearing the worst, I tried something and hoped to the Mother I was wrong.

Don't panic. Pretend nothing happened, I sent out through the connection of magic surging on a river between us.

Alys scrambled backward, hand clenched to her chest.

Please—I begged through the connection—*If anyone notices, we're dead.*

"What's going on?" Yori asked, examining our bizarre interaction with a frown.

"I need more air," Alys blurted and whirled for the door.

You better have a fucking good explanation how you—a Night Witch—are my twin, she snarled into my head.

Just go outside, I snapped back, glancing through the archway toward Morgenna. Thank the Mother, the queen was deep in conversation with a magistrate. *We have to get out of the palace and far from Morgenna before she notices.*

The moment we stepped outside, I dragged Alys toward the barracks, intent on the umbranation point and Rilessa.

She shivered violently, mouth in a tight line. *You're not a Night Witch, are you?*

I leaned into a gut feeling to trust her. To believe that she was the ally I'd been waiting for. I took a deep breath and threw away a lifetime's worth of caution.

No, I am not a Night Witch.

Then what *are you? Gods, what am I?*

With my head on a swivel for any onlookers, I shoved her toward the open barracks door, thankful she had enough sense not to speak any of this aloud. She tottered under an archway and into the barracks main hall.

We're an aberration that comes from a Night and Day Witch union—You and I are Dual Witches. We're not meant to live amongst other witches. Our power is a threat to both realms.

She paused, panting as she wiped sweat from her brow. I could see the pieces falling into place behind wickedly sharp brown eyes. *That's why you masquerade as a Night Witch. That's why you're so oddly powerful, you have both sets of magic in your veins. Your mother, the headwitch, is she—*

She's not my mother. Not by blood anyway. Our father entrusted me to Rilessa's care and then vanished. No one but Rilessa—and now you—knows what I am.

Leading her down another empty hall, I peered around each corner, praying no one would stop us. *We're not the only ones, but Morgenna hunts us all with a beast at her command. I've tried to save as many as I can find, but . . .* I thought of the red line slashing Seren's throat. *If we're discovered, it doesn't end well for our kind.*

The rumors of the families killed in the Blackwood—they were Dual Witches.

I nodded, but Alys shivered violently again. Sweat beads slid down her cheek. Even in the dim light of the barracks hall, she looked too pale.

"Are you all right?" I whispered aloud, checking for listeners.

A wry grin twisted her lips. "Everything I thought I knew about myself is wrong. So . . . no, not really." She laughed but the motion pitched her forward.

I lunged for her, barely catching her before she struck the floor. Shadows rushed us and helped me prop her against the wall. "I meant physically. Are you ill?"

She shook her head, trying to push me away but only succeeding in slipping further down the wall. *It feels like something is trying to crawl out of my skin.*

I'm going to try something. It will feel as if I'm taking over your body. Don't shut me out.

She curled her lip but nodded.

Diving into the river of magic surging between us, I tried to find her on the other end but was instantly blocked. Her magic sprang forward and snapped at my intrusion. The furious power snarled like a caged beast finally bursting free. I stumbled from her head and sank beside her, almost as pale as she was.

You've been bound. Your magic is untethering from whatever bound you. My magic must've served as leverage to break you free. If it's anything like mine, and as my twin it should be, we need to get out of here before your magic explodes from you.

She groaned and slumped to the floor. *Lovely. Not only am I not a Day Witch, but I'm also not even magicless. Bleeding, lying Mother couldn't have mentioned that?*

I ignored the sprouting seed of hope and seized Alys around her middle, tugging her up with shadows. We had to leave *now*. She threw an arm around my shoulders, muttering something about how tiny I was. As if she had any room to talk.

A single guard guarded the umbranation courtyard. He didn't bother to question me when I told him Alys wasn't feeling well, and I was umbranating her to see a healer. I joined his snickers with a weak laugh as he crowed about Day Witches needing a healer because of a bit of Night Realm liquor. He waved us through to the umbranation point. I let loose a slow breath of relief.

"Bleeding knew the Mother hadn't meant metaphorical power."

Don't you dare say anything aloud, I snapped internally, reaching for umbranating shadows.

She gave a snort. *I hope you're better at this than Maddox.*

I'm better than him at a lot of things.

Her delirious laughter followed us through the shadow plane. The school's umbranation wards shifted and screeched, confused by our double approach. Heaving through the shadows, I forced the protection wards to search *my* blood. Maddox and Rilessa's magic was strong, each originating from powerful lineages. But mine was stronger. The opalescent wall shimmered in the shadow plane, slowly bending around us. A deep moan reverberated through the cracking magic. I shoved harder. With a creak like an opening door, the wards gave in to Alys, accepting her as a part of me.

How oddly right that seemed.

We landed in Rilessa's sitting room in a heap on her rug. I pulled Alys up and gently guided her onto the faded sofa. She shivered violently again, mumbling thanks before sagging motionless into the cushions.

"What on the Mother's green earth?" Rilessa cried from the doorway. She hurried toward a convulsing Alys. Concern quickly replaced shock.

"What indeed, Mother," I replied scathingly. "Did you know? When my father dumped me on your doorstep, did you know there was another? A *twin* sister?"

Rilessa paled.

She dropped beside Alys and pressed a hand to her brow. "You were never supposed to meet. Your father said—" She broke off staring at Alys.

Shadows erupted *from* my sister. She didn't pull them from dark corners, but from herself, like some beast that dwelled within her burst free. The whipping shadows exploded across the sitting room. Half-wind, half-shadow, they knocked over chairs and rattled windows.

I scurried onto the sofa and summoned shadow to hold the feral darkness in place.

"She's been bound all this time," I choked out, trying to decipher what was mine and what was Alys's in the river coursing between us. "She thought she was born magicless, but *this* has been living inside her." Our shadows struggled, trying to dominate the other. "The binding couldn't even hold it all back. She could fly while *bound*."

"Quick," Rilessa hissed. She pointed to the fire storm launching from Alys's limp palm. "*Sigillum magicae*." A pearly bubble formed around Alys, shrinking around her in a second skin.

But Alys's magic far exceeded Rilessa's. Cracks instantly splintered the seal in an inferno.

"Corryn! Help me!" Rilessa held both hands out in vain, straining to contain Alys's magic. Flames shot through the cracks. Red-hot serpent tongues slipped through the seal, searing the sofa.

Anchoring my magic to the words I spoke aloud, I pooled my soul into my own pearly bubble. Alys pushed against me. The well inside her howled with desperation to break free and bring the walls down on our heads.

I wasn't the only one battling the animal.

Barely conscious, she pushed on the surging magic with me, keeping the flames from exploding and devouring everything.

Only one thought streamed toward me.

Protect the Amethyst Hall. Protect the children.

Her nose began to bleed, blood flowing down her chin.

Ever the soldier protecting everyone before herself.

Something cracked inside me.

Let it go, I whispered, hoping she'd hear me, praying I hadn't foolishly spent too much time getting answers from Rilessa. *Break the binding magic, or it'll destroy you. We're safe, I can hold it. Trust me and let it go.*

A small voice, thin and faded in a melodic brogue, answered. *It hurts. I—It's too much. My skin—it's too much magic. I can't hold it in.*

Then don't. We're twins. Mirrored souls of one another as the Mother designed. Whatever you have, I have too. Trust me. I can hold it back. I'll keep you and everyone safe. For once let someone else save the day, Captain Sathos.

A bitter laughter floated on the river between us. *I don't even know the surname I was born to.*

Destroy the rest of the magic binding you, and I'll tell you everything I know. Careful what you promise.

Let it go, Alys.

I alone knew how much magic I'd hidden from the world. I knew the dangerous perplexity inside me.

I thought I'd been alone.

I was so very wrong.

Whatever beast lurked beneath her skin burst free, roaring into the world. Pure, unfettered magic ripped from her soul, shredding through her body. She toppled from the sofa, screaming and writhing with a snapping of bones. Tears and sweat streamed down my cheeks, but I held onto the thin seal. I understood the beast, knew what drove it, what it wanted more than anything else. Freedom—a chance to stretch and live amongst the shadows *and* clouds.

Rilessa sank to the rug, hand over her mouth, watching in horror as Alys broke free of the binds that'd held her soul for twenty-eight years. She was free.

Alys collapsed onto the rug's remains, ash floating over her unmoving form.

"Potions, Mother," I urged Rilessa, who scrambled to the kitchen. Falling on my knees beside Alys, I heaved her head into my lap. "*Sana corpus.*"

My magic sensed what I wanted, latching onto the river between us and careening downstream to Alys. Creaking pops echoed off the walls, her bones mending.

"Dear Mother, I've never seen such healing," Rilessa whispered, dropping at my side, vials clinking. "How are you healing her all at once without touching her injuries?"

I shook my head and stroked Alys's sweaty hair. "I'm not passing my magic onto her in a healing cast. She's taking my magic directly through the twin bond."

My healing magic faltered at the entrance to her mind. Cold frost crept over the river between us, barring any more healing.

"I can feel her compulsion. It's—it's awful. Layers upon layers of it."

Alys's eyes fluttered open, and she croaked, "Why didn't I hear you in my head until tonight?"

"I can answer that," Rilessa said, helping Alys tip back a tea magicked with energy. "Your father told me your mother refused to allow you two to touch after birth. She wanted the twin bond to remain hidden, to protect your identities from Morgenna."

Alys slowly sat up, wincing. "How did I end up in the Day Realm?"

Rilessa glanced down at the empty potion vial, thumbing the cap on and off. "That was Zelah Zerrata—your mother's—doing. She and your father split you up. Olyvr Felumbra was a neighbor of my mother's. We grew up together. We hadn't seen one another in nearly twenty years when he showed up with Corryn. He entrusted me with her. Your mother—a Day Witch—took Alys. I knew another babe was born to Zelah and Olyvr and that both Morgenna and Lilain would either prey on your power or kill you for it. You had to be hidden. But I had no idea you were bound. Zelah was meant to find a safe, secure home for you, far from Lilain's prying eyes."

"Instead, she dumped me on Kazadorah's streets, right on Lilain's doorstep." Alys snorted, then cocked her head. "Felumbra? You're telling me I'm the blood relative of a *magistrate*?"

Rilessa winced. "Your uncle, in fact. Not that he knows his younger brother bore any children. As a powerful second son, Olyvr was a Night Guard—a captain, I believe."

Like father, like daughter.

I reached to help Alys when she began rising on unsteady feet, but she shrugged me away. My hand fell to my lap. Captain Sathos didn't need help. But she wasn't only Captain Sathos. She was my *twin*—a blessing of the Mother, a reflection of her dual nature.

The number two was the most powerful in magic. A natural binary balance. Two twins from the same conception. Two words to spellcast. Two realms. Two kinds of magic. Even two queens. One always reflected the other. A perpetual balance.

I didn't see balance in the shrewd eyes of Alys Sathos. Instead, I saw a stranger who'd cut down countless lives, who was more comfortable with a sword than a pen. A stranger who didn't fully trust me, who knew nothing about me, nor I her. I didn't know her deepest fears nor her greatest triumphs. But I *wanted* to. Mother curse me, I wanted to know my *sister*.

"All this time," I whispered, "I thought I was alone, all others bound or dead. The last of my kind—a freak."

"The world is full of freaks." Alys's words held a test in them, evaluating my response. An image floated down the river between us. "But some of us freaks were born to serve a greater purpose than the ordinary Creatures of this world."

The image cleared. Light and shadow streamed from a glowing being in a forest. Two eyes of different colors swirled with ancient power. One blazing fire, the other a starry night sky. A goddess—no—not any goddess. The Mother of all Creation.

You, my child, the Mother said in Alys's memory, *are the answer to the north.*

For the first time that night, I smiled. Hope surged through me greater than the new river of bottomless magic. Without a shadow of a doubt, I'd found one of the fated six—my *last hope of refuge*, as Nyx had predicted.

Find your hope and you shall find the rest.

30

THE JUNGLE'S MIRAGE

Alys

*H*ave *you always been this reckless? I've known you for less than a month, Alys, and I've already begun prematurely graying.*

Corryn's unusually snarky admonishment prompted me to snort into my tea. Flecks of scalding hot brew flew up my nose, and I hissed.

Across the long table in Maddox's office, Maddox and Yori looked up from Day Realm maps scattered across the table. I signaled I was fine, and they returned to discussing the best time and place to umbranate in order to travel across the island.

Setting the teacup onto a map of the Vinnith Mountains, I shot back at Corryn, *I said I was going to the Sorrelikah Jungle with Maddox to find the novelist. You'd think I'd said we were planning copious amounts of sex in hopes of impregnating me with a little Dual Witch baby for Morgenna's hunting pleasure. I know what I'm doing, Corryn. Trust me.*

I felt her long-suffering sigh on the lazily flowing river between us. I smothered a grin behind my teacup.

In the past month, I'd come to understand why Elenna took delight in vexing Ansil. Corryn's straight laced, no-nonsense attitude was gloriously rigid, and it didn't take much to send her into a tizzy. It was still odd to call her sister. *Elenna* had been my sister, blood or not. For now, Corryn Stellanati was simply my stern conscience come to life inside my head.

I do trust you. It's him *I don't trust.* Something lingered unsaid in her words, but I didn't push, and she didn't offer. This odd new relationship balanced on a fine line of curiosity and wariness—at least for me. She puffed another sigh and snapped, *A witch can't dangle off Morgenna's hand and not come away tainted. I simply ask that you think with your head instead of other parts. Don't let stolen kisses cloud your judgment. Besides, what about your magic?*

I've got it handled. Our secret is safe.

At every opportunity, we had umbranated somewhere isolated to practice magic. Too slowly, I learned to rein in the massive buzz pulsing beneath my skin. A lifetime without it meant I didn't have the automatic instinct to reach for it. *Something that will change,* Corryn had warned. She was terrified the instinct would appear around Maddox. *He'll have no choice but to run to Morgenna, and then we'll* both *be doomed.*

"Any chance you'd like to join us from the clouds, Sathos?"

I jolted and offered Maddox an irreverent grin that yielded a scowl. "Not really. Your sources say Agria Grafeas is in the jungle. I've shown you what parts are inhabited. Are you suggesting I do the umbranating for you too?"

Yori let out a booming laugh.

I probably *could* umbranate us to the Sorrelikah Jungle, if I hadn't adamantly refused to navigate the shadow plane on my own. I forced Corryn to navigate us each time, no matter her insistence I learn how. I'd rather fly blind through an electrical storm than pick my way through shadows that may or may not be shadows at all.

Rolling up a map, Maddox snubbed my quip and said, "Let's go over this again."

For what felt like the hundredth time, he drilled us with the plan. Exploiting compulsion loopholes, Maddox and I would take a few days of leave, telling no one but Yori where we were headed—together. We'd search the few inhabitable bits of jungle and find the novelist. If the worst happened and one or both of us ended up dead, well, then Yori could sound the alarm.

"Well, if we're dead at least we're free," I muttered and picked up my tea, careful to blow across the teacup's rim.

Maddox studied me with an odd expression—a sifted mix of exasperation and desire. For a long moment he said nothing, as if my flippant remark offered a puzzle he could piece together. A flurry of butterflies hatched from their cocoons within my belly. I stirred my tea with unnecessary vigor.

Yori cleared his throat and whatever spellcast I seemed to have inadvertently cast broke.

Maddox blinked and bent to roll over a map, but I caught the faint pink reaching for his cheeks. "You're not dying. This plan is ridiculous and probably won't work, but it's not dangerous."

Clearly, he'd never been to the jungle.

Rather than umbranate south in multiple trips, Maddox and I hiked to the nearest, darkest shadows to make the umbranation trip in one go. The beach on the north end of the bay was our best bet. In the early hours before dawn, we trekked from the city and down a set of icy, worn stairs an ancient witch had once carved into the cliffside. More than one curse had been yelped in the dark. Neither of us had the foretelling to bring a torch, and I couldn't very well light the stairs with magic.

Somehow, we reached the desolate beach beneath the cliff's shadows with every bone intact. I wiped a thin streak of sweat threatening to freeze on my forehead and shivered. The winds billowing off the silent sea blew more frigid this close to the water and even our exertion down the cliffs wasn't enough to offset the chill.

I started to make for a pocket of deeper shadows when Maddox caught my arm and slid his hand into mine. "This is dark enough."

Bracing myself, I burrowed into his chest and used the steady rhythm of his heart to soothe the creeping fear. Deep shadows sprung forward and sealed us in a black bubble. In a wave of horror, screeching shadows swept over us. Howls tore the thin air. Claws sank into my cloak, yanking me backward. I tightened my hold on Maddox's waist and held my breath. Any hope of listening to his heartbeat for assurance died. As if feeding off my fear, the screams grew louder, more insistent. They wanted to keep me, to press me down to whatever waited at the bottom of the shadow plane's abyss. I buried a strangled whimper in Maddox's cloak.

As quickly as the shadows had swarmed us, they vanished.

We burst into humid heat and the buzz of insects. Maddox was definitely worse at umbranating then Corryn. At least, when I umbranated with her, the shadows weren't trying to maul me.

Beside me, Maddox began unbuttoning his cloak. I copied him and shoved my heavy cloak into the bag slung over my shoulder. My cotton tunic and pants beneath hadn't given much protection from the Night Realm's chill, but in the jungle, the lightweight fabric offered relief.

The scent of wet leaves and decaying wood flitted up my nose in a familiar scent. I slowly spun and took in the jungle with a wide smile. *Welcome back, Captain Sathos*, the jungle seemed to purr. Hanging moss and vines draped thick trees shooting high into a woven canopy of leaves and limbs. Reflective eyes blinked like tiny stars above us. Beneath the lush undergrowth, a soft din of chirping insects made themselves known. Somewhere a chimp howled, and others soon joined.

"It's winter. Why is it hot?" Maddox wiped his neck and glared down at his sticky palm. "If this is what you're used to, it's no wonder you're always cold."

I laughed and handed him a square of linen before wiping my forehead with my own. "It's the trees. Their humidity worsens the heat, but it's preferable to the dry desert. At least there isn't any sand here."

"No, but there are these." He slapped at a mosquito buzzing at his ear. Another quickly replaced it. A hair-raising shriek somewhere to the east drowned my snickers—a river nymph. Maddox's brow quirked with annoying superiority. "And those."

Searching for the tallest nearby tree, I began our search. Hunting for a single witch in the Sorrelikah was next to impossible, but we had a plan—*a foolish plan that will sap all my magic by the end of the day*, Maddox had sniped. If we umbranated from one vantage point to another where Agria was rumored to be, then perhaps we had a chance of finding her.

He was about to learn all my plans were good ones.

"Come," I called. "Help me up this tree." I pretended not to hear what he muttered beneath his breath. I knew what I wanted, that didn't make me a tyrant.

Shadows boosted me up the tree's branches, one always watching my back. His spellcast kept the branch firm beneath my feet as he followed, snarling and swearing at mosquitos. We broke the tree canopy to a brilliant dawn of golds and pinks. Emerald tree canopies stretched in every direction, a gently rolling carpet as far as we could see.

But not a single cottage.

Balanced on a branch, I pulled a rolled map from my pack. "You landed too far south. We should be able to see the southernmost peaks of the Vinnith Mountains."

"*You* try umbranating across an enormous island to a point you've never been and see how accurately *you* land. It's impossible."

Corryn did it all the time.

We spent much of the morning bickering and umbranating from one point to another. Sometimes we paused and spent far too long arguing over the uses of various plants—how he thought he knew more than *me* about a *Day Realm* plant baffled me. When a pair of jaguars leapt in our path, we'd dove into a bush, only to spend half an hour there utterly mesmerized by the beautiful animals and their lazy antics.

As the day rolled on, I could almost see Morgenna's hold slip off him. His dry humor he rarely showcased in Morithia, drifted in and out of our easy conversations. I told him about Ansil and Elenna, how we grew up as pages under Federikka's ever patient eye. How she'd taught me not just how to read and write, but philosophy, mathematics, and the science of magic and nature. Her one constant motto forever rang in my ears—*Think with more than your sword.*

In return, he recounted stories from Amethyst Hall, of mischief he and Yori brewed as young boys. Melis occasionally made an appearance in his tales, but he skated over her parts too quickly, leaving painful gaps in all his stories. As often as he could, he took my hand, absentmindedly sweeping his thumb over the thin skin at my wrist. He had a peculiar habit of searching for my pulse, as if needing to reassure himself I was alive and real.

By midafternoon, we hadn't found any sign of Agria's cottage.

I didn't mind.

I wasn't foolish enough to think I could ever be seen in public with the Night Prince without consequence, but here in the jungle, on the other side of Efelldor, there was no one to judge or go running to Morgenna. Here, I could pretend I hadn't stupidly given a piece of myself to someone who could never keep it.

We crested a modest hill overlooking one of the few human settlements. Far below, treehouses peeked in and out of the canopy below. Trailing woodsmoke pierced the leaves and something delicious wafted to our hilltop.

"Let's stop and rest here." I scratched at a mosquito bite on my neck before remembering that would make it worse. "You need to sleep for a bit anyways if you're going to continue umbranating without draining your magic."

Maddox nodded and shrugged off his pack and sword, letting them collapse to the ground in a heap. While I spread my rumpled cloak out over the mossy ground as a makeshift blanket, he rummaged in his pack and pulled out a wrapped lump. He pulled off the beeswax-lined wrapping and tossed whatever was inside to me.

I caught it and stared down at the apple with something between horror and a tingling softness. "The barracks cooks claimed I had to wait until the next harvest if I wanted one."

"Yes, I know. They said you asked. *Twice.* When she was heir, my grandmother installed a royal orangery in a northern village. They keep fruit trees in harvest yearlong for royal use." He threw me a slight grin and plopped down beside me on the cloak. "Might as well take advantage."

"I can't eat this. I'm not a royal—"

"Don't make a big deal out this. Just eat it."

"But—"

"*Alys.*"

I scowled down at the offending apple. It did look scrumptious. Thick, red skin glistened in a swath of sunlight, promising to be sweet and juicy. I held out the fruit. "We'll share it."

He side-eyed me and shook his head. He pushed the apple back toward me. "You go first."

I threw a hand up in the air and snapped, "I thought we were long past this! How could I have poisoned it in the last minute?"

"We *are* past this. I trust you with more than my life. That's not—" Familiar irritation slashed across his face. He bit his lower lip and focused on the mossy earth beneath his boots. "Can we *not* have this conversation now?"

When I didn't answer, he tensed his shoulders and sighed. Pink stained cheeks already flushed from our hike. "I have a challenging time eating anything before you do. It feels—I don't know. Wrong? I know I'm not guilty for how you grew up but imagining you starving and alone on the streets is . . . distressing in a way I can't explain. I just can't bring myself to eat before you do."

Oh.

I took the first bite. A sweet tang hit my tongue but something else chased the tart flavor—a deep unseated longing. We never spoke of how we felt for one another. It had become an unspoken rule to live in a frozen moment between the night in the library tower and the end waiting for us. There was no progression or hope for the future. I thought I'd accepted it, but the aching sorrow wringing me like an old rag said otherwise.

I handed the apple to him without a word and pulled out a small loaf of honeyed bread. Out of my periphery, his shoulders dropped with relief I hadn't pushed for more. We ate in comfortable silence, each lost in a chasm of thoughts and dreams. I didn't have to press to know we were thinking along the same lines of *if only*.

Soon, the chattering insects became a lullaby my heavy eyelids couldn't resist. Maybe I hadn't expended any magic, but rising before the sun and tramping through a sticky jungle encouraged a nap. I yawned and unbuckled my dimachairi, setting the swords beside my pack. The cloak wasn't much, but it offered a thin pad between the ground and my weary bones.

Behind me, Maddox raised my head onto his lap, shaking his head when I offered a feeble protest. He lifted my braid from the dirt and coiled it onto the cloak. Without looking at me, he leaned against a tree and shut his eyes, forbidding any more conversation.

Something had changed between us.

Sneaking through the palace or barracks to steal a few forbidden kisses wasn't enough. Out here, alone and far from Morgenna, something budded like a fragile blossom. Whatever was between us wasn't purely physical. It was indulgent and tender. Like friendship that had progressed into something more powerful.

More dangerous.

Wiping the dimwitted smile from my face, I studied the canopy above, trying to find answers in the mess of vines and moss. Gods, I wanted to tell him everything. To share the dark secrets I carried—my magic, my origins, my *twin sister*. Hiding secrets from him felt like forcing a verdant seed to remain in the dirt. We could never bloom. He was a dagger held over me no matter how gentle the hand that held it.

"Stop thinking so loud," Maddox chided without opening his eyes. "You're supposed to be resting."

I huffed a laugh and snuggled deeper into him. Long fingers smoothed over my temple, winding around the tiny curls twisting with humidity. The Mother had claimed I had one chance of picking the right path or else I'd fuck over witchkind. I knew finding Corryn was part of the right path—but Maddox? No matter how he felt about Morgenna, Maddox was on her side and falling in love with a witch who was more compelled than even me was fatally stupid.

S omething smelled like rotting fish.

I opened my eyes to rows of sharpened yellow teeth, each dripping with venom. The bulbous black eyes of a river nymph squinted down at me.

A scream caught in my throat, unable to push out past a lump of terror.

I threw my hands high.

Fear exploded from my palms in a golden ball of fire. Blazing flames struck the nymph's chest in an awful fleshy sizzle. With a hair-raising shriek, it sailed into a clump of bushes.

At the shriek, Maddox jerked awake and flung me off his lap. Thanking pure dumb luck he'd been asleep, I scrambled for my dimachairi. If he had awoken a second sooner . . .

The nymph crawled from the bushes, panting and swiping at its raw chest. It threw back a domed head and let loose a deep, gravelly howl.

Lovely.

I'd pissed off a nymph looking for an easy meal.

Uncoiling to its full height, it rose on skeletal legs far taller than any witch. The female river nymph might've passed for a witch if it weren't for white-less eyes dominating a thin, scaled face. Amphibious gills fluttered at its long neck. Scales of brilliant sapphire covered its agile body from its clawed fingers to webbed feet—except for the bare patch between its breasts.

Bulging glare on me, the nymph dashed forward.

My heart swung with my sword, and I set my feet in the moss, ready to run it through. Halfway to me, it jolted to a halt. A shadow crept from the tree where we'd taken shelter. The slithering magic inched for the nymph's webbed feet. But the nymph swerved with the grace of a dancer, one leg tucked behind it as it focused on Maddox. It bared slimy fangs in a growl. Two sets of claws flexed at its sides.

It was going to use those powerful thighs and leap for Maddox.

I took the opening and launched, heaving the dimachairi over my head. With a grunt, I swung the swords down onto the exposed leg. The river nymph toppled to the mossy ground, clawing at the spurting blood from its ruined stump. Ear-bursting screams shattered the silent jungle, but the nymph wasn't finished.

It bolted upright, ready to spring at me.

"*Frigidus motus*." Hissing a spellcast I'd never heard, Maddox froze the nymph and swung. His blade sank through the center of the singed scales of its chest with a spray of red. The nymph gurgled once before falling limp into the slick moss.

Maddox cocked his head and withdrew his sword with a squelch. He nudged the black-tinged patch with the blade's tip. Wary of drawing too close to the venom dripping from the nymph's open mouth, he crouched and examined the wound.

"We were not the first witches it found."

I couldn't trust my voice. With trembling hands, I sheathed my dimachairi and strapped it to my back. Corryn would be pissed. Rightly so. Half-asleep and pumped with fear, my magic had sprung to defend me. A life without using it made no difference. To a witch, magic was as instinctual as breathing. I *had* to be more careful around Maddox.

"We should make for the village." I pointed down the hill. My finger still trembled. I hoped he chalked it up to the nymph's attack. "Perhaps someone there can direct us to Agria's cottage."

Maddox nodded, peering at the sun through the canopy. The sun had lowered further into the sky. *A little rest* had become a couple of hours. At least, Maddox's magic wasn't dwindling anymore. I snuck a glance at him to find him already watching me thoughtfully.

Raising a brow, I asked, "Is this adventure everything you hoped for?"

He didn't answer immediately, shaking his head with one of those rare indulgent grins.

Massive tree roots stuck out from the hillside like a training obstacle course. Some jutted out higher than I was tall. I climbed over a particularly gnarled root, hoping I didn't topple over headfirst and make a fool of myself. A cedar-scented shadow darted forward and hooked around my waist until my feet were back on the ground.

Maddox followed me over the root in quiet contemplation. This unseen side of him might've been sweet if it wasn't slightly unnerving. I'd been excepting a dry quip or snide remark. Instead, he reached for my hand and threaded his fingers through mine. He pulled me to a halt and my stomach sank like a stone in water. I needed only one look at him to interpret the determination stamped across his perfect features.

He brushed the back of his hand across my cheek and said, "I hadn't hoped for anything beyond time with you away from *her*. Whether or not we find Agria, I'm glad we got this day. If this is all we ever get, then it's enough. It has to be." He dropped his palm to rest against the fluttering pulse at my throat. "I know what you've been thinking. It's written all over your face—what you want, what you wish for. There's nothing I want more than the freedom to give it to you."

My heart fractured along the line between my fate and my longing for another path. I managed to whisper, "What does freedom look like?"

His grip tightened around my throat.

Something dark shifted in his gaze, deep and unrelenting as it tracked my pulse beneath his palm. It should have frightened me, but I wrapped fingers around his collar and tugged him closer, wondering what it would be like to fall *up* into a pool of gold and emeralds and never resurface.

"Freedom is a sharp-tongued witch more lovely than any on this island and beyond. It's someone too clever for her own good. It's a light in my darkness that I hope to the gods never goes out." The gold hardened into a frozen layer of impenetrable stone. "Most of all, freedom is entirely out of reach. Wishing for anything else will get you killed, and I won't allow that to happen."

"*You* won't allow it? I've told you before and I'll tell you again—I chose this path with you. We'll walk it *together*. No matter what waits at the end."

He tried to argue, but my lips were convincing enough he didn't say anything else for a long time.

31

THE NOVELIST BIAS

Alys

"Where did you umbranate us? The humans said Agria's cottage was on the other side of the lake."

"This *is* the other side of the lake. Have a smidge more faith in me. The cottage is *here*."

"Why is it so dark? I can barely see my hand in front of me." A sheet of hanging moss looped around my neck in response, provoking a yelp as I ripped out its hold. Through the thicket of vines, I caught a faint patch of light ahead and picked my way toward it through the darkness.

The light turned out to be a sunlit glade.

At its center, surrounded by unbound nature, sat a cottage. Vining briars snaked across two stories of cracked and faded stone. Weeds threatened to overtake the splintering porch, and I wondered if one wrong step would break an ankle. To the side, an overgrown garden of white trumpet nightshade oozed into a weedy thicket leading to the jungle. An overgrown path of steppingstones began at the tree line ahead of us. The chipped stones meandered through the wildflowers, leading to the rickety porch that might kill the wrong person.

Making sure Maddox's hooded cloak covered him, I ignored his snide, silent, *I told you so* and strode across the rickety porch. I didn't expect him to be recognized, but I couldn't risk anyone second guessing his short hair. Few Day Witches kept hair that short, even if his remained long for a Night Witch man.

Taking a deep breath, I squared my shoulders and knocked on the door.

After a moment, a woman peeked out from the cracked door.

"Who are you and what on the Mother's green earth are you doing out here?" she snapped in a blurred accent. The door widened and revealed the speaker. Agria Grafeas was a soft, rounded woman with the sort of envious never-fading beauty some women would kill for. Her silvered hair was pulled into a loose topknot with thin tendrils trailing a billowing magenta dress.

"Good evening," I began in a practiced smooth tone. "You must be Agria Grafeas—"

"I know who *I* am. Who are *you*?"

"Edara Makim." I forced a probably manic smile. Who knew Elenna and Ansil's bratty cousin would serve a greater purpose?

Agria's face softened. "A Makim. You must be from Kazadorah."

Alarm bells instantly went off. "Um—yes?"

She huffed. "Even in the jungle we've heard the sad tale of the 22nd's ambush. A horrid tale. The realm lost a number of good witches that day. Except for their captain. Rumor claims there's a deserter's bounty on her."

Blood roared in my ears, memory bleeding into reality.

Lightning. Arrows. A great big bolt. Ansil falling. His broken body. Elenna's final smile.

A warm hand on my lower back lurched me back to the dilapidated manor. From beneath his cloak, Maddox lifted a questioning brow.

I cleared my throat and said, "Yes, my cousins. But to the point, we're here on behalf of the realm's Council of Scholars in Kazadorah. Would you mind if I asked you a few questions on vampyres?"

The softened features resharpened. This time Agria glanced at Maddox, trying to peer beneath the hood. He tugged it lower. "Why would desert academics care about the jungle's vampyres?"

"A simple study," I answered smoothly. "We may be in the middle of a book ban, but knowledge waits to be gleaned."

Agria harrumphed but stepped back and waved us through her door. "Inside then, before the mosquitos suck us dry."

An odd tingle went through me as I stepped through. *An effect of your new magic,* Corryn had explained. Powerful witches could sense and—with some practice—pick apart runic wards of lesser witches. Beside me, Maddox said nothing to indicate he'd felt anything.

Together, we followed Agria into the dilapidated cottage.

"Let's try this once more," she said, flicking her wrist to shut the door behind us on a draft of lemon-scented air magic. "The truth this time." Another flick and Maddox's hood fell back. "What business do a Day and Night Witch have together in the Sorrelikah?"

Shadows leapt into the air from the room's corners.

"No, wait." I sprang between Agria and Maddox with upheld hands. "We're not academics, but we *do* need your knowledge of vampyres. Innocent witches of the Night Realm depend on it."

"Pity for them," Agria sneered. "But they have nothing to do with me any more than they do with you."

"Is pity not enough?" I lowered my hands. "Would you let *children* die by ancient prejudice because you refused to share your knowledge? Should I remind you who else hoards knowledge?"

A muscle ticked in her temple. "I don't know how a Day Witch ended up in the Night Realm, but you know as well as I how they see us. We're vicious brutes to them. They hate us because we're stronger than they are. They have numbers, but we have might." She turned her scorn onto Maddox. "It's not prejudice. It's self-preservation."

I hadn't noticed when my attitude toward the Night Realm had changed. Maybe before Maddox. Maybe before the Water Wheel. Faced with Agria's prejudice, I swallowed the nasty flavor of hypocrisy. No wonder the Mother was ready to give up on witchkind. The Creature made in her image couldn't see beyond the magic flitting in a palm.

Trying to be reasonable, I said, "How is that any better than how we see them? Think of the threats we tell children. *The Night Guard will snatch you from your bed if you don't eat your porridge. Be grateful we don't feed naughty children to nymphs like Night Witches do. Best you speak correctly, or you'll end up with a boorish accent like a Night Witch.*"

Maddox snorted at the last threat. The shadows flitted back a hair, but he remained no less alert. "Was it self-preservation that trapped us here? Seems odd to seal us behind wards with you if you're bent on saving yourself."

"Maddox," I hissed. For once, couldn't he pretend not to be the most powerful thing in the room?

The disdain melted from Agria, and she flicked her gaze between us, reminding me of a silver swan who found itself trapped by two cats.

Shit.

I shouldn't have said his name.

Wary of the lazily whirling shadows, she took my hand between her thin, papery ones. "But if he's—if *you* are who I think—"

The buzzing beneath my skin slowed to a hum.

I frowned and bit my lip, puzzling her plea. She wanted confirmation. "If you know, why bother asking? Why bother keeping us captive if you suspect who I am?"

Maddox tilted his head and the room's dark corners crept closer, slithering like snakes between Agria and me. I shot him a glare he returned with equal fervor.

As if the last few seconds hadn't happened, Agria straightened with a long sigh.

She dropped my hand and mumbled a spellcast. "The wards holding you in are gone, but I wouldn't advise leaving yet. It's nearly night and that's when the vampyres wake. That bit of jungle you two fools blindly trampled through is called a dark ward. It's safe nest for a handful of vampyres high off goblin magic while they sleep."

She opened a side door and pointed us through to a sitting room. "Bless Fortuna's luck for sparing you from stumbling into a sleeping vampyr on your way here."

Bless Fortuna, indeed. Maybe Nyx and Baldyr weren't the only gods on our side.

Maddox and I each sank into chairs, eyeing one another with unease. The inside of the cottage was nothing like its exterior. Intricate wickerwork chairs of varying sizes scattered the polished tan-and-cream checkered floors. Potted palms and various small trees waved in cool air most certainly not coming from the quality linen-covered windows.

Agria whizzed a carafe and service tray on a gust of air from another part of the manor. With a scowl reserved for Maddox, she poured a familiar bitter brew of *kafeh* into tiny clay cups. Cinnamon and cloves wafted from the steam in a delicious aroma.

I had to sit on my hands to keep from clapping in glee.

Tea was delicious. *Kafeh*, on the other hand, was life-giving nectar.

Spotting my excited wiggle, she smiled, passing me a floral painted cup.

"I'm surrounded by vampyres out here, hence the wards. I've trapped more than one with them. The only way out of the glade is to fly, but you can't do that with a Night Witch." She offered me the sugar bowl, but I passed it to Maddox. "Now, unless you want to fight your way out in the dark when they're most active, I suggest waiting until morning to leave and staying the night here. You have a better chance of crossing their dark ward in the daytime while they sleep."

Maddox sipped his *kafeh* and made a face before spooning an inordinate amount of sugar into his cup. "We could umbranate home tonight."

"I'm not lowering my umbranation wards on the glade for you two. I've made my fair share of Night Witch enemies in my day and won't leave myself open to them, not for a minute. You want to traipse into the jungle and risk the vampyres prime hunting hour? Be my guest. I'll be snug and safe in my warded cottage. See if I save you!"

He twisted his lips into a soft snarl but caught my narrow-eyed warning and scowled instead. I could practically hear his petulant, *"fine,"* before he attempted another sip of his sugared monstrosity. He added more sugar. Mother help me. By that point, his *kafeh* had to be more sugar than brew.

Hoping we weren't falling into some bizarre trap, I said, "Then we'll intrude on your generosity a little longer, but you *will* give us answers on the vampyres. For my sake?"

Agria released a long sigh, like I'd asked her to eat a mouthful of sand and not a half hour of conversation. "Very well, but in the *morning*. You two have disrupted my nightly routine enough."

She ushered us to the single guestroom upstairs and pointing out the bathing room to Maddox, practically shoving him inside, claiming he stunk worse than a dead nymph. Before shutting the door, he raised one brow in question. I nodded. I'd be fine alone with Agria.

"You two move with complete synchrony," Agria muttered as pulling me back down the stairs and into another room. "It's uncanny. He reaches for something; you're already handing it to him. You step forward and those damned shadows might as well be yours with the way he anticipates your movements."

Instead of a retort, my mouth dropped open. Her illegal library could've rivaled any room in Albulus Tower. Shelves lined each wall, from the floor to the high ceiling. Glass cases of ancient books and scrolls filled every available space along the floor, saving room only for a worn wickerwork sofa.

Agria hurried to a glass case and, with a quick spellcast and a bloody thumb, unlocked the door. She paused and aimed beady eyes at me. "You're Alys Sathos—just say it."

I crossed my arms. "And have you try to claim a bounty on me?"

She snorted and eased a book from the case. "I'm a novelist with an enormous library in the middle of a book ban, unlawfully selling *my* books to the Night Realm. Do you honestly think I would go anywhere near Lilain?"

"Fine," I hissed, dropping a hand to my thigh where a stiletto waited. "I'm Alys Sathos."

Instead of pleased, her rounded shoulders drooped. She patted the book.

"After all this time . . . Feels strange to be handing it over." She held a finger to her lips and cast a sound sealing bubble before shoving the book at me. "What passes between us cannot make it back to Lilain *or* Morgenna. You must swear not to tell that boy what I'm about to tell you nor let him know you have this book."

"Why?"

"Because I know how tightly Morgenna controls her heirs."

Shit.

"Heirs?"

"Oh, please. He looks exactly like his father."

"You knew Prince Mendrick? You knew an *heir of the Night Realm*?"

"My dear girl, did you not come to me for my experience across this island?"

"I don't understand how—"

"That part doesn't matter. What matter is this—decades ago, deep in the Blackwood, a goddess came to me in the form of a doe, more beautiful than any Creature. She wouldn't give her name, but she bestowed a task on me and offered her blessing in return. I took both, enjoying her blessing with a profitable career in love stories. Today, I fulfill her task."

She stroked the book in my hands with a mournful huff. "The goddess left this in my care and amongst other things whispered your name in my ear. Alys Sathos would come one day, accompanied by a prince—not very many of those on Efelldor. She would require this book to fulfill her own god-given task. No, no. Don't ask questions. I want no more part in this game of gods and fate. Tomorrow, I'll help you save those who would sooner see you die."

Great. What else had the damned gods embroiled me in?

She marched from the room with one last scathing glare, taking her sound bubble with her.

What an odd witch—Corryn in forty years if she didn't pull the stick from her ass.

32

AN ORDINARY DREAM

Alys

A lone in the novelist's guestroom, I opened the book but found the Mother tongue mocking me from the first page. Godsdamnit. Another barrier to cross. I upended my bag and tossed the book into the empty bottom before replacing the bag's contents. Satisfied with its concealment, I paused before raising a single finger at it.

Why wasn't fate simple and easy?

At least this proved I was on the right path. I hadn't fucked up fate—yet. The night was young.

Reaching for the flowing river of magic, I recalled the book's title and asked Corryn, *What is* Dualitas Maleficarum?

As I waited for her answer, I traded places with Maddox coming out of the bathroom, taking a giant inhale of spiced cedar and soap as he passed. I let out a breathy groan and ignored the odd look he shot me.

Why did he have to look like he did *and* smell like temptation itself?

I stripped off my grimy clothes and wondered how I hadn't drowned in my own sweat when I'd been stationed here. Thank the Mother Agria had modern plumbing. The water-wielding Night Realm had no need for it, but I wasn't so far removed from Kazadorah that I'd forgotten what it was like to want for hot, clean water. Snickering as I scrubbed my scalp, I wondered how long it had taken Maddox to figure out the bathtub's handful of knobs.

It's the Mother tongue for The Duality of Witches, Corryn floated into my head. *Is that a book title? I thought you were in the jungle.*

I quickly explained Agria Grafeas's task from the unknown goddess and her ominous insistence we read the book to complete the Mother's fate.

What could be so important the gods fated you to find in an old book?

Splashing from the bath, I wrapped my wet hair in a linen towel. *You don't think it's a way to stop compulsion, do you? That would be uncharacteristically helpful of them.*

It would be a good step in the right direction. She didn't sound sure. *But without the rest of the Mother's fated six, we shouldn't consider taking on Morgenna.*

Slipping into a borrowed nightgown, I brushed my teeth with a scowl. If twins were supposed to be mirrors of one another, Corryn was certainly the wise turtle to my rash rabbit. She wouldn't hear of any plans to take on Morgenna until we at least knew who the other fated four were—a plan she'd ensnared Maddox in with the portents in the temple.

Sparing a quick glance in the mirror, I shot her, *When I get back, we'll dive into this book. Perhaps we'll find some desperately needed answers.*

Alys, Corryn began with a low warning, *please, be careful tonight. Don't let your heart get ahead of your head. Think of the path you are meant for.*

I rolled my eyes and made for the bedroom. *You're allowed to say, 'Don't think with your lady bits and fuck the Night Prince. You and the rest of Efelldor might end up dead if you do.' Perfectly acceptable.*

Don't snipe at me. I didn't design your Maddox-less path, sister dearest. Besides, I can say all that without vulgarity.

Mirrors indeed.

I grinned and opened the door.

Maddox paced the small room, prowling before a solely decorative fireplace of white stone. The mantle above it was lined with some of Agria's more famous literary works. With his nose buried in a book of Gilgadorian elvish fables, he barely raised his head when I strode into the room.

I took advantage of the quiet and sank into a plush high-backed armchair. Linen curtains gently billowed from the window. A dim buzz hummed from the open air—most likely yet another ward intended to keep out mosquitos.

Beyond the sill, the stars flickered. Their tiny pin pricks lit a black canvas as fathomless as the one in the north, but the jungle didn't quite capture the aloof nature of the night like the Eastern Sea in Morithia.

Maddox lowered himself to the floor at my feet in a graceful folding of long legs beneath him. I nearly called him out for being on his knees before me yet again, but he snapped the book shut and said, "My father had this book. He used to read from it when Melis and I were barely old enough to understand the fables' moral."

Absent-minded, he set his arm on my knee, running his fingers along the hem of my nightgown. His gaze was fixed on the false fireplace, but it didn't take much imagination to delve into his head. He rarely spoke of his parents, and I never pushed. Knowing our fathers had most likely known one another left me unsettled in a way I didn't dare probe. Fate was a fickle thing. One small twist and I had ended up on the other side of the island—alone—while Corryn and Maddox grew up together.

Maybe it was rude to watch him while he was woolgathering, but I couldn't pull my gaze from the lashes sweeping over the faint dusting of freckles on pale skin. Even without a fire in the hearth, his eyes glittered like specks of gold inside an emerald with a hypnotic call nearly as powerful as compulsion.

His calloused hand glided up and down my leg below the borrowed nightgown's hem, leaving a trail of gooseflesh inching high. Beyond kissing me, he hadn't touched me like he had on the balcony. I hadn't brought it up. Not because I was afraid of the consequences of intimacy. I had no fear of creating a child Morgenna would hunt—Lilain had made sure it could never happen.

But there were other consequences I hadn't allowed myself to think about—until now. The single bed loomed behind me. Corryn's warning rang in my ears. Realization impaled me in a violent blow—I had no idea what I was doing.

I'd let Maddox get too close, and now I was on the cliff's precipice, looking down to find the deadly shallows waiting for me to lose my balance.

Fear stalked my new realization. It sent a wave of panic washing down my throat in a fiery burn, stoppering my lungs. I couldn't breathe. Couldn't draw in enough air in the humid room.

I was going to doom every witch on Efelldor because I couldn't control my longing heart.

Gasping, I jerked to my feet and sent Maddox's arm flopping into his lap. He blinked up at me, and his eyes widened.

Heat scorched a path up my cheeks to my ears. I spun from his reach and sucked in a wavering breath. Putting several steps between us, I wrapped arms around my torso, trying to regain feeling back into my lungs. The world pushed in. I squeezed my eyes shut and concentrated on what my body felt. The magically cold tile beneath my feet. The soft cotton on my skin.

Something hot trickled down my cheek, and I swiped at it with the neckline of my nightgown.

Gods, I was *crying*? No wonder he looked panicked.

"Are you—are you all right?"

"I can't." The words came out rough and wet. Shame flooded me and I cleared my throat. "We shouldn't . . . you know." I flung a hand toward the single bed. "Not tonight. Not when—Morgenna's compulsion—If we could be freed—Maddox . . . *I can't.*"

Gods. I couldn't even speak through the bubbling panic.

How the bleeding Mother was I supposed to explain the idea of giving myself fully to him terrified me in a way it never had with anyone else? That if I gave him this final piece of me, I'd risk losing myself to him forever. Mere hours ago, he'd warned we would never find the happiness I sought. I'd pushed it out of mind, but here in the silence of a cottage in the middle of nowhere, the injustice of it all came crashing down on me. It went beyond fate, beyond risking witchkind. If I ignored every warning tonight—Corryn's, the Mother's, even Maddox's—I wouldn't just lose the fate of witchkind. I'd lose *myself* to someone who could never fully be mine. There would be no coming back from that. Like every fable writer claimed: heartbreak was the one sickness not even magic could cure.

I couldn't risk everything for happiness. I was destined for something else. Perhaps I was destined to be alone—where I was safe.

At some point, Maddox had risen from the floor. He guided me to turn, never applying more than gentle pressure to face him.

"Look at me."

I couldn't. He'd see the shame and misery. I studied the linen-covered buttons scaling his tunic to the divot at his throat. He'd changed into another tunic. This one plain cotton, but black as always. I didn't think I'd ever seen him in any other color.

"Alys."

When I finally met his gaze, he pried each hand from my sides and unwound me until I was limp and raw between his arms. He held me too gently, as if terrified I was going to break apart in a weepy heap at his feet. My throat burned with humiliation and the threat of unshed tears. I held them back with sheer determination, but he cradled my face between his hands like I was made of priceless glass and a single tear spilled out to prove I was just as breakable.

He smoothed it away. A pained line appeared between his brows. His grip tightened to hold me like I might slip and shatter anyway. "I will *never* expect anything more from you than what you're willing to give. You are already a gift I never deserved and anything between us is precious, no matter the end. If it's only friendship you're willing to give, then it's more than enough."

I *wanted* to give him *everything*. My body. My secrets. My future. But I couldn't and it felt like a knife twisting inside me.

"Right." I pulled away from his reach. "We should go to bed if we want to rise early enough to umbranate home."

He bit the inside of his cheek and slowly nodded, clearly not as eager as I was to finish this conversation. "You can have the bed. The floor is—"

"Don't be ridiculous. I said I wasn't going fuck you, not that I was going to have a conniption like some virginal maid if we shared a bed." The sharp words snapped whatever vulnerable cord had sprung between us. Maddox's gentle contemplation evaporated into more familiar irritation.

I held back a relieved sigh and climbed into the overstuffed bed. "Besides, I can think of at least half a dozen species of jungle spiders that come out at night to crawl across floors. Two of them are venomous."

That sent him flying into the empty space beside me. Apparently, even terrifying princes weren't fond of spiders.

Half an hour later, we were both wide awake, and I was beginning to wonder if the spiders were worth getting a few hours of sleep.

He was *everywhere*, and my poor mind couldn't shut him out. Not his breathing. Not his damned alluring scent. Not his shifting mere inches away that reminded me each second I was lying in bed next to the witch that tended to shatter my rational thinking on a good day.

Sleeping next to him had been a terrible idea.

"Stop moving," he hissed when I sat up to fluff my pillow for the fifth time. "You'll never fall asleep if you can't be still."

"I'm *trying*, but I'm drowning in this ridiculous bed. It's too fluffy. I'm sinking onto your side because your five times heavier than me, and after everything I said tonight, touching you feels godsdamned awkward."

He let out a long-suffering sigh and through the room's darkness, I thought I saw him pinch the bridge of his nose.

"Come here."

Well, that finally stilled me.

"Don't you have any trust in me?" he snapped. "I'm trying to settle your fidgeting so we can *finally* fall asleep—" He broke off, and I could practically hear him wincing. "Gods, I'm sorry, Alys. I shouldn't have said it like that."

A soft laugh bubbled free.

"Don't apologize. Perhaps we only needed a bit of bickering to make everything between us feel natural once more."

I scooted closer. He raised one arm, and I curled into his chest. Warmth and cedar enveloped me nearly as tight as the arm sliding around my shoulders. Beneath my ear, his heart raced for a few moments before slowing back into a gentle lull. He smoothed my bare arm, tracing meaningless patterns down my elbow and back up again.

The millions of thoughts that had scoured the inside of my brain finally quieted at his touch.

Damnit. He'd been right.

My yawn prompted a soft snicker out of him, but I ignored it and said, "Morgenna truly ruined us, didn't she? We're finally alone, far from her, together in a bed with no one to judge, and I ended up deep in my head. Ordinary people would be bent over the bed right about now, you know."

He let out a strangled bark of laughter into my hair, and his heart sped back up. "Nothing about either of us is ordinary."

"Maybe I prefer we were ordinary."

"And what is *ordinary*?"

I thought about it, afraid I didn't know, but a clear picture formed in my head as vivid as a memory. "A cottage like this one in the middle of nowhere. Maybe tucked into the Vinnith Mountains with a lake nearby, like Grelgesco but without the mob. There's a cloudless blue sky and the sun shines onto a quaint little porch with a swing where I can read all day and not think about training or swords or anything violent. There's an apple tree or two in the back heavy with red apples, ready to be plucked.

"I've never gardened anything in my life, but I think I'd like to try. Bring things to life instead of killing. Not just apple trees. Maybe flowers that are pointless for anything but their beauty. It would be nice to clean soil from under my fingernails instead of blood." Another yawn interrupted me. "I just want to be boring, Maddox. Be the kind of uninteresting witch no one ever thinks twice about."

I didn't make out what he whispered into my hair. Something about if wishes were fishes—another Night Witch idiom that went over my head. A final yawn tugged me from reality's hold, and I drifted into a world of gardens and cozy cottages with fluffy beds that I didn't think twice about pushing Maddox into.

33

LIGHT OF THE WORLD

Alys

S omething gave my hair a sharp tug, jolting me awake.

I sprang up in bed with a hiss, reaching for the knife I kept tucked beneath my pillow. The figure dodged my swipe, and a familiar snicker broke the room's silence as Maddox strode for the door. The guestroom was dark but for a single candle on the mantel Maddox must have lit. A clock beside it said dawn wouldn't yet show its face for a little while.

"Get up and get ready. We need to get our answers before we dawn. Fingers crossed your Day Witch novelist is an early riser."

He didn't see my single finger salute. I should have aimed the knife at his back for waking me like that, but the door closed, and the moment was gone.

Groaning, I slumped back into the bed, muttering curses. Maddox was a *terrible* bedmate. For all his complaints about how I fidgeted, he was just as bad. More than once, I awoke to find one of us sprawled across the other. But *he* wasn't going to suffocate if I was on top of him. *I*, on the other hand, had to heave his two-ton bicep off my neck before he accidentally strangled me in his sleep.

He also had a bizarre habit of randomly waking to pad around the room and do gods knew what. At least he was mostly silent about it.

We would have to find a way to make sleeping together work. I could always make him take a sleeping potion or—I slowly swung my legs off the bed and shook off the cobwebs of sleep. There would be no making *anything* work.

Time to wake up to reality.

Drowsy and gloomy, I dressed and made a quick stop to the bathing room. When I returned to the bedroom to blow out the candle, something on the bedside table on Maddox's side of the bed caught my eye. He'd taken his knapsack with him but had left a slip of paper behind. Ever the prince, expecting someone else to clean after him.

Muttering about entitled asses under my breath, I went to retrieve it.

I picked up the paper and sucked in a gasp, clapping a hand to my mouth.

He'd drawn a cottage. In soft strokes vastly different from the sketches I'd glimpsed in his office, he'd brought to life *my* little cottage. A porch with a pair of rocking chairs wrapped around the ivy-covered stone cottage. Apple trees peeked from the behind the porch, dotted with flowers of varieties I'd never seen. In the back, the Vinnith Mountains stood watch over the quaint home beside a glass-like lake.

But it was the tiny, shadowed figures in the front window that made the backs of my eyes burn. No more than the size of my thumbnail, the entwined shadows swayed to music they alone heard, free and utterly ordinary.

Maddox couldn't have meant for me to see this. Unable to sleep last night, he must have sketched my vision still burning in his mind to try to settle himself and promptly forgotten about it. I couldn't leave it behind for Agria to discard. I upended my bag and pulled out *Dualitas Maleficarum*. Careful not to crease the sketch, I tucked it in between two pages and wetly sniffed.

Damn him. He was turning me into a watering pot.

Downstairs, Agria was up and . . . laughing.

I half expected to find a bloodbath below. I should've remembered Maddox knew how to charm anyone when he set his mind to it—he was the queen's right-hand diplomat after all. Instead, I found Agria flittering like a butterfly in her kitchen. From a clay pot over the iron flat stove, she ladled steaming oat *atoleh* into a bowl.

The novelist gave me a nod when I entered the airy kitchen. I plunked onto a stool beside Maddox and gave him a crisp greeting he returned with a slight grin. He sat at the tiled counter, intent on Agria's cooking with a curious tilt of his head. I supposed he had never had *atoleh*. Lucky for him, she appeared to be making it with mounds of sugar. Notes of cinnamon and star anise wafted from the pot, filling the kitchen with the smell of home.

The willowy witch continued chatting about the religious Jansk District and the scandals of the Second Order Priestesshood. Apparently, the high priestess had a string of lovers the realm found outrageous. Poor woman had needs. Nothing to be ashamed of.

With a flourish, Agria stuck a piece of sugar cane into the bowl and set it before Maddox. "No doubt nothing like what you're used to, but *atoleh* is hardy food for a traveler."

He side-eyed me, no doubt wondering how he could make me eat it first without offending Agria and losing our chance at a vampyr answer.

I took pity and snatched the bowl off the counter. I hadn't cared for *atoleh* in Kazadorah, but after months away from the Day Realm porridge tasted divine.

Agria clucked her tongue. "I see time in the Night Realm hasn't cured your DRAS airwitch manners." Rolling her eyes at my indignant protest, she ladled another bowl for Maddox who tucked into it with obvious glee.

Next time I'd let him squirm in his odd protectiveness.

Steepling her fingers, the novelist peered at us from across the counter. "Now, let's get to it. The sooner I send you two out my door, the better. I've heard rumors of vampyr attacks in the north, but I want to hear it from you."

Between bites of *atoleh*, I recounted what I knew of the countless sightings at the border, of the village they'd drained. When I described the vampyres' feeding and stolen magic at the Nyxinthi attack, Agria frowned and held up a hand.

"They fed on witches and didn't *die*?"

"Not these vampyres."

Maddox rose and took our empty bowls to the washbin. "We have reason to believe the legionnaire attacking the realm is from the continent. Could a Gilgadorian vampyr feed on a witch without consequence?"

"Absolutely not," Agria huffed. "While more powerful than their exiled kind in the Sorrelikah, the vampyres of Gilgador are still below witches in Creational order. They cannot feed on witches or elves without deadly consequences."

"We already know they shouldn't," Maddox shot back, rolling his sleeves up to reveal deliciously corded forearms. He plunged his hands into the soapy water and began scrubbing our bowls. I gaped at his back. What happened to my arrogant prince? "Clearly, that's not accurate. They drained an entire village without a single vampyr death."

"Then they're in league with a powerful Creature. Or a god. Someone with enough magic to change their nature. I would say it's impossible, but there are rumors of books hidden in temples within this very jungle claiming such perverse magic—for example compulsion."

I blinked from the miracle unfolding before the washbin.

A thought sparked alive, and I turned to Agria to ask, "Would these temple libraries contain books powerful enough to alarm a queen into a realm-wide book ban?"

"If you're asking me if the Sorrelikah priestesses found a way to subvert Lilain's magic, I'd wager her reaction was answer enough."

If Lilain was in league with the Gilgadorian vampyres, there was no telling what she'd done to destabilize their Mother-given nature. And if the answer to compulsion lay in those libraries . . . Well, I couldn't dwell on that. Those books were long ashes.

"But how do we *stop* the vampyres?" Maddox pressed. "If you've lived amongst them, you know their weaknesses. It doesn't matter if they're from Gilgador or not. We just need an advantage."

Agria threw him an icy glare to rival his own. "It's so straightforward, I'm shocked you've missed it. The sunlight they're cursed to avoid? They fear it in every form. Firelight, witch-made light, a reflected light off a mirror. It's light that burns them, not the sun. Keep your villages and cities well lit. Only in darkness do they advance against a witch."

I huffed an incredulous laugh. Well, now I understood why the vampyres never bothered with the Day Realm, preferring the dark and unpopulated jungle. A single magicked flame from a child would send them scampering.

Thanking Agria profusely for her knowledge and hospitality, Maddox and I strapped on our swords and made for the jungle. At the door, Agria seized my sleeve and held me back.

"Be wary of that one." She nodded to Maddox stepping over an over-grown swath of thorned violets eating into the path. "Morgenna's heirs are never whole when she's finished with them. I've heard rumors of Prince Mendrick and his wife's true fate. All the rumors end with Morgenna's rot. She feeds her heirs a darkness that goes beyond shadows."

I shrugged her off and rubbed the scar on my chest. "I know what she's capable of."

"No one knows what she's capable of until it's too late. She's not ostentatious with her cruelty like Lilain. Therein lies her danger."

34

DUALITAS MALEFICARUM

Corryn

H ands on her knees, Alys heaved in gulps of salty warm air. She sur-
veyed the crumbling temple with a greenish mien and snapped, "I
take back all the compliments. You're as awful at umbranating as Maddox."

More than likely, Alys's aversion to cramped spaces made umbranating
through the suffocating shadow plane more difficult, but I had no intention
of bringing her worst fear to light and bickering.

I pushed past her and squinted at the primeval ruins. The white sands
of the beach sank under the heels of my pointed boots. Soft waves of warm
aquamarine sea lapped behind me.

Alys had told stories about this ruined temple deep in the uninhabited
wilds of the western coast she and her mother had discovered years ago, but
when she suggested this place to practice our Dual Witch magic and read
the book Agria had given her, I hadn't expected it to be half-falling into the
Western Sea.

A statue jutted into the sky at the temple's entrance. Time and salt had
swallowed their features, and I could no longer discern which god it had
once been. Corrugated pillars, some crumbling before my eyes, lined the
portico. Shaking the uneasy feeling something was watching me, I ambled
behind Alys up the sea-slick steps.

"For someone who made a living out of balancing on a strip of wood in the
air," I began, "you have a terrible inner ear. It's normal to feel disconcerted

in the shadow plane, but I've never seen it affect anyone like you. Perhaps it's like those who don't have sea legs. You don't have shadow legs."

She snorted and ducked under a toppled pillar angled over the temple's entrance. "If I can balance a thousand paces in the air with goblin arrows aimed at my head, then I have the balance to journey through the shadow plane. I'm telling you, there's something *wrong* in there. It's like it's sick or dying."

"I won't disagree, but it's pointless to complain when you can't fix it."

Her reply made me wonder how many iterations of the word *fuck* were out there.

The circular temple walls were in little better condition than the outside. At some point an earthquake had split the ivory marble floor in a gaping chasm through the center. Spiky crimson hellebore poked through from the earth beneath, the only proof winter had come to the warm western side of the island. One marble wall had crumbled to reveal a beautiful view of the sea lapping at the edge of the ruins. A salty breeze threaded with wild rosemary whipped through the opening, lifting the ends of Alys's unbound hair.

One hand to her roiling stomach, she plopped onto the cracked altar and tossed aside the double swords she'd insisted on bringing. Sea nymphs were unheard of, but that hadn't deterred her from bringing weapons into a temple.

I joined her and tried—and failed—to dust sand off my skirt.

The book she pulled from her patchwork of a bag wasn't particularly special. Black leather stretched over the cover, slightly worn at the corners with a spine showing signs of a careless reader or two. Faded gold foiling displayed the title in a typeset I'd seen a thousand times in Amethyst Hall's library rotunda.

Alys handed me the book with bony fingers nearly identical to mine. Where I had ink stains and calluses from writing, she had scars. Hatch marks of white against soft brown continued up her knuckles, disappearing into the cuffed sleeve of her black Night Guard tunic. Another sign of her violent life.

I shot the swords a wary glare. How was I supposed to form a bond with someone who had existed on the opposite end of life's spectrum?

Biting back a sigh, I opened *Dualitas Maleficarum* to the title page and scanned the author's name for anything familiar.

An ear-splitting shriek exploded out of my chest.

"Mother help me—Alys! Look, it's dated 76AE—that's After Efelldor. After we conquered Nordith's reign and renamed the island. Do you know what this means?"

Alys's brows flew into her hairline. "That it's a nearly a thousand years old and clearly has a dozen spellcasts on it to keep it pristine?"

Huffing with impatience, I jabbed a finger at the book's printing date. "76AE means it's part of the Lost Five Hundred Years. That time period spans the turn of the millennia to 500 AE. This is one of them. Merciful gods."

Alys sat up straight. "Go on. What else does it say?"

I flipped a few pages, searching them with a frown. "It begins with the story of Creation. *'The Mother of all Creation began life with a seed of hope. Planted in the fertile soil of Gilgador, our blessed Mother grew life from such a seed.'* Then it recounts the elves' Creation, but it wasn't enough for her. The Mother wanted another Creature, one made in her image . . ." My brain spun like top, trying to simultaneously translate and makes sense of the next passage. "This version has witch Creation all wrong. It's missing the bit about dual Creation. One witch born under the Mother's moon, one born to the Mother's sun."

Alys leaned over my shoulder and drummed her fingers against the altar—an impatient habit whose origins I had little doubt of. "Read it aloud."

"*The new Creatures born of bitter soil were not of one but two. A Creature of the sun's womb and the moon's seed as Created in the image of the Mother who was born to the twilight and dawn, baptized in nature's duality. And so, one hand wreathed in sunlight, the other in shadow, the first witch arose.*"

What the cursed Mother did that mean?

"I don't understand, my translation is accurate, but this version makes little sense."

A haggard laugh snuck out of Alys. "Oh, it makes perfect sense and—fuck—does it explain a lot. This is why Lilain erased years of history. Why both queens keep a tight hold on books. Within a few centuries, they erased witchkind's entire identity. *That's* their true source of power—truth."

I wrenched my nose from the book. *Truth?* I shook my head and sent curls bouncing in my periphery. "But—"

"Think! There's no such thing as a Night or Day Witch. There are only witches—us, Corryn—a Dual Witch *is* a true witch. We're meant to carry both light and shadow. What does every version of Creation say? Witches were Created in the Mother's image. We reflect her duality, her double-sided nature, her rocky temperament. Both warm and cold, bright and dark."

"But the realms—How did the queens split up witchkind into two realms? How did they tear our souls in half from birth? Every Night or Day Witch is missing half their magic." An awful thought snaked around my throat. "Missing half their soul."

I shoved off the altar and sent the ancient book tumbling to the sandy floor. Dimly, I was aware of Alys diving for the book and recognized I shouldn't have let it fall, but my mind had latched onto something I hadn't let myself think about in years.

Ignoring my pacing, Alys cradled the book to her chest, brushing sand off the ancient leather. "Gods, are you trying to ruin our only source of lost information? I thought you said this was a priceless treasure. Who knows what other life altering secrets it's carrying." Her voice dropped and she narrowed her eyes, pinning me in place. "This is why I was fated to find the book. *Everything* Efelldor knows is a lie perpetrated by two queens who have gone to forbidden lengths to cement power. They destroyed our identity to sit on dual thrones built on lies splitting witchkind's soul in half."

Split in half.

I unclasped my pearls from my wrist and held it up. The stand caught the breeze floating in through the gaping wall and began to swing, beautiful in a despondent sort of way.

"What if the Night and Day Witches have always felt something was missing? Melis gave this to me a week before we ended it. She meant it as a promise, a symbol she was trying to be better. More than once, she wished she'd been born a Day Witch. If she'd been born with light in her soul like a Day Witch, then she would have found balance. But because she was made from darkness, she deserved what waited in the dark."

A sob clawed up my tightening throat, as bitter as the poison that had wrecked my life and started me down a path I'd been meant for all along. That didn't mean I was happy to walk it.

"I hate Morgenna," I whispered. The sea breeze snatched at my words, but it didn't matter. Alys heard them all the same when the words echoed on the river between us. "They say hatred is the first step toward defiling your soul, but I hate her for what she did to Melis. Morgenna stole more than her light. She broke her until all that remained was that bitter shell. She—she took her from me. Our future, our dreams. All of it shriveled and died because of her."

The pearls rattled harder. A deep sob erupted from my chest, dry and unrestrained, like after nearly ten years it had finally worn down its cage. The *if only* that had haunted me broke in another sob, this one wet.

I was undoubtedly embarrassing Alys with this display. A tough soldier like her didn't cry.

I turned to hide my blotchy skin, but she took a hesitant step toward me, and then another until she was close enough to touch. She raised her arms then yanked them back down.

"Do you—Can I—"

I eyed her through blurring tears and let loose a watery giggle. "Is this you asking me if I require comforting? It looks as if you're debating tackling me."

She crossed her arms tight over her chest, flexing her fingers. "Don't make it more awkward than it already is. Just say yes and let me hug you."

"All right, but don't squish—Oof."

She hugged like she was headed into battle, aggressive and desperate. But she was warm and solid. She smelled like the spiced honey I drizzled into my tea, sweet and comforting—like who she was behind the thorny exterior. Relief smoothed the ache inside. It didn't altogether vanish. Nothing would cure me, but at least I wasn't alone. We were different, yes. Different and balanced.

"You already know how I feel about her," she whispered somewhere by my ear. "But I don't have a right to tell you how to live your life. I can only say after all you've risked for this world, you deserve happiness. Move on or don't. Whatever you choose, I'll be there. We're each other's only constant in this world. If blood is all we share, then let's make sure nothing taints that bloody bond."

"Including royals who maneuver their way into our hearts?"

"Especially those." She pulled back with a roguish grin, but she didn't meet my eyes.

I cleared my throat before returning to the altar. Grabbing the book from where Alys had left it on the altar, I said, "Right, well the book answers some questions but raises more. Are the queens Dual—or rather *true*—Witches? And where does compulsion fit? Is it meant to be magic born to witches?"

She toed the hellebore reaching for her in the gentle breeze. "Agria mentioned Lilain might have found perverse magic that changed a vampyr's nature. Suppose she changed them to feed on vampyres to take our magic without dying. That's awfully powerful magic. It explains how the vampyres are getting around undetected. They're umbranating with stolen magic given by Lilain in exchange for hunting me. Now, imagine Lilain *and* Morgenna found a way to pervert witches too? Like splitting witchkind's soul into two?"

"That's a lot of supposition."

Alys shrugged.

She was right. If Lilain had access to lost ancient magic who knew what she was capable of.

"I suppose this is why Morgenna hunts Dual Witches," she mused, peering over my shoulder at a sketch of a witch bathed in both shadow and light. "She must be one too. It's not only our power like hers that's threatening, but we pose a risk in revealing witchkind's true nature and what she tried to destroy."

"Tried and failed. Meanwhile nature's brought balance to her perversion. It explains why Night and Day conception comes so easily." I offered her an apologetic wince, recalling my not-so-gentle warning I'd given her the night she stayed at Agria's house.

"I told you I was never a problem. Lilain wards the DRAS against pregnancy." Lifting her tunic, she tapped an iron-inked conception rune tattooed on her hip. "We're sterile. Makes it easier to control us if we can't create outside ties."

I pressed a hand to my heart, all horror aimed at the inverted triangular runes. Lilain was a monster. A tyrant of the worst kind who abused those she should have protected.

Alys bit her lip and yanked her hem back down with a nonchalant shrug. "Amongst the atrocities Lilain's committed, forcing sterilization onto her soldiers is a drop in the bucket."

She tugged the book from me, flipping through the pages at an alarming speed. She was going to rip the vellum pages if she wasn't careful. Not that I had any room to talk.

"What are you looking for?" I asked. "What could be more shocking than revealing witchkind's true nature?"

"Ending our exile crossed my mind."

"The exile spans two millennia. We don't even know what happened to Gilgador and its people. What would be the point of ending it?"

She gently closed the book and said, "Nature works on a balance, right? Dark and light. Life and death. One upholds the other, or the balance tips. But witchkind's scales have been broken for millennia. Between the exile and the split, we're a poor imitation of the original witches. Who better to bring back balance than the fated gift of the Mother herself—us. A perfect balance. One witch raised by Day, the other Night. One of death and war, one of life and salvation."

I bolted upright from the altar. All the blood rushed from my head, leaving me lightheaded.

"That's why we need six. We're the Dual Witches, the center counter-weight to each side. We need to find the others—two witches of Day and two of Night."

"Then you better hurry and find those portents so we can warn the other four."

35

HEED THE PORTENTS CALL

Corryn

The Night Flame above the Mother's marble temple reminded me of a black-and-silver flag. The eerie flames had burned for centuries above the ancient temple—a symbol of the Night Realm's enduring power—a lie. The flame indignantly sputtered silvery sparks into the evening sky.

"What's your point? You're nothing but a meaningless icon," I muttered, hunching deeper into my cloak as I attempted to shelter from the pelting snow. "Only good for burning the dead as a symbol of pretentious grief."

"Are you talking to the Night Flame?"

I spun and found Maddox behind me, peering up at the flame with a frown. "I didn't mean—I was only—" Pink flooded my face, recalling the last time the Night Flame was used. "I'm sorry. I didn't mean to be insensitive about your parents."

He shrugged, expression smoothing into neutrality. "It *is* pretentious. The dead don't care if you burn them with Night Flame or toss them into the Quies." He pointed to the temple's marble entrance of a dozen winding columns. "Speaking of pretentious—are you ready to meet the Second Order of the Priestesshood?"

Not particularly. But I *was* ready to find the portents. And steal them. *All for the good of witchkind,* I reminded myself as we passed though the temple doors. I wasn't a criminal; I was a revolutionary. Or so Alys tried to convince me.

"Let's go over this again," Maddox insisted.

"I'm here to take notes on runic inscriptions throughout the temple as a runes instructor from Amethyst Hall. The tour also includes runes etched in the portents. Should you draw their attention, I would find the need to relieve myself. What happens then is certainly none of your business."

He nodded sharply, a sign his compulsion remained untriggered.

"Don't leave a trail," was his only warning.

He needn't worry. Alys and I had spent the past week searching through old runic books to find the rune I needed to pull this off. The night before, she'd found it. Without this rune, my trip to the temple was useless.

Heart hammering, I entered the temple to more blinding white marble. Apparently, the ancients hadn't believed in lumber or stone. Only marble. A crystal sculpture of a wide-hipped figure holding aloft a sun in one hand and a crescent moon in the other loomed over the sanctuary of worshippers. I craned up to study the top. It must have been four stories tall.

Mother bless the sculptor.

Beneath the crystalline moon, a priestess in white robes waited. Her round ebony face was pinched and even her crisp bow to Maddox couldn't hide her disapproval. To be fair, we were probably the least religious witches in Efelldor. Thin bands of gold-infused tattoos circled the priestess's naked scalp like a crown, swirling with runes spellcasted for painful subjugation. I admired the Mother, but clearly not as much as the Second Order.

I eyed Maddox and wondered if the rumors he had the same tattoos in iron ink held any truth. Mother help him, I hoped not. Not even he deserved that sort of penance.

The priestess hurried us to a sitting room off the sanctuary. For a temple, the furnishings were terribly ornate. Apparently, living humbly before the Mother didn't apply to decor. Velvet fabrics and amethyst with inlaid gold covered anything that wasn't marble.

"We meet again! Greetings and may the Mother bless you, Prince Maddox," a woman chimed as she rose from an indigo quilted armchair. Like the first priestess, she wore a naked creamy scalp of tattoos with buttoned, white, floor-length robes—although she'd left significantly more buttons undone. Rounded and full, she exuded the ideal femininity of the Mother.

With a sideways glance at me, she said, "I am High Priestess Helenae Noxavis of the Second Order." She may have been addressing me, but her deep, button-threatening bow was for all for Maddox who looked as if he'd swallowed a vial of the bitterest potion.

I rearranged my wool blouse over my flatter frame and offered her a smile. She ignored me, fawning over Maddox, and leading him to her vacated armchair. She tried to press a tea service onto him, but he firmly declined, neatly avoiding her wandering hands when she took his cloak. If the priestess had an inkling who held his heart, she may've been more circumspect with her hands—provided she wanted to keep them.

The pinch-faced priestess watched the display with growing disgust, all but baring her teeth. I inched toward her, hoping to ease her tension.

"I'm Instructor Corryn Stellanati." I held out a hand, but the priestess continued observing the other woman's impressive bosom jiggle with laughter. I tried again. "You must be our escort. Sister Del, is it?"

"I know who you are, Instructor, and why you are here."

My heart dropped to my feet.

Del whirled, dark eyes splitting me in half. "You academics are all the same. You plunder knowledge like miners with gold, ripping it from our temples, bringing to light what was put to rest. You may have fooled Prince Maddox, but I see you for what you are—a thief."

The accuracy of her words smarted. I spun my bracelet and kept my smile tightly glued. Nothing I could say would change her opinion, but I couldn't squash the part of me that longed to be praised for what I was about to do.

"Perhaps Instructor Stellanati can begin her tour now? Perhaps with the Hall of Murals?" Maddox asked, smoothy twisting his arm from the high priestess's reach.

Helenae gave a merry laugh and waggled a finger. "Not without an escort, she cannot. Come, we shall *all* enter the Hall of Murals." Her hips swayed with each step, and she pulled her robes tighter over her behind. She took female embodiment to the very edge, willing to plunge into obscenity. I might've not minded a second or third look if it weren't for her wandering hands on someone who was noticeably uncomfortable. No amount of beauty was worth a narcissistic temperament.

I fell into step beside Maddox as Del brought up the rear of our party. "Why do you look so glum?" I whispered with a wry grin. "Sister Helenae looks like she wants to shove you into the nearest closet and convince you of her commitment to the crown."

He shuddered, shoving his hands deep into his pockets. "You're hilarious. Shall I be your wingman and turn her onto you instead?"

"Do so at your own peril, Your Highness. I prefer not to be smothered between her . . . *commitments.*"

That drew a soft laugh out of him.

Mother bless Alys. What had she done to the prince made of stone?

I'd studied the Hall of Murals and its runes many times, although never in person. I knew each mural from memory: The gloomy tale of the elven queen whose tapestries hung in Amethyst Hall; the fable of the giant squid and the sea nymph in their struggle to conceive. Each mural portrayed useless runes, their accompanying spellcasts lost with time. I didn't need to pretend fascination. They were beautiful works of ancient art, and I sketched them, nonetheless.

"You mustn't touch them," Del hissed, rounding to stand between me and the sea nymph.

I snatched my hand back, heat crawling up my neck. "I was merely using my hand as a reference—"

But Del had already steered me from the hall. Maddox shot me a pained look as Helenae wound her arm through his, jovially cackling at a joke she'd made. We rounded a corner and came before an arch of more marble. A ward glowed over the entrance, protecting its contents.

"Here we have the divinationists chamber, where all recorded portents are stored. Just let me open this teeny poison ward." The High Priestess whispered a spellcast with a smear from her bleeding thumb and the glowing sapphire ward fell away. "Not that anyone would get past the Second

Order, but if they did, they'd find a slow, miserable death upon triggering the ward."

Helenae finally acknowledged me. Shrewd calculation replaced her smiles. "We cannot permit you to study the portents alone, Instructor. The Second Order takes the security of Queen Morgenna's property most gravely. You will be closely monitored by Sister Del, but you will not sketch, note, nor touch anything within the room. Am I clear?"

Ignoring the pinching in my stomach, I nodded. "Of course. I understand the severity of the situation. I am most thankful for what you'll graciously allow."

Del followed me through the archway, close enough her breath whispered over my neck.

The room wasn't much larger than a classroom. Narrow tables formed rows with narrower aisles, barely leaving enough room to pass through. Scroll after scroll lined each table, all behind age reducing wards or glass. Some portents were incredibly short—a line of numbers and runes and nothing more. Others were countless pages, threaded and bound into books.

Peering at a scroll barely legible against decaying parchment, I said to Del, "I suppose this one is positively ancient, isn't it?"

Her pinched scowl grew tighter. "Can't you read the inscription plaque below? It's from 239BE. As in Before Efelldor. It's the only portent we have before the Lost Five Hundred Years and before witchkind overturned the elves."

"Oh, yes. Of course." I squinted at the tiny inscription as if confused. "But if this is your oldest portent, which is your newest?"

Del huffed a low sigh, pointing at a portent behind me. "For an academic, your reading proficiency is sorely lacking."

I released a nervous titter and turned. Three portents were lined together on a muslin cushion beneath a glass case. "These three?"

My heart sank. Where were the other three portents?

Del sucked air through her teeth and jabbed at the inscription. *Portents of Alistyr Fidustella as recounted to Queen Morgenna in 999AE.* Twenty-nine years ago. The year before Alys and I were born, right when we'd been conceived.

I'd found them.

Each portent spanned a piece of parchment no bigger than my palm. Tiny, cramped writing surrounded numerical equations and sloppy sketches of astrological symbols.

I held back a groan. They would take me ages to translate.

Del's frigid fingers circled my wrist. "You've had your fill. Out."

Maddox waited by the archway, the high priestess pressed against his side like a second skin even as he continued sidestepping her. The glower he sent me screamed I'd owe him far more than simple forgiveness.

"Shall we have that tea now?" he asked Helenae, prying her claws from his undoubtedly sore arm.

We followed the beaming priestess to the velvet sitting room off the sanctuary. Del never strayed far from my side, breathing—literally—down my neck. Maddox gave her a small frown, turning back to study Helenae. Whatever distraction he was concocting, I hope he thoroughly ensnared Del, or I would be walking out of here in chains.

Helenae took every effort to bend forward and backward before Maddox as she served him tea, utterly oblivious to his irritated sighs or dark glares skewering me with threats I'd be indebted to him for life.

Del saw it all. Every taut tendon in her neck prepared to snap as Helenae nearly upended the tea service with her swaying bottom.

When Helenae leaned too far over an armrest and toppled into Maddox's lap, Del darted to her feet. She shook from head to toe, screeching something about undignified whores of House Noxavis.

Quietly as I could, I rose and crept toward the door just as Maddox shoved Helenae off his lap. Hard. The buxom woman crashed into the tea service, scattering pastries and teacups. I ambled a few more steps from the chaos.

Stony as ever, Maddox stood and pointed at Del. "I do not expect much decency from the fallen House of Noxavis. But you, Del, belong to a house older than the realm, and yet you stoop to her level by allowing her to continue her sordid displays without a word. No wonder you were passed up for the high priestess role."

I ducked from the room to Del's ear-piercing shrieks defending her and her house's honor. Helenae's muffled sobs followed at a much quieter decibel. Trust Maddox to turn the courtier houses against one another.

All the easier for me to get in and out of the portent room unnoticed.

The corridor to the archway remained empty; the sapphire pulsing ward reactivated. Praying to Fortuna Melis's trick worked here too and that my magic superseded Helenae's, I roused the shadows tucked beneath a nearby hall table. Thin, black wisps prodded the arch, searching the place Helenae had resummoned the ward. With a fizzle, the shadow pushed through a button-sized hole. Following Alys's suggestion, I called the portent room's shadows to my wisp, doubling its size.

I glanced back down the corridor, making sure Del hadn't followed. But the shouts continued. Releasing a slow breath, I eased open the portent case with a flick of shadow. After months of fruitless searching, three scraps of parchment waited with answers. A shiver wormed up my spine as I released my shadows.

Now came the hard part.

I'd practiced all morning with Alys, sneaking her into my rooms at Amethyst Hall to get it right.

Breathing shallowly, I pressed a summoned stream of water through the ward's button-sized hole. The rivulet swirled for the waiting portents, trembling with my concentration. But the water jerked to the side, curious of a portent behind a violet glow. Gasping, I halted and steadied my breathing. I was already debasing myself with criminality. I wasn't about to ruin centuries worth of knowledge and destroy the surrounding portents. The Mother-cursed water and its unruly nature. My shadows never misbehaved.

"Focus," I muttered to the summoned water. "You can't touch anything but what I command."

Like a reprimanded child, the water wavered then thinned to the finest line I could muster. With it, I traced a replication rune Alys had found onto the back of the first parchment. A drop bled through to the front.

Hissing, I yanked the water back and held my breath. But the parchment's ink didn't bleed. Seconds ticked by as the drop evaporated. I let my breath whoosh out.

Maddox had wound up the priestesses, but he couldn't hold their attention forever. I had to get the portents out. Guiding the water back to the parchment, I finished the replication rune.

An identical parchment sprang from the first and drifted to the floor. I'd done it. I swallowed a gleeful giggle and moved onto the second portent. Another success. As the last replicated portent fell to the floor, the screeches began fading.

I was out of time.

Dissolving the water into mist, I rammed shadow back into the ward's weak spot. I snapped the glass case closed and scooped the replicated portents, guiding them back through the ward. The pulsing blue light trembled but remained untriggered. Gently, the shadow deposited the portents into my outstretched hand.

I shoved them up my skirts, into the deep pocket I'd sewn into my petticoat. Footsteps sounded and I smoothed my face, striding to meet them. At the corner, I narrowly avoided sailing into a furious Del.

"Oh, pardon me, Sister." My throat clogged around my frantic heart.

"Where were you?"

I smiled and glanced at my boots, trying my best to appear sheepish. "Well, I'm no member of a distinguished house. It seemed Prince Maddox wanted words with the high priestess, and I didn't feel it prudent to participate in such a conversation when I myself belong to no great house. I made myself scarce and sought the lady's room."

What a load of hogwash.

Del bought it, nose reaching for the air. "No, you certainly did not belong. At least you had enough sense to see yourself out. But you shouldn't have strayed. Simply waiting outside would do. Just in case"—she peered again at the pulsing ward, eyes narrowing—"empty out your bag and pockets."

"I don't think—"

"Now, *Instructor.*"

Hands trembling, I upended my satchel of pens and notebooks onto the marble floor. A fistful of coins from my outer pockets followed. Nothing incriminating. I held my breath, but Del merely harrumphed. She allowed me to return my belongings before gripping my wrist, dragging me to the chamber where a beetroot-red Helenae stared down at her tea-stained robe.

Maddox extended his elbow and muttered, "I hope you're well *relieved* because I am never coming here again and not a soul could convince me otherwise."

Well, maybe *I* couldn't convince him, but I could think of a witch who could, should the need arise. I would pay good coin to see Alys put Helenae in her place.

I smiled brightly and bid the sullen priestesses good night.

Outside the temple, Maddox wiped his hands repeatedly against his pants and snarled, "You owe me more than *forgiveness*, Stellanati. Gods, that woman has bleeding tentacles."

I chortled, pulling my rabbit-lined hood over my head against the snow. "Helenae was rather determined, wasn't she? I nearly felt sorry for you when she fell into your lap—" I broke into peals of laughter only made worse by Maddox's hissed curse. "All right, then. Name your favor."

He followed me from the Jansk District in quiet contemplation, his attention far from Morithia's streets. I thought he'd changed his mind, when he finally said, "Answer me this and we're even. How well do you know Alys Sathos?"

I stumbled over the cobblestones, catching the heel of my boot in a crack. His expression was too blank. Devoid of any hint to his intentions.

"Erm—well, I—I met her at the Harkening Ball."

He sighed and a spark of irritation broke the blank wall. "Yes, Yori told me. Didn't *I* tell *you* to stay away from her?"

Relief flooded me. He didn't know. This stemmed from his earlier warning and my willful defiance.

"You also said she was dangerous," I snapped back. "And you were wrong. Perhaps she's a bit more calculated than most, but it's well-earned if you know how she grew up. I happen to enjoy her company very much. Good thing I didn't listen to you, or I wouldn't know her hidden sweetness beyond the thorny exterior."

Maddox's lips twisted painfully tight. Like he'd swallowed the bitter taste of jealousy.

I halted in the street and rounded on him. "That's your first thought? I'm *stealing her away*? I told you she was lonely and needed a friend beyond your goons. If I happen to be that someone, who are you to take her from me?"

Contrition glimmered briefly before splintering into burning ice. He turned away and trudged down the nearly empty street. "She isn't a possession to steal. If you think that, you don't know her at all."

"I seem to know she's much better off without you."

He whipped his head back with a glare that could've skinned me alive. Alys must've been short a few marbles to look at that expression and feel gooey. "That was never in doubt. The true question is—is she any better off with *you*? Or will you backstab her if she hurts you?"

My mouth dropped in an unseemly gape.

He released a strangled sigh, running a hand through his hair with a slightly abashed expression.

When he tried to explain, I held up a hand. "I don't know what she sees in you, truly. But something encourages a sweet smile onto her face whenever she speaks of you, and I can't bring myself to say anything negative for fear of bursting the rare contentment she rightly deserves. So, I'm begging you, Maddox—don't let us force her to choose between us. It would destroy her."

He reared back as if I'd slapped him. He might not have known exactly what Alys and I were to one another, but the desperation in my tone gave him pause. Apprehension and longing warred across his features before he finally bit out, "I—I agree. But . . . At least soothe my worries and tell me she's not caught up in your portent *studies*."

A thin laugh warbled out and his narrowing eyes said he saw right through it. "Alys might be more intellectually curious than most, but why would she bother studying portents? She's a guard, not an academic—"

"Don't say another word, Stellanati." He kicked at a loose cobblestone with a soft snarl. "You're an awful liar, and it's going to get you killed. Gods help you if it gets *her* killed."

Silent and brooding, he escorted me to the city's gates. I shouldn't have said anything. Even he realized the precarious situation I'd put Alys in, and he knew next to nothing. Alys would shrug and say Maddox was too bright to ignore our connection forever, but I knew better than to believe the nonchalant attitude she wore like armor.

At the onyx gates, he cast a narrowed glance toward a nearby guard before whispering, "Tell her to be careful. Both of you. Morgenna is always watching and while I might cheat some of her compulsion, not everyone can. Just—make sure she's careful."

I stepped through the ward's reach and felt its grimy hold slide off. "You know as well as I do—no one tells Alys Sathos what to do."

Except for maybe Morgenna's compulsion.

36

THE RAGE OF A MOTHER

Maddox

"Keep glaring at the window like that and your face will freeze—eh ... too late."

Yori's jibe cut through my spiraling thoughts. Without turning from my office tower window, I raised a single finger. Frost glazed the windowpane, but I saw enough of the long braid peeking from the pacing cloak below to know Alys was anxious about something.

Yori came to stand beside me, squinting out the window with an informant's letter in hand. "She nearly bit off Sylinia's head in training this morning and made another page cry. She's never been one to hold their hand, but dangling a page off the catwalk for failing to understand the proper sword progression is a bit much—even for her."

Alys tilted her chin to the sky, eyes shut against the snowfall. She was utterly mesmerizing. I could've spent hours studying the indention in her bottom lip, the faint dimples when she truly smiled, the wispy lashes framing doe-brown eyes and never come up for something as trivial as air.

Conjuring her from memory came as easy as breathing. She was a permanent cycle of examination in my head. How she spoke melodically faster when she was excited. Her enthusiastic love of apples. Her honeyed scent lingering on any surface she touched, stronger than ever. How any semblance of control irked her, yet she longed to belong. Her soft mutterings in her sleep. The way she twisted the second earring in her left ear when she was nervous. The never-ending restless fidgeting that would send me to an early grave.

I'd memorized the feeling of her racing pulse against my lips. Knew if I bit the sensitive spot below her ear she'd arch into my arms, pliant and warm. Only then would the noise in my head finally fade. I knew the sound she'd make if I ran my fingers along her lower spine—a faint hitch in her breathing, barely audible, but I would've ruined my own realm to hear it again.

I wasn't modest enough to think she didn't want me, but the blatant panic swimming with her tears the night we spent at the novelist's cottage spoke of how deep Morgenna had forced herself into Alys's psyche—and I knew I was partly to blame. All because I hadn't stayed away from her and now, I was risking both our lives.

Below, Alys snapped her eyes open and wistfully watched the shifting gray clouds—perfect conditions for a flying witch. Guilt twisted my gut. The clock tower rang the evening hour in a series of clanging blows. She straightened her shoulders and nodded once before marching for the doors, determination clear on every delicately sharp feature.

I wrenched myself from the window and strode back to the overflowing desk. A quick stretch had become twenty minutes of reliving every moment I'd caught alone with Alys since the night of the balcony. Not that I didn't spend each night making sure each second was committed to memory, but somehow it was never enough. Not enough to stop me from reaching for her in an empty corridor or creating excuses to sit with her in the barracks dining hall.

The most dangerous part of Alys wasn't that I wanted her beneath me in bed, but rather that I was just as content to sit hours with her and bicker about meaningless topics.

I still waited on her to admit she'd stolen the sketch I'd left for her to find.

As I'd drawn the quaint little cottage for the witch muttering in her sleep beside me, I'd realized how difficult it must have been for Melis to simply put down the bottle and walk away.

Yori plunked in the chair across the desk and stroked that ridiculous beard he refused to shave because, "*Some women like a little extra friction.*"

"I tried suggesting Alys should find you and a balcony to lighten her mood. In return, she suggested I go fuck a nymph." He grinned at my rolled eyes. His observant nature was going to get him in trouble. He tapped the letter against the desk. "Whatever you did, you should try apologizing. A novel concept for you, I realize, but worth a shot."

I scowled and motioned for the letter. "What makes you think I did anything?"

He extended the letter only to snatch it back. "Oh, I don't know. It's not as if I've endured your charm for over fifteen years. I was getting rather used to a mellow Alys. I'd rather she not go back to using her creepy stare when she looks at you. It gives every man in her radius the willies."

"What creepy stare?"

"The one where she can't decide if she wants to fuck you or stab you."

I choked down a laugh. "Give me the letter, you git."

Scanning the informant's sloppy writing, I yanked a plain cloak off a hook and muttered a spellcast to repel snow from the wool. The stacks of grain reports would wait until morning.

Yori rose to his feet. "Want me to come? We can get rip-roaring drunk afterward."

I shot him an indulgent grin but shook my head. Rip-roaring drunk meant waking somewhere in the seediest part of the Black Wall District, wondering how we were still alive. Lord Felumbra and the other magistrates wouldn't appreciate a hangover at the next day's meeting.

He clapped my shoulder with a dramatic sigh. "All right then. Go meet your informant. Alone. Miserable. Doing your best not to obsess over Alys Sathos's hair and failing spectacularly." He caught the sketchbook I lobbed in his direction and chuckled. Heading for the door, he tossed back, "Stop ogling out of windows. Get on your knees and apologize."

I hurried down to the city, deep in thought on what I could do on my knees or what kind of new gasps I could draw while there. I was more than aware how often the little demon had me on my knees, but I couldn't find it in me to mind.

As I shifted to what lay ahead, an icy hook tugged at my mind, a subtle reminder I'd do nothing but watch the once bustling Water Wheel District die.

The letter in my pocket claimed the resistance Morgenna had tried to kill was stirring. Osrin Atercruor was missing, presumably hiding, the letter claimed. Bodies drifting down the Quies no longer belonged to innocents, and known thugs had gone missing.

The Water Wheel's restless witches represented everything Morgenna hated—independent thought, steel will, and a hunger to survive. Somehow my father convinced her wiping out an entire district was political disaster. When Osrin Atercruor rose to power, she seized an opportunity. How could the district turn against her if they were too busy keeping Atercruor at bay?

Veiling from sight, I followed the Quies River through the Water Wheel until I found the discreet tavern tucked against the city's wall and a long-abandoned butchery.

Hectir Albanox, a tanner—and my informant—waited outside beneath a wooden plank depicting a bedraggled man holding a dragon's egg. Hectir took a drag from rolled paper stuffed with tabacum. The smoke danced into the swinging sign, slithering up the golden dragon egg before fading into the sooty air.

Unveiling beside the barrel-chested witch, I offered a quick nod.

"Better veil back up, Highness." He tossed the tabacum roll over his shoulder. "Ervik Noxos's inside. Don't trust the creep not to slit your throat. Usually this little tavern's dead, but tonight's drawn in a rowdy bunch. Ervik could get away with anything in a crowd that size."

Ervik Noxos was an alleged vigilante, but he had never been witnessed committing a crime. At least not by anyone willing to rat him out. That alone saved the terrifying witch from Morgenna's compulsion.

Hectir, on the other hand, didn't seem to mind occasionally selling his district out for coin.

He led the way through the cramped Villager's Egg, head down as he avoided a table of witches urging on an arm-wrestling pair. The overwhelming scent of unwashed bodies clashed with the sticky sweetness of mead coating the floors. In this corner of the city, no one looked twice at the hulking Hectir pushing his way to the back.

We settled into a corner, tucked away from the bustle of the tavern's open floor. A propped-open side door swept in desperately needed fresh air. Grunting a warning, Hectir deepened the table's murky shadows, obscuring all but his silhouette from view.

"Two more brothels went under this week," he began, glancing to the bar where several cloaked figures huddled together. "Both burned to the ground."

"And the women inside?"

"Pulled out in time."

"Any word who did it?"

Hectir grinned, sitting back and propping his feet on the table. "You wouldn't believe me if I told you."

"Tell me anyways."

He fixed his stare on a group of young women dressed in men's tunics. Jeering loudly, they tossed back tankards of mead, as coarse as the table of men beside them. Daggers sharp as any sword glittered at their sides. One of them, an owl-eyed blonde, tossed a dagger between her hands, staring at the door with a peculiar unblinking yearning. Rolling her shoulders, she rose and sheathed her dagger. She nodded to a cloaked figure at the bar and hurried out the tavern.

"Wind's shifting, Highness." Hectir pulled out another tabacum roll. "Gone are the days them young girls sit by and let the world run roughshod over them. That lot runs with Ervik Noxos, as eager for blood as the mad witch himself. 'Course, they got more reason."

I leaned forward, holding my breath against the burn of tabacum. "Why did you bring me here, Hectir? What's Ervik planning with those girls?"

Hectir's laughter grated like knives against glass. "Ervik? He's no mastermind. You want to know who holds the Water Wheel's reins? Find Matilda

Noctem. Used to rule our district's council with an iron fist. Well, until Osrin raped and butchered her only daughter. Went a bit mad after that. Seeing your kin that way does things to you."

"Nah," Hectir continued. "Matilda's a bit dodgy, but she still holds the district in her grip. Dissolved council or not. You mark my words—whatever trap's being set for Osrin, it starts with Matilda Noctem. Ervik's nothing but a blade."

Unveiling, I tugged my hood further over my face, careful even in the dark to keep my identity obscured. The Lexsidus line wasn't received well here. Sliding a sack of coin over the table, I demanded, "What trap?"

Hectir eyed me over his smoke, his cocky attitude slipping as he once again glanced at the bar. "Ervik claims Osrin's after some girl. Wouldn't say which. Only that Matilda intends to lure him from hiding with her. You can guess what happens then. That's not all." He narrowed his eyes and took a long drag. "That Day Witch the queen compelled?"

The world slowed, blurring to a halt.

"What about her?"

"She's often at Matilda's tavern. I think she befriended Matilda's grand-daughter." He pointed to the table of young women. "One of those wildlings slinging back mead. Sometimes the two of them eat with the girl's father, Rugard. Sometimes Matilda joins. Maybe it's nothing. Maybe Rugard's got a thing for the Day Witch. She's pretty in an odd sort of way. *Or* maybe she's in deep with Matilda and Ervik."

In a practiced voice, I drawled, "She's compelled like any guard not to move against Osrin." My heart hammered like a chisel against my ribs.

Hectir raised an eyebrow. "So are you, yet here you are, two fingers deep in the Water Wheel's business. I've met her, y'know. Mouthy, but sharp. If anyone could wrangle compulsion's loopholes, it's Sathos."

He let out a snort and nodded toward the door. "Summoned like the demon she is. Guess she's in deep after all."

In a punch to the gut, Alys walked into the tavern.

She meandered through the tables with a lazy grin. She'd thrown off her hood, the gold in her ears catching the candlelight. Witches called to her.

Some clapped her back. She knew each by name, scowling at some, laughing with others. Perching on a stool at the bar, she waved away a tankard of mead. With an exasperated groan, the barkeeper poured her a glass of apple wine instead.

The figure beside her flipped their hood to reveal a wiry witch, a stiletto between his teeth. Ervik Noxos spat out the knife and grinned at Alys. Beside him, an older woman turned. There was no mistaking the weathered face of Matilda Noctem beneath the hood.

The final hooded figure rose to stand beside Alys, placing a massive hand on her back as he bent low to whisper in her ear. Something twisted my insides. But Alys shrugged his hand off and glanced at the tavern door swinging open.

The blonde girl with the iron dagger stepped inside, nodding once to Matilda. She lowered onto the stool beside Alys, breathing hard. Alys wrapped an arm around the young girl's trembling shoulders and offered her a rare, soft smile. The girl gripped her dagger, jaw clenched as they both watched the door.

The tavern was a trap for Osrin.

Ice struck and my will misted into nothing. Morgenna needed to know. *I* needed to tell her. Alys had skirted the line. Alys plotted—

No. Alys had done nothing wrong. She was merely sitting at a bar.

No—I should leave—I needed to rise. Slip out the open back door. I should—

Sit, an icy voice seemed to hiss, wrapping icy talons around my legs. *Stay and watch, report what you see to your queen. Watch Alys disobey and make sure she is punished.*

I couldn't. I—I had to leave. I couldn't hurt her. Never her. I pressed my hands against the table, trying to rise.

My legs had frozen.

The tavern door opened, and the Villager's Egg fell silent. Osrin Atercruor ducked through the door, snow swirling in behind him. The sides of his shorn head gleamed almost as bright as the curved dagger at his hip. A shoulder-length braid fell from the golden strip on top. Two men followed, paid thugs watching Osrin's back. The monstrous witch scanned the silent tavern before fixing on the bar.

"Oh, fucking Mother." Hectir shot from his chair, dashing for the back door. "I'm not a part of this, Highness. Whatever's going down here, remember it wasn't me."

I couldn't reply. *You can't warn Alys*, the icy compulsion cooed. *You must watch it play out and report* everything *to Morgenna. Alys must be punished.*

Frozen, I watched Osrin swagger to the bar where the blonde girl shivered. Alys and the others had vanished, and Osrin plunked onto Alys's vacated stool. He dragged a languid gaze over the girl's body. Her dagger clattered to the ground. Face in flames, she lunged for it, but Osrin laughed, kicking the knife from her reach.

The girl whirled and slapped something onto his wrists.

He flicked his hands, frowning at the metal encasing his wrists like two perverse bracelets. Warded manacles to hold in his magic. Roaring, he spun onto the girl and shoved. With a scream, she careened into the bar, glass and mead crashing to the floor.

Shadows exploded at the tavern door. Reams of black slashed through the two thugs in a spray of blood. Soundless and grim, Rugard and Ervik stepped over the fallen bodies. Their stony expressions turned onto a heaving Osrin.

Screams should've ripped through the tavern or feet stampeding for the door. But no one moved. Not the witches of the Water Wheel. They eyed the manacled Osrin then the dead thugs and something merciless and dark bloomed. One by one, the witches crept closer.

"You," Osrin snarled, kicking aside a chair to reach the broken bar. "You did this. You poisoned them against me. The women, the district. You ruined everything."

He ripped the curved dagger from his hip and lunged for Alys.

The table jerked beneath me, but I couldn't rise.

A flash of steel sailed through the air. Osrin fell to the floor with a bellowing crash of wood and glass, a knife deep in his thigh.

Ervik strolled to the fallen witch and retrieved his stiletto. Razor-sharp shadows sliced tendons in Osrin's shoulders and then behind his knees. The giant screamed but the sound baited the tavern closer. Hungry shadows inched across the sticky floor.

"You air-humping bitch. This won't end here." The knife tumbled from Osrin's limp hands. He wormed his way to Alys, clawing the ground with useless arms. He rolled to his side, unsuccessfully sitting up. Features scarred by evil and malice twisted into inextinguishable fury, lips drawn back to reveal a snarl. "Morgenna will know. She'll find out, and she'll punish you until you're begging for death, you worthless piece of shit."

Alys crouched just out of reach. "Who will tell Morgenna? You?"

Osrin paled and whipped to the circling witches. "Help me. She's not one of us Water Wheel folk. She's not even a fucking Night Witch. She'll kill me! Don't stand there watching!"

Matilda limped her way through the parting crowd who ducked their heads as she passed. "Don't be silly, Osrin. Sathos is compelled to never harm a hair on your head."

The older woman crouched beside Alys and pointed to a woman with scars stemming from her lips to her ears. "Remember Sorsha? You sold her sister to a brothel and left her for dead when you'd finished with her." She pointed to another woman, a hunched, white-haired witch with milky eyes. "Surely you remember *her*. You killed three daughters and sold two more to a whorehouse. Still no recollection? Too many to remember, I suppose."

Osrin struggled on the floor, alternating between pleas and obscene curses. Someone summoned shadow and wrapped a cord of darkness around his mouth.

Alys helped Matilda into a standing position and wrapped her arm around the older woman, her angular face soft and warm. "Do what brings you peace. There's no judgment in whatever you choose."

"Judgment is nothing when you've lost a child."

Alys nodded once. "I think I'll enjoy that glass of wine now." She slipped through the crowd, pressing her dagger into the hands of the heavily scarred woman. Silent, the crowd of Night Witches watched her settle onto a stool at the bar, her back to the tavern.

The crowd of mothers and grandmothers, sisters and husbands, inched forward, eyeing the squirming witch on the floor. Shaking hands wiped wet cheeks. Aprons revealed kitchen knives. The group of tunic-clad young women pressed forward, starved retribution corrupting any remaining innocence.

But Ervik held up a hand and pointed at Matilda. "To the victor goes the spoils, my friends. So shall the greatest amongst us claim the first spoil."

Matilda tucked her hand into an apron pocket, pulling out an unadorned iron knife. "My daughter was slaughtered with this," she told Osrin. "You must've dropped it when you left her broken body behind. I've kept it all these years, waiting—*hoping* for a chance to use it."

Osrin swiveled his head, wildly seeking an ally that wasn't there. A lifetime of butchery had come to collect, and it would be paid in blood.

Rugard stepped beside Matilda, his arm tightly wrapped around one of the tunic-wearing young women. Cheeks damp, the three stared down at the monster who'd shattered their lives.

"For Amalie," Matilda whispered and plunged the knife.

Another woman stepped forward and another knife dropped.

And then another.

Names were choked between sobs. Blades flashed in the dim light. A thick sludge of blood and grime gathered beneath Osrin. Dress hems turned scarlet, brushing against sticky floors.

Finally, only the young, wide-eyed blonde remained. In an over-sized tunic, she held a quivering knife over a heap of a man. "I watched you brutalize my sister. She died hiding me while you—you"—she choked on a sob, tears pouring from enormous blue eyes—"you don't deserve this mercy. But I'll give it to you anyways because then at least I'll be saving someone else's sister." She drove the dagger through his chest, crying out as she crunched her weight down past bone, sinking the blade into his heart.

The witch who'd wrought impossible anguish let out one final grunt and stilled.

Alys faced the wall, jaw clenched, tears dripping from her chin.

Suffocating silence pressed onto the tavern. Then a sob broke. The cry of a heart breaking all over again ripped through the tavern. Memories swarmed, thick and oppressive. One by one, the witches turned from the body, heads hanging with the weight of justice. They'd killed a witch deserving retribution, but there was little comfort if justice couldn't bring back the dead.

I'd failed them. My father and the Lexsidus line had failed them. How many Water Wheels had Morgenna thrown to the wolves to keep power? I could keep my realm fed and warm, keep our lands protected and thriving, but I couldn't protect them from their queen.

And I couldn't protect Alys from Morgenna any longer.

Alys who served everyone above herself, who faced heartache after heartache and still chased hope's light. She deserved much more than life offered her. And gods, I'd turn the world upside down to give her everything. But I couldn't even save her. After all I'd sacrificed, all I'd endured to make sure she was safe from Morgenna, I couldn't save her from her kind heart.

Mouth compelled shut, my legs unfroze.

I tried—gods, I tried—to run back, to roar out a warning. To make her run. To save herself from what came for her.

But I couldn't do anything but get up and walk out the side door.

37

CAGING A WINGLESS BIRD

Alys

C eremonial remembrance pyres dotted the city below the Onyx
Palace's stained-glass windows like a twinkling reflection of the starry sky. The winter solstice festival honoring the dead came once a year, but
each year the same thought occurred—only the dead escaped their cage.

Pulling my elbows from the windowsill and the celebratory lights of the
Water Wheel, I continued up the stairs to my rooms. This year, a few of the
living had found a sliver of more freedom. Osrin was gone, and the dawn had
birthed a lighter, freer Water Wheel. Spending the day in the Water Wheel
had lifted a weight off me—no—a *mountain* I'd carried since that alley in
Kazadorah Federikka had rescued me from. Simone, Jorlenne, and the girls
of the next generation heralded a new world at their fingertips. They were
free to explore the stars without fear of the dark.

The tiny bud of hope inside me sprouted a new leaf, fragile and precious.

We could do this.

I could bring about the earth-shaking transformation across the island,
even if I began one district at a time.

"Alys."

Yori waited at the top of the stairs, bearded face drawn. He held himself
like a statue of carved umber. Swallowing, he said, "You've been summoned
by the Night Queen to her rooms."

The precious bud shriveled.

She couldn't know.

Not one witch at the Villager's Egg would have betrayed their district. Ervik had posted a girl at the tavern door. Gretta flagged no one. Each witch who entered hated Osrin more than the next. He was dead. His thugs were dead. The remaining few had fled the city.

Yori moved his mouth to speak. Tight lines radiated from his lips. He ripped a hand through his already mussed curls. I'd never seen him angry. Even in the middle of a battle, a hopeful resilience always graced him. Not now. He clenched his hands and tried to speak again. His mouth snapped shut in compelled silence.

I laid a hand on his arm. "It's fine. I've survived this long, haven't I?"

"Don't blame—Maybe if—*Godsdamnit*." He slammed a massive palm against a wall. A portrait rattled against hand-painted wallpaper.

Head hung low, he gestured me down the long corridor of royal apartments to whatever fate awaited. Once, I might've believed myself invincible, but hadn't the Mother warned even fate wasn't set in stone? Failure could come for a fated witch as it came for any ordinary Creature.

We trudged down the never-ending corridor in foggy silence and knocked on the door.

Every fable cast the villain in a dark, dank hovel, but the muted pinks of Morgenna's rooms painted a portrait of tranquil rest. The royal apartments somehow tied beauty into grace with none of the palace's darkness. Ethereal landscapes of the realm hung in gilded frames, painted by a master of pastels and oils. Her sitting room window stretched across the end of the castle wing, spanning the bay and the city's glowing fires. Perfumed oils in glass lamps burned in a relaxing melody of florals.

It might have been beautiful if it hadn't been for the witch reclining by the fire.

"Ah, thank you for fetching her, Lieutenant."

Morgenna lounged on a damask chaise in frothy robes of pink over tight sage pants. Her black curls fell loose across her shoulders, the tips skimming her breasts. Bare feet dangled over the edge of the chaise where gold chains glinted from the crackling fireplace behind her.

I skated over her and settled on the shadows swirling at the wide window across the room. Serpentinian lines of translucent darkness swirled against the glass, nearly hiding the witch within their churning mass.

Maddox didn't turn at our entrance. Each line of his long, lean frame was pulled taut. Hands deep in his pockets, he watched the Jansk District's enormous pyre burn in remembrance of the last heir, Prince Mendrick.

"Sit," Morgenna insisted, pointing to a high-backed chair across from her chaise. A tea service waited on a low table between us. She righted and began pouring two cups of tea.

I lowered onto the dainty, rose-printed chair feeling like a nymph in a china cabinet.

"You've been busy, Captain Sathos. Risking your life for that quaint little village, offering valuable intelligence to my Guard, and even teaching my young pages. An untrained eye might've believed your loyalty to the Night Realm true, so ready were you to give your life for my realm." Morgenna passed me a teacup with a small, sad smile. "Then you ventured into the Water Wheel's filth. You became homesick, didn't you?"

Fear spiked the rushing blood in my ears like the hardest liquor.

She knew.

I placed my untouched tea onto the table and sank deep into the surging river of magic inside me. The tides flowed both ways, but by catching Corryn unaware, it didn't take much to flip the entire river toward her in a massive rush. I'd practiced for this moment, to block her from me even as I sent her everything that *was* me.

A final way to share my last moments.

Damp mountain air hurled against the river tides as she tried to scramble upstream. I sensed her fear, her frantic words that couldn't reach me over the double tides. Unprepared, she couldn't fight my overwhelming wave. My thoughts, my sight, my hearing—my fear—all of it streamed for Corryn.

I'm sorry you have to see this, I sent her. *But I owe it to you to see what's coming. Whatever happens, know I wish we'd had more time.*

To Morgenna, I managed in a miraculously unaffected tone, "How did you find out? It should've died with Osrin."

Her brows soared beneath her burgeoning smile, thrilled I didn't bother denying what I'd done. She sipped at her tea before cooing, "You seem to forget Prince Maddox's ability to veil, my dear. Nothing is secret in this city. Not disobedience to your queen. Not trips to a novelist. Not even sweet, misguided words on a balcony."

Maddox finally tore from the window.

I could've counted each flicker of the pyres behind him. Brief warning flashed across his face, a tiny shake of his head. *Don't react.* But a nauseous film coated my stomach. Morgenna knew *everything*. Every word, every kiss—rushed back to her ear.

A great mallet of doubt smashed through my fear.

"Was this always your plan?" I couldn't rip myself from the void where golden stars once glittered for me, but never when Morgenna was nearby. "Was any of it real or were you merely waiting for me to fail?"

He jerked back like I'd struck him.

Raising a hand as if to reach for me, he said, "What—*no*. I didn't—You think I wanted this to happen? I warned you—" He shot a sideways glance at a beaming Morgenna, before slamming down his icy shield and dropping his hand. "I had no choice."

The queen's laugh held the decadent confidence of an upper hand. "He knows his limits well. But you, my dear, do not. Compulsion loopholes are not without consequence. The moment you manipulated those pathetic witches into ridding themselves of Osrin, you became a liability I could no longer sustain. Our game must come to a close."

The room's dark corners exploded and raced for me. Long, black ropes looped around my body. I pitched backward and tried to claw upright, but the ropes wrapped like vines around my chest, flattening my arms to my sides.

Maddox lunged and was on me, tearing at the shadows, trying in vain to loosen their hold. He couldn't get his finger beneath them. The harder he tried, the tighter they became. One curled around my throat. Black floated onto the edges my vision.

Yori ripped and pulled on his knees beside Maddox, but the ropes slithered like slime beneath his thick fingers. With a flick of Morgenna's wrist, a shadow dropped from the ceiling and slammed Yori into the window. Cracks spiderwebbed under the pressure. He slumped to the carpeted floor, blinking hard even as he tried to stand beneath wobbly feet.

Magic roared beneath my skin, begging to burst free.

I couldn't touch it. Couldn't reveal myself. Not if it could lead back to Corryn.

Tighter and tighter the vines wound. I was gasping, taking in only thimblefuls of air. My lungs burned, clawing to expand against the ropes slowly crushing my ribs.

"*No*," Maddox snarled somewhere above me. The room's remaining shadows hurtled toward us on a wave of cedar. Razor sharp, they sliced through Morgenna's vines. Like decapitated snakes, her shadows flopped to the floor. Maddox's breath rushed out in ragged torrent. I'd barely managed a great big inhale when he hauled me to my knees and shoved me behind him.

I fell on all fours, gasping, heaving, pumping air into my burning, greedy lungs. Yori crawled from the window, helping me stand. The room spun in a pink muddle, and my belly gave a nervous lurch. Too much air at once.

Mountain air magic pounded at my head, threatening to crest my river dam.

Not yet.

Morgenna studied her limp shadows squirming on the rug with a delicate crease of black brows, as if puzzling out a perplexing riddle on the floor. She held out an arm. A fallen shadow slunk around it—an eel through the reeds of firelight.

"How odd. Prince Maddox, I don't recall the exact verbiage I used to compel you, but I'd assumed *will not work against me* was all encompassing."

"I didn't work against you," he said, breathless. He fumbled behind his back, reaching for me. "Killing her doesn't work in your favor. It would raise too many questions. Especially in your court. You know how restless the magistrates have become. They'd want answers you can't give them. You can compel a few of us at a time, but the entire magistrate council *and* the court?"

He found my shaking hand and gripped it tightly. I could sense his pleading through his fingers intertwined with mine. *Go, leave. Let me deal with her.*

Morgenna's depthless eyes found me, two black pools drowning everything they swallowed. "What do I care what courtiers think? A sly loophole, but wrong, nonetheless. I warned you, Maddox. Alys must be punished."

She swiveled her life sucking gaze onto Maddox and tilted her head. I'd seen Maddox cock his head the same way a hundred times, but it never struck fear into me. Not like it did then, realizing how Morgenna intended to punish me.

I tore my hand from Maddox and pushed my way past him. Using my body to block him, I begged Morgenna, "Return me to Lilain. Your problems vanish with me. There won't be any fuss, your court will understand. Me for the vampyres retreat."

"What are you doing?" Maddox hissed. He wrestled with my twisting limbs, trying to push me back behind him. Horror and fury saturated each clipped syllable. "The moment you return to the Day Realm, Lilain will take your head."

Inside, the mountain air pounded harder at the river.

I ripped from his reach, but he was quicker and captured my arms, pinning me to his side. Struggling to free an arm, I snapped up at him, "If it's me or you—"

"I'll pay for Alys's mistakes," he said over my head. Morgenna finally blinked. "For the Water Wheel's. Whatever your price, if you spare her, I'll pay it. Send her to the border with Melis. She can stay there forever."

Forever.

The word rattled alone in my head. Maddox alone with Morgenna *forever* because of me.

"Don't do this. Please."

"If the price is blood—take mine. You have another heir. Just spare Alys."

"*No*—" I pushed harder against him. But he spun me and pressed me into his neck, my words lost against his speeding pulse.

He couldn't do this. I wouldn't let him.

Morgenna sighed through her nose. Maddox let me shift barely enough to catch her sitting back on her chaise and crossing her legs, unaffected by his martyrdom. Tapping a single finger against her chin, she said, "This feels oddly familiar. A sacrificial montage I swear I've seen before." A cruel smile tugged at her pale pink lips. "Ah, I recall now. Prince Mendrick and his wife, the beloved Princess Amira."

Maddox sucked in a slow breath.

"Do you know the full story of his parents, Alys, dear?" Morgenna purred, raising her teacup for a sip. "I suspect not. Prince Maddox keeps a veritable trove of secrets. Even from you. Perhaps, *especially* you."

Yori had crept forward and stood alongside us. His enormous, muscled arms tensed and angled for the door, ready to snatch me and run at Maddox's signal.

What was the use?

Morgenna had snared us in her web—with or without compulsion.

"Mendrick was one of my favorite heirs. Powerful. Quiet. Rarely questioning—until he met that insidious little mouse. A daughter of some lesser son, Amira was a nobody. But Mendrick was a faithful heir, and she came from noble enough stock. Why should I deny their marriage bond? Whatever she lacked in status she made up in powerful breeding. Her magic *almost* rivaled Mendrick's. I thought what harm was there in a powerful little mouse? Perhaps she'd bear me a powerful heir."

She turned her mocking smile onto Maddox. "And she did. Two of them. Then the mouse stumbled upon her own backbone and the mouse became the snake. Morithia and the Onyx Palace were no longer enough. She wanted her family far from the capital and tried more than once to steal them away. Mendrick, loyal heir that he was, would not leave."

"*Could* not leave," Maddox corrected hoarsely.

Morgenna's smile widened. A frigid wave passed between them. "No, he could not," she said softly. "Not even for his precious Amira. When the twins left for Amethyst Hall, she fled Mendrick and the city. To where, I didn't care. She'd begun to test my patience, enticing Mendrick with wild ideas and pushing him to deep melancholy. She broke the poor man with her incessant needs."

At this Maddox shook his head, brushing stubble across the top of my head. "No, she was trying to save him—"

"From what?" Morgenna asked when he faltered. She quirked a brow and gestured for him to continue. His mouth moved, but compulsion wouldn't let any sound free. She threw him a pitying smile before continuing. "Amira appeared on and off for the next few years, never long enough to see me, the little snake. The twins completed their studies and returned home. All was as it should be. But then—Oh, my poor heir. Amira returned unannounced with an ultimatum for her husband. Either she took the twins from the palace, or she'd kill him. What a choice. Well, he rightly refused to allow the twins departure with a mad woman. True to her word, with their son watching, Amira buried a knife in Mendrick's heart."

Maddox was shaking his head. His hold on me grew painful. His breaths sawed in and out against me, on the verge of inhaling too deep and bursting with unrestrained emotion he never liked baring.

Morgenna carried on with a morose sigh, one hand to her chest. "I wish I could say it was over then, but the awful woman couldn't live with what she'd done. She threw herself out the nearest window and over the cliffside."

Into the sea Maddox had always been transfixed with.

I knew Morgenna's story had seeded lies amongst half-truths, but I couldn't discern what was real and what was lie. Compulsion had played a role in this tragedy. The taint of it bled through her twisted words.

I sank into Maddox and offered wordless comfort. He buried his face in my hair, breathing me in. Warmth to warmth, I hoped the negative space between us conveyed my thoughts. *I'm sorry. I didn't know.* He'd experienced firsthand what came of Morgenna's jealousy. The fleeting happiness she was capable of destroying. If she suspected I superseded her influence as Amira had with Mendrick, I was dead. We both were.

Morgenna tilted her head again, this time examining us with a curled lip. "Do you see now, Alys? Your sacrifices mean nothing to me. Only death and the Crone win. Still . . . from death we learn. Maddox did. Perhaps that is how you too shall learn obedience to your queen."

Black pools flicked to Yori half-crouched at my side. Yori who'd seen me before anyone else, who'd recognized the terrified woman behind the infamous DRAS airwitch. The only one who'd never once been afraid of what I was capable of.

Together, as if pulled by one string, Maddox and I sprang for Yori. A shield of intertwined bodies tried in vain to place ourselves between him and Morgenna. I grabbed Yori's arm and tugged as Maddox shoved him toward the door.

With a startled grunt, Yori tumbled onto the rug. But I hadn't let go. Neither had Maddox and all three of us tumbled to the rug.

"Get out!" Maddox hissed. A vein ticked in his jaw. Somehow, he managed to shove both Yori and me behind him. "Before she—"

"*You will all be still and quiet.*" Morgenna's compulsion severed Maddox's pleas.

Ice froze everything but my heaving chest. One of my arms tangled between Maddox and Yori's smashed legs, and I could already feel its circulation cutting off. We were going to die in a mess of limbs.

Rising from the chaise, the Night Queen sauntered to our heap on the floor and studied us. She attempted a contrite smile, but it revealed too many teeth.

"Foolishly, I believed compulsion alone would control *you*, my dear Alys. Perhaps it would've been enough, but then compulsion cannot control what the heart wants. A pity. I tried to warn Maddox away, for your sake. To his credit, he tried. But again—that silly heart will do as it wants. Now, here we are. Consequences must be met. Hearts shattered. And so, my melodrama ends as a tragedy."

Above Yori, I met Maddox's eyes. What had we done?

"*Alys,*" the queen called, eyes glowing. "*Unsheathe Maddox's dagger.*"

No, I couldn't. Not Yori. He was blameless. Innocent. He hadn't foolishly ignored all reason and diverted from his fated path.

I should die. *I* should pay the consequence. I begged the Mother, Nyx, even Fortuna, pleading for any of them to reach an interceding hand and stop me.

My mental pleas rang silent.

Like I was watching a marionette come alive, my numb hand jerked from between Maddox and Yori and reached for Maddox's hip. The ring of steel might as well have been my trapped scream.

"I cannot bear to watch such pain unfold," Morgenna said, fingertips skimming over her lips, "but lessons must be taught, no matter how excruciating. It is the burden of a ruler. *Alys, drive the dagger through Yori's heart.*"

No, no, no. I tried hauling my hand back. Tried to cleave the ice between my mind and arm—but the dagger rose. A choke lodged in my throat, stuck between horror and agony. I couldn't plead aloud, couldn't even offer final words of apology.

Tears splattered Yori's cheeks. *Kill him*, the ice screamed. Time became nothing as the knife fell. On and on it went toward Yori's chest. He smiled, a tiny twitch fighting compulsion. His gentle amber eyes spoke the imprisoned words he couldn't release. *This isn't your fault.*

The dagger plunged straight through his heart. Red bloomed over his chest. It stained the pink rug crimson. He sank backward, each breath more ragged than the last. He blinked twice and tried to smile again, but a muscle spasmed in his cheek.

"Poor Alys," Morgenna moaned softly. "What guilt you will bear. *I release you all.*"

I threw myself over Yori, cradling his head. Sobbing. Mumbling incoherent apologies. I was dimly aware of Maddox yanking out the knife, muttering the healing spellcast that wouldn't work. I did this. Because I pushed for what I wanted. Because I didn't listen. I'd killed Yori. My pride, my so-called cleverness—I was the monster.

"Use me," Yori garbled through blood. "Use me to f-find a way out."

An unseeing glaze coated eyes who had seen through my walls, and his head fell toward the crimson-stained rug. He didn't move again.

Cold fingers lifted my chin. Dazed, I met a pair of black, bottomless pools. "This guilt will haunt you forever but perhaps good can come of this? Hm? Perhaps this shall serve as a reminder of who holds power in this realm. When you think of undermining me, perhaps you will think of Yori and remember nothing, not even love, happens unless I grant it."

Artificial gentility slid from her countenance, revealing the monster many had warned me waited beneath the surface. She sank her nails deep into the tender skin beneath my chin. In a low whisper, she mocked, "You belong to *me*, Alys Sathos. Not Lilain, not the people of the Water Wheel. Not Maddox. There is not a part of you that isn't mine. Not even your heart."

Whirling, she stepped over Yori's body and curled back onto her chaise. *"Tell no one what you have witnessed tonight,"* she compelled.

A cool mountain breeze gently pushed at our dammed river, and I nearly laughed, half-manic, half-sobbing.

Morgenna dismissed us with a wave, ringing a bell for someone to take Yori's body.

Stumbling from her rooms, I couldn't recall how I made it to my apartment's door. My hands were sticky. Why was blood sticky? I felt rather than heard Maddox behind me, but I couldn't look from my crimson-stained hands.

"I did this," I whispered.

"It's not your fault." Maddox reached for me, but I lurched back. His face crumpled. "You can't let her inside your head. Please, Alys—"

"You weren't my path. I knew that, but I was so fucking lost, and you saw me like no one else had. I just wanted—I didn't think—*This* is my path. Death." I was rambling now, desperate to cling onto the last of my reasoning. "I *killed* him, Maddox. Our friend. He'd be alive if I'd died with the goblins. I *should've* died. I'm not worthy. He was good and kind and everything I'm not. I was made for death. It's my only path. I should've accepted that long ago."

Guilt roared in my ears, shooting poisonous thoughts through my veins. I lived when so many did not. Fate had made death my path.

"No." Maddox reached for me again, trying to tuck my flailing fists into his chest, trying to soothe my panic reflected in his expression. "Think about how many you've saved. Nyxinthi. The Water Wheel. You are much more than death. You're everything *life* represents. That hope I've been looking for? It was always you. You are my resilient, never-dimming light in the darkness. You're—you're *everything* good in my life."

If I could reach it, I would shut the door—on him, on this awful monster enslaving us to Morgenna. I pitched for the door. Wet, red palms slipped against the wood, sliding for the handle. The hall's shadows reared. They grabbed my sticky wrists as Maddox gripped my waist from behind, holding me more gently than I deserved.

"Please, Alys. Don't let guilt destroy your light. Let me in, let me help you find yourself the way you've helped me."

"Just—let me go, Maddox." I slumped against the door and swallowed a sob. "I haven't helped you. Look at what I've done to your life. I'm everything you thought I was. I'm the monster you found in the Blackwood."

His hands fell away, and the shadows skittered back as if my words had hurt them too.

Two accusing smears of blood gleamed on the door.

The mark of a murderer.

I threw the door open and stumbled inside before slamming the door on Maddox, on the unmasked panic stamped across his face.

His only friend dead because of me. The only one who saw Maddox as more than Morgenna's right-hand witch.

I slid down the door to the onyx floor. I couldn't see the hall before me, only the dagger in my hand falling—over and over. Each time the blade ripped through Yori. Each time blotting out the life from the familiar laughing creases of a kind man.

Magic bubbled beneath my skin, clawing, screaming for freedom. A sob finally broke and power exploded. Darkness swallowed the entry hall, pouring in from the single window at the end of the hall. Howling shadows dashed into a mirror above me and silver shards rained. I threw up my hands. Unguided air exploded from my raised palms in a low boom. Glass became sand, puddling at my feet like a dark reminder of where I belonged.

This is who I was, a dangerous Dual Witch, capable of powerful magic and destined by the Mother to destroy the island's tyrants. Nothing else.

My story didn't have a happy ending, but if I knew anything, neither did Morgenna's. Not if I could help it.

38

SIX SPOKES ON THE WHEEL OF FATE

Corryn

S ilver dusted Night Flame consumed Yori's body in the same way time consumed Alys and me. The longer we took to undo Morgenna's hold over the realm, the more witches died.

A dark smudge of smoke floated from the pyre and over the cliffs, staining the bay. Morgenna's council of magistrates claimed Yori's special service to the crown merited the Night Flame. The large crowds gathered on the cliffs wanted more than that, but no answer was given. Few knew the mockery behind the regal funerary rite.

Holding tight to Alys's wrist, I flitted through the crowds of every life station. Night guards, shopkeepers, magistrates, powerful lords, and villagers—every walk of witchkind found their way to the clifftop to pay tribute to the gentle giant who accompanied the Night Prince everywhere and always with a beaming smile.

The whispers began long before Maddox set a Night Flame torch to the pyre. The path to the cliffs had hissed with rumors. How did a healthy man in his prime die of sickness when the finest healers resided in the city? How did a supposed sickness strike down a man close to the prince? The loudest rumors came within the Guard—Yori had been murdered, and the court had hidden it.

I stood on one side of Alys, far from the front. Two young guards flanked her other side. In hushed whispers, they hissed over the pompous courtiers swathed in silk and velvet on the cliffs beside the shopkeepers and villagers. Each time someone offered condolences to the young guards they were met with sneers. Occasionally, they'd eye Alys. She never spared them a glance. Like a strung bow, she aimed all her focus on the sooty clouds.

Dark shadows rimmed her eyes, her skin as dull as her gaze. Every symbol of her heritage had faded. A tight knot at her neck's nape hid her hair. One gold nugget remained in the swirl of her ear; the rest had vanished. Drawn in misery and guilt, she looked like every other witch in Morgenna's court.

The Second Order Priestesshood of the Crone wafted sweet smelling herbs from swinging thuribles. The poor attempt to cover the stench of burning flesh wasn't compatible with the clifftop's gusts. At least we were downwind. Here, we were lost in the crowd of mourners, not special enough to warrant a spot near the pyre.

As crown prince, Maddox stood at the front beside Morgenna and the pyre holding the remains of his closest friend. His typical icy expression was replaced by blank steel, like the world pressing in on him ceased to exist. But his carefully constructed mask couldn't hide the flash of unadulterated anguish each time the body occasionally shifted with the crumbling wood.

Beside him, Morgenna searched the crowd. She skimmed past me and settled on Alys.

The queen's watching you, I mentally warned her.

Alys peeled her thoughts from the sky. She refocused on the surrounding world and all at once suffocating hate hurtled down the river between us.

I gasped and pressed a hand to my breathless chest. I felt as if I'd been dunked beneath her rage. Far too still, she met Morgenna's stare. The gnawing hatred surged harder. In spite of the leviathan howling inside, Alys's expression mirrored the frigid landscape. Cold and empty as the snow melting into her high cheekbones.

She was as terrifying as the thrumming magic desperate to unleash on the cliffs.

The wind shifted and sickly-sweet air wafted over us.

Her nostrils flared and blood drained from her cheeks as she spun from the pyre. On the river, rage plummeted into regret and settled deep into my skin like a blanket of stinging nettles.

Morgenna gave Alys's back a mocking pout and dabbed her dry cheeks with a lacy handkerchief.

One of the guards at Alys's side bristled. "Did the queen have anything to do with Yori's death?"

A new voice, cutting enough to pierce my soul, answered for Alys. "Don't be an idiot, Nik. You know better than to voice certain things aloud. One never knows who's listening."

Nik pursed his lips and gave Melis a short bow. With one last withering glare toward the queen, he muttered something to the young redhead, and they melted into the crowd.

Melis swung to Alys, taking in the drawn-up hair with a soft huff. "Death isn't new to you, Sathos. Besides, you barely knew Yori more than a few months. Why do you care if another Night Guard dies?"

I inhaled sharply. Drawing my arm around a stiffening Alys, I blurted, "She has as much a right to grieve as you."

The dark forest in Melis's gaze blazed to life and something inside withered a little more. "The way you keep showing up tells me you *must* be a glutton for punishment. But then . . . intelligence doesn't translate to sense, does it? Perhaps you're too simple to see where you're not wanted."

"Projecting our inner weaknesses, Princess?" Alys cut in. She squared her shoulders and took a step toward Melis. "Why don't you do us a favor and go swallow a tavern?"

Refusing to engage with Melis's poison or Alys's growing itch for a fight, I pulled my sister from a rash mistake and led us to the quieter edges of the clifftop. For once, the bay's waters were smooth glass beneath an azure mantle. Only a pillar of smoke over the water marred the landscape.

"I know I'm not entirely to blame for Melis's bitterness," I began, studying a speck of a village across the bay. "It began long before me. Morgenna irrevocably broke her, but I delivered the final blow with my pettiness."

Alys shook her head, pulling my arm closer against the glacial gusts. "You were through with her before . . . Maddox. You didn't owe her allegiance. The moment she broke it off with you, you could have kissed whomever you wanted."

"I know, but I wanted to *hurt* her, to break her the way she broke me. But of all the witches I could've used against Melis, I blindly chose the only one who could've pulled her from her darkness. Poor Maddox was a casualty of our toxic war." I winced and shook my head. "I'm sorry. This is stupid. After everything—you and Maddox—this is nothing compared to what you've gone through."

"It's not stupid." She snuck a glimpse through the crowd, past the pyre. After a moment, she shuddered and whirled to give the pyre—and who stood by it—her back. "Don't hold your pain inside because you think your life isn't as dire as mine. Pain isn't competitive. What hurts you, hurts me."

I desperately wanted to believe that was true.

Swallowing my discomfort, I said, "Do you know what Melis said the night we fell apart? She didn't know why she was attracted to me when she could have any other witch. I was lowborn, quiet, and awkward—barely pretty enough to tempt *her*. I didn't have connections or money. She said she held all the cards in our relationship. If I suddenly died, there was little she or the rest of the world would miss in my absence."

Rage streamed back down the river, and I had to plant my feet not to be carried away.

I shot a wary glance at a stone-faced Alys and pulled my cloak tighter around my chest. If only I could've suffocated the threatening sob. "She was right, of course. My academic career failed miserably before it began. My only saving grace was obtaining the instructor job by some Mother-made miracle. Perhaps I should've tried harder to fend off Maddox's vengeful rumors. But part of me accepted them as punishment for what I'd done to Melis *and* Maddox."

"You made one hurtful choice against another witch whereas she's made hundreds. She doesn't deserve you. You're better off without her venom."

I smiled, a thin watery thing with little sincerity. I appreciated Alys's fierce loyalty, however misplaced. My words had been as awful as Melis's that night—words I refused to think on. Truthfully, I missed her. Nine years wasn't enough to forget the sweet girl who'd planted wild dreams in my head, who encouraged me to reach for the furthest star. I hadn't given up hope someone would draw the dreamer back out of her.

But I no longer believed it was me.

"**M**other fucking—"

"Alys," I snapped, peering over the cover of *Dualitas Maleficarum*. "Do you not know any other words to express your frustration?"

She clenched her jaw and flung a thick mist of water onto the small fire spreading up the vine choked marble pillars. Her control on Night magic was impressive, but her fire was unpredictable. No doubt a product of her volatile emotions.

We'd retreated to the abandoned temple on the Western Sea. Cross-legged on the altar of carved white marble, I was determined to uncover the portents' secrets—but *Dualitas Maleficarum* sitting open in my lap proved as equally fruitless. If there were more secrets to glean from it, I hadn't yet figured them out. The armless statue of the unknown god looming over me agreed, if its stern frown was any indication.

"Let's go over this again," Alys said for the dozenth time.

I refrained from pointing out how much she had begun to sound like Maddox.

She climbed onto the marble slab, her silky hair a flat curtain down her back against the ivory blouse she'd chosen, and picked up a portent copy. Pointing at a line on the parchment, she said, "You said this series of runic equations translates to the two queens and their time ending. These further down indicate a completion, something made whole. We know that means uniting witchkind and restoring our true nature. But how is this supposed to help identify the others?"

"It doesn't." I shut the book and picked up another portent. "Those runic equations don't have anything to do with identity. I'm confident that's in the numerology. But I'm stuck. They all equal two, no matter what I input in the astrological variation."

Alys squinted at the portent, visibly biting her tongue in effort not to ask what an astrological variation was. Her pride rivaled any courtier's, which made sense considering she should have belonged to Morgenna's court through House Felumbra. Not that their crone of matriarch, Lady Evangelyn, would welcome two bastard granddaughters with open arms.

"Basically, I'm struggling to translate the meaning of the number two in relation to identity. All three portents have different equations, yet each one equals two. I think the answer lies further on, but the equations are far more complex than anything I've seen. My specialty lies in runes, not numerology."

"Do you think this means three of the fated are Dual Witches too? Are we wrong thinking they might be Night and Day?"

I shrugged. "More likely it's a reference to the Mother and her dual nature, or even the true dual nature of witches. Two is the most powerful number because it derives from the Mother herself. Nature balances on two halves and all that." Sitting up, I tugged the portent from her. "Give the portents a rest for a moment and listen to this passage from *Dualitas Maleficarum*.

"A thousand years ago witches hadn't needed brooms to fly nor shadows to umbranate. Water and fire weren't all they wielded, but also earth and lightning. The very fabric of reality split open to other planes under their hands. A powerful few could even spin fate like a spider with silk, binding the future's will to their own."

Alys wrinkled her nose. "Sounds like evil magic."

I stared at an illustration of a witch with upraised hands, lightning forking between her fingers, splitting the page with blue and silver. "How did the queens fracture such powerful Creatures? Surely there would've been resistance. Morgenna has never wielded this sort of magic."

"Nor Lilain." Alys frowned, peering at the illustration. "More forgotten magic from the Lost Five Hundred Years. It wouldn't shock me if much of those Lost Years are actually hidden in the forbidden levels of Albulus Tower or Amethyst Hall. Seems like something the queens might squirrel away in case they ever needed more power."

Shaking my head, I turned the page and found a passage on Death Runes. I hadn't told Alys about Maddox's odd behavior with the Death Rune book. I didn't know how to bring it up without shoving that knife in deeper. What was I supposed to say? *"The witch you're hopelessly in love with and can do nothing about? He might be up to something evil, but I can't be sure."*

A civil war in 50BE had spurred the creation of Death Runes according to the book. Spurred on by their elvish overlords, the ancient witches slaughtered one another vying for power until they discovered a way to steal magic from another witch without repercussions. Then they'd joined together and overthrew the elves in a great and bloody war—and thus Efelldor was born. I'd always assumed the civil war had been between Night and Day Witches. Too few books existed on pre-Efelldor history. Now, I understood why.

A sketch of a familiar Death Rune decorated the next page. I held the book up to my face with a squint, trying to recall where I'd seen it. The jagged circle slashed the parchment, two arrow tips pointing in opposite directions sat atop and below the circle. There was no script to go with it, but someone had drawn a crowd beneath it. Their hands were held up as if worshipping the rune and whatever power it bestowed.

"Well, that's a tad disconcerting," I muttered under my breath.

Alys let out a startled shriek from my shoulder. I clapped a hand over my ear, but she yanked it away to say, "I've seen that rune before. Yes, look. Here it is." She slid one of the portents over the illuminated page of Death Rune worshippers. "It's on this portent. Gods, it's identical to the one in the book. It has to mean something. What does it do?"

I shook my head and explained I needed time to translate its lines' measurements and angles into words. "Death Runes don't need spellcasts like other nature-driven runes since they latch onto another witch's magic. Most of them have lost their meanings or abilities. Partly because modern witches refuse to study them and partly because they're lost to time. Odd that it's only on this portent and not the others."

Alys tilted her head to the side, peering at the portent. She pointed to a smudge of ink spots. "That's the month of Leon's star chart, isn't it?"

I snatched the portent, holding it up to the sunlight streaming through the cracked temple roof. She was right. Flecks of ink mapped out the position of the stars showcasing Leon's prancing lion during that month.

Mother curse me, how had I missed that?

Alys thrust out the other two portents, grinning for the first time in days. "This one is different. It's a Taura star chart. And this one—Look, Corryn. This portent is for one of us. It's a chart for the month of Scorpius."

I released a breathless laugh. So, we were on the right track then. We needed to search for a witch born under Taura and Leon. Tracing the lion, I whispered, "Melis was born under Leon." Alys whipped to look at me, and I raised a hand in defense. "Not that I think she's one of the fated, just that—"

Alys's eyes grew huge. She seized the portent from my hands, arranging them side by side on the marble slab, nearly touching her pointed nose to the parchment as she inspected them. "Oh, shit. You've been looking at the number two wrong."

I didn't bother to chide her for her language, leaning closer. "I don't understand."

"Twins, Corryn! The number two you keep equating? It doesn't signify the Mother's dual nature. It's *twins*. Think. What's the most precious gift the Mother bestowed onto witchkind? The conception of twins—a powerful force of magic, *two* mirrored and *balanced* souls."

I scanned the portents, heart racing faster than my brain. She was right. *Again*. This was why I wasn't making sense of the numerology. I already had the answer, but I was looking at the equation expecting a different outcome. Three portents for three sets of twins. All the portents were here.

A sickly green came over Alys. "This means . . ."

The river between us crashed to an awful halt. I scanned the Leon portent trying to find something to prove her wrong. Twins were rarer than the most precious stones. How many twins in the Night Realm had been born under Leon?

I tentatively reached for Alys, smoothing back hair from her bloodless forehead. "I think we've always suspected, haven't we? Why else do our paths consistently cross theirs? It's as if the fate itself shoved you two together over and over. Maybe it was a step in our path we somehow missed."

One hides behind a veil of self-hatred—in hindsight, undoubtedly Melis.

One is caged, the bars sealed by malice and woe—Maddox caged by Morgenna's compulsion—again, utterly apparent. This would teach us to keep our heads—and hearts—out of the sand.

Alys shoved me away and choked out, "All this time—I rejected my own path trying to stay on that *fucking path*. I wouldn't have failed witchkind if I'd let myself be happy. I wanted to do this alone and prove I was worthy of fate's choice. Not some useless street rat with nothing to offer but stubborn pride. Yori *died* because of my pride. If I'd realized sooner—"

"No, don't go there. You couldn't have known. Nor did Maddox. Whatever broke between you two is not your fault any more than what happened to Yori is your fault. That blame belongs solely with Morgenna."

"Maddox and I are not broken," she snapped, throwing her hair over her shoulder. "It's just impossible as long as compulsion holds our strings." Glaring at the limbless statue, she pressed her lips into a thin white line. "That bitch. She knew all along. She saw what I hoped for, what I thought I'd lost and said *nothing*. She let me walk away thinking there was nothing but death ahead, doomed to loneliness."

"Who—"

"*The Mother*! Her cursed little trees, her neat little path to Maddox. Waiting for me to make this connection. For *what*? I can't so much as *think* of him now without guilt. I'm terrified of who Morgenna will come after next with her gods awful compulsion. And Maddox! How can he be one the six? He's more Morgenna's will than his own. And how do we—"

Spinning, she nearly tumbled off the altar, her elfin features stark with panic. I reached out to steady her, but she seized my shoulders, squeezing until they throbbed. "Morgenna knows, Corryn. She may not have deciphered who the rest of us are—or else we'd be dead—but Maddox and Melis? Her *heirs*? Twins born under Leon shortly after the portent was divined? She knows. And she *doesn't care*. Why should she? None of us stand a chance against her compulsion."

I squished the urge to scold her rambling. She was stunned, grieving and close to losing hope. Fate was a tricky thing. Not quite carved into stone. The chance of failing loomed too near. But fate had chosen us as the best chance for witchkind to succeed. I wouldn't allow doubt's blade to whittle witchkind's only hope of survival.

"Let's think of this revelation another way," I began in a mellow tone, grabbing the abandoned Taura portent from the altar. "As uncommon as twins are, surely you know of a pair in the Day Realm. It can't be difficult to track them down."

Somehow, Alys's dusky, olive-gold skin managed to further pale into gray. She swiped the back of her hand over her mouth. "Yes, I knew a pair. A Taura pair, no less. But you better hope they're not the final set of twins."

"Why not?"

"Because they're dead."

39

ELEUTHERIA

Maddox

One day Morgenna's appetite for pain would bite her in the ass. Every bone in my legs screamed like it had been snapped—which it had. I stumbled from Morgenna's rooms on barely mended legs and tried not to faceplant. Her healing spellcasts were a lazy bare minimum to hide any permanent damage. The world may've known Lilain for her cruelty, but Morgenna's hidden streak surpassed it.

Nik waited outside the door, catching my unsteady sway toward the floor. Easing me against the wall, he muttered, "*Sana corpus,*" as he'd done since Yori died. Discovering Morgenna's punishing cruelty had been an accident. He'd been waiting for me outside her rooms, insistent on answers about Yori's death. The bloody mess he'd discovered instead answered most of his questions and silenced any more. Since then, without any request from me, he'd waited outside Morgenna's rooms until I emerged—in a variety of states.

Nik picked at imaginary lint on his sleeve while I regained my breath. "Would you permit me to ask what—ah—incited your injury this time, Your Highness?"

A hard lump inched up my chest. Gods, where did I begin?

Shutting my eyes, I imagined Yori clapping my shoulder; he'd urge me to give the younger guard answers. He'd been thick as thieves with him, considered him a friend—his replacement should things go sideways, he'd once joked. Maybe he'd somehow divined his early end and prepared the younger guard to put up with my future shit. Or maybe he'd seen the writing on the wall and known we were all well and truly doomed.

"Yori is . . . missed by many," I began, stumbling around the ice skating over my tongue. "The effect of his loss is greater than expected, and the queen's . . . platitudes . . . haven't been enough. They want answers and she—" I paused and worked through the scorpion tail spearing my thoughts. I couldn't even think ill of her after she'd murdered my oldest friend—my only friend. "She cannot give answers without . . . repercussions."

Nik's sleeve became infinitely more interesting.

I pushed off the wall, testing my mended legs. Slowly, with Nik dogging my steps, we ambled down the corridor. "I haven't managed to quell questions of his death as well as she hoped. My failure to pacify the grieving means . . ." Compulsion wouldn't even let me gesture at my legs.

No one shall ever know what punishments I deem worthy of your failures, Morgenna had once compelled.

Nik was one of the angry, grieving witches questioning everything and unsettling the Guard. Why was Yori not healed of his supposed illness? Why had Morgenna given him royal funerary rites? Melis had asked questions too, but one knowing look from me snuffed them.

Familiar footsteps, quick and purposeful, broke the awkward quiet.

Alys appeared around the corridor's bend, head down, patting her pockets for her key. Dressed in an unadorned black skirt and blouse, she'd drawn her hair into a simple knot, something she once told me she hated. She stared vacantly at the rug, oblivious to everything but her thoughts. No sweeping watch. No calculated glare, thinking two steps ahead.

Nothing like the snarling fox I'd captured in the Blackwood.

She could've been walking into a Day Witch-hating ambush for all she knew. A DRAS captain knew better. The airwitch champion who'd maneuvered to high rank without magic would've never let her guard down. Since the night of Yori's death, she hadn't so much as looked in my direction.

Hadn't made one snide remark. She was fading into Morgenna's darkness where the rest of us lived, and I'd let it happen.

No.

She wouldn't drown in this pit the rest of us had long given up escaping. Not her. *Never* her.

Nik shot me a sideways glance and read whatever intention lay there. "Good luck."

Offering a wry salute, he trotted down the hall past a startled Alys. She swung her gaze and found me. All blood drained from her face, and she shot for her door. Back ramrod straight, she moved too precise, too measured.

"Skirts again?" I drawled, shoving my hands into my pockets to keep from reaching for her. Knowing what irritated her was easy. Hoping it would snap her from her docility was something else. "If I didn't know any better, I'd think you've begun preferring them to pants. I'm not sure you pass for a respectable lady of the court, if that's your intention. It's your fidgeting that gives you away."

My gut twisted uncomfortably.

I aimed for the prickled pride jugular behind her grief. If I had to prod her with cruel words, then so be it.

Key in hand, she barely turned over her shoulder. The full lips that haunted my nights, thinned into a pale line. A wisp of irritated smoke began behind the numb weariness.

Progress.

"What do you want, Maddox?"

Her beside me without guilt or fear. Freedom from compulsion. To take her to my favorite secondhand bookstore tucked in the Worth District and watch her eyes light up. In that order.

But I skirted any answer and, instead, said, "You've managed to look like every other witch in this godforsaken realm."

"Wasn't that your goal from the beginning?"

I scowled and any plan to make her snap vanished. "Forget what every other idiot in this realm demanded of you, I *never* wanted you to be someone you're not. You were always better than the rest of us—a light we reached for."

Her thin shoulders drooped like I'd heaped the world's expectations onto her.

I shoved my hands deeper into my pockets, willing her to look up, to fight with me. "How are you calm? Morgenna *killed* him. Used *you* to kill him."

She reared back.

Startingly white rimmed irises pinned me in place, and she reached for me before yanking back with clenched fists. "I'm one wrong word from burning to ash with hatred and taking this godsdamned world with me. I want her—" Compulsion strangled *dead* from her. "Who's next? Who else could she steal? Corryn? Matilda, Sylinia, Nik? Gods, even Melis." Her eyes became impossibly wide, drowning me in prisms of umber. "You?"

I abandoned logic and cradled her face. Anything to wipe the desperation blooming pink into her cheeks. Beneath my fingers, her soft, smooth skin was a promise and threat in one. A promise of the life I hadn't realized I wanted until her smart mouth wandered into my path. And the threat that could break everything if I tried to reach for that life.

"Don't let the darkness win. Fight with me."

"*How*? Her malice controls every facet of our lives. We can't be the reason someone else dies. As long as her compulsion remains, you can't—you shouldn't touch me anymore."

She shoved my hands away and went for her key.

"Only this summer," I pleaded, "you would've never accepted her control. You stood before her throne with defiance and refused to let her win. You saved a village, then the realm. You *freed* an entire district on sheer determination regardless of compulsion. She hasn't changed. *You* have. You gave into her and handed her a win."

Inserting her key into the lock, she whispered, "Well, then I'll add it to my list of failures." She stepped through and shut the door on my hope.

What happens when Morgenna finds out about you two? Yori had asked late after the Harkening Ball and one too many tankards of mead. *I don't think there's ever been anyone who's looked past your title and your godsdamned face long enough to see who's underneath. Who cares where she was born? Fuck the consequences and let's make a stand. You, me—shit, Nik too. I trust him with my life and Alys's too. He worships her. Bet he'd do anything to keep her safe. Not like that, jealous prick. I'm serious, Maddox. Maybe she's the key to getting out. Another big-headed brain—like you.*

Alone with every miserable thought, I headed for my rooms. I bathed and made ready for bed, but too many memories pushed to the forefront of my loaded conscience. I poured a generous helping of whiskey into a glass tumbler. Bits of barrel floated in the amber liquid—a disgusting trait Yori claimed made it the finest whiskey in all of Efelldor. Careful not to spill a drop, I balanced the tumbler on a severely squashed armchair—Yori's favorite because it supported his massive frame.

There. A semblance of normalcy.

Now, he just had to walk through the door, complaining how I should hire a secretary instead of dragging him everywhere with me—as if he hadn't loved traveling the realm. The people had loved him right back.

That had been obvious at his funerary rites.

Getting out, he'd said.

Compulsion prevented me from plotting to overthrow Morgenna, or even complaining, but Yori had seen the effects enough to understand it tore at me. For years he'd spoken of *getting out.* Well-meaning, but useless.

Until Alys.

Yori would never know his insistence I fight for Alys her first night in Morithia would awake a deep-seated memory.

You must remember, my mother had said, golden eyes brilliant even beneath a cloudy sky, *whenever this witch enters your life, you must keep her within reach. For the sake of witchkind, it's imperative you work together. You will break the Night Queen's hold with her, and it will test you both in many ways.*

Mum, I'd whined in the cracking voice of a thirteen-year-old boy. *I'll be the Night Prince* and *the heir* and *the commander of the Night Guard. I don't need her—whoever she is. Everyone says I have more magic than anyone has seen in centuries. I'll save us all from the queen myself. Besides, you've no idea who this witch is. How am I supposed to recognize her?*

She'd smiled, indulgent as the picnic spread on the mountain above Amethyst Hall. *When she comes along, you'll know. Fight for her, Maddox. You don't yet understand how much you'll need her. Or she you. But you* must *fight for her. Use everything in your arsenal. The darkest magic can free the light if used with a pure heart. But do not let Morgenna win.* Her smile had grown tight, as if stretched thin by her many secrets.

My mother's divination had been remarkable. Her brilliant mind found patterns in the stars and numbers where most saw coincidence. I'd begun to wonder if she'd predicted Alys was more than my mother had let on. If she divined I'd gladly leap in front of an arrow for Alys, sacrifice my freedom to keep her safe. Alys had become more than a means to ending Morgenna.

Not that any of it mattered if I didn't have a way to keep her safe.

I eased my way through the rickety stacks of runic books cluttering the sitting room and found what I was looking for. Returning to the sofa, I gingerly opened the goblin-skin book for the hundredth time, trying not to think about the buttery-smooth cover.

The book remained as worthless as every other time I'd studied it. The same pointless runes unable to break Morgenna's compulsion stared back. I could topple realms with the power they offered, delve into the darkest of magic and mangle every Creature's mind within my radius. But what good was power when Morgenna held it all on a compelled leash?

An icy sting pricked my mind. I gritted my jaw and reminded myself *and the compulsion*—I wasn't undermining her realm—I was opening myself up to more power to *save* her realm. The flimsy loophole soothed the frigid pinprick. At least for now. Gods only knew what would happen if I found a way out—*if.*

My mother had claimed pure hearts could freely use dark magic. Well, I certainly didn't have one of those, but I had a book on the darkest runic magic. That should have been enough.

I'd translated each miserable rune over months, spending every available hour trying to find something, *anything* to sever compulsion. To keep Alys safe from me, from Morgenna. Over and over, I'd failed. Until Alys was a shell of herself. Until Yori was dead. If there was a freeing Death Rune, it wasn't in this pointless book.

Inhaling sharply, I flung the book into the fireplace. Sparks cascaded from the hearth, threatening to bite the nearby books. A violet-and-gold ward flared to life around the book, but age had weakened the magic. One flick of my wrist sent the ward crumbling against the enveloping shadows. Greedy flames licked at centuries of academia. All of it *wasted*. A sick sense of control twisted around me like a comforting blanket. No one would translate those runes. No one would use their perverse magic again.

Goblin skin crackled and popped, charring black in the roaring flames. Shrinking, the leather revealed gleaming bone binding. In between the leather and exposed bone, something fluttered. Was that—a piece of paper?

Shit.

Heart in throat, I scrambled on all four for the fireplace. Secrets in ancient books made out of goblin skin had to be a good thing. A shadow dropped from the ceiling. The black wave dragged the book from the fireplace and tossed it onto the stone tile. With a sickening sizzle, the cover fell apart and plopped onto the tile. I tucked my nose into my tunic's hemline and grimaced.

The ancient witches had been sick bastards.

The smoking scrap didn't want to give. It took a minute of prying and tearing at the binding before I finally tugged it out. Another Death Rune and an inscription. This one sloppily sketched by hand, unlike the book's printed press interior. A circle and two arrows—one below, one above—took up most of the singed scrap.

The inscription read, *Eleutheria*, the word for independence in the Mother tongue.

The next line forced me to read it two—three times.

I sat back on my heels and read the words again. Something foreign unfurled wings in my chest—hope. I read the inscription one more time.

For when the puppet is ready to cut the puppeteer's strings.

Clambering from the tile, I knocked into a stack of books, littering the rug. Blood pounded in my ears as I sprinted for the apartment door. My focus centered on one witch, on the wicked smile I wanted more than anything to spark alive, to see uncaged and freed of the crippling terror bowing her shoulders. I focused on the only witch who'd bothered to see what lay beneath the mask of the prince and understood the mangled mess inside.

Eleutheria in one hand, I rushed for the door and for the waiting freedom.

When I opened my door, Alys was already on the other side, hand on her hip, the other ready to pound down my door.

"First of all—how dare you try to bait me into a fight."

Her sharp-edged voice sliced a breathless laugh out of me. I searched the empty corridor before yanking her into my rooms and into a new freed era.

40

A NEW DAWN AT MIDNIGHT

Alys

F ew things rankled me more than admitting Maddox was right. I'd played into Morgenna's hands and crowned myself with guilt. But the bitch had missed something important. She didn't understand Yori's effect after death. Not on me. Not on her own people.

Sinking deeper into the tub, I sent the water rippling with a long exhale. From the beginning Yori had seen through the magicless nobody to the hope I could wield—like Ansil and Elenna had seen in me. He saw a witch capable of saving a village, a district and even a realm. I didn't just wield hope, now. I wielded *power*. Sure, I couldn't quite control my Day magic, and maybe my water control remained untested, but I could *wield magic*.

For Yori and all the Dual Witch children her beast hunted, I should have been flaying Morgenna alive on a—

Compulsion skewered that thought dead.

All the power in the world meant nothing under her compulsion.

Jerking upright, I sloshed from the tub. Goosebumps flourished across my arms in the freezing bathing room. Summoning a gust of magicked warm air, I dried my hair before dressing in a deliciously soft silk nightgown. I ran my fingers over the fabric and managed a smile. Sylinia's expensive taste in clothing had rubbed off on me. Good thing Nik's family's massive coffers barely noticed. My smile bloomed wider, remembering Nik's horrified yelp when he'd received the bill. The trip to the Black Wall clothing market had been his idea. A sweet attempt to cheer me up after Yori's funerary rites.

"My father is going to think I'm supporting a mistress with the way you two take advantage," he'd groaned. When Sylinia stepped out in a plunging dress of forest-green velvet, he'd ate those words. More like he'd ate his words plus any insistence Sylinia was merely a friend. He hadn't looked twice at me and spent the evening sighing like a witch whose heart had gone missing.

My smile dimmed as I passed my apartment door and the door beyond. Part of me longed to shove Nik and Sylinia toward one another, impatient with how they danced around their feelings. I wanted to scream, *Don't squander your time.*

The bitter taste of hypocrisy coated my tongue. Wasn't that what I was doing? Squandering what I felt for Maddox because of Morgenna's compulsion? I couldn't use fate as an excuse anymore. My path and the fate of witchkind were intertwined with his. But what about my fear? If I stayed away from him as Morgenna intended, was Yori's death nothing but a casualty of her cruelty?

I glared at the door, imagining Yori walking through, ducking beneath the doorframe and cracking a joke. Right behind him came Ansil and Elenna, squabbling as always. All three would turn on me with hope brilliantly lighting them from within as it did in life.

Yori would say, "*Mother curse me, Alys. I told you to use my death to find a way from under Morgenna. Don't waste my death. Find the happiness you deserve.*"

Ansil would fling his braid over his shoulder and huff, "*The world will always be colored in moral grays, whether you succeed saving witchkind or not. If you don't move against her, she'll find another reason to hurt those you love. Make up your mind and do something.*"

Never one to be outdone, Elenna would push her way past the men and grab my shoulders, black eyes twinkling brighter than any starry sky. "*Move before the bitch does and take your happiness back. Damn waiting to be saved.* You *go and save* him."

"It's not that easy," I snarled, breath ragged.

No one replied.

A sob slipped out and I slumped against the wall of the empty hall. If they were here, alive at my side, they would've been right. Whether or not I gave into fear of Morgenna, she'd continue to destroy. Dual Witches would die, innocents would be sacrificed as punishment, and another Water Wheel would suffer.

I couldn't live in a cage of fear forever. At least, not alone.

Mind made up, I threw open the door and stalked across the corridor in my bare feet. First, Maddox needed to understand provoking me to reason hadn't gone unnoticed. I raised my fist to pound his door, but it opened before I could touch it.

"First of all," I snapped, "how dare you try to bait me into a fight."

I didn't manage another word before he pulled me inside.

"Yes, yes, I provoked you." His perfect features were lit by a strange grin, feral like the thrumming shadows slithering up the walls. "You can scold all you want, for as long as you want, *after* I show you something."

I'd never been inside his rooms. Stepping into them felt as if I'd stepped into his woodsy, spiced soul. It fogged any irritation toward him. I didn't get a chance to examine the jumble of books on an entry table before he'd gripped my hand and dragged me into a sitting room.

Maddox was annoyingly neat. Everything from his outward appearance to his office desk presented a perfect picture of elegance and grace. Stepping into his sitting room, I realized his orderliness was yet another mask.

Books covered every surface of the simple, unadorned room. They hid the dark blue rug peeking from beneath towering stacks of books. More haphazardly scattered a table by an arched window overlooking Morithia. Bookcases lined each wall. Shelves bowed under the weight of dozens of double-stacked books. A lone green leather book lay on the onyx tile before the fireplace, singed and partially burned.

That explained the odd scent of charred meat faint in the air.

I sank onto the lone sofa cushion not piled with books. I rather liked knowing Maddox was as messy as I was, if not worse. At least my books stayed on the shelves.

Maddox had abandoned me in a manic search through a bookcase beside the window. Running a long finger across their spines, he threw over his shoulder, "Do you know what a Death Rune is?"

I blinked and dislodged a fantasy of that finger skimming across *my* spine. "Yes?"

"Then you know how they work?"

"Something like stealing magic from one Creature to boost another through a rune carved onto skin."

Frowning, he dropped his search and came to slump beside me on the crowded sofa. I squashed the urge to lean into him. He was already touching me from thigh to shoulder. It wasn't enough. "It's only stealing if that's what one intends. Death Runes facilitate *sharing* magic between two Creatures. Magic can go back-and-forth depending on the wielder, the one who carves the rune."

He sounded as if he was trying to convince himself. I peered at the piece of parchment he hadn't released since I walked in. "Are you telling me you have one?"

His mouth quirked into a smirk, one I remembered tracing my collarbones. Swallowing, I resisted the budding guilt in my chest. I wanted this to be easy, to fall into him without the terror of compulsion's consequences plaguing me each time I thought of kissing him.

"Perhaps I have one."

Recalling the Leon portent and the odd Death Rune inscribed on it and in *Dualitas Maleficarum*, I reached for the parchment, but he snatched it from reach. I huffed a breath through my nose. "Show me and stop being so damned cagey."

He shot me a glower but extended the parchment. "You have to realize, they're dangerous. Deadly. There's a reason they're called Death Runes. But I think"—he twisted his lips and slouched into the sofa, going wan as if hardly believing himself—"I think it's a chance at cutting Morgenna's compulsion."

I unfolded the scrap of paper and choked on my gasp. The same circle rune from the Leon portent was sketched in black ink. There could be no doubt now. Maddox and Melis were two of the Mother's six. This had been Maddox's path—forced to undergo Morgenna's horrors to find hope. While I hunted Osrin and vampyres and Corryn hunted portents, Maddox hunted escape from compulsion.

"We'll do it together. Right now," I whispered, heart tripping over itself. "We'll carve the rune into one another's skin at the same time. Your rune frees me and mine frees you. We can't risk this working on one of us while the other goes running to Morgenna. Two runes, two streams of passing magic."

Maddox set aside the parchment and laced his fingers through mine. Once, I would've misunderstood the ice in his expression. Now, I recognized the concern behind it. "Death Runes work on a forceful overthrow of one Creature's magic. Yes, it can be a back-and-forth flow, but it's difficult to control. One of us will overpower the other and it will feel *good*. Therein lies the danger. Good intentions turn into draining someone until they're dead."

He thought he'd overpower me. Without saying so, he gave me an out. Giving me his trust and asking for the same in return. Our fate in *our* control. Not Morgenna's.

"Wait"—I sat up and frowned—"aren't Death Runes illegal? How do we get around Morgenna's law?"

His crooked grin melted any ice. "*Are* they illegal? I searched the law codes and found nothing. We've convinced ourselves they're outlawed based on centuries-old code. Code that burned along with the rest of the books from the Lost Five Hundred Years. *Technically*, those laws no longer exist."

We could end compulsion's cruelty on a godsdamned technicality.

Leaning into Maddox and his firm warmth, I gave him my trust and my future, whispering, "Let's do it." I could've forever basked in the brilliance of his returning smile.

He retrieved two small blades from a drawer in the table, no more than sharp letter openers. He hesitated before kneeling on the floor before me. He really needed to stop doing that. Princes didn't kneel before captive nobodies. "If this ends wrong, I need you to know something."

"It *won't* go wrong. Don't you dare say that out loud. You can tell me whatever you want when we're free—"

He grabbed my cheeks between his hands. My blathering fell silent. "I love you, you obstinate little demon. You don't have to accept it or do anything with it. I just need to make sure you know so that you can see yourself the way I see you. A heart that never falters and perceptive to a fault, but never for your own benefit. You get under my skin, you push me in ways no one else dares, but, Alys, you alone see me, even when I can't see myself. All this time and until the last star blinks out—I'm yours."

Time bent around him like a crux of fate.

Yours.

Mine to have while the world pressed in. Never alone.

I launched and wrapped around him. We tipped backward in a mess of fallen limbs. Books toppled like playing dominoes around us, but neither of us bothered to look. Lips pressed tight against his, we sank to the floor.

Safe and loved, I burrowed into his embrace.

A slow warmth edged into my bones, daring to grow where ice had lived for weeks now. But the lurking Death Rune waited, beckoning us onto our intertwined path.

Firelight fell on the blades, as if fate impatiently pointed with a finger. We knelt on the stone tile, ready for whatever came. Maddox took one knife and handed me the other. Rolling our sleeves back, we offered the other an arm.

"Together?" he asked.

I pressed the trembling tip of the knife to his forearm. "Together."

The sting in my arm was nothing to the wrongness of splitting Maddox's skin. I cut Eleutheria's circle, then a line, then the arrows into his arm. Blood pooled then slid over pale skin and onto the rug. My stomach sank with each falling drop.

We waited, eyeing the other with bated breath.

Eleutheria's power didn't waft across my skin like the air runes on my broom. No, the Death Rune ripped open my center and clawed inside in an onslaught of cedar talons, intent on tearing apart my soul. A Maddox-marked wave of darkness stormed my vision, cutting off the world until there was only his magic plundering me.

My magic stirred at the intrusion. Emboldened by my own Death Rune, it awoke in a fury, clawing to the top of our magics' struggle. Bit by bit, honey overpowered cedar. Poisoned sweetness surrounded his cedar storm, feeding his magic to the purring beast within. More. More. Until I vibrated with unimaginable power.

And it was mine.

For the first time in my life, I felt unstoppable. Strong. Infinite. Like I could break this plane and the next. I could remake the world in my own design. I could wipe away evil. I could *fix* this broken world. The power waited in my hands.

Something sagged against me. A heavy weight threatened to knock me backward.

Maddox.

His magic—no—his *soul* rested in my grip.

I didn't want his power. I wanted *him*. His unerring ability to make me simultaneously scream and laugh, to make me *feel*. I wanted the rare smiles and the irritating sighs. The boundless wit and intelligence that met mine again and again, pushing me to reexamine myself. My match. A wall and a path all at once, a safety net and a gentle push.

I wanted to fix this broken world *with* him.

Flinging his magic toward the soul on the other side, I fumbled for reality. It felt like wading through a bog of churning power. I latched onto the feeling of the bodily weight against me and pushed past the haze until Maddox's sitting room came into view.

Terror flooded me. He wasn't moving.

I pushed him into an upright position, muttering frantic curses when he swayed back toward me. His eyes didn't open. Holding my breath, I searched for signs I hadn't pulled too much. I shoved my hand beneath his tunic, seeking for the rhythmic beat against my palm.

A yelp burst out of him and his eyes flew open. Golden, precious proof of life. "Why are your hands always godsdamned cold?"

Whimpering a curse, I threw my arms around him.

He rested his forehead against mine and he whispered, "And here I thought I had to be the one to hold back. Don't ever stop surprising me, Alys Sathos."

Choking on a giggle, I pressed kisses to his forehead, his faint freckles, along his scar, anywhere I could reach. We were alive. Thank the Mother and her twisted, fated path. We were *free*.

The icy grip that hadn't faded from my head in months was . . . gone. I thought of the impossible, of running to the beautiful western shores with Maddox and disappearing together. Of a lifetime spent together in the open without repercussions. Only the warmth of the future's hope met my defiant thoughts. A future with Maddox, with Corryn. Happy and free.

Delighted words stuck to my throat, unable to form, spilling instead from my eyes.

Morgenna had no control here.

Maddox blinked once. Twice. He searched the room as if waiting for compulsion's cage to reappear from behind the sofa.

"I don't—it's gone. The compulsion, the ice. I can't—I can't feel it any-more." He rose from the tile floor, swaying slightly, fixed on the door. When nothing happened, he dipped and yanked me up with him. His laughter surged free, loose and incredulous. He swung me in a wide circle, stumbling drunk on hope. Stacks of books collapsed in our wake. They scattered across the rug in unnoticed heaps. Everything seemed . . . more. The fireplace hotter. The sparkling stars in the window brighter. A new untethered world waited, one where we could move without Morgenna pulling our strings.

He dropped onto the sofa and pulled me with him, breathless and light. Reality crept in but this time I wouldn't face it alone. "Maddox, now that we're freed, there's about a thousand things I need to explain."

His smile dimmed, but he nodded, already expecting this. The shadows rushed from the corners and out the door. A moment later, they returned laden with clean linens and a roll of bandages.

"You can start by telling me how you lied to Morgenna and said you didn't have magic."

He took the supplies from the shadows and began wiping the torn skin on my arm I'd all but forgotten. I suppose we couldn't magically heal our Death Runes if we wanted their protection to be permanent. Unlike mineral-inked tattoos, Death Runes worked without nature. If we left them as permanent scars, we could be impervious to compulsion. A giddy thought.

"I didn't lie," I insisted. Pursing my lips at his cocked brow, I allowed him to wrap my arm in a tight bandage. "When she first asked, I didn't have any magic. Not until the Harkening Ball."

"Alys, I've smelled your magic since the ravine in the Blackwood. How do you think I didn't fall for your little trick with the splashing water? I smelled you right in front of me."

I frowned. How *had* he always smelled it when no one else could? "I don't have an answer for that, but I can tell you how I accidentally awakened my magic." Quickly, I explained touching Corryn and discovering we were twins separated at birth.

He shook his head slowly, brows dipping low. "Corryn is Night Witch. I grew up with her. I've seen her magic. You can fly, that means you're a Day Witch. You *can't* be related."

Nerves struck at my chest, wrapping tightly. Moment of truth. How far had Morgenna pulled him into her web? "Do you know what a Dual Witch is?"

He blinked owlishly.

Relief, thick as honey, rolled over my nerves, squashing any apprehension. He didn't know. Corryn had been wrong.

Smiling gently, I took his hand and explained what Corryn and I were. Of the queens' deception. Morgenna's hunt, Corryn and Rilessa's defiance. What the queens hid in the Lost Five Hundred Years. I told him of the portents and the Mother's fate for the six. How Corryn and I had discovered he and Melis were destined to destroy Morgenna and Lilain. This was why we'd all been gifted extraordinary magic. We would free our people and restore our kind from the perverse magic of the queens as Lilain had done with the vampyres.

Mouth twisted in concentration, he rose to pace the sitting room. I let him mull it over in silence, recognizing I'd probably upended his world.

"We are *all* meant to be Dual Witches?" A note of despair cracked his voice. I wondered, if like his sister, he'd longed for light in Morgenna's shadow. It would have been natural, after all, to seek the half missing from their soul.

I nodded and summoned his shadow. It uncurled from the tile, sweeping up his legs, before dashing shyly to me. A flicker of light from my palm floated out to meet it and they swirled into one another in an orb of gold and black. The orb lifted a bandage from the heap on the sofa and wound it around his bloody arm. He studied the dual magic with a terrifying intensity, chest heaving, as if debating whether or not to extinguish the ball of shadowy light that made me Morgenna's target.

Seeking to smooth the line between his brows, I rose and raised a hand, but he snatched my wrist.

He tipped my chin to meet his unblinking stare. Before I could alleviate the darkness easing up the walls with his thoughts, he crashed his lips to mine in a bruising kiss. If I thought I knew what it was to be kissed by him, I was wrong. The panic from the Death Rune, our freedom, my magic's reveal—I felt his relief in his hand gathering my nightgown to my bare hip, the other wound tight in my hair. In how he pressed his thigh between my legs, leaving nothing between us.

Ripping away from me, he dropped my nightgown and took a staggered step back.

Heat rushed to my face. All I had told him at Agria's cottage came rushing back.

Always so damned noble.

"No," I whispered, reaching for him. Uncertainty dipped his dark brows in a rare show of vulnerability. I slid arms around his waist and anchored him to me. "We're free, Maddox. I won't be afraid of her anymore. Not ever again. This time I want you to take me to your bed. This time I want you to take all of me, and then I want to lose myself in all of you."

For a long, uncertain moment neither of us moved. Slowly, the shadows inched back down the walls to their natural corners.

Maddox swallowed hard.

"Alys," was all he managed before he swept me into his arms. His mouth found mine again, and this time, he didn't let go.

Somehow, we made it to his bedroom. Halting. Stumbling. Tongues encouraging groans. Fumbling fingers unbuttoned his shirt and pushed it off his broad shoulders. I needed to touch him, craved his burning skin on mine.

My back barely hit the bed when my nightgown rose, rucked up around my hips. Higher and higher. The silk elicited a path of pebbled skin up my neck he chased with his tongue.

I need more. More skin. More fire between us.

His hand trailed down my hip, down the inside of my thigh. A burning path followed his touch. Locking my legs around him, I rolled my hips into his, creating delicious friction. He let out a deep groan and it sent new waves down my spine. Sharply inhaling, he pinned my hips to the mattress and pulled back.

A faint hitch in his breath ignited something low beneath my navel. The small sound was nearly as undoing as the hungry way his gaze blazed over me. My hair spread in a mess on his pillow. Every bare inch of me shivering under his stare. Roving. Discovering. Claiming. His fingers traced the path his eyes tracked, and my breathing became little more than shallow pants.

Gliding fingertips along the V-shaped planes above his hips to the runic tattoos, I breathlessly teased, "Shouldn't we savor our hard-won compulsion victory a little longer?"

"I *am* savoring my victory." He ducked and grinned against my skin. Focusing on that damned weak spot below my ear, he licked and sucked my neck until I couldn't remember my own name.

His calloused palm cupped my breast and brushed a thumb over my hardening peak. Fire threatened to burst from my veins. Every inch of skin thrummed alive beneath his touch.

I groped for the buttons at his pants.

The hand tracing idle circles around my nipple shot for my clumsy hand, stilling it flat against the line of dark hair at his stomach.

Lifting his head to brush the tip of his nose against mine, he took a ragged breath and said, "I've thought about this nearly every night since I met you. Imagined you a million ways. You are not a simple, quick fuck. I want to revel in you, worship you. I need to *show* you what you mean to me. Please."

A prickling sting of vulnerability threatened to pierce the spell between us, but the heady weight of all I felt for him drowned out my deprecating self-worth.

I nodded.

His mouth found mine again, his tongue moving slower than the hand sliding down my stomach. Long fingers danced lower until they parted me, gliding to my center. He swallowed my moan, drawing more whimpers when he slid a finger into me. No midnight fantasy had ever come close to those deliciously long fingers.

Rasing my hips, I sought more friction, silently begging for a faster pace, but he continued his unhurried torture, easing in and out of me. Minutes turned into lifetimes. When he slid a second finger into me and a third finally granted me friction against my most sensitive spot, I arched into him and cried out.

Every nerve in my body sang to life, throbbing before I plunged into bliss.

His fingers languidly slid from me, and he pulled from my lips to watch me come back down with a dark, possessive gaze. Boneless, I sighed dreamily and threw an arm over my eyes.

There was a very strong possibility he'd just fingered my soul right out of me.

He let loose a soft laugh.

Oh. I'd said that out loud.

His breath hot on my skin, he shifted lower down my body. A wet finger drew a line around my navel. I uncovered my eyes to find my stomach damp with patterns.

"Shall we go again?" he asked. Again? The answer was yes, *obviously yes*, but I hadn't even yet managed to find my breath. He lay on his side between my bent legs, propped up on an elbow. His intense focus was on whatever he was writing on my skin with the effect of my pleasure.

"What are you writing?"

He pulled back, a hand on each of my knees, slowly pulling them further apart as he lowered a dark, hungry gaze. "It says *regina mea*."

I had an inkling of its translation, but I asked, "What's it mean?"

His answering smirk sparked another flame deep in my core. "It means you're mine until the last star blinks out, Alys. It means our world might be burning but I'll gladly burn if it means standing beside you."

Then he bent down and drew his tongue through my gleaming belly.

My queen.

Something hazy in my brain preened before thought became impossible.

He kissed a wet path to the valley between my thighs. I was entirely at his mercy as he raised my hips high and brought me to his mouth. He dragged his tongue from my center to the aching point still tingling from before. Lightning arced through my body in delicious waves. As if grasping a life-saving raft, I sank a hand into his hair, pushing him down, desperate for more. Deep low moans sank vibrations plummeting into my core. Liquid fire spread with each one, all more potent than the one before.

My spine arched, threatening to snap to the rolling waves of lightning. But his grip tightened, hands holding me open, showing me what it meant to be worshipped.

I couldn't breathe, his name a barely audible chant. The building heat leapt to unfathomable heights, lunging higher with each stroke, each nip and ragged breath and groan. Every time I neared the ledge of oblivion, he lifted it higher.

When his tongue curled inside me, I grasped oblivion's ledge and fell over it, fragmenting into a thousand stars. The sound that left me was unnatural, unrestrained as he plundered me. Supported by his strong hands, I rode a wave of stars and all-consuming pleasure.

I couldn't speak. Couldn't think.

Only a mind-numbing fog remained in the aftermath.

"You, my darling *mea*, are in for a very long night." Maddox gently set me back down and crawled forward to surround me on all fours.

Mea.

Mine.

"Again," he ordered with the self-satisfied smirk of someone who knew who was in control. At some point I'd wipe it off—once I could remember my own fucking name.

He bent and pulled the tip of my breast into the heat of his mouth. A new fire began, burning through the fog. His fingertips and lips wandered. Exploring. Ravenous. My shoulders, my spine, my sides—my *thighs*. He stoked an all-consuming fire with soft, filthy words in my ear, drawing gasps each time his long fingers dipped between my legs. It took him no time at all to discover what made me stutter and gasp.

When I couldn't handle his promising threats any longer, I locked my legs around his hips and pressed him against me until I found what I wanted. He dropped his head onto my shoulder and released a wavering exhale, one hand fisting my hair.

Well, it turned out he didn't have the control he let on.

Good.

I wanted him uncontrolled. In my hand. In my mouth. In me.

This time, he didn't stop me undoing his pants and together we clumsily pushed them to the floor. Bare above me, my breath hitched. He was achingly beautiful. Not because he was perfect, but because he wasn't. Because the series of scars and tattoos across his body matched the imperfect map of my life—broken and battered, inside and out.

He was mine and I was his. *Together.*

"Wait," he rasped.

I was going to erupt into a thousand flames, but I flopped back onto the pillow with a loud sigh.

He traced the contraceptive tattoo ward on my hip with careful strokes as if worried it still hurt. "If you get pregnant and Morgenna—"

"Maddox, look at me." I cupped his cheek and turned him until he was fixed on me. "We're free to do whatever we want and face the consequences however we want. *But* I promise, however awful it may look, the ward works."

He locked eyes with me, every thought, dark and light, clear to me between golden stars. Slowly, he pushed into me, stretching, filling, stirring something new within, and, right then, I knew no one would ever compare.

I was gloriously ruined by him and his touch.

"You," he groaned through clenched teeth, sinking until we were hip to hip, "are—perfect and warm. You're utterly *perfect.*" He slid an arm beneath my waist, raising my hips at an angle that forced a new set of whimpers out of me.

Abruptly, he pulled away.

Before I could protest, he sat up and lifted me onto him, spearing me. Electric bursts, sweet and agonizingly wonderful, shot up my spine. His low, velvet words of praise broke through my panting cries. I clenched his shoulders as though he was the only anchor to this world. Gripping my hips, he rocked us together, moving in synchrony toward the same high.

I gave up on breathing. Frantic to reach that place of totality. Every part of me screamed to let go.

"You are—gods—*Alys,*" he whispered hoarsely against my throat. "You're everything I will spend the rest of my life trying to deserve." Fisting my hair, he yanked my head down to meet his lips. Urgently, desperately, we thrusted—bodies and tongues.

Higher and higher, past the moon, past the stars.

Together, we fell off the ledge.

Unbearable bliss erupted, not a part of me left untouched. Crying out, gasping, unable to catch my breath, I fell deep into his soul and everything he offered.

Maddox buried his face in my neck with a choked groan. His hands fell to my thighs, digging, finding his release deep inside me. Cedar and cloves swirled within as if I could feel his magic—his soul—within mine.

I'd never felt more weightless, more unburdened, floating in brilliance. In comparison, the stars were nothing but stagnant light in the sky. *This* was an echo across time, harkening through ages of misery. As if a part of him had always been a part of me and now it awoke in recognition. A call to home.

No longer alone—I was free, and I was home.

"What do these runes mean?" I rolled off my belly from the plush rug and traced black tattooed lines over his ribs with a fingernail and hid a smile at the erupting goosebumps.

After washing away the slick of sweat and sex, we'd ruined our bath before ever making it back to the bed. Twice. Although to be fair, the thick bedpost was technically a part of the bed. The rug before the fireplace I'd smugly lit with magic, however, offered a much slower pace.

Remaining flat on the rug, Maddox gently pried my hand from the tattoos and examined a scar across my wrist where a stall merchant had tried cleaving my hand as payment for a stolen jug of goat's milk. After a long while, he said, "They're penitence runes. A permanent reminder of regret."

I blanched. Penitence runes were used by priestesses in self-flagellation to the gods as penitence for their sins. I'd never guessed Maddox for religious. Certainly not one who took such harsh measures against his body.

Careful of my words, I asked, "And have you triggered them with their spellcast before?"

He lifted his gaze to mine, once more icily bland. Weighing the truth over placating me, he finally said, "Yes."

"How badly does it hurt?"

He dropped his head back onto the rug, dark hair spread like a twisted crown around his head. Contemplating the ceiling, he said, "Like hammering a chisel into your bones."

I bit my lip. How had I missed the true weight of his guilt we spoke about on that tower top all those months back? At the heart of his pain was a desperation for control. Anything to subvert Morgenna. Even awful agony. Her compulsion had ruined any sense of self-worth, and I never wanted her dead more than when I looked at the runes staining his sides.

"I won't tell you to stop," I whispered, laying back down and crawling into the crook of his arm, "but you're not alone anymore, Maddox. Talk to me. Let me share your pain. If anyone understands guilt and regret, it's me. I have bloodied hands and a bloodier heart, but they're yours."

He released a shaky breath and wound his fingers through my hair, holding them above us like a black spiderweb. "You already have the important parts of me, Alys. My respect, my love. Why would you want my pain?"

"Because I chose all of you. I won't be inconsistent with which parts I love. What makes you Maddox isn't merely the neat, orderliness you show the world. It's the scars and the struggles too. I want the messy bits because I want all of you."

"Even if I'm the reason you're here? Alone, and far from your people?"

I raised my head and found the fireplace flames reflected in his wary stare, comforting and dangerous as the heat billowing off the fire. But easy serenity floated through me, content in knowing I walked the right path alongside him.

Cupping his cheek, I brushed my nose against his long aristocratic one, and softly said, "I'm not alone. Because of you, I found my sister, unbound my magic, and discovered a path to free *our* people. Every witch is ours to protect, Maddox. I'm going to do it *with you* because you are *mine*."

"I'm yours," he repeated to himself, almost too low to catch. He bracketed his hands around my waist and flipped me onto the rug. Caging me on all fours, he dipped his head over my throat and breathed in deeply. "I hope you realize you bound yourself to someone who will never let you go. No matter what comes, nothing will take you from me."

If he meant that as a warning, he should've tried harder, because nothing was going to rip *him* from *me*.

41

EVEN SHADOWS GLIMMER

Corryn

"For the last time," I hissed, ready to throw my bracelet at the hooded witch across the lace-covered table. "Moving against Morgenna *now* is a terrible idea. With the Nordith elf delegation attending the ball this evening, the entire city will be on high alert."

Alys's nostrils flared and she slammed a palm down. The fine china on the spindly table rattled but no one in the nearly empty shop looked up. She'd done a fantastic job with her soundproofing ward. Even I had to admit she was getting better at her spellcasting—when she didn't let her magic explode out her.

"Damn the elves," she snarled. "We're *free* and the sooner we act the more lives we save. We've broken compulsion, we know four of the six. The last two don't . . . exist. Why wait?"

After she had shared the meaning of the Death Rune on the Leon portent, I'd immediately enacted it with Rilessa, and at Alys's behest had met her the next morning. She'd balked when I suggested this tearoom. Seeing her and in her Guard uniform, I understood why. We sat in a shadowed corner of a posh tearoom in the Black Wall, waiting for Maddox. I didn't doubt the other two would collaborate against me to move on Morgenna, but I wouldn't give up my ground.

"You only found out last night how to break compulsion. A grand total of *four* witches are free. Us, Maddox, and Rilessa. *We need more time.*"

"More time? For another Yori? Another Seren?"

The opening tearoom door saved me from a reply. A towering witch in hooded cloak brushed past the tearoom's serviceman and prowled for our tucked away corner.

Alys shoulders relaxed, and the fingers fidgeting with the lace tablecloth went still. A ping of annoyance shot through me. Maddox could do what I couldn't with nothing but his presence. I reminded myself he'd had more months with her, and it didn't necessarily mean she trusted him more.

Across the tearoom, their gazes collided and in spite of their eerie intensity, neither smiled. Each stone-faced, as if animosity lingered between them—a perfectly enacted lie in case of Morgenna's spies. I almost believed it. But Maddox's stare dipped to the mouth-shaped bruise above Alys's collar I'd actively avoided looking at. If I'd blinked, I would've missed his smirk.

I wrinkled my nose and took a delicate sip of tea as he sat down beside her. If I could go the rest of my life without thinking twice about what they did alone, I'd be Mother blessed.

Alys tugged her hood lower and recast the soundproofing bubble before aiming a narrowed glare onto Maddox. "Do princes not adhere to the same standards of time as the lowborn?"

"Forgive me for being unable to excuse myself from the city magistrate—or should I say your uncle—to plot a coup." He turned to study me and then Alys again. "You two look nothing alike. No wonder no one's guessed you're sisters."

We each shot him a glare.

He lifted a brow and muttered, "There it is. Same judgy attitudes." Ignoring Alys's suggestion where he could shove our attitudes, he pulled something from beneath his cloak. The charred remains of the goblin bound book slid across the table. "Turns out it was worth it."

"Keep it." I poked the book back at him with the end of my fingernail. "What about Melis? Did you give her the Eleutheria rune?"

"She won't let me in her head." He adopted a marginally softer tone at my crestfallen expression. "It's fine. We'll catch her tonight at the elven delegation."

I grimaced and downed the rest of my tea, wishing for a glass of wine. The longer we waited, the more we risked Morgenna's compulsion on others. I didn't enjoy leaving Melis out in the open, but if her stubbornness made her inaccessible, what could I do?

Alys snuck a sideways glare at me and leaned toward Maddox. "Don't you think the delegation ball is the perfect time to strike against Morgenna? Preoccupied with the elves, she'll leave herself open to attack."

"*No*," I snapped, boring holes into her. "Too many innocents remain in the city and palace. If we move against her during the delegation ball, we risk hundreds, if not thousands, of innocents in the city below. I won't put another in harm's way to get what I want. That's Morgenna's role, not mine."

Alys released an incredulous laugh. "Should we politely offer Morgenna an invitation of attack instead?" Face puckered into a simper, she mimed knocking on a door, " '*Please clear the city of all civilians so that we may rip off your fucking head without interference.*' We need to move while she's preoccupied—*tonight.*"

My cheeks burned as I spun my worn pearls. "So, you two would sacrifice a city of innocents—of *children*—to kill her?"

Maddox sharply angled his head. "Of course not. You know us better than that. But people die in war, even innocents. Yes, death should give us pause, but everything has a price—including freedom."

Stiffening, I sat back, violently shaking my head. Maddox held up a finger and pointed at Alys.

"But . . . she's right, Sathos, and I think you already know that. We need time *and* Melis. With four of the six, we stand a better chance. Morgenna won't give us two opportunities."

Her face crumpled, and she slumped into her chair.

He curled his hand inches from Alys's drumming fingers on her teacup but pressed his own flat against the table. Soft enough I knew I wasn't supposed to hear, he added, "What matters is we're free, *mea*. Together."

Her cheeks flamed at the unusually sweet endearment, but she nodded without looking up from her empty cup, admitting defeat two to one. If only *I* could talk her down that easily.

Maddox poured her another cup of tea and tossed in two sugar cubes—the only way she'd take tea. With a remorseful smile, I passed her a slice of apple tart. A pathetic apology for our squabble. She took it with a quiet, "Thanks."

As she tipped the teacup to drink, Maddox shot me a warning frown and mouthed, *Don't push.*

He was right. Judging her ruthlessness would be too easy. Guilt was a grueling taskmaster and revenge fogged her path, obscuring the upcoming twists and turns. If she wasn't careful, she'd let it drive her—and the rest of us—right into a blade.

I didn't know what terrified me more—Melis's slow inebriated sweep down my body or Morgenna watching me enter the delegation ball. The elf lord twirling Melis in his arms gave his own perusal of my less than elegant courtier robes and whispered something in her ear. I tugged the hem of my hip-length robes further down my plain navy-blue dress. Their only adornment were the ridiculously long sleeves that skimmed the floor in decade's past fashion.

She tossed her head back and laughed. The throaty sound slid across the floors like a soap bar over bare skin.

I pressed the pearls higher up the inside of my sleeve and swung from the dancers. The easiest way forward meant letting go of the past. No matter where fate took us, I'd remain steadfast and keep my heart guarded from her poison. If only that same heart listened to my brain.

Alys hadn't arrived yet. The plumed crowds parted around me in low whispers. *Isn't she the headwitch's daughter? The odd quiet one who teaches runes? I heard she's a bastard by-blow of a nobody and the self-righteous Rilessa Stellanati.*

Heat washed up my neck. Without looking any of them in the eye, I ambled toward the only witch who didn't despise my lowborn status.

Maddox maneuvered through political muck as if he'd been born to do it—which I supposed he had. He calmed the hysterics, neatly avoided the traps and listened to the never-ending praise with ears that heard the critical words in between.

When the sycophants thinned, I swallowed my pride and said, "I've been meaning to say thank you. Whatever you told Alys yesterday to bring her back to us worked. I prefer her scathing obnoxiousness over her silence. You pulled her from her grief, and I'm thankful you could do it when I couldn't."

Maddox threw me an odd look, a combination of pity and irritation. "There's no such thing." At my bewildered frown, he lowered his voice. "Grief lingers forever. You don't overcome it. You grow around it or change to accommodate it, but grief remains woven into the fabric of who you are. I reminded Alys how to live in spite of it, but I didn't take it away."

That had never occurred to me. But then, what did I know of grief and loss?

I bit my lip, focused on the smooth pearls, counting them to hide my pink cheeks. Losing Seren was the closest I'd come to death, and I'd barely known the girl beyond the secret she carried.

"Don't be embarrassed," he said quietly, studying the dancers. "Not understanding the complexity of grief is a gift. One day soon, you'll find a clearer understanding than you'd like."

"What do you mean?"

"You and Alys have it in your heads this is six versus two. But politics and two realms lay between us and our fate. I don't see a way through this that doesn't end in a bloody war."

Movement at the dais caught our attention.

Morgenna rose from her throne and smiled brightly toward the door. Several Night Guard in evening clothes entered with little commotion. A witch pressed her way to the front, and they parted for her. Midnight hair waterfalled down her back, unadorned but for a simple golden comb of holly leaves tucked behind one ear. Traditional knee-length Night Realm robes of black silk and golden embroidery fell over her slight frame.

The combination of realms on one witch sent a signal to anyone who understood Alys's true nature—*here walks a Dual Witch*. A message aimed right at Morgenna.

She *had* to be missing a marble or two.

Dipping low in mocking bow with an arm outstretched to the side, she kept her gaze trained on the stiffening witch on the throne.

"What exactly *did* you say to her yesterday?" I muttered to Maddox.

He dragged a slightly glazed stare from the doors. He had to blink several times down at me before he spoke. "I reminded her of who she was."

"Or did you awaken something else entirely?"

A black-and-gold fox slunk through the henhouse, sizing up colorful chickens. Without magic, she'd been formidable, but with it . . . the throne room's shadows perked up, sniffing the air to the new entering power.

Maddox tilted his head to the side and watched Alys part the crowd. "I don't know why you're surprised. Yes, she doesn't think twice about throwing her life away for another. She's softer than she appears and can never say no to anyone. But there's another part of her you purposefully overlook because it makes you uncomfortable." He fixed steel and ice on me, and I fought the need to step back. "We both know why the gods chose her. Out of the six, she's the most likely to choose the darkness if it means saving witchkind. But most importantly, she's the only one who can return to the light unscathed."

An unfamiliar grin overtook the ice and rose with mischief. "I'm sure she'd leave a piece of Morgenna for you if you asked nicely.

"You're as demented as she is. You deserve one another."

A shadow fell over me and stole his retort.

"Why are you torturing me?" a new voice slurred in my ear. "Can't I enjoy a proper revelry without your mousey little face invading every thought?"

Melis slung her arm around my waist and bent down to breath me in. Expensive cherry wine washed across my neck. Gooseflesh prickled in response. My panicked yelp prompted a low laugh. The sultry sound shot straight into my veins, deeper than I would admit.

I shoved her off me, but it threw my center of gravity off balance. My foot caught on my ridiculously long sleeves, and I toppled toward the floor.

Maddox's righted me with a frown over my head. He gave me a light push toward Alys who was already angling toward us from across the throne room.

Don't, I mentally warned her. *You'll grab unnecessary attention if you dive through the crowd. I'll be fine. Maddox won't leave me with her.*

She bit her lip but slipped back into the group of young Night guards.

Melis snatched my hand, but the sudden movement disturbed her already precarious balance. We tottered backward, wine sloshing onto my arm in a wave of overbearing cherry sweetness. She let loose a garbled giggle and gripped me harder.

Maddox began prying her pale fingers off me. "This isn't what you want to do, Melis." He lowered his voice, pleading and bringing back a wave of memory. "You're drunk and you'll regret this in the morning."

How many times had he said those words before?

She wriggled from him and pressed me closer into her warm, hard body, inhaling my hair. Poisonous familiarity stung the backs of my eyes. "What is it about you? I've seen your little claws. Like a shrew dressed as a mouse. Have you sunk those claws into Sathos? Does she know what kind of a backstabbing, petty thing you are?"

"Enough," I whispered. "I hurt you, and for that I'll always be sorry, but I won't be your whipping post anymore. Stop weaponizing your bitterness and leave me alone."

A cherry scoff caressed my cheek. "What do you know of bitterness?"

Something cracked inside and anger seeped out. "I know it destroyed us long before that night. You ruined me as surely as you ruined yourself. If anyone is to blame for what happened, it's *you*, Melis. I loved you enough to forgive anything, but you didn't want forgiveness. You wanted to hurt and hurt others in return."

Melis jerked back, sloshing more wine over her sleeve. "I never asked for your *forgiveness*." She hissed the word like it burned. "How is it my fault you couldn't see beyond a few stupid kisses?"

"Don't make it out like I was nothing to you. I'm worth more respect than that." I raised a trembling hand but yanked it back when she flinched. Instead, I went for my pearls. "You wanted to drown in your misery, and for years I sat with you at the bottom of that misery, gasping for air in hopes you'd forgive me and we'd both be freed. Now, I've realized, you have no intention of surfacing."

I ripped off the bracelet and lobbed it at her. "I won't wait for someone who wants to wallow in misery to avoid facing the truth. I choose to find peace and it's not with you."

Sobriety hit her before the pearls did. Staring at the bracelet in recognition, the Night Princess's expression crumbled into something almost familiar behind the bitterness.

The hurt there didn't bring satisfaction.

Hating the heat inching up my neck, I glided through the crowd for Alys, doing my best to emulate my mother's grace.

"Well done."

I offered Maddox a watery smile. "You should go back to her. Maybe warn her about the rune. She shouldn't be unprotected."

"In her state? I'd have better luck convincing a nymph. Go find Sathos and keep her from eating a courtier alive. Or maybe let her loose on them. Might be fun." With a final assessing grin, he vanished into a sea of feathers and silk.

Alys found me first. Emotion streamed warmth downriver toward me and her soft, proud smile meant the world. She threaded her arm through mine and wound us through sneers. Catty remarks on her hair or Night robes sailed past on whispers. She offered equally haughty sneers in return, scrutinizing their outfits and feathered hair like she'd spent all her life amongst them. She was half-aristocratic brat, after all.

Like a mother duck with a duckling under her wing, she pressed me into her side and never let go. She and Maddox would have to learn I could cope fine on my own, but it was nice to be cared for all the same. Who would have thought I'd have found it in a captured DRAS airwitch and the boy who'd tormented me in school?

Fate had some nerve.

Morgenna began a pretty speech on elven and witch cooperation. Mostly platitudes and nonsense. Not a single elf bothered disguising the blatant contempt they swept over the witches. Well, then what was the point of their delegation to Morithia?

"And now," the Night Queen called, clapping her hands. "As a little demonstration of our realm's fine law code at work, I've arranged—"

A boom rattled the castle.

I staggered across the trembling floor, yanking Alys with me. A moment later, the clang of alarm bells sounded outside the palace—the signal of attack.

42

NO REST FOR THE BLOODY

Alys

T he boom came first. Glass in the dome above groaned with an ear-tin-
gling creak. The courtiers froze, staring uncertainly at one another.
Some squinted out the wall of windows to the city below. More than one
edged for the doors.

Like a hammer, Morithia's siege bells shattered the pause.

Screams followed. A wave of courtiers charged for the doors, each frantic
for the barracks' umbranation point and the safety of escape.

The elves, too, shoved their way through to the front, aimed for the
barracks without a spared glance for the witches they pushed to the floor.
Selfish pricks. We could have used the magic of the most powerful Creatures
on Efelldor to face whatever waited below.

Heaving Corryn off me, I scrambled upright.

Chaos exploded all around the throne room. Candle wax and crushed
flowers splattered the floors. Witches cried out, trampled to the floors. Broken wine bottles and shards of ice sculptures created a dangerous maze to
the doors. Above the din, frantic bells called the Guard to the barracks.

Get to the umbranation point when the crowds thin, I ordered Corryn as I
squeezed out the doors. *Then umbranate home.*

No. I won't leave you.

Please, Corryn—

I need to know you'll come back safe. She sounded breathless. *I'll wait behind the palace walls. Whatever's happening below, the palace remains safe. Morgenna warded it herself.*

Sylinia found me in the barracks. Speaking rapidly, she helped me into leather armor and twisted my hair into a low knot. "Vampyres blew two holes in the city wall in the Black Wall District. Two patrolling units are all that's stopping their breach for now."

"They *blew up* the wall? *Twice?*" A rare few Day Witches could manipulate and propel fire into explosions—like Ansil and Elenna. If Lilain had fed her own soldiers to the vampyres, they were capable of more than Night magic. It didn't shock me that a few vampyres sacrificed their lives to blow open a hole in Morithia's defenses.

Sylinia strapped a thin sword to her back and crossed her arms. She angled her chin, daring me to stand her down. The giggly, pink-faced witch dancing with Nik minutes ago had disappeared. A soldier ready to defend her home to the last breath stood before me.

"Don't make me regret this," I snarled and slammed a helmet over her fiery hair.

Dust and charred stone chunks scattered the remains of the once vibrant Black Wall. A thick haze blotted our path. We could barely see more than a pace ahead through smoke and ash, but we zigzagged through the ruptured streets for the gaping hole in the wall.

Disembodied shrieks ruptured the gray haze. Shadows rose and swallowed the trivial protection of a few torches left untouched in the ruins. The roaring fires Maddox had directed to burn each night along the exterior wall were gone. Nothing remained but pillars of smoke.

What should have been an easy path took us twice us long to traverse through debris. Streams of rushing Guard clambered over a fallen wooden wall that looked like it once belonged to a tearoom. Heart thudding, I hollered to Sylinia, "Prince Maddox? Is he down here?"

She leapt over a toppled wagon, landing on nimble feet. "No one knows where anyone is. The officers are in chaos. We're struggling with long forgotten breach contingency plans."

He was fine. Clever, competent, wonderfully terrifying with his magic. He'd be fine.

We rounded a corner and came face-to-face with a unit of Guard taking on a flooding horde of snapping teeth.

"Remember, they die easy," I yelled, praying to Mother I hadn't fucked up letting her fight. If something happened, Nik would undoubtedly send me to the Soul Lands after her. "Quick, simple strikes. Don't bother with fancy footwork. Just live, Sylinia."

The young woman straightened her shoulders and nodded. Together, we tore into the fray. Our swords never faltered. Blood sprayed. Bodies fell. A call for aid sounded through our ranks. It wouldn't be enough.

More bodies. More blood.

Vampyr shrieks swallowed witches' screams. The shadows thickened. Vampyres flowed in an endless stream through the broken wall. Two replaced each one struck down. A never-ending river of carnage.

We needed my fire.

But from the palace dome Morgenna would have a clear view. I wasn't ready to risk exposure. Not yet.

The ground beneath us rumbled. Further down the wall, the Quies River heaved. Foam bubbled the surface.

With a warning shout, I grabbed Sylinia's collar and lurched from the banks. White, churning water sprang over the ruined market in a thick paste of ash and debris. Tiny stinging droplets pelted my face. A freezing mist settle onto my leather armor as the waves threatened to slip over the tops of my boots.

Downriver, something roared.

Clawing waves swept a nearby guard off his feet and sucked him into its murky depths. More waves hauled over the riverbank. Filth and debris washed over the ruins in a nose-numbing stench. The breaking river didn't discern witch from vampyr. It engulfed all in the rising flood.

If the Quies was breaking its banks . . .

Shit.

I yanked Sylinia from the water and shoved her toward the Water Wheel. The embankment there was meant to hold the Quies from flooding the city. But if the embankment grate in the wall had also been blown open, vampyres could enter the city through the river—and right through the Water Wheel the Guard never bothered patrolling.

Screaming an explanation over my shoulder, we raced for the forgotten district. A blanket of dust and ash covered empty streets. In some places, a paste had formed where the creeping river oozed into the city. We ran blindly through burning smoke. I ignored my pleading lungs and pushed harder toward the faint sound of screams.

We sped through an alley and burst into the main square. Without warning, I halted and Sylinia slammed into my back. I stumbled into the square, but Sylinia caught my collar and wrenched me back into the alley.

Vampyres held one side of the square. Pressed against the looming shadows of the city wall, they seethed with snapping jaws. Razor-sharp shadows hurtled toward the witches on the opposite end.

Rugard, Ervik, and a few others had pieced together a monstrous shield. The patchwork wall of shadows blocked the vampyres' attacks, but cracks had begun forming. It wouldn't last long. Behind them, Simone and the group of girls I'd trained lay siege to the buildings. Flaming bottles of liquor hurtled into buildings in explosions of light.

Pride surged for my little demons. The vampyres couldn't cross the square without risking the firelight from the blazing buildings.

The same firelight shone on the littered bodies at the square's center. Each lay unmoving in the shallow floods. Blood swathed them in great brushstrokes of crimson. Sorsha, the brave and beautiful witch with scarred cheeks, faced me. Water lapped into her gaping mouth. Her neck had been ripped open.

Swallowing past the tightness in my throat, I scanned the street beyond the square to the rushing river flooding the district. Water gushed through the gaping onyx wall in torrents. Vampyres rode on the flooding tides. With stolen water magic, they shot into the streets. If I could find a way to dam the river, I'd seal the hole from vampyres *and* stop the river from flooding the city.

I motioned to Sylinia, and we dashed across the square. Shadow-tipped arrows screamed past our ears. With a cry, Sylinia flung out an arm and a thin wall of shadow surged from the alley behind us. The wobbling shield flickered and hissed over us, but it managed to fend off the arrows long enough to reach the witches.

The massive shield opened, and Rugard's enormous hands shot out to drag us inside.

Ervik's hands shook with the strain of holding up the shield, but he managed to hiss, "*This* is what the Guard sent to protect the Water Wheel? A page and a magicless Day Witch?" Black gore smeared his cheeks. Much of it centered around a mouth twisted into a sneer.

I briefly wondered if one of his ancestors had actually managed to fuck a nymph.

"We need to dam the river," I said to Rugard, ignoring Ervik's painful jab. "If we can shift the rubble back onto—"

"Day Witch!" high-pitched shrieks called from the other side. "Come out and face us."

"Your ears," Sylinia whispered, eyes wide. "We forgot to take out your earrings."

Shadows boomed against the shields, doubling their efforts to rip it open. With one long howl, the vampyres ran across the square. They threw hands up against the glare of the flames, screaming in agony when the light fell onto them.

But they didn't stop.

They threw themselves at the shield, trying to rip it apart with bare hands.

The cracks lengthened in the patchwork of shadows.

Ervik and Rugard lunged to reinforce the shield. Their arms shook and even in the winter night air, sweat poured down their temples. Sylinia and Simone rushed to join them, adding depth to the cracks like plaster.

Witches cried out and dashed behind the failing shield. Chunks of shadow fell at their feet. A few old men unsheathed rusted swords with trembling hands. Someone called for the young girls to run. Too few wielded shadows in the Water Wheel—as magicless as me.

But I wasn't magicless.

Not anymore.

Morgenna be damned.

I wouldn't risk more lives to keep her off me. Corryn was right. We were better than her.

Sunlight erupted in my soul, filling me with peculiar warmth, like the dawn had emerged deep in my gut. It spread through my veins, focused on finding a path to my hands. Gold lightning forked across my knuckles—waiting.

Inhaling, I threw the warmth into the sky. Orbs of daylight launched from my fingertips. They exploded into glowing fat drops of sunshine rain and poured onto the bloodied streets. The square glowed like a sunlit morning at midnight. Somehow brighter than even the summer solstice.

Vampyres fell to their knees, dropping swords to claw their eyes. Agonized screams cut across the square, glass against my eardrums. Each hair on my neck rose and every witch flinched.

"Now, Ervik," I cried, straining to control the light pulsing from my hands. "Kill them!"

He snapped his dropped jaw shut and whooped. Shouting for Simone and the young women, he threw himself at the blinded vampyres.

More witches crept from hiding places beyond the square. Shopkeepers and tavern-goers. Hectir and his ilk. Old men with rusted swords.

And the women.

Women of every age who'd seen one monster ravage their streets. They wouldn't allow another. They would hold their streets—their homes—against any who threatened them.

The sound of witch snarls wove through the squelch of torn flesh. Black vampyr blood stained the flooded river darker than night. Morithia had never shown the Water Wheel mercy, and they fought like it. No other monster would defile their hard-won peace.

Alys! Corryn's horror filled my head. *Stop! Morgenna will know. She'll see—*

I won't sit idly knowing I can save hundreds. I'd never forgive myself if I did nothing in order to save my skin.

My soul prickled, an itchy feeling spreading through my arms. The pull to erupt with all my magic at once was strong. I was using too much.

But—

I'll risk her wrath for them.

The last vampyr shrieks became gurgles before falling silent.

For a moment, silence pressed on the Water Wheel. Scattered witches sagged against swords. Some knelt over bodies. A few let out halfhearted cheers.

Slithering strands of sunlight slowly twisted back into my hands. With a grunt, I slammed the door on my soul and its seemingly bottomless well of magic. The beast wasn't satiated. It wanted more. Breathing hard, I sank to my knees and rubbed at my chest. Everything felt inside-out. I wanted to claw at my chest and scratch my soul until it bled.

"What in the godsdamned Soul Lands was that?" Rugard's wary glare dropped to my hands where golden light flickered at my fingertips before fading.

"Told you she was a shifty little bitch," Ervik called from across the square. He wiped a trickle of black blood from his chin and hobbled toward us. "Matilda was right about you though, wasn't she? You saved us. Though probably not what she meant when she laid eyes on you."

Accepting Sylinia's help, I rose on unsteady feet. "Where is she?"

Rugard frowned and pointed in the direction of the Dueling Dragons, deep in the Water Wheel. "Last I saw Matilda, she was at the tavern. I hope the siege bells kept her inside."

A piercing shriek from beyond the wall snatched our attention. The vampyres on the other side of the wall had begun regrouping. I doubted it'd be long before they attacked again.

"Help me shift the rubble."

Summoning a smoky windstorm, I sucked debris and ruined homes from smoldering heaps. Rugard and Ervik joined me and shadows sprung to lift the remains of a butchery. I caught sight of a sign with an upheld butcher knife before it vanished into a cloud of dust and mist.

The river held and sighs bloomed from a dozen mouths.

I turned to slap Rugard's back but a low groan from the watery ruins halted us all.

As one, the people of the Water Wheel scrambled over the dead and lifted hands toward the charred ruins of their homes. Grunts of concentrations filled the square. One by one, chunks of stone and cracked timbers dropped onto the trembling dam.

The Quies roared back. Thin spigots in the dam's clefts became shooting streams. Another rumble and the river threatened to blast back into the city.

"More," Rugard roared, enormous chest heaving with the strain of magic. He let out a roar to rival the river and hurled a chunk of stone onto the dam.

Side by side, Simone and Sylinia worked on the water. They pushed against the river's flow, quaking hands outstretched, slowing the coursing streams to give the others time to heap debris onto the slowing dam.

Together, we heaved what remained of the Water Wheel into the gaping hole. Slowly but surely, the water began to thin. Streams became trickles. Trickles became droplets. Piled high and nearing the top of the looming wall, the makeshift dam shuddered. But it *held*. If it held for the night, then it would do.

Cheers boomed louder than the angry screeches on the other side of the wall. But the cries faded, probably headed for the hole in the Black Wall.

I slumped and reached down to rest my hands on my knees, breathing deep through the burn in my chest. Rolling my body upright, I called to Rugard, "I've got to go back. The Black Wall is overrun, and it won't be long before the vampyres seize the main road to the city. If I can use my light there too, maybe I'll give them an advantage."

He pursed his lips but didn't argue.

I nodded to Sylinia, and we took off down a side street.

We'd made it a block before Ervik's drawl forced us to halt.

"I might've been all right leaving the rest of this godsforsaken city to die like they've left us. But then I thought, how else we going to prove we got bigger balls than to save their sorry asses?"

He tucked a stiletto into his boot and jerked his thumb over his shoulder to the crowd of approaching witches. Rugard and Simone pushed into view and came to stand by Ervik who grinned with tiny, black-stained teeth.

"We win this thing for them, who knows? Maybe we get a modicum of respect in return. Maybe we get our district council seat back. And maybe"—his wild grin stretched—"maybe we get the Night Queen's attention."

"You sure you want that?"

He snickered and wiped black blood from his mouth. Sauntering past me for the Black Wall, he threw over his shoulder, "Her attention would be nice. Her head might be better. The Water Wheel's got a long memory, Sathos. Trust me when I say we keep score."

43

BLOOD IN THE WATER

Alys

B lood, receding waters, and ash made up what remained of the Black Wall market. Guards wearing more blood than armor pushed against the vampyres spilling into the streets. By the time we returned, the scourge had spread beyond the market. The vampyres ducked into houses, drawing terrorized screams of trapped witches. Unlike the Water Wheel, the more affluent witches hadn't thought to sacrifice their homes. Sitting alone in the dark, they waited to be saved.

We hurried down a collapsed side road, mildly cursing when we realized it forked into two directions. A heavy gust pounded down on us, but weaving in and out of the smoke was the unmistakable scent of cedar and cloves. Relief burst out of me in a garbled laugh.

Maddox was alive.

On one end of the forked road, a worn Night Guard unit stretched across the narrow cobblestones. They stood shoulder to shoulder against the on-slaught of vampyres bearing down on them from the other side. Sweat beaded each witch's face, sliding past bared teeth. Wavering arms cast thin-ning shadows. Blood crusted swords swiped and parried, each time a little slower. Maddox held their center with Nik at his side, roaring for the unit to press forward.

Behind them, the cobblestone road flickered with torches someone had haphazardly stabbed into the rubble. I knew in an instant why they'd barricaded this road—behind them lay a path to the city's main road—a key to seizing the rest of Morithia.

Maddox poured his focus into his razor-sharp shadow snaking around a vampyr's neck. He paused to wipe his bloody cheek. The shadows tightened and the headless torso toppled to the wet cobblestones. Another leapt forward to replace the fallen. The shadow slammed the newcomer to the ground. It flattened into a wall, pushing, pressing, squeezing. Then a squelch like a tomato bursting. Maddox didn't bother to check if he was dead—he was already onto the next one.

He was beauty and horror wrapped in destruction, and somehow, he was *mine*.

Maddox spared one glance up the side street and, like a magnet, found me. A quick scan over me confirmed I was fine. He followed it with an irritated glare, as if to say, *What took you so long?*

Under no one's command but their own, Ervik and Rugard plunged into the vampyres, shadows sailing to clash against stolen magic as they relieved the guards who sank to the cobblestones from sheer exhaustion.

I didn't bother drawing my dimachairi.

A breeze floated smoke through the narrow street. On my command, it swelled into a gale. Circling. Building. Then it lunged. Like a swarm, it gathered the vampyres into a shrieking mass. I could rip them apart. Or paint the cobblestones with their blood.

No—I wanted to watch them burn for what they'd done to my city.

To my people.

Flames sparked midair. Gold and red all-consuming tongues lapped at the blinded vampyres. Whirlwinds shot high above the ruined street, flaring to the rhythm of my rapid heartbeat as if I was the one breathing fire onto them. Another breath, and the winded flames vanished. The smoke drifted to the sky and revealed a cleared street of charred bones.

The itch had returned, more pressing this time. I couldn't breathe. Something weighed on my chest. Within me, the beast howled, desperate to rip my ribcage open and escape. I sank to my knees, ready to claw out my soul onto the cobblestones to make it stop. The itch became a burn, swarming my insides, spreading through my limbs.

"Pace yourself," a low voice hissed in my ear, intoxicating and familiar. Maddox slipped an arm around my waist, pulling me up against his chest when my legs wouldn't hold me. "Control it. Don't let your magic explode all at once, no matter how good it feels."

I shoved him away, blinking through the fog his scent wrapped around me. "I *can* control it. I haven't reached the bottom of my soul. I can push them from the city with my light."

"You can't burn them if they're hiding in the buildings. Let the Guard flush them into the streets where more Guard wait. I'll deploy a few more units here to protect the main road. The rest will fight in the streets and hold them from spreading."

"Let me do that. I'll reorganize them in the streets—"

"No." He gripped my shoulders. "Nik and I shut one hole in the Black Wall but he's about out of magic. I need *you* for the other. It's massive, Alys. I can't hold the vampyres off *and* shut the hole. I need *you* and your beautiful, powerful magic."

Blood, black and red, smeared his cheeks, obscuring his faint freckles and the good witch beneath. I saw him just the same—as I always had—I realized. That was why I'd never been afraid of him. Sure, he irritated me, and some days I fantasized tackling him to the sparring ring floor, but I'd seen straight through the mask to the tired witch doing his best to survive in a world where fate had turned on him the moment he was born—like me.

"Together?" I asked. Bloodied gloves found mine and squeezed.

"Together."

Leaving Nik and Sylinia in the Water Wheel's capable hands to hunt the streets, Maddox and I took off toward the wall. We sloshed through the streets, climbing across ruined, wet stalls to the remaining hole. Bottle-necked, the vampyres climbed like a mass of spiders through the opening, descending onto the city.

The nearby ruins weren't enough. I didn't have to fight against the river here, but the crumbling remains of the sodden market were not strong enough to block the yawning gap. The vampyr hordes were thicker here too.

Climbing onto the remains of a tavern, I gathered light and aimed it toward the opening.

But the vampyres were ready.

A wave of shadow shot from their outstretched hands, spreading like a parasol over the gap. They'd learned from the Water Wheel. Creepy, thieving bastards.

The light hissed and sputtered, transforming into golden-red fire. Gritting my teeth, I guided the flame into a four-legged beast, trying to recall the exact dragon Elenna once created.

But as I flung the flaming mangled dragon, Maddox sent a blade of shadow. Gold collided with black. A scream like metal on metal pierced the ruins, worse than any vampyr shriek. Above us, shadow and fire swallowed one another in a calamitous, slobbering mess.

With a pathetic wail, it swooped low.

I leapt for Maddox, throwing us to the cobblestones with a painful smack. We ducked, hands over our heads. Burning air singed the tiny hairs on my neck and the awful stench of Quies sodden wood bloomed around us.

A fucking *black* dragon roared silver flames over the ruined market.

This was nothing like the burning behemoths Elenna and Ansil conjured. The black dragon moved like water, gliding on paper-thin shadow wings against a smoky-filled sky. Wispy legs of smoke trailed a narrow body. But the silvery black fire hurling from its mouth was unmistakable—Night Flame.

"What did you do?" Maddox hissed, trying to coax the dragon with shadow toward the vampyres instead of the market. The beast careened in zigzags. First for the ground, then shooting for the sky. Incapable of command.

"*Me?*"

"It's part fire, part shadow. You're the—" He shot me a dark look.

"That wasn't me, nitwit. I summoned *fire* at the same time you summoned shadow. That thing is part *you*."

Confused by two masters, the dragon snaked through the ruined market, hacking out silver flames as if strangled. The strange fire devoured everything. Wood, metal, flesh. Only when it found earth or water did its peculiar flames fade.

The vampyres screamed, racing for cover. But it didn't take them long to realize the dragon was useless, uncontrolled. The nearby waters of the Quies rose and with a great ear-splitting shriek, the vampyres flung the river onto the dragon.

"No!" Something tugged inside my soul. I *felt* where the dragon had been. Felt the rush of cedar-scented magic leaving me. What the bleeding Mother had that thing been? Witches weren't supposed to share magic. Not like that. Only twins—

Horrified, I scrambled to stand, my eyes wide on Maddox. "How are we sharing magic? Are we—"

He pulled himself upright, furiously shaking his head. Without missing a beat, he flung another shadow toward a nearing vampyr, sending its head into the mud.

"Are you seriously asking me that?"

"Then *what* was that? Only twins combine magic."

"Obviously that's not true. Now, help me shut the godsdamned wall."

I eyed where the dragon had vanished in a cloud of vapor and inhaled, flaring my nostrils before spitting out, "All right, but we use a dragon again. This time don't release your shadows. We'll push the vampyres back, and I'll hold the dragon's leash."

"Why you?"

"Because I'm a fucking Day Witch, and I've seen them a thousand times!"

"Gods, fine. You hold it." He lowered his voice to mutter, "No need to yell at me."

After the vampyres, I was going to murder him.

This is what came of falling in love with a pig-headed git. I could murder him, and he'd come back to tell me I hadn't done it properly.

As if he heard my thoughts, Maddox shot me a wicked grin. My insides squirmed in reply.

No one needed to look that attractive covered in blood.

On the count of three, I flung a dragon's fiery form right into Maddox's shadow. This time there wasn't a metallic shriek. The flames melted into the shadow, writhing to form the details of the dragon. Sparks showered the market, peppering the vampyres. A head formed, long and sleek with a half dozen drooping whiskers of smoke. Golden eyes burned, sweeping the ruined landscape with a smoky huff. Wings of paper-thin smoke materialized. Three times larger than a horse, its massive body solidified, followed by legs and a tail of snaking shadow.

I could sense the dragon like a flickering flame inside me. A living cedar tether in my soul. I tugged it toward the hole, pulling on the cedar magic flowing through the tether.

It wasn't anything like the Death Rune. Whatever this odd new tethered magic between us was, I could feel Maddox's magic ebbing and flowing inside me, as if he could control what he gave.

He shuddered and snaked an arm around my waist, no longer caring who saw. If they knew we could intertwine magic, everything else was laid bare. He dragged me closer until his chest lined my spine, ragged breathing hot in my ear. Through his racing heart against my bones, I knew he felt my pull on his soul.

A hand slid up my chest to my throat's base, solid, warm, and searching. He poured more magic into the shadow, into *me*. A raging storm of cedar wind roared inside my soul.

This was exhilarating. Connected from soul to soul. It was like he was moving inside me all over again.

I fought to focus on the dragon.

Liquid fire licking at my core during a vampyr siege wasn't—ah—prudent.

The dragon soared over the Quies River, spraying silver fire onto the vampyres below. This time, I wouldn't let them cut the dragon from me. I'd keep the river within its banks.

A spark of an idea began forming.

"Hold the dragon," I whispered. "Keep it fixed on the vampyres at the wall. I'll raise the river and drown the rest."

"Do it."

I concentrated on moving the flickering flame inside me down the cedar tether. Maddox's eyes widened the moment he felt the flicker. The dragon remained in the air. Cedar flooded deeper inside me, and the flicker vanished.

This was nothing like the river to Corryn. This was a tethered knot, tying me to Maddox. Like another piece of myself was deep inside him, and I had connected to it and he to me.

Gods, this was eerily euphoric magic.

Most certainly not meant for siblings.

The dragon flapped enormous wings above us, rushing a gale and flattening us into a crouch. Trained on the dragon, Maddox guided it to the wall with a soft frown. Silver flames engulfed the base as the cries of blind and dying vampyres harpooned the air.

Entrusting our dragon into his hands, I shut my eyes and felt for the river and the natural magic within its waters. Horror swelled and I stumbled backward over a slab of broken wall. Inside me, the Quies's magic groaned, sickly and marred, searching for the sea's relief. Thick oily anger streamed through the waters. That ancient powerful rage readied to flood the world clean—unstoppable as the flames above.

I funneled its silent rage, diving into overbearing fury. The earth beneath the cobblestones trembled. Water sloshed from the banks. Bubbling from beneath, the river churned murky water over its confines. But it didn't slide toward the cobblestones. Instead, I guided it high into the air.

The remaining vampyres shuffled backward, blood-red eyes widening. With ear-splitting shrieks, they spun and raced from the liquid tower.

Inhaling deep, I hurled the Quies toward them. Whoever Maddox missed; I swallowed whole. Twisting midair, the river shot through the shattered wall. Air joined water and a howling whirlpool formed above the city, sucking in smoke, fire, and a thousand screams. The Quies swallowed gurgling cries on each side of the wall, offering no mercy. Water delved into lungs, ripping them from inside out. Bits of gore fell like black rain.

I pulled more, fueling the Quies's twisted rage with my own dark fury. Lilain had sent the vampyres. Used them. Wielded them to find me. She was afraid of this power. Of mine, Corryn and Maddox's magic. Of the chance we would tear her and her perverse magic apart.

The water roared, smashing stone and wall. Devouring everything in its greedy path. More. We needed more. Wipe away the city, the hills, the bay. Make it clean.

Alys.

If I could reach the outer hills, I could clear the northern end of the realm. Purify the realm—no—the world.

Alys.

I'd let Lilain know she was *nothing*. My magic, my will—I'd pour it onto her destruction. She'd drown in the fear she'd wrought on the streets of Kazadorah. I'd wipe the gods-awful desert off the island, every grain of sand.

"*Alys!* Let it go. Come back to me." A voice snapped the water's hold, breaking on my name.

Gasping, I released the river. The raging waters stormed back into the muddy banks with a heaving splash. River water misted the ruined market, dampening anyone in the open air. I gulped in heavy breaths, sucking air like I'd been dragged hours underwater.

"Gods, I'm sorry." Maddox guided me into the shadow of a ruined wagon, keeping me upright against his firm warmth. He dropped a dozen kisses onto the top of my head, whispering into my hair, "I should've warned you. Night magic and its power is new to you. Water—it's not like shadow. It takes as much as it gives, and it's full of ancient emotion. That's why you've never seen any of us wielding it on a grand scale. Shadows are less sentient."

"The river is *angry*," I croaked, burying my face into the wet crook of his neck. "I could sense its rage, its horror at what we've done to the natural world. I almost destroyed everything."

"But you didn't."

"Because of you."

He pulled back with a familiar scowl I adored and cupped my cheeks. "Listen to me. Either we save this world, or we burn it down, but we'll do it together. Whatever comes at you, I swear to you, *mea*, I won't let you battle it alone." His intensity softened. He wiped my damp cheeks and tucked wet strands of hair behind my ears. "Now, let the rest of the Guard take on the few remaining vampyres while we find dry clothes and a fireplace."

I looked around and realized at some point in the water's hypnotic sway, he'd let the dragon go and the tether had vanished. Rubbing my chest, I peered up at him. Feeling unusually shy, I offered a hesitant smile. Sex was one level of intimacy. Sharing magic to form something new? That was something else entirely and it left me feeling bare in the most primal way.

What the bleeding Mother did it mean?

I shoved it from my head and focused on our surroundings. The vampyr's storming of the wall was over. The few remaining in the city would soon meet the Guard's blade. Or Ervik's. Better they find the merciful Guard than a witch of the Water Wheel.

Alys, oh gods. Alys!

I froze.

Corryn? Where are you? What's happening?

44

UNFURLED AND
UNFETTERED

Corryn

T he dragon howled at the obscured moon, reminiscent of the wolves who'd created it, uncaged and loosed upon the world.

Shivering, I drew my cloak, wishing I'd worn more than the thin robe beneath. On the palace walls overlooking the city, the winter winds tore skin to bone. But I couldn't look away from Morithia as it burned to the cobblestones. The Water Wheel was a flooded, charred mess. The Black Wall nothing more than dust and rubble. Even the Jansk's white marble temples on the city's opposite side were barely visible beneath a layer of soot.

Alys's lifeforce hummed on the river between us, thank the Mother, but my relief came in waves of lung-crushing anxiety. She'd exposed her magic, undoubtedly becoming Morgenna's next target. We had hours before she turned on my sister and then onto Maddox and me. Onto Melis.

The dragon soared into the sky, spinning on a hairpin curve to spew a line of Night Flame. I squinted and tried to find something about it to disprove my theory. A beacon of ancient, joined magic returned to modern witches. Alys couldn't know the merged dragon confirmed my speculation about her and Maddox's entwined fate. The Mother wasn't the only god toying with them. The Maiden was supposed to be little more than myth to the modern witch.

Until now.

Finding the Mother's final two of her six was paramount to completing our fate, but as I watched the dragon's shimmering black scales glow with silver firelight, I finally believed Alys.

I knew where the final two were—in the Soul Lands.

Dualitas Maleficarum spoke of old magic the ancient witches in Gilgador possessed long before the exile. Creation magic was a pale mimicry of the Mother's original Creation. Massive, powerful creatures of gold or blue flames Created by powerful witches to prove their worth to the gods. Dragons, phoenixes, gryphons. None of them quite as sentient as natural Creatures.

According to the book, the ability to Create went to a select blessed few. Even amongst the ancients, Creation magic was barely more than legend.

So where had Alys learned to Create a fire-breathing dragon?

A scream pierced the wind before cutting off—dead—like the last of the Mother's six.

Elenna and Ansil Makim had once held power beyond any Day Witch in centuries. Magic that should've belonged to Mother-blessed fated witches. Watching Alys wield magic she'd learned from the Makims vanished any disbelief who they should've been. They'd borne magic unseen in millennia. Magic Lilain must've recognized. If she knew the portents fated her doom, suspecting the Makim twins would've been a fairly easy assumption once she saw their incredible power.

But how had she recognized Alys?

Faint sweetened cedar rose on a gust and barreled into me. I snatched at my cloak as another dragon materialized below. Even from a distance I made out its burning golden eyes. This new dragon soared over the city wall. Silver flames shot from its long snout, aiming for the hills and beyond.

Night Flame was beautiful. It spread in an arc of moonlit flame, hissing glimmering smoke into the air. No longer confined to a meaningless icon above a temple, the Night Flame spread untamed, serving its true purpose.

"*This* is what you were made for," I whispered into the wind. "A symbol of strength and protection. Not vanity."

The fire devoured the countryside beyond the wall, taking vampyres with it—serving its destructive purpose. How could I fulfill *my* purpose if I was fated to fail? The Mother-fated six against the island's queens. Before I'd even heard fate's call, two were dead.

A muffled whimper intruded on my gloomy thoughts.

The sound came from behind, from the palace. Shoving aside my misgivings, I crept down the stairs to the palace's main wing. Another, louder, cry split the air. This time a sob followed. A woman's plea begged for mercy.

It was coming from the throne room.

The gold-hammered doors were cracked open, a sliver revealing the candlelight inside. I prayed to Fortuna for silent movements and stuck my head inside. Then yanked it back out, clutching at my heart threatening to give.

Alys, oh gods. Alys!

45

FIRST COMES SHADOW

Alys

M atilda held a knife to her throat. She wasn't alone. Half a dozen women trembled in a line before Morgenna's throne. Courageous witches of the Water Wheel who'd seized justice when no one else offered. Each holding knives to their necks. Jorlenne stood beside Matilda, back straight, shoulders proud. Unfailingly defiant despite their quivering knives.

Too late, I saw we weren't ready to face the Night Queen smiling from her perch on the throne. Maddox and Corryn were right. We needed more time. We needed Melis. But in chaos of the vampy attack, Maddox had never given her the Eleutheria rune.

Our odds didn't matter. I wouldn't leave the women to Morgenna's cruelty. If I offered myself instead, if I could placate her, perhaps I could take their punishment.

"Come, come," Morgenna called, waving us in from the doors. "I must admit I'm rather put out. I'd hope to surprise the delegation ball with an example of what happens when my law breaks. The grisly murder of a witch in a public tavern is a most grievous example. Alas . . ."

Beside me, Corryn crept forward. Her lacy dress gathered in one hand, she kicked aside ruined flowers and glass with dancing slippers. On my other side, Maddox dripped water and blood. Footprints of wet ash marked his path.

We were all that stood between Morgenna and more needless death.

Maybe without compulsion we had a chance.

Maybe I could somehow make sure Maddox and Corryn left the throne room alive to find Melis.

The Night Queen smiled brighter. White, even teeth sparkled in the dim candlelight. A mass of black shadows swirled behind her throne—a show of indolent power. She rose with an unfurling of black-and-crimson silk, like a black widow extending its legs.

"Did you think the women of the Water Wheel would go unpunished, Captain Sathos? Perhaps you thought you'd taken their punishment for them with dear Yori."

How dare she speak his name.

She stepped off the dais. Lazy shadows drifted from behind her and gathered at her feet. She studied the three of us with a delicate tilt of her head, her elaborate coiffure as unmoving as the monster beneath it. "The Mother chose her fated well. I will concede that."

Iron skewered my stomach with an arrow of dread.

She let out a soft laugh, wagging a finger as to scold us. "Vampyres and goblin ambushes. Stolen portents. The stars all but screaming impending change. Did you three expect I wouldn't know of the coming fate? And you, Alys Sathos . . . when you first stepped into this room, I knew exactly who you were and what you came for. How could I not? It was as if your mother, Zelah, was alive, walking these halls once more. The same defiant smirk and reckless arrogance hiding an insecure witch."

My mother had been *here*? I stopped breathing. Corryn clutched my elbow, pressing against me, erratic breaths heavy in my ear.

Morgenna's smile deepened. "The Day Witch Zelah Zarrata was a double spy who amused Lilain and I, refusing to pick a side. We had great fun with her and her cunning schemes to trip us both up. But then she went and fell in love with a Night guard. Another clever woman lost to the fellowship of lovesick fools." She made a face and flicked a speck of lint off her robes before continuing.

"Soon after, she and Olyvr Felumbra vanished from both realms. Lost to the hidden unknowns of the western coast, I suppose. Oh, the delicious scandal that rocked my court. It was almost worth the annoyance of Zelah finally picking a side—her own. But then a portent revealed the twin children she was destined to conceive and the power those babes would wield. Well, I couldn't have that."

Bottomless black pools flicked to Maddox then me. A slow leer twisted porcelain-doll features. "Prince Mendrick, my faithful hunter, searched for them and found Olyvr first. Inconveniently, he and Zelah had separated, and the children gone. But Mendrick had his orders, and Olyvr died alone face down in his blood."

Corryn's grip became painful, but I scarcely felt it through the pounding in my blood.

Morgenna stretched an arm to Maddox who had frozen in place. "What a trial it must have been for Mendrick to hunt Dual children for decades and then come home to his own sweet children. All the while knowing when he died his boy would be forced to pick up his mantle of service to the queen. It's what my crowned heirs are meant for, you must realize. They are my hunters, my beasts in the night."

Everything went oddly blank, like a rough canvas gone smooth.

Corryn slowly turned.

She fixed wide eyes on Maddox and whispered, "*You* killed Seren?"

Blood drained from Maddox's high cheeks, and he took a step back. He shook his head slowly, holding trembling outstretched hands as if to keep us from advancing. "I—I didn't—I couldn't stop . . ."

The river between Corryn and I churned. Greasy rage lapped the edges, threatening to flood us both with her shock and fury. Her shadow twisted into a jagged inkblot. It skittered up her lace robe to swallow her trembling hands.

"*No!*"

I leapt between her and Maddox, stretching to take his hands. He yanked from my reach, stumbling over an ice sculpture cracked in half. A chord of recognition snapped inside, and the crush of weighty realization toppled onto me.

The penitence runes.

"Oh, Maddox." If I could touch him, if I could show him understanding through my fingertips . . . "It wasn't you. Your hand, but not your will." I lowered my voice, praying to the useless gods I could plunge into him and prove what was inside didn't match the outside. "Don't let her win, remember?"

Corryn inhaled sharply. "He *murdered* people like us, Alys. It was *him*. Innocent children. Entire families. Dead because of him and his father—who murdered *our father*."

Her words bounced off. She couldn't comprehend the terror of watching one's hand dangle off a lethal marionette string.

"He certainly did. Your mother too," Morgenna called with a heavy sigh. A tiny smirk destroyed any pretense of remorse. "Eventually, Mendrick found Zelah deep in the desert with a single babe in her arms. Both were destroyed, and I breathed a sigh of relief. Mendrick had lost one child, yes, but I convinced myself without the other, the portents no longer meant anything." Morgenna rubbed her forehead with a scowl.

Again, I tried to reach for Maddox, but he took another step back, not meeting my eyes.

"I should've expected Zelah's trickery," Morgenna wearily told Jorlenne, patting her cheek. "Clever women with moral ambiguity are cunning things. When you stepped into this throne room all those months ago, I realized the infant she'd carried was a decoy. She shrewdly hid you beneath Lilain's nose in Kazadorah and by the time Lilain recognized Zelah in you and predicted your fate, it was too late. Too many questions would rise from the execution of her most infamous airwitch. She'd risk making you a martyr. Worse, a rebellion. Instead, she devised a convoluted scheme of goblins, vampyres, and traitors."

Morgenna tucked a blonde wisp behind Jorlenne's ear and smiled kindly at the shivering girl. "My sister always liked her twisted schemes."

No one dared move.

Sister.

Morgenna continued seamlessly. She walked forward, studying each knife-wielding woman, occasionally adjusting their knives closer to their throats. "Did you think you were first, Alys? Corryn? That the Mother chose you twin sisters to redeem witchkind first?"

She turned to us, head tilted to the side.

"Lilain and I were chosen to bring witchkind back to Gilgador, to end this long exile. But . . ." A hunger crept over her doll-like features. "Lilain and I discovered something better, and it didn't involve risk without compensation. We found power to finish what the ancients couldn't—end our exile *without* the gods—the fools who had exiled us to this forsaken rock and abandoned us *all* to die. Do you really think the gods are on your side? That they'll allow you back on Gilgador if you unite Night and Day?

"Think, girl. We could rip apart their barring magic and once and for all take Gilgador by force. A punishment for our exile. With new power and vampyres seeking a cure to their own curse, we stand a chance. Or we did, until the ridiculous portents appeared in the stars. First Maddox and Melisandre, then you, Alys. You fell into my lap. At first thought, a hindrance to our plans, but then I realized—a power, waiting to be awakened and wielded. Perfect soldiers for our march on Gilgador. We could have had two more if Lilain hadn't panicked and sicced the goblins on them."

She was close enough to make out the intricate braids spun like a spider's web in her hair. I had to know, before she struck. "Why didn't you kill me? Or Maddox or Melis?"

Her voice dropped, its low timbre sinking into my skin, deep and monstrous. "Haven't you been listening? Unlike Lilain, I saw you for what you were. A powerful tool to manipulate. Under compulsion, I'd use your immeasurable power to bring down Gilgador."

Strawberries rode on her breath, as mocking as the smile she gave me. "But mostly, I kept you alive because you're amusing, as your mother was. A silly little bird puffed up on its self-importance. You have no power against me. Lilain sees peril, but I see no threat." Her dark gaze swiveled to Maddox. "None of you are. I claimed two of you for twenty-eight years, used you and found only *power*. Not death. You are nothing but pretty caged birds who will sing for me. How could you think you stood a chance against *me*?"

Spinning, the Night Queen strode to her dais. She flicked her wrist at the shadows swirling behind the throne. With a hiss, their cage parted and revealed the witch lying in wait.

Melis slunk down the dais stairs, utterly sober and unsmiling. She drew her sword, jaw tight. The bitterness festering within the blonde princess bloomed alive. It rose on the jagged shadows encircling her arms, as treacherous as the rot inside her. Maybe she was compelled. Or maybe—like the queens—Melis had chosen a different path than the one fate had set.

"Don't." Corryn's whisper broke the weighted silence.

Something shifted in Melis's gaze. But before I could pinpoint what it was, she curled her lip and crouched to brace her feet into an offensive stance. Maddox's ringing steel sword echoed hers.

Heart thundering, I lurched to shove Corryn behind me.

Morgenna was quicker. She pointed to Matilda with glowing eyes, and hissed, "*Slit your throat and die.*"

The world took in a long breath. Everything slowed to a snail's pace. As if running through sand, I ran. I tried to open my mouth to scream.

With a jerk of Matilda's wrist, it was over.

I was dimly aware of Melis leaping for me. Of Maddox's sword blocking a blow for my neck. Magic flooded my nose. Shadows lunged and wrestled.

Everything faded in the thin spray of blood.

Matilda fell slowly. First to her knees. Then to the floor. She never dropped her defiant glare. Choking, she pointed her dripping iron knife at the Night Queen. Unadulterated hatred poured out with her blood. A gurgle swallowed whatever words she aimed at Morgenna. The same knife used against her daughter, against Osrin, clattered to the floor.

I sank to the puddle and cradled her head in my lap. Not again. I begged the Mother, the Crone, *Please, not again.* Matilda grimaced in a gruesome stretch of bloody lips. Fury blazed hotter and hotter. And then it vanished into nothingness.

Resuming her seat on the dragon throne, Morgenna's voice soared over the sound of the twins' clanging swords. "The blame is on you, Alys. You convinced a caged bird it can fly. How wrong you were."

The itch of unused magic floundered in me like a bee with wings soaked in blood. It struggled to find the will to spring out of the well it was drowning in. But it hadn't drowned yet. No, it wasn't a bee. It wasn't even a bird. It was something so much more and Morgenna couldn't touch it.

"I wasn't wrong." I rose and met her gaze unblinkingly. Matilda's blood trickled from my fingertips, dripping onto the floor. "A caged bird can see beyond the bars. It can hope and it can dream. Haven't you ever read a fable? Hope is powerful, not only because it can spread, but because it can inspire even the most insignificant person."

"*You will cease your speaking and be still.*"

The ice didn't come. I smiled and summoned the itch, ready to *finally* give it relief. "We were never caged birds, Morgenna. We were snakes. A snake only has to realize it can slither through bars."

Eyes widening, she leapt from the throne. The thundering howl beneath my skin soared to meet her. Night Flame howled through my body. With a gasp, I released decades of pent-up magic into the world. Black-and-silver flames flared for the queen, intent on ridding the world of her malice.

Morgenna launched a wall of matching black fire. My flames snapped and clawed, but her ancient fire knew bounds I did not. In a great swoop, they swallowed my Night Flames, leaving behind nothing but smoke. Gods, I hadn't even realized Night Flame extinguished Night Flame. She prowled down the stairs, fixed on me. Her smug smile had twisted into a snarl. The simpering doll queen had finally gone.

"Do you wish to play this game, Alys Sathos?"

Behind me the shriek of steel on steel bounced off the onyx floors. Even if Maddox placed the Death Rune on Melis, it wasn't a guarantee she would stop once freed. No, it would be Corryn and me against the Night Queen. *Two* of the Mother's six against Morgenna.

Corryn's voice coursed on the river. *Alys, the women. They're compelled to be still. What if they're hit with stray magic?*

Get them out with the Eleutheria rune, I mentally threw to Corryn. *I'll hold off Morgenna as long as I can.*

I withdrew my dimachairi and tossed them aside with a clatter. "I don't mind games. After all, what's fate but a long, twisted game?"

With a baiting grin, I launched at the Night Queen.

Shadows enveloped her, and she vanished, leaving me grasping air. She'd broken through the wards—ones of her own making—a guaranteed way of escape should she ever desire. She reappeared by the windows. The burning city cast a reddish glow over her ivory skin, pink and glittering like river nymph scales.

I fumbled deep in my soul's recess for a whip of black fire. The itch exploded and the whip nearly snapped out of my hold. At least it was actually a whip. Maybe I should've spent longer hours testing my magic at the ruined temple. Not that it mattered. I wasn't foolish to believe I'd last long. Just enough to get Corryn and the women out.

The whip snapped again, but Morgenna caught the tip with a flash of smothering light, yanking me closer. She *was* a Dual Witch—no—an original witch. An ancient with untold magic of light and shadows. Caught, I let go of the whip and stumbled onto all fours. Shards of broken glass sliced my palms, drawing a hiss through clenched teeth.

Somewhere behind me, Corryn scrambled for the first woman, her voice soft and assuring as she explained her plan.

A boom came from my right, and I spun in time to catch part of the wall of windows exploding with Melis's shadows. Maddox summoned a darkened corner, trying to catch her from behind. She knew his mind too well and predicted his movements, dodged before throwing herself at him. In a blur of swirling shadows, they swept across the throne room. Blood against blood.

The Night Queen studied them and let out a soft snicker. "I'm curious, Alys. What is your plan?"

She circled me, ebbing in and out of the darkening shadows. Flashes of crimson robes flickered in Morithia's burning glow. Smoke trickled through the shattered dome behind her.

I rose, breathing hard and unspooled the itch inside. "I don't have a plan. I have faith I'm where I should be. Fated for this moment, to free the island from you and your miserable sister."

"Pity. Faith is food of the weak. The conquerors feast on power."

She struck from the shadows, a whirlwind of too-sweet roses and malevolence. The gusts snatched me off my feet, flinging me into the air before hurling my limp body to the floor.

Pain splintered up my spine with a horrifying crack.

Swallowing a whimper, I rolled onto my feet and lunged only to find a wall of shadow waiting. The wall collapsed, sucking me into a black void. But the void opened and dumped me onto Matilda's body. Crying out, I clambered off the corpse.

She'd sucked me into the shadow plane. Umbranated me *without* her. What else could she do? We didn't stand a fucking chance against her magic.

Morgenna chuckled at my panting horror as I backed away from Matilda's body. Her stagnant black eyes sparked, and Matilda's body rose on a web of shadow. The Water Wheel women let out muffled groans through frozen lips. Matilda's head rolled back, exposing the slash of red across her weathered skin.

With a flick of her wrist, Morgenna flung the body through the serrated open window, sending Matilda to the burning Water Wheel below.

"Let them see what you brought down on them," she said, peering to watch the body land far down below. "How long do you think before they turn on you, Day Witch?"

"I'm no more a Day Witch than you are a Night Witch."

A freed woman stumbled past, fleeing the throne room on numb legs. Morgenna's hungry gaze followed.

I hurled a wall of Night Flame, creating a barrier between the flying spear of shadow and the woman. The wall wobbled, silver flames snapping, stretching to reach the waiting fuel of dead flowers below. I sucked them back, fearful of reducing the palace and its inhabitants to ash.

Lip curling, Morgenna demanded, "Where did you learn Eleutheria? I made sure every book with it was burned long ago."

"You should've realized Maddox wasn't Mendrick. He was never going to take your compulsion lying down. Of course, he searched for a way out—and he found it." I threw a fist of shadow at her flaring nostrils. She flew back into an overturned table, careening through glass and wax. But her slight frame was deceptively quick.

A second later, another spear soared for me, barely halted by my air typhoon. The shadowy tip squirmed, intent on my heart. My upraised arms shook with the strain, scraping the sides of my soul. Slowly, it drew closer. Cracks spiderwebbed my wall of air.

Morgenna merely lifted a brow.

A muffled bellow boomed from beyond the broken window, low and thunderous. A death knell. As one, the people of the Water Wheel roared. Their cries fell away in the pounding rhythm of angry steps.

Dropping her spear, Morgenna tossed her head back and cackled. "Not long at all before they turned on you."

The muffled cries grew louder. A sound of furious grief. Rugard. Simone. Ervik. All they fought for. All they'd given. Only to lose their matriarch, their leader and guiding star—dead. I'd brought death upon them. With the vampyres, with Morgenna. I hadn't given them justice. I'd given them grief. I *deserved* their retribution.

Pounding booms met flashes of shadows as the Water Wheel mourned Matilda. Mourned the last bit of hope.

"Listen to them," Morgenna cooed, angling her ear. "Listen to the Night Realm come for the witch who took their lives and destroyed their homes. You ruined everything, and now, it is they who must pay."

46

THEN COMES THE LIGHT

Corryn

B lood slid down my arms, matting my dangling sleeves. Throbbing fingers clutched a broken glass shard. It was *working*. I'd carved Eleutheria into a woman. Her magic, soft and sparse, buckled under me. High on the power I could give, I'd released her from compulsion and burst into triumphant tears. *I could do this.* I could save them.

An arrow of light screamed past, hitting the hammered-gold doors like a gong. Morgenna shrieked in frustration, barely missing Alys who sprinted to the open window. Her face had gone too pale, and she was panting hard, clutching her chest. She was letting too much magic out at once, and it was waning.

I needed to hurry.

Alys was clever and shrewd, but she couldn't win. Morgenna merely toyed with her in a sick game. How long before the Night Queen lost interest and flung the full force of her power?

A young woman was next, wide blue eyes fixed on Morgenna. I ripped her sleeve, but the girl hissed, eyes flicking to the woman on her side, her demand clear. Not her, not yet. Save the other woman first.

The other woman sobbed. Her quivering hand was drawing a thick stream of blood at her throat. Careful as I could with a shaky hand, I sliced into her tawny skin. First the circle, then arrows.

Like a kick to my heart, magic howled through my soul in a forest of pine needles and sap. It tasted incredible, as if lapping from nature's core, smooth and feminine. I could take a little more to hold off the darkness—*No.* I wouldn't *be* the darkness. Squeezing the glass shard, I focused on the sharp pain. This was nothing to what Morgenna would do if I didn't get the woman out. I hurled my magic into the forest's core. *Take it,* I wanted to scream. *Take Eleutheria and run.* The ice inside her shattered and she shot for the doors.

I broke the skin of another woman. This one wasn't nearly as powerful at the last. In my growing confidence, I worked my fingers quickly. I could do this. I didn't want their magic; I wanted their freedom. Again and again, I passed on Eleutheria, and again the women ran.

Only two more were left. I could save them. I hurried for an elderly woman, a white-haired wizened witch with clouded eyes. Her feeble magic didn't put up a fight, but I pushed into her, giving her new life in Eleutheria. "Go on," I whispered. "The queen's distracted. You can make it to the door."

She hobbled off, one limping step at a time. A blur of black hurtled for the hunched witch. Without thinking, I gathered air magic and flew between the blur and the woman. The blur slammed into me and smacked the floor. A heavy weight slammed after me. Lightning pain shot through the crook of my elbow.

Shifting above me, Melis's eyes flew open; widening, they flew to my arm, and her lips parted in a horrified *O*. My trusty shard had burrowed deep to the bone. Dark blood poured from a severed vein. A strong inclination to gag heaved my belly, but I held it back with a swallow. Whimpering at the fire in my arm, I yanked the glass out and bucked Melis off me.

Murmuring worthless apologies, I dragged the old woman toward the doors, never taking my eyes from Morgenna and Alys, still caught in a battle of Night Flame. We'd nearly made it to the door when another blur tackled me to the glass-strewn floor. It sliced into my gown and robes, stinging my legs.

"I can't—Get out, Corryn." Melis wavered between the terrified tears streaming down my cheeks to my dripping arm. *"Please.* Forget them and *get out."*

Maddox crashed into her, sending them flying toward the door. The old woman had vanished. Safe. I used a precious half-second to find Melis. She's rolled from Maddox, jaw gritted, lifting a sword to run him through. She lunged, but not before yelling a warning. With a nearly identical expression of stubborn will, he spun and threw a wisp of shadow, trying to pin her.

Hope burgeoned in the place she'd broken it with her supposed betrayal. She was still in there.

Beneath the layers of poison, the sweet dreamer of giggles and smiles had survived Morgenna. She wasn't fighting Maddox on her own will. He would free her. He had to.

Only Jorlenne, the young woman Alys admired for her resilience, remained. I snatched another shard of glass and etched into her arm—first the circle, then the arrows.

Before I finished, a body hurled into Jorlenne.

The poor girl crashed into me with a muffled shriek. We slid through glass and spilled candlewax—right for the broken window. Terror and smoke crammed my lungs. My bleeding hands flailed against slick floors until I jerked to a halt.

Out of the corner, a body toppled out of the window and plunged to the city below.

Alys.

Screaming, I crawled to the gaping window, heart ready to vomit from my mouth. I couldn't lose her—I'd just found her.

Alys floated like a specter into my line of sight—flying.

Blood spilled from a dozen gashes on her face and neck. Flecks of glass still clung to her leather armor. But she was *alive,* and she was bloody *flying.*

She flew like the ancients—without a broom—thousands of feet above the city. Leaning forward, she shot like an arrow for Morgenna. The queen crowed in delight and leapt to meet her midair. The two soared high into the glass dome above us. Shadows and fire danced in a tumultuous reflection in the remaining windows.

With a gasp, I remembered the young girl.

The girl teetered on the broken threshold; a statue caught in compulsion. Yanking my hand from a puddle of half-hardened candle wax. I crawled toward the window's edge. Glass stung my tender palms and knees, but I hurried for Jorlenne. Her upper half jutted over the burning city, motionless. Panicked tears slid from her cheeks to the fire far below.

I rolled her to safety, whispering soft words of nonsense. The jagged windowpane had broken the thin skin at her neck. More glass clawed my bare arms through my ripped sleeves as I pulled her free. If I survived this night, I'd burn this Mother-cursed robe.

Completing the Eleutheria rune, I plunged into the girl's magic and obliterated Morgenna's compulsion. The moment she was freed, I hauled her up, and we wobbled for the doors.

An enraged shriek high above the throne room preceded the black arrow aimed for Jorlenne. The shadow nicked her shoulder, and the girl stumbled with a hoarse scream. Blood spurted onto the pale freckled skin of her neck. Freckled skin like Seren's. She would die like Seren, forgotten as another unfortunate death in the struggle for power.

Echoing Morgenna's shriek, I hurled a surge of air toward the girl, shoving her through the doors. I wouldn't lose another witch to Morgenna.

I dug into that itching fire I never touched, never dared as a pretend Night Witch. Every bit of helpless frustration I'd ever felt poured into the heat. Every lonely day, every worried hour trying to pass as a Night Witch.

Never again.

Fire burst free with golden claws, trapping Morgenna against the domed windows. Their roar rattled the glass, demanding she stand down. But she flicked her wrist, and the Eastern Sea's waves howled for the dome's shattered windows. The foamy water enveloped my flames, raining salty steam onto the ruined delegation ball.

A snicker bounced off the shards of broken glass reflecting the queen floating to the floor in the mist's rainbow fractures. Unharmed. Unmovable.

Alys dove, but Morgenna flung out her arm and she soared into the remaining glass, splintering the dome with a chilling crack. She hurtled for the floor, limp.

Maddox cried out and darted to catch her. Melis lunged just as he wrapped arms around Alys and slammed all three to the floor. She clawed a grip around his ankle with a snarl of frustration. Shoving Alys from him, Maddox aimed a kick for Melis's head, but she twisted out of reach and yanked a knife from her boot. They'd both lost swords at some point.

"Stop trying to save her. She's *Alys fucking Sathos*," she roared as she raised the knife. Maddox slammed the heel of his palm into her elbow and the knife clattered to the floor. "Focus on staying alive or your beastly little witch will hunt me down. Then we'll both be dead."

With a grunt, Maddox managed a hand around her neck and threw her off. She crashed into a partially collapsed table and disappeared behind a thicket of summoned shadows.

Racing to Alys's side, I hefted her up. She blinked groggily but let me guide us to the cover of a pillar.

"More than once," Morgenna called, "I've wondered how the regal Rilessa Stellanati birthed such an odd witch. It made no sense, even as a mere by-blow of a passionate night as she claimed. It wasn't until the forged portent was discovered and your name brandished when I recalled the lost babe Mendrick never found. Maddox had no inkling of what you were up to, as much as I . . . demanded an answer, but I knew then the lost babe had returned for her sister and her fate. I realized then, why Olyvr concealed you among the academics. A little mouse hidden amongst the shrews. An insipid, little wall flower no one paid any mind—exactly as your father intended."

She meant her words to sting, but I heard past their cruelty to the meat within. Morgenna didn't know what Rilessa and I had done, who we'd stolen and saved from under her nose.

Laughter bubbled out, loud and high-pitched. From it, the pain of losing Seren, the doubt of binding young witches, and the ever-present fear of being caught burst free. The world blurred. The sounds of Melis and Maddox fighting softened as they slowed to listen.

"Beware the wallflowers," I chided Morgenna. "Some are worth only a smile. Some nothing more than the greenery boosting another's beauty. But you forget an important lesson the Mother's nature teaches us—not all Creatures bear colorful marks to warn of their danger. Some of us hide in plain sight."

A nudge from the roaring river broke my mania.

Here. Alys rolled the river's currents toward me. On them rode a well of spiced-honey magic. *Pool it with yours and strike her down.*

Night Flame flickered at my fingertips, curiously reaching for me. They didn't burn. I glanced down at the fawning flames gliding up my arm like shadows. *Use us,* they seemed to purr. *Show us* both *our true purpose.*

Teeth clenched, I flung the Night Flame into the air. From the river within, I pulled at the honeyed currents and released a ray of blue flames, gilded in white light. Our magic coiled around one another, a vortex of ravenous heat.

Morgenna soared for the ceiling, but the whirlwind monstrosity roared and followed. Licking tongues lashed at the queen's shield. Her wall of black began to flicker. One by one, cracks formed, and hope spread with each ragged line.

"*I* stole the Dual Witches from under you," I spat at Morgenna. A single fiery tongue skewered past her wall. Then another. "All these years, *I* kept them safe. *I* bound and hid them. *I,* the insipid wallflower, defied you right under your nose for years."

Another whip of fire broke her wall, setting her robe's hem alight. I pushed harder and something scraped inside me.

"Odd and quiet does not mean weak. It means the chance to observe, to see others for who they truly are. Perhaps that chance is now lost to me. Perhaps I can no longer hide in the shadows. But then, neither can you. The whole world will soon know exactly what you are and what you've done."

For the first time, Morgenna looked uncertain, and it was all I needed.

47

LAST COMES HOPE

Alys

The itch inside me exploded into a curling eel of Night Flame—hotter and brighter than any star. This feral beast had always lived inside me. Every blood boil spellcast I'd endured. Every icy word of compulsion. All the nights I'd spent wondering if the Mother chose wrong. Wondering if a Kazadoran street rat deserved untold power.

Never again.

Hurling every doubt into the ribbon of Night Flame, I splintered the fire into a volley of arrows raining on the Night Queen. Eyes wide, she threw out a hand. Shifting shadows darkened above her, swallowing the black-and-silver arrows. She'd created an umbranation point outside her body. Without going into the shadow plane herself, she'd opened a hole and sent the arrows through.

She didn't catch every arrow. One sank into her arm. Her scream rent the air and blood squirted onto her crimson robes. With her head tossed back in agony, the golden dragon crown slipped off her head and vanished into a spilled table of roses. The remains of the glass dome cracked under her howling winds. Lines crawled like drunken inchworms across the glass.

Shit.

I released my arrows and dove for Corryn. Together, we tossed a shield of shadows over us just as the dome shattered. Sand poured from Morgenna as she destroyed her way through the raining glass. Her intricate braids had begun unraveling, her ruby crown gone. Burn marks and blood scoured the length of her robes.

We were gaining on her.

It had come too late. We'd found the bottom of the river. Every piece of magic I drew from my soul no longer itched. It *burned*, as if I dragged my soul across a coarse rug. We were close to the bottom, close enough to start draining the life magic keeping us alive.

An orb of black flames struck a fallen table beside us, devouring the littered remains of a vase of roses. Each rose went up in silver flames, taking with it Morgenna's signature cloying scent.

I copied her and flung my own orb, narrowly missing her. Instead, it flew out the window. I immediately evaporated it. The city didn't need more deadly flames.

The chants of the Water Wheel had grown louder. More voices added their howls to the brewing fury. More than the Water Wheel pounded their feet. The other districts had added their cries.

Morgenna flung a razor black scythe, any pretense of toying with us gone. Corryn's taunt had made sure of that. I dropped and rolled across still-warm candle wax. The scythe flew overhead, whistling inches over the top of my head—

Mother fucking . . . Too close.

Corryn threw up a solid wall of black over our hunched position, barely blocking more Night Flame blades Morgenna sent our way.

"We can't do this alone much longer," I whispered, searching the near barren river between us. "Unless you can think of some rune or spellcast that deepens our souls, we need the rest of the six. Otherwise, we won't live to see the morning."

Corryn whimpered, lifting trembling hands high. She tugged harder at my soul, but I had little to give. "Maddox will free Melis. She'll help us, I know it. Then we stand a better chance."

But Maddox couldn't pin Melis down. Wrapped in a funnel of shadow, the shrieking steel and thuds at least proved they both lived—a poor relief, but relief, nonetheless. As long as compulsion held Melis, we couldn't rely on either of them. No matter what Corryn's unfailing hope insisted.

"It's gone horribly wrong," she panted, straining against the shadow axe hacking through our shield. "We've failed, haven't we?"

"Don't think like that. You saved those women; you gave them a way out *and* their freedom. That alone is worth everything." I offered a weak grin. "But we're not dead yet, and I have an idea."

With a deep breath, I rolled beyond the wall and shot into the air, gathering wind to hold me aloft. Corryn watched below, her dark brows dipping.

Grinning, I fumbled with the shadows and formed a set of stairs. *Let's force her to the open sky above,* I said into her mind. *Force her to reveal to the Night Realm who she truly is. If she wants us dead, she has to come get us.*

Corryn rocked on her heels, arms straining. She bit her lip and squared her thin shoulders. The shield vanished as she raced for the stairs. She'd nearly reached them when Morgenna released a volley of arrows. The sharp tips raced for Corryn, ready to sink into her heart.

"No!" I dove into Morgenna's umbranation ward, ripping through the strands of roses and glittering malice-made magic until I reached the pulsing cord of the ward. With a scream, I ripped it in half and opened a hole in the shadow plane. The shadows screamed alongside me, begging me to enter with them. But only the arrows vanished into the abyss.

The burn of powerful magic frayed my drained soul, but Corryn was *safe*. She raced up the stairs to the domed palace top and the city's smoky breath. Eyeing the night sky, her ashen face tightened into a grimace.

Now, Corryn.

Eyes squeezed shut, Corryn leapt from the stairs and plummeted. For a moment, I was sure I would throw up. But air snapped around her slight frame and threw her to the open night sky. She opened her eyes beside me with a wild, untethered smile—freed.

Below us, Morgenna's black pools flared horribly wide. She shot into the air, following us past the shattered dome and into the smoke-ridden stars.

Hand in hand, Corryn and I soared over the burning city. Morgenna followed. We wove a shield of air to trail us, but the thin glimmer wouldn't last long. It was meant to buy time. If the city caught sight of Morgenna, long enough for rumors to begin, then this was enough. We would create a foothold for an uprising centuries in the making.

Wind and smoke blurred the lights below, but the familiar airborne sensation curled around my soul and released it from a hold I hadn't realized weighed me down. Gods, I'd missed flying. Beside me, Corryn freed a breathless laugh, squinting against the burning air.

Flashes of shadow followed us, but we held onto the flimsy shield together. Cracks appeared. An arrow snuck in, grazing my leg. We soared over the city, looping around towers, down past the burning Water Wheel, past the Night Flame mockery over the Mother's Temple in the Jansk.

I've always wanted to fly, Corryn whispered in my head. *I never had courage to try. Now, it's too late. I wasted so much time hiding. All alone and miserable.*

No, I chided softly. *If we die, then we die together—free. If we die feeling more alive than ever, then it was worth getting here.*

I sank into the dregs of the river between us, to the drying bottom. Corryn fell in beside me. A sob rattled the river's remaining magic. Her fear, her joy, her unfurling emotions saturated my soul. She was me. I was her.

A glimpse of young Melis ran past my memories, giggling and trailing a kite on a wispy shadow, yelling for me to chase her. Older memories poured into my head. The first day of Amethyst Hall as a student, not an outsider and the hope the day brought. Rilessa combing my unruly curls, gently reminding me I couldn't leave her rooms until dark, not until I had my Day magic under control. A sadness, all encompassing, reminding me I would always be alone. I was a hunted abomination.

Corryn's memories blurred, faster and brighter. Loneliness and guilt. Terror and confusion. Tears streamed down my cheeks, whether mine or hers, it didn't matter.

Blinded by tears and smoke, I whispered into her head, *You're not alone anymore, sister. Whatever awaits, I'm here to the end.*

She squeezed my hand. The dimming light in her eyes paused, then flared bright. "Alys, listen."

The chants boomed louder as we drifted over the streets of thronging people. They weren't calling for the Day Witch. Chilling roars, rhythmic and pulsing, called for Morgenna's head.

They had never called for me, not when they knew the true monster.

Clenching Corryn's hand, I spun us to a halt, facing Morgenna. In the thick smoke, I made out the bottomless black pools peering below with confusion. In all her pride, it never occurred to her flinging Matilda's body into the city would backfire.

I choked back a sob and thought of the flashing blue eyes hungry for justice, not for herself but for her people and said, "Matilda Noctem was more than a tavern owner with a tragic past. She was the soul of the Water Wheel, a matriarch the city once listened to. You know well what power the Water Wheel holds over the city. That's why you sicced Osrin on them. You knew their brewing passion and power would leak to the other districts. But by killing Matilda, you murdered the last voice of reason in a people starving for justice."

"Those people can die as easily as she," Morgenna hissed and shot for the crowds below.

"*No!*"

I wrenched from Corryn and shot for the black shadow plunging into the city.

Morgenna never had any intention of saving her realm. She knowingly brought vampyres to the city. She'd known Lilain schemed with them, that they fed on witch magic in exchange for a Gilgador invasion, and she never lifted a hand to save them.

She would sacrifice her people if they satiated her hunger for power.

A hunger her people saw in the burning Water Wheel, in the shattered wall, and hundreds dead. Most of all, they saw it in the Night Queen soaring for them. Three figures flying in and out of the smoke may've been alarming enough, but when Morgenna swooped under the smoke to the city below, no one would mistake her for anyone but the Night Queen.

Screams cut off the chanting roars. Witches ducked into buildings, diving to the cobblestones to avoid her flinging shadows. Corryn and I threw shields at random, swaying in the air, scraping the last bit of magic to save the Night Realm from their murderous queen.

A voice, manic and shrill, pierced the smoky air.

"Fuck the queen!"

Ervik emerged from a burning inn, bloodied to his boots. He cried out again with an upraised fist. His shadows soared to meet the queen's in a metallic screech. Another voice joined him. And then another and another, until the new chant drowned the screams. Shadows, some deep, some wispy, shot arrows into the sky, aiming for the flying phantom dodging in and out of their city.

As one, the people of Morithia turned on their all-powerful queen. But power didn't equate status or magic. Or even coin. In the Water Wheel, power meant heart and passion. A need for more than survival. Like Ansil and Elenna had once said, witchkind wanted to thrive. The powerless were worthy, not because of what they had but because of how far they'd go for never-ending hopes and dreams.

The powerless like me.

Maddox. Corryn. Yori. Ansil and Elenna. They'd seen what I saw now. *I was worthy.* The magicless orphan fighting for garbage in filthy alleys, the skeletal page who couldn't read—she hungered for more, strove against all odds to rise against her circumstances. She was worthy of the Mother's fate and the enormous power given her. More than any of the Mother's six, she knew the misery and pain that waited for Efelldor if they failed.

That night the powerless saw what they could be without Morgenna, and they wanted it more than they feared her—a queen with unfathomable power who'd let her city burn. There would never be another district left to tear itself apart. She would never hold an axe over their heads with tales of murderous beasts.

As one, they tore after her, following through the charred streets. Bloodied, ash-smeared faces contorted with rage, mouths stretched wide as if they could swallow her whole.

Morgenna faltered, sending magic heaving into the crowd, but more came for her. Shadows ripped her robes, her skin. Tearing through silk she believed worth more than their lives.

A howl split the screams, and Morgenna wrenched herself from the city's grasp. She shot into the sky until she was a pinprick. Whirling, she examined Morithia. Half the city was ablaze; the other half teemed with Night Witches screaming for her head. There would be no going back. Not even fear could hold the rebellious city. The arrogant control she'd held for centuries went up in the smoke drifting toward the hazy moon.

As the Mother fated, so it happened.

The Night Queen Morgenna fell from her throne.

With one last narrowed glare in my direction, she spun south. She passed the city wards, summoned shadows, and vanished.

The city fell eerily quiet.

Slowly, awed gasps rippled the streets. Horror crept over some, realizing they'd turned on their queen. Necks stretched in search of her. Instead, they found Corryn and me, floating above the street, wide-eyed and wondering if the mob would turn on us too.

Ervik grinned at me and threw his fist into the air. "Fuck the queen!"

The city followed his cheer with wailing laughter, half-tears, half-finality. Anger dissolved, melting into watery smiles. Arms were tossed over shoulders. Excited tales of bravery began. Above the chaos of celebration, a wave of air, powerful as any magic, rushed from a thousand lips. Relief.

On the cliffs, the silent Onyx Palace beckoned.

Corryn and I floated to the cobblestone using the final dregs of the river between us and vanished into the crowd. Sleepiness dogged every slow and ambling step. My soul begged me to lay on the cobblestones and refill its well with magic found in sleep.

I couldn't give in. Not yet.

Wordless, we ran through the streets, aiming for the hill and what might remain above.

Don't, Corryn snapped in my head. *Whatever dark trail you're starting down, come back. They're fine. No matter the compulsion, Melis isn't capable of killing him.*

The cliffs never seemed higher. The path to the Onyx Palace spiraled into the stars, never ending. We passed the gates, the courtyard. Everything centered on the hammered-gold doors and whatever waited.

I shoved the doors open and nearly collapsed with relief.

Maddox and Melis sat back-to-back in a puddle of fallen candles. Haggard and bleeding from a dozen wounds, they passed a leaky bottle of wine between them in silence.

Corryn rushed past me and fell to the floor beside a wide-eyed Melis.

Babbling about the city's overthrowal of the queen in a voice that rivaled a chattering chipmunk's, she shoved aside Melis's protestations and rolled her sleeve back to inspect Maddox's crude work. Through blood and bits of wax, a circle with two arrows shone on Melis's pale arm.

Corryn halted mid-sentence and let out a weak groan. She slumped to the floor and dropped her forehead to the bloody arm.

Melis threw me a panicked look, but I had turned my focus behind her.

Maddox lowered the broken bottle, already fixed on me. The room's shadows slithered from their corners to find him. "Don't ask why I never told you. You know why."

I nudged him with my boot. "Get up."

Corryn lifted her head and frowned, but before she could rise, Melis slid an arm around her waist and pulled her roughly against her chest, never taking catlike eyes off me. Corryn shot me a bewildered glance, but I nodded at Melis. Good. Regardless of their past, her priority would always be Corryn's safety. Even against me.

Maddox stared down at his bloody hands, smearing sticky blood over the pads of his thumbs. Slowly, he got to his feet. He shot a hand over the gash at his thigh where blood trickled through the torn fabric in a persistent stream.

We were toe-to-toe, my heart strumming my ribs like a morbid stringed instrument.

"How dare you?" I hissed. He flinched but didn't back down. "Didn't you tell me only a short while ago you would be there for me no matter what came? That you and I were in this together? I suppose that only applies to me, right? I'm the only one allowed to fuck up and fail because you love me, is that it?"

"It's not that simple—"

"I said I chose all of you, didn't I? Does that mean nothing to you? I am *choosing* to be here for you. *Choosing* to hold your pain and help you find the way out of its darkness because *I love you*. Godsdamn it, Maddox, if you can't let me into your head, how can I trust you in mine?"

He shook his head, jaw brittle and tight. "Because you don't deserve the weight of what's in my head. You've had enough in your life without bearing more pain that isn't yours."

"I killed Yori. I held that Mother bleeding knife and no matter how badly I wanted to drop dead, I shoved it through him and watched the life leave his eyes. How could you not realize I already hold the same pain you bear?"

He lunged and seized my shoulders. Horror broke through his mask to reveal raw, unfiltered pain. "*Because it's not the same*. Yori understood the danger of living near Morgenna as we all did. Alys, I've murdered hundreds of unassuming innocents—most of them *children*. Do you know what haunts me every waking moment I'm not busy? Mothers screaming for mercy, shielding their infants. I think about the fucking sword I couldn't stop from coming down. Memories where I dragged my feet through the mud, trying in vain to stop advancing on a group of crying children with their dead parents at my feet. Wishing the boy who gave me this scar"—he raked a finger down the side of his face—"had finished me off."

The sounds of the city evaporated. Corryn's soft sobs, the thick stench of smoke drifting from the shattered dome—all of it fell away.

A brutal hammer struck at my chest. It pounded on my heart until only fragments remained. I took in the torment darkening the gold in Maddox's broken gaze. The guilt I thought I understood in him paled in comparison to the avalanche he'd hidden from the world.

"I-I'm so sorry. I can't begin to fathom—That's more than any witch should bear over a hundred lifetimes," I managed in a thick voice. When he wouldn't meet my eyes, I gripped his cheeks and forced him to look at me. "But it doesn't change how I feel because it wasn't *you*. You are not to blame for what she compelled you to do. I'm going to fix this, Maddox. I'm going to find a way to heal you so that *you* see what *I* see—a selfless witch who used himself to keep Morgenna's attention sated. A witch worthy of being loved. One day you'll look at your penitence runes and realize you never want to speak their spellcast again. You're going to reach for me instead, and we'll go through whatever fate throws at us *together*."

He let out a shuddering breath and tore my hands off his face, but he didn't let them go. He'd convinced himself that if I discovered he'd been the beast hunting witches like me, he'd lose my love. Each piece of him clicked together to form a sorrowful picture. Morgenna had ripped him apart at the seams and crammed in her own malice before stitching him back up. She'd forced him to believe no good lay within. That he truly was a beast of evil.

She wouldn't win.

I'd rip apart her work and undo what she'd done to him—one day at a time.

I threaded our fingers together, clinging harder when he tried to pull away. He let loose another sigh, this one more irritated. The familiar sound sparked warm hope. He was in there, the witch who occasionally saw past his heavy guilt because of the irritating little witch who got under his skin and refused to leave him alone with his dark thoughts.

"Get it through your thick head, Prince. I won't give up on you."

He shook his head, lips tightly twisted, but he gripped my hand and said, "We have too much to do to worry about the state of my head. The fate of an island is ours to save, and we have *two* queens with unlimited power to destroy."

Corryn's hesitant voice cut off any retort I prepared to launch. "But how? There's only four of us. We don't even have the fated six. And those people down there will be looking to us for guidance. They'll want answers."

Muffled celebrations punctured our uneasy silence.

Morithia would want answers for the flying witches, the vampyres storming, their queen's betrayal. The courtiers would begin circling Maddox as the heir presumptive. And the elves? What had been the point of the delegation? Who benefited their agenda—whatever it was.

With my free hand, I threaded Corryn's bleeding arm through mine, careful not to touch the torn skin. Dragging her and Maddox behind me, we picked through the ruined ball to the open window overlooking the city. Somewhere behind us, I could feel Melis watching with heavy longing.

Much of Morithia lay in ruin, but the sounds of relief spoke of a people who looked to the new world awaiting them. One where freedom was within reach.

A gentle wind sifted through my loosened hair, caressing my scalp. Through the smoke and smell of blood, I caught a soft scent of lavender on the wind. The unfamiliar magic scent reminded me of a still night as it rushed past me and fluttered Corryn's curls. Eyes wide, she watched the wind crush the forgotten rose petals and carry them out the shattered window before vanishing into the night.

Our paths were not finished. The gods may have been on our side, but they couldn't carry out our fate for us. We didn't need them. Witches were a stubborn lot. Our pride had got us into this exile, and it would get us out.

The witches below held their fists high. Echoes of their crude chants floated up the cliff to the shattered Onyx Palace. A shadow depicting Morgenna's obscene execution formed over the burning city. As I watched the people climb out of their centuries' long cage, they transformed into the impassioned witches the Mother Created us to be. The prey had become the predator, and they would not rest until Morgenna's head sat on a pike sharpened from their grief.

I let out a dark laugh and nodded to the shadowed head of Morgenna tumbling from her body. "How do we defeat the queens? We take a freed people, and we ram them down Morgenna and Lilain's throats."

THE END

Acknowledgements

Dearest reader, if you would like to leave a review, please, please, please do. Make it honest, make it sweet, make it brutal—just make it, pretty please. You'll have this author's love forever and ever. <3

When they say it takes a village—y'all, they mean it. Writing is a community effort and I'm about to roll out the red carpet for my community.

First, an enormous thank you to Chersti Nieveen at Writer Therapy for taking a baby writer under her wing and explaining how to craft a story. I will forever appreciate our many Zoom calls and all the homework you assigned!

Thank you to Heather at Simply Spellbound Edits for fixing all my weird ellipses and inappropriate fixation of semi-colons when they should have been em-dashes. Not to mention, hyping me up a dozen times and giving me all the "LOL" comments that stroked my sad, little ego. Seriously, I'm beyond lucky to have such a patient editor. You are a true gem, and I'm thankful not only for your work but for your friendship. (Next time I'M buying lunch...)

My Chaos Discord group girls! You all deserve a medal for reading everything I threw at you for nearly three years. I couldn't have picked a more encouraging group to start this writing adventure with. Our weekly/monthly check-ins have been a highlight of this journey, and I would have probably quit if it wasn't for you ladies. An enormous thank you to our faithful leader, Nicole, who keeps us glued together no matter what life throws at us.

Thank you to all my beta readers who pushed me or held me up at each stage—Ema, Alisha, Lindsey, Sabrina, Kelly, Nicole, Stefanie, TJ, Bailey, Rachel, Taylor, Tori. I appreciate each one of you and am so thankful for your time.

Kristen . . . Listen, bestie, I truly don't think this book would have happened without you. You read *every* draft and lifted me up so many times your arms *must* be exhausted by now. You were the OG cheerleader, telling me what worked and what didn't, and you helped me chase my dreams. A million thanks! Now, put this book down and go get back to work on your own novel!

The world's biggest thank you to my husband. Thank you for never giving up on my dreams even when I wanted to, even when the universe seemed to say "no", even when I disappear into my head at the worst times or cry at the drop of a hat because I just realized who has to die in the next book. Your never-failing support (and all the treats that miraculously appear when I'm in a writing cave) means this book is possible, and I will forever be grateful for a spouse like you.

Finally, thank you, dearest reader, for supporting this author's wildest dreams! I hope you enjoyed Eleutheria! Stick around for books 2 & 3!

ABOUT THE AUTHOR

Ruth Cantu is an adult fantasy novelist who adores all things romance. After setting aside fanfiction writing during college to pursue other goals, she rediscovered writing during the pandemic, but this time to create her own worlds. *Eleutheria* is her debut novel.

When not dreaming up fantastical worlds, Ruth can be found thrifting, collecting rare books, or elbows deep in a garden. Writing maybe her first love but a sun-warmed garden tomato is a close second. She resides in the middle of no-where Oklahoma with her spouse, pups, and kids.

Follow Ruth on social media for updates on her next books under @ruthcantuauthor.

www.ingramcontent.com/pod-product-compliance
Lightning Source LLC
Chambersburg PA
CBHW020649110726
47901CB00001B/103

* 9 7 9 8 9 9 8 8 8 5 5 1 8 *